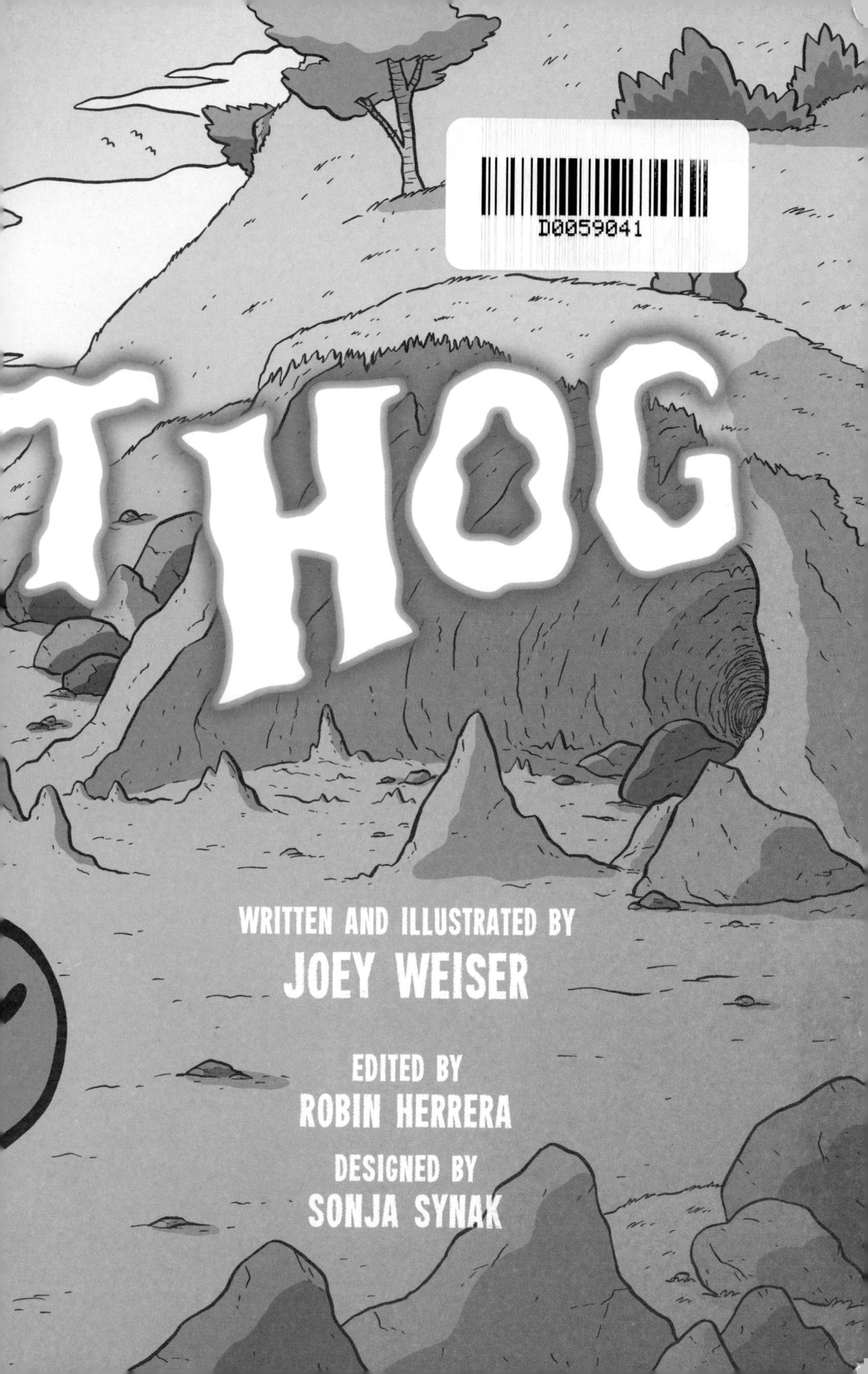
T HOG

WRITTEN AND ILLUSTRATED BY
JOEY WEISER

EDITED BY
ROBIN HERRERA

DESIGNED BY
SONJA SYNAK

Published by Oni Press, Inc.

Joe Nozemack, founder & chief financial officer

James Lucas Jones, publisher

Charlie Chu, v.p. of creative & business development

Brad Rooks, director of operations

Melissa Meszaros, director of publicity

Margot Wood, director of sales

Sandy Tanaka, marketing design manager

Amber O'Neill, special projects manager

Troy Look, director of design & production

Kate Z. Stone, senior graphic designer

Sonja Synak, graphic designer

Angie Knowles, digital prepress lead

Ari Yarwood, executive editor

Sarah Gaydos, editorial director of licensed publishing

Robin Herrera, senior editor

Desiree Wilson, associate editor

Michelle Nguyen, executive assistant

Jung Lee, logistics coordinator

Scott Sharkey, warehouse assistant

onipress.com
facebook.com/onipress
twitter.com/onipress
onipress.tumblr.com
instagram.com/onipress

tragic-planet.com
@joeyweiser

First Edition: May 2019

Paperback ISBN 978-1-62010-597-9
Hardcover ISBN 978-1-62010-654-9
eISBN 978-1-62010-598-6

Printed in China

Library of Congress Control Number: 2018960492

10 9 8 7 6 5 4 3 2 1

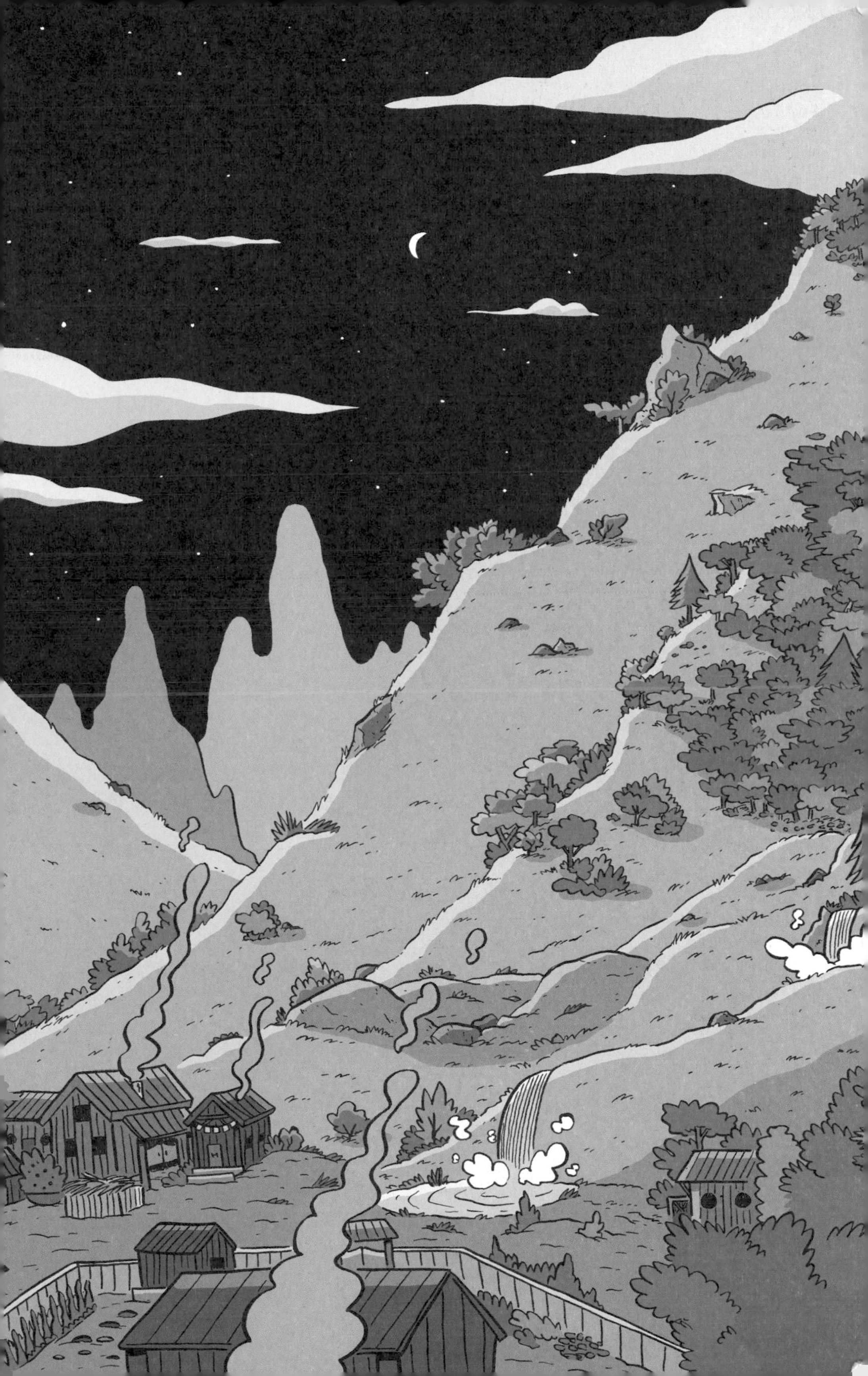

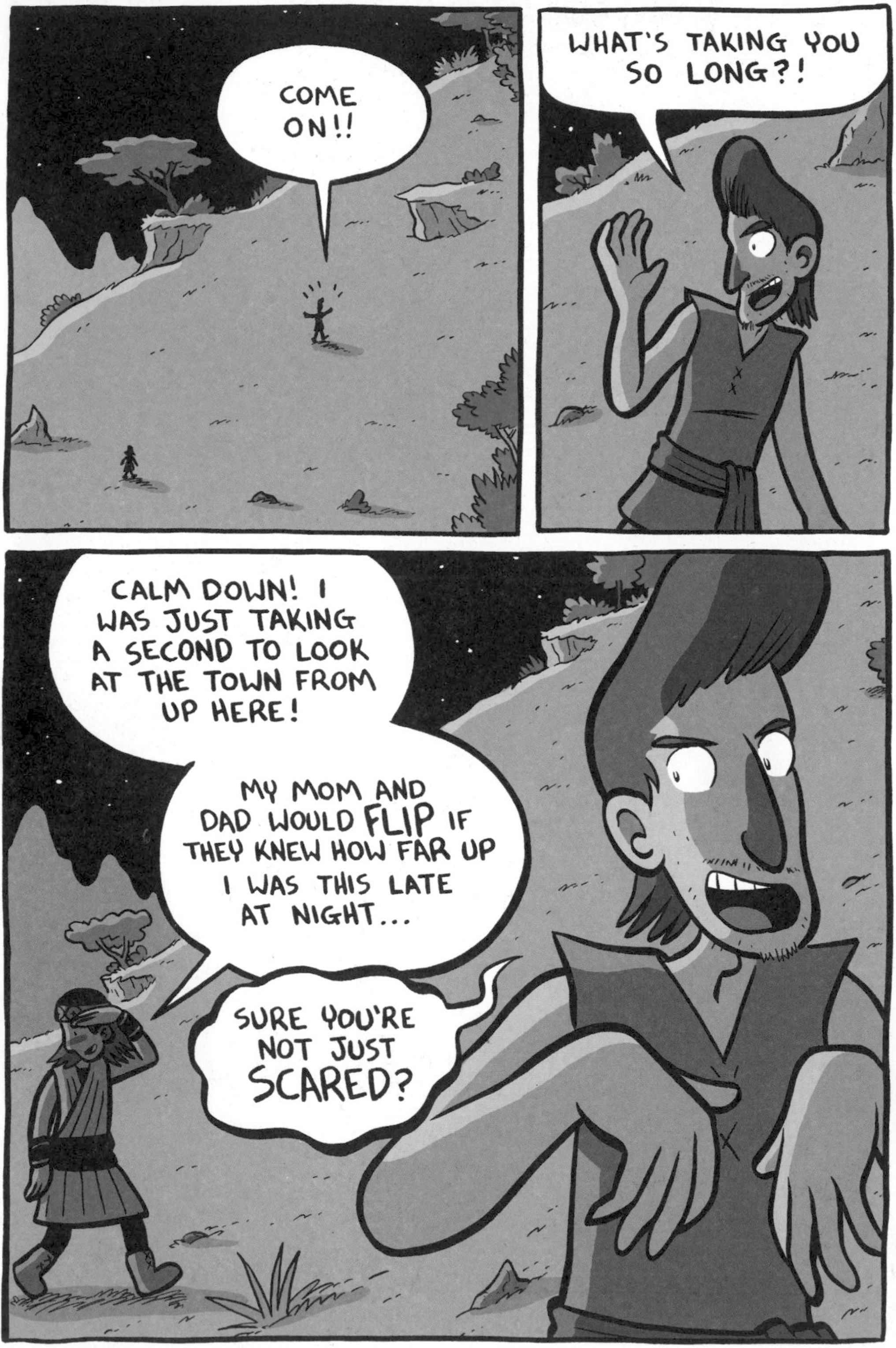
COME ON!!
WHAT'S TAKING YOU SO LONG?!
CALM DOWN! I WAS JUST TAKING A SECOND TO LOOK AT THE TOWN FROM UP HERE!
MY MOM AND DAD WOULD FLIP IF THEY KNEW HOW FAR UP I WAS THIS LATE AT NIGHT...
SURE YOU'RE NOT JUST SCARED?

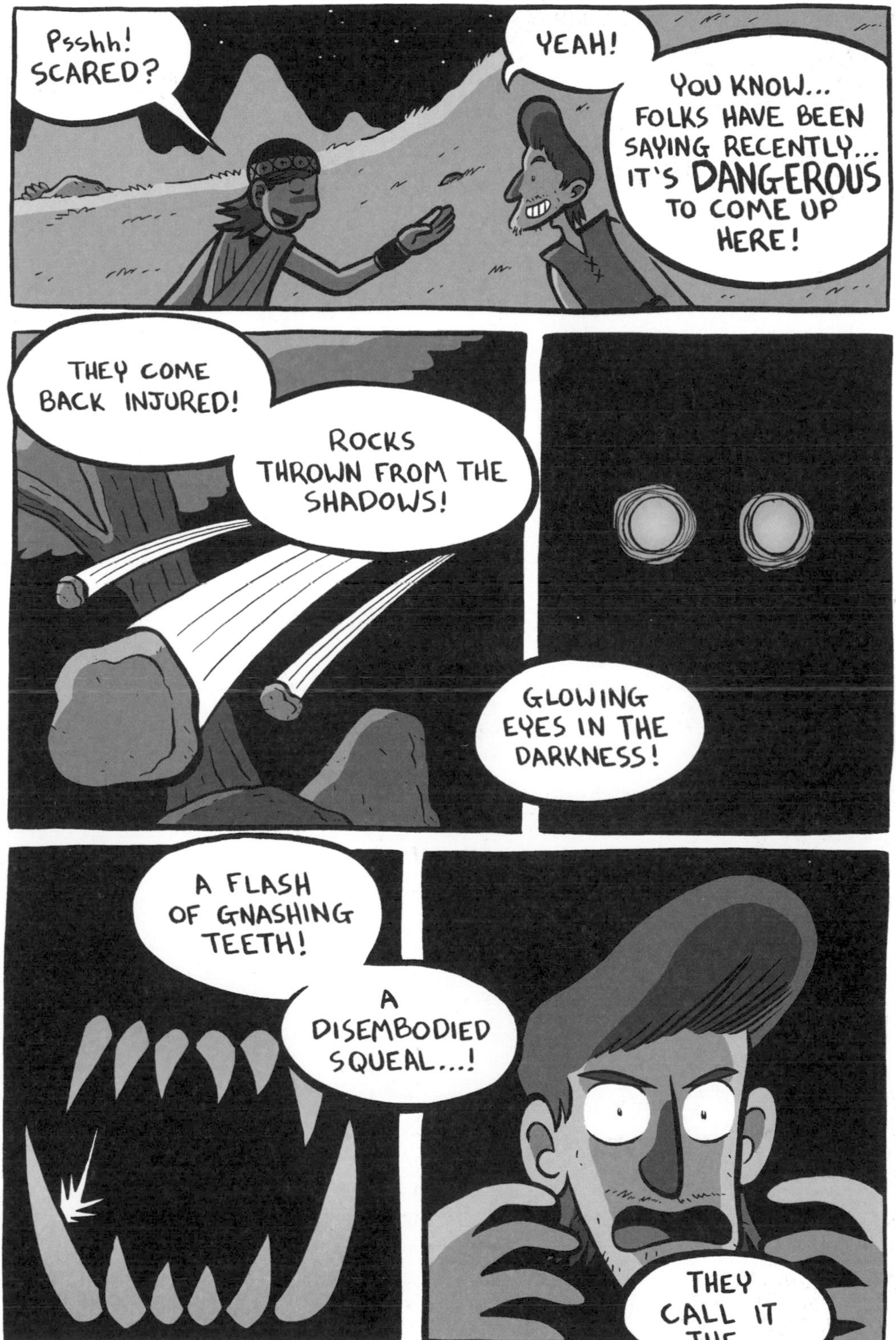
Psshh! SCARED?
YEAH!
YOU KNOW... FOLKS HAVE BEEN SAYING RECENTLY... IT'S DANGEROUS TO COME UP HERE!
THEY COME BACK INJURED!
ROCKS THROWN FROM THE SHADOWS!
GLOWING EYES IN THE DARKNESS!
A FLASH OF GNASHING TEETH!
A DISEMBODIED SQUEAL...!
THEY CALL IT THE...

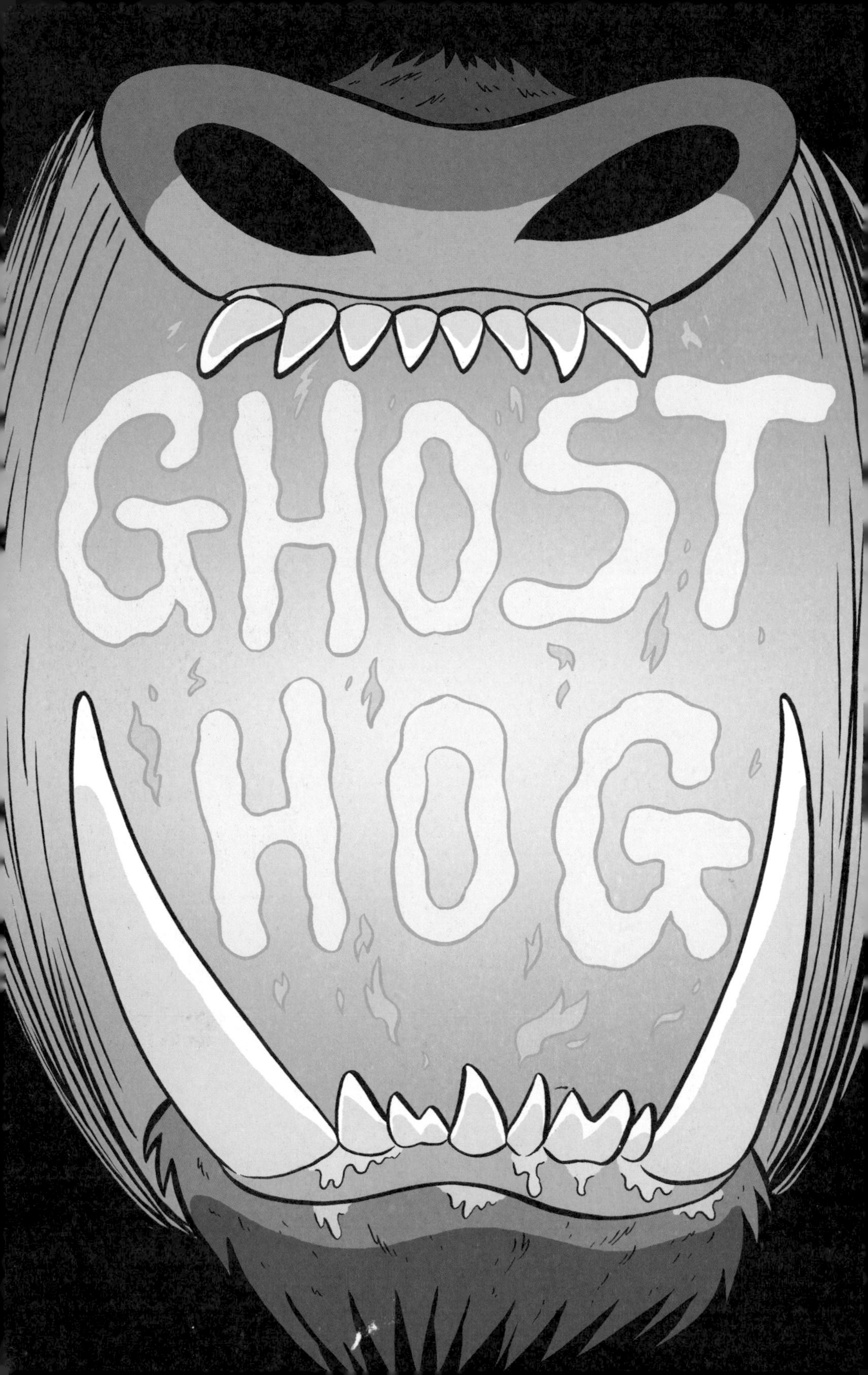
GHOST
HOG

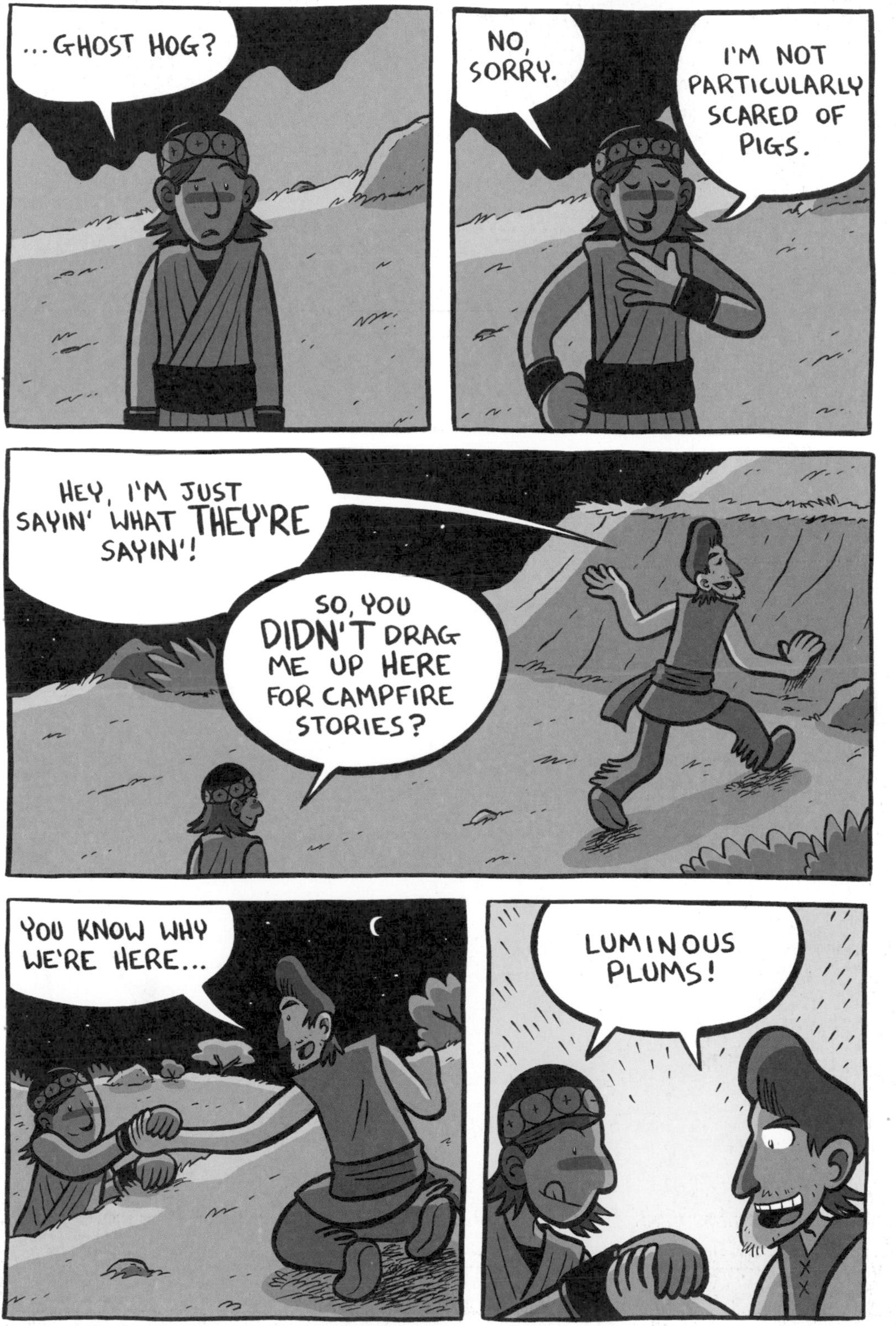
...GHOST HOG?
NO, SORRY.
I'M NOT PARTICULARLY SCARED OF PIGS.
HEY, I'M JUST SAYIN' WHAT THEY'RE SAYIN'!
SO, YOU DIDN'T DRAG ME UP HERE FOR CAMPFIRE STORIES?
YOU KNOW WHY WE'RE HERE...
LUMINOUS PLUMS!

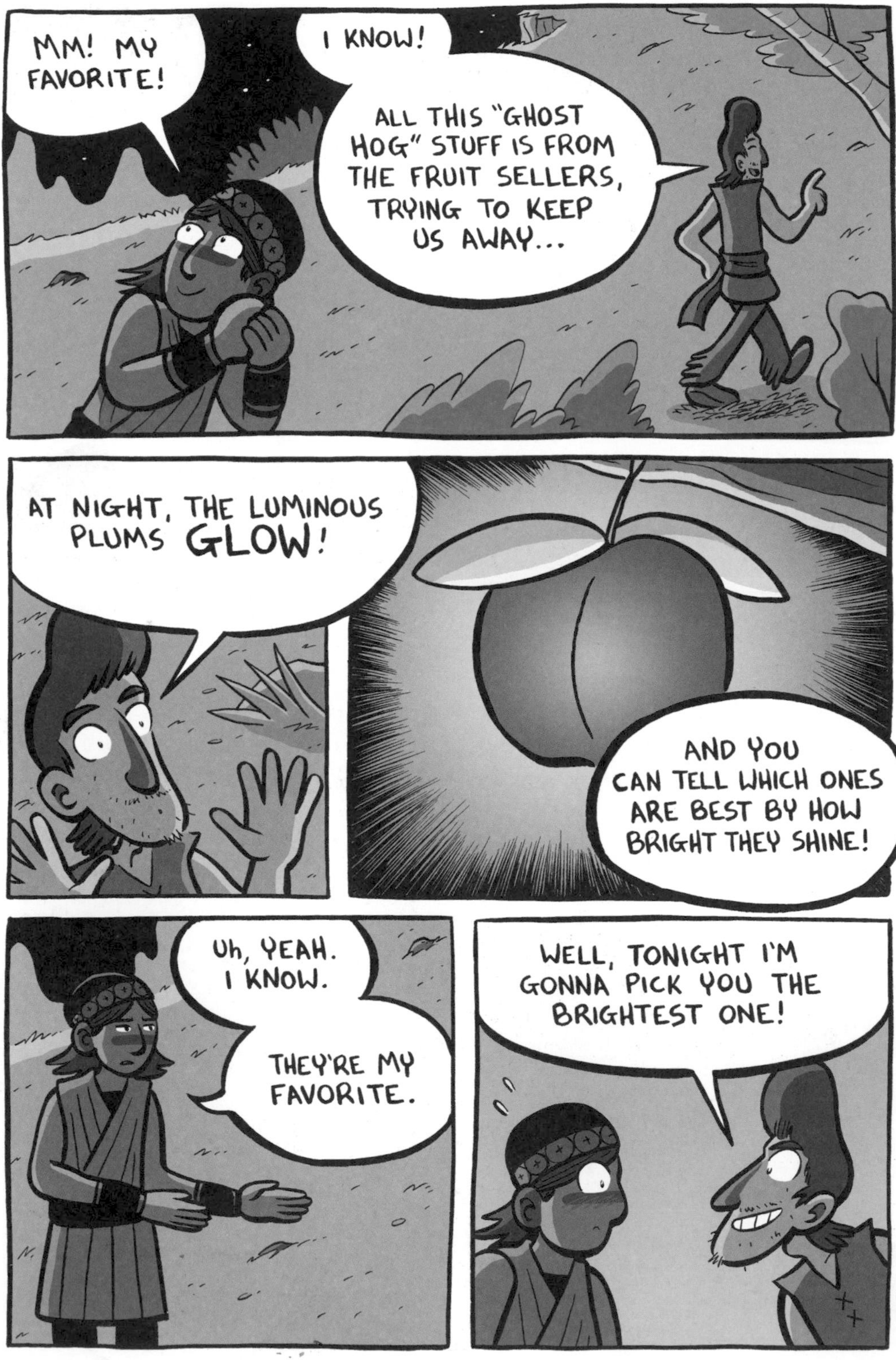
MM! MY FAVORITE!
I KNOW!
ALL THIS "GHOST HOG" STUFF IS FROM THE FRUIT SELLERS, TRYING TO KEEP US AWAY...
AT NIGHT, THE LUMINOUS PLUMS GLOW!
AND YOU CAN TELL WHICH ONES ARE BEST BY HOW BRIGHT THEY SHINE!
Uh, YEAH. I KNOW.
THEY'RE MY FAVORITE.
WELL, TONIGHT I'M GONNA PICK YOU THE BRIGHTEST ONE!

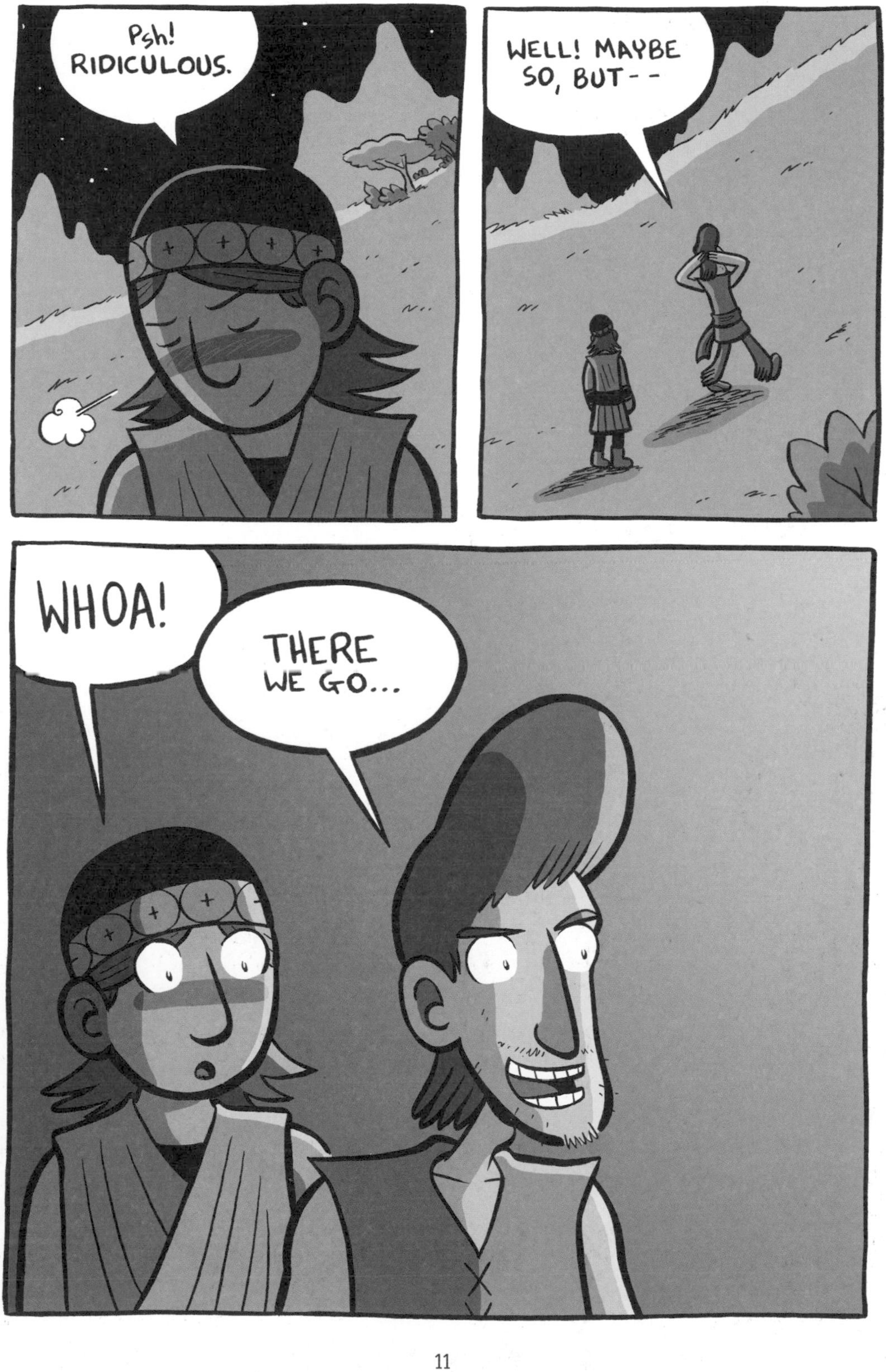
Psh! RIDICULOUS.
WELL! MAYBE SO, BUT--
WHOA!
THERE WE GO...

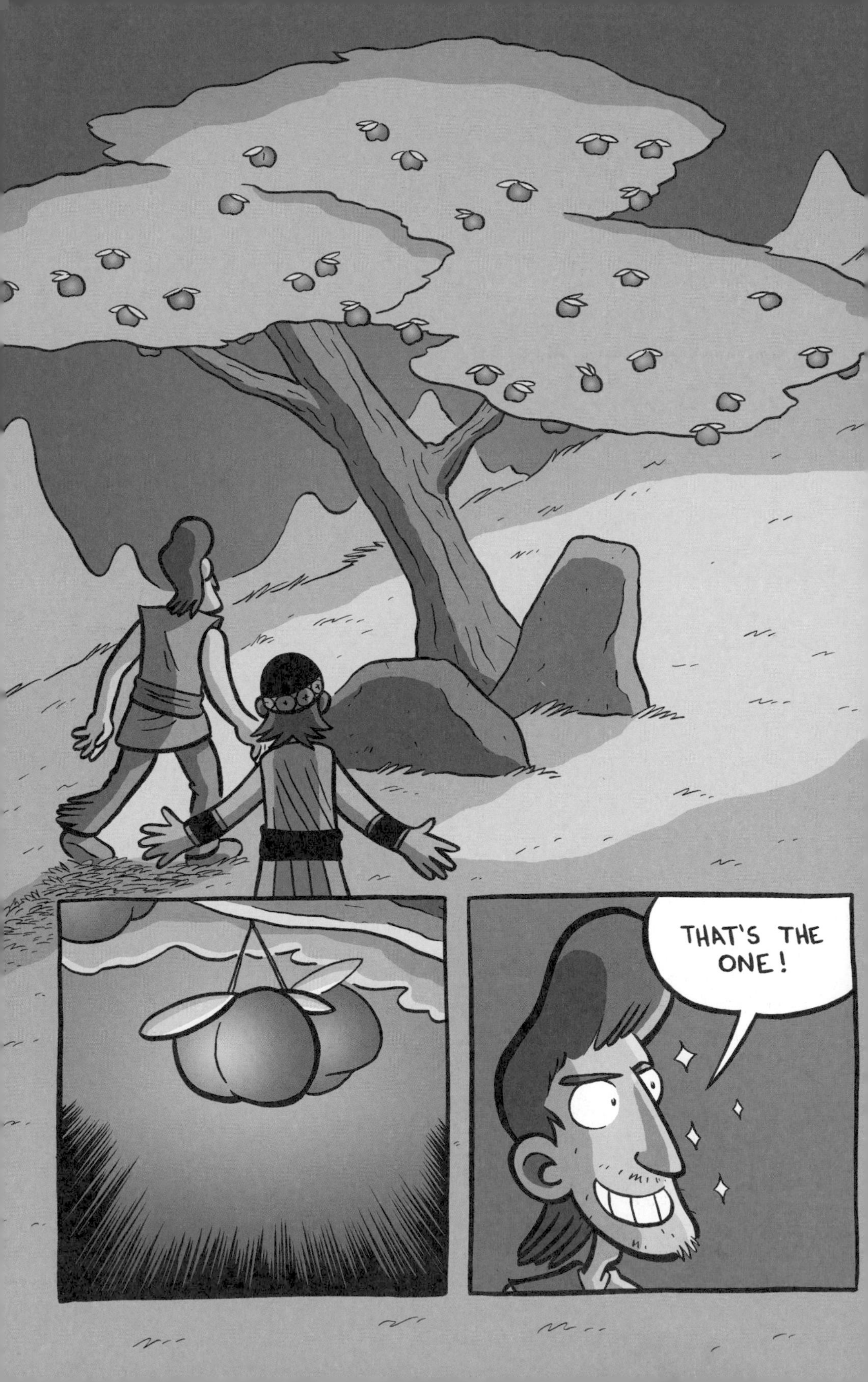
THAT'S THE ONE!

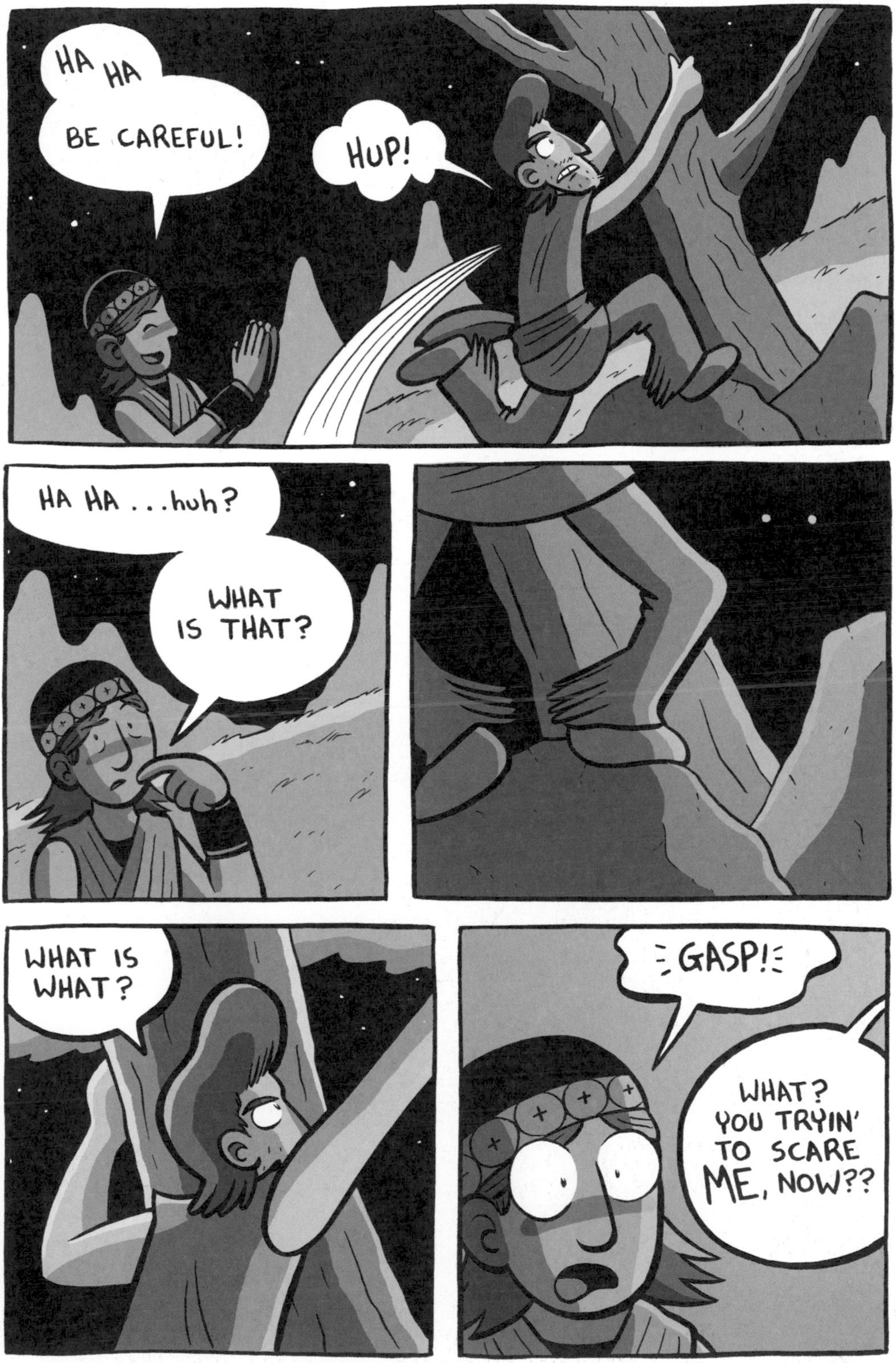
HA HA
BE CAREFUL!
HUP!
HA HA ...huh?
WHAT IS THAT?
WHAT IS WHAT?
GASP!
WHAT? YOU TRYIN' TO SCARE ME, NOW??

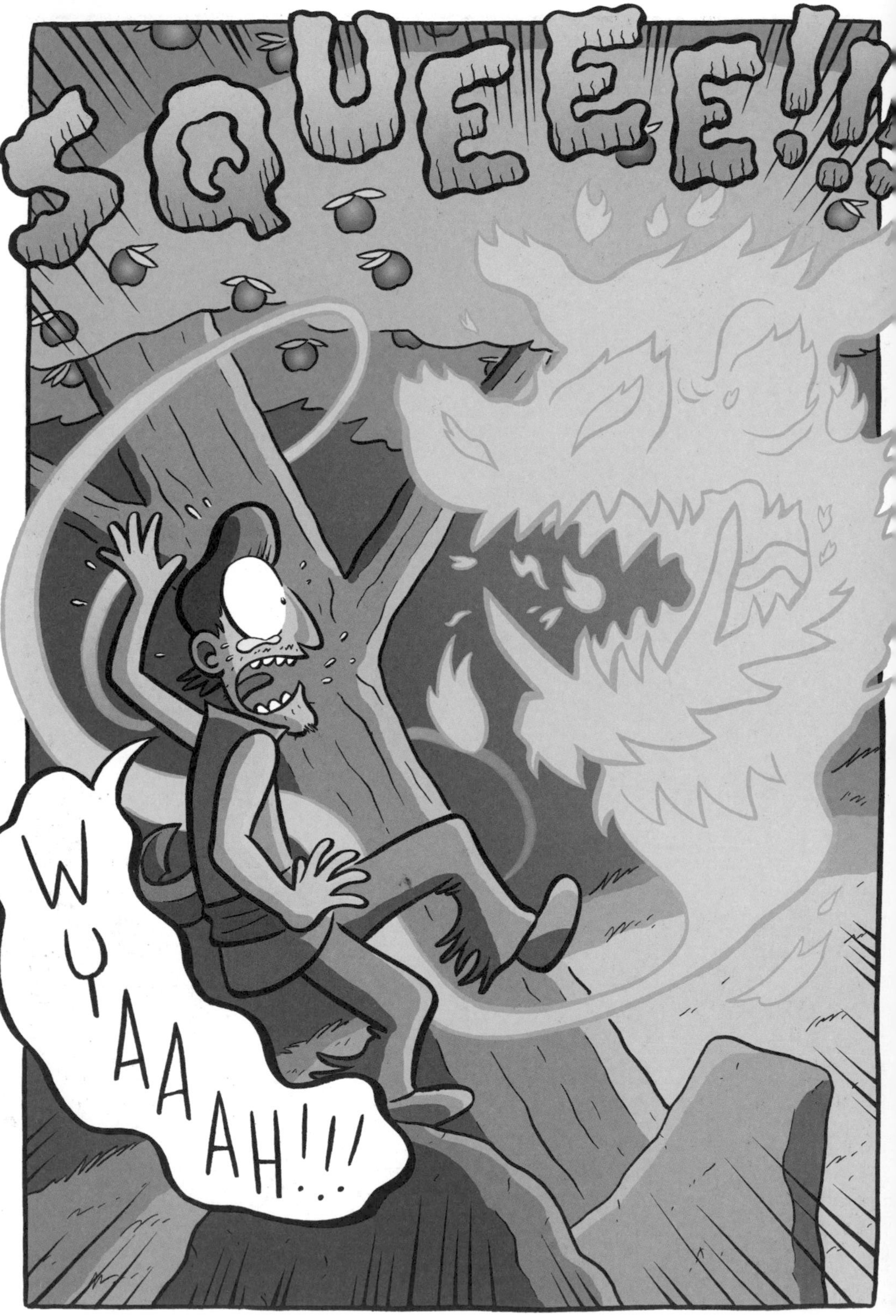
SQUEEE!!!
WYAAAAH!!!...

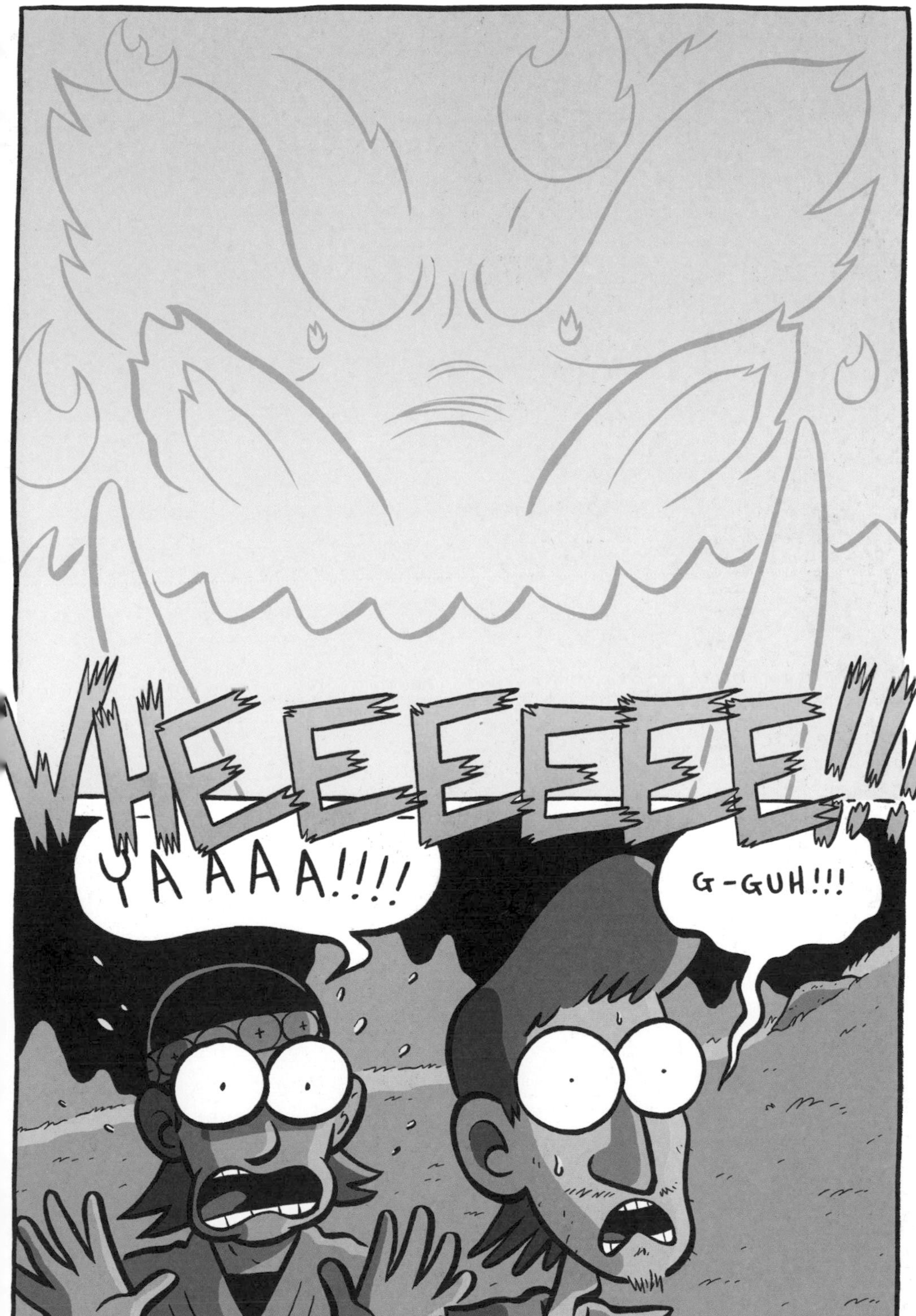
WHEEEEEE!!!
YAAAA!!!!
G-GUH!!!

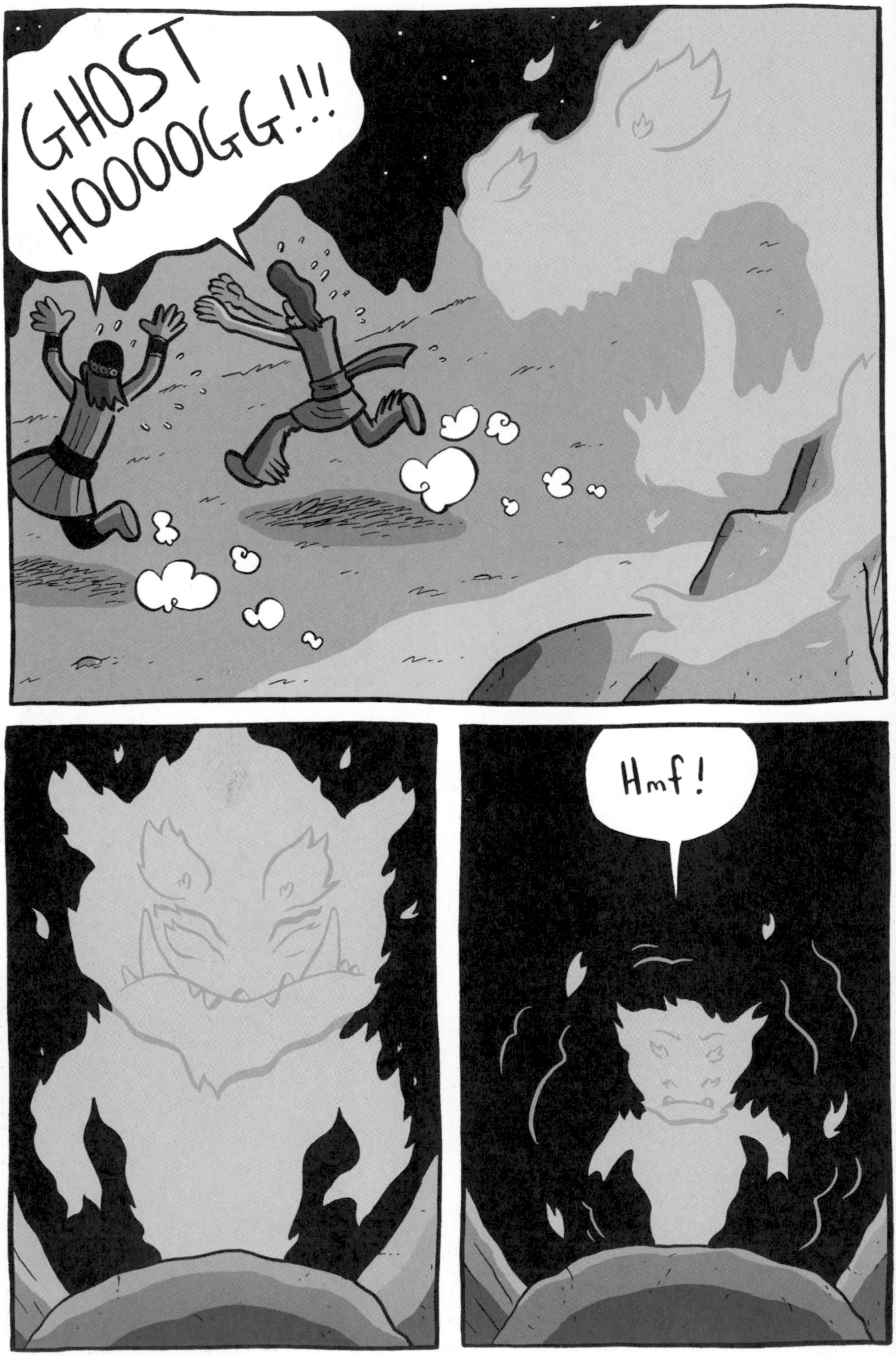
GHOST HOOOOGG!!!
Hmf!

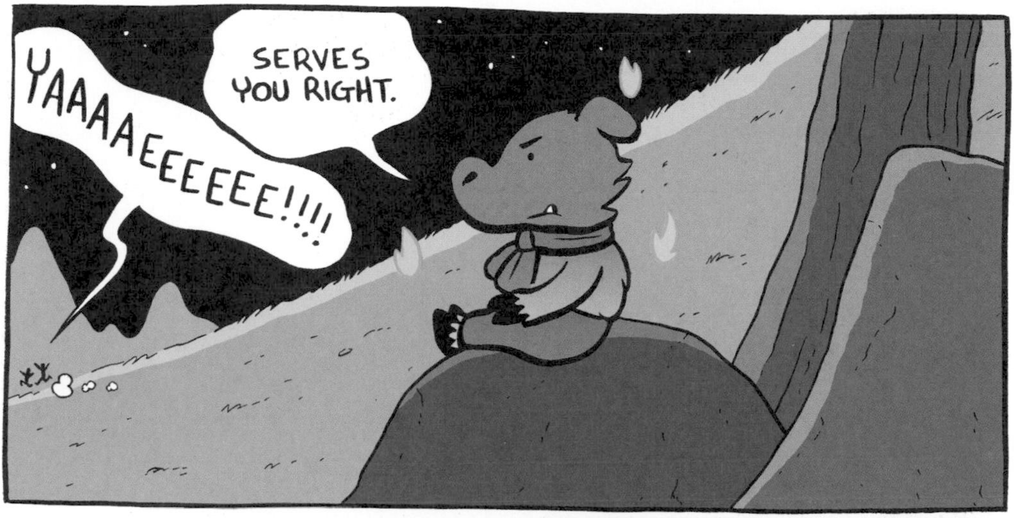
YAAAAEEEEEE!!!!
SERVES YOU RIGHT.

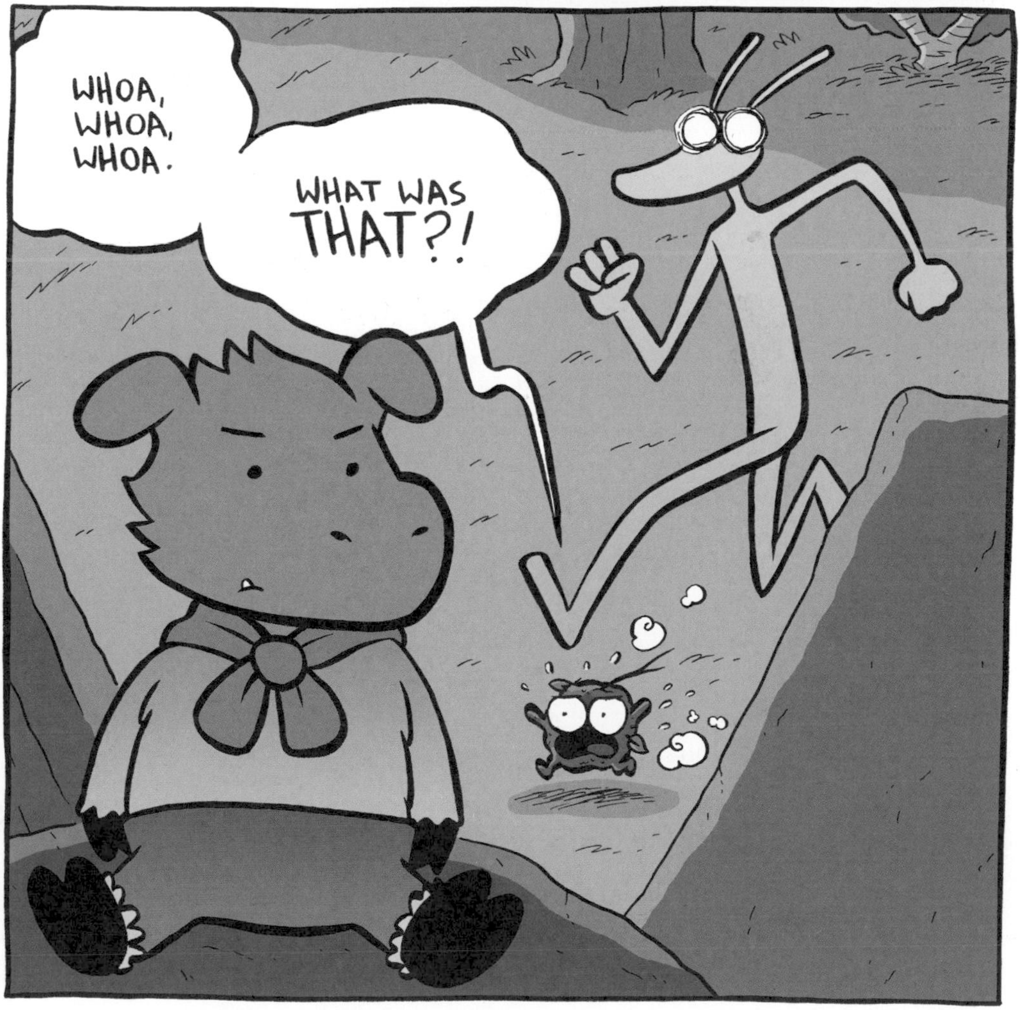
WHOA, WHOA, WHOA.
WHAT WAS THAT?!

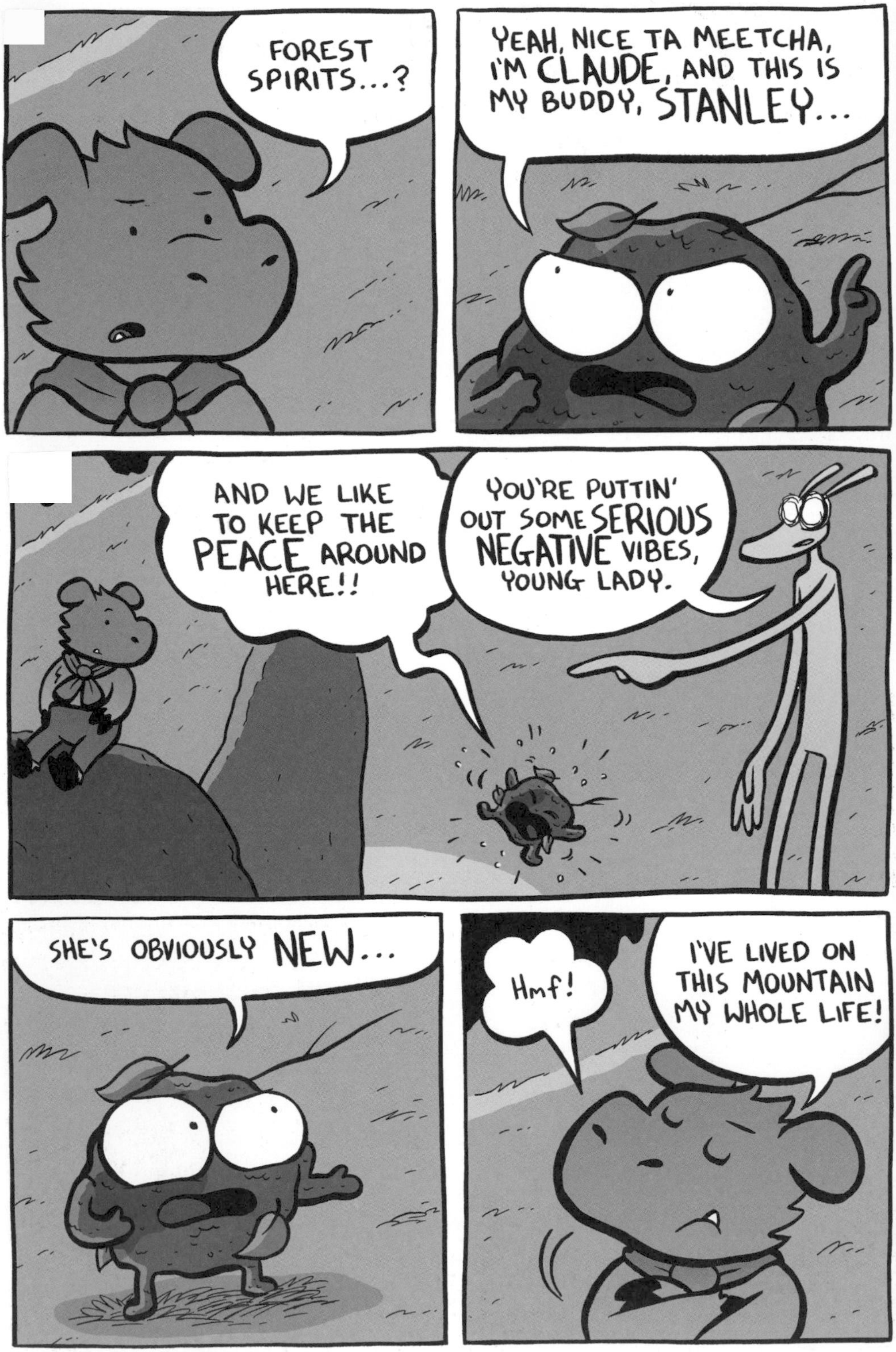
FOREST SPIRITS...?
YEAH, NICE TA MEETCHA, I'M CLAUDE, AND THIS IS MY BUDDY, STANLEY...
AND WE LIKE TO KEEP THE PEACE AROUND HERE!!
YOU'RE PUTTIN' OUT SOME SERIOUS NEGATIVE VIBES, YOUNG LADY.
SHE'S OBVIOUSLY NEW...
Hmf!
I'VE LIVED ON THIS MOUNTAIN MY WHOLE LIFE!

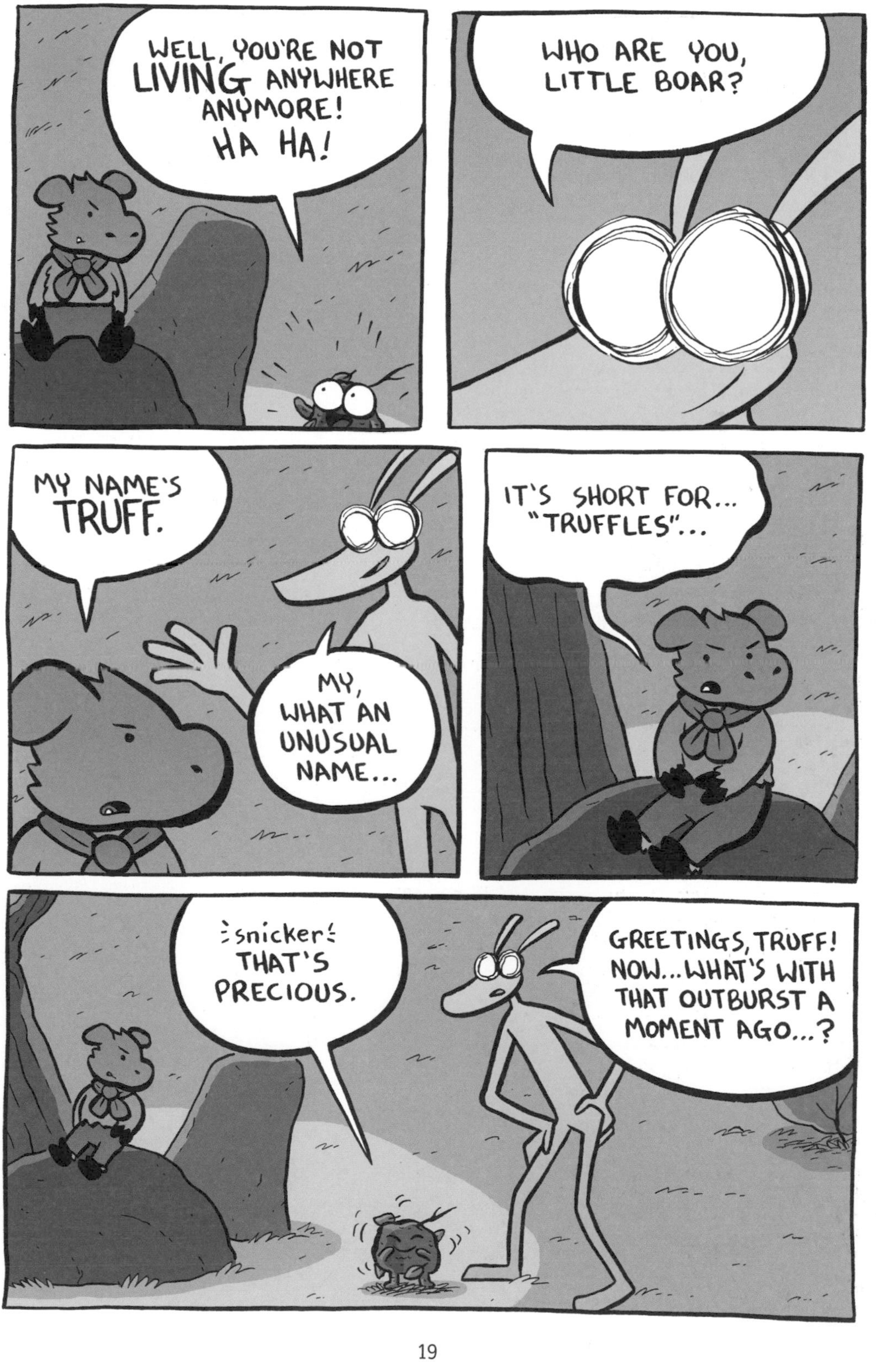
WELL, YOU'RE NOT LIVING ANYWHERE ANYMORE! HA HA!
WHO ARE YOU, LITTLE BOAR?
MY NAME'S TRUFF.
MY, WHAT AN UNUSUAL NAME...
IT'S SHORT FOR... "TRUFFLES"...
snicker THAT'S PRECIOUS.
GREETINGS, TRUFF! NOW... WHAT'S WITH THAT OUTBURST A MOMENT AGO...?

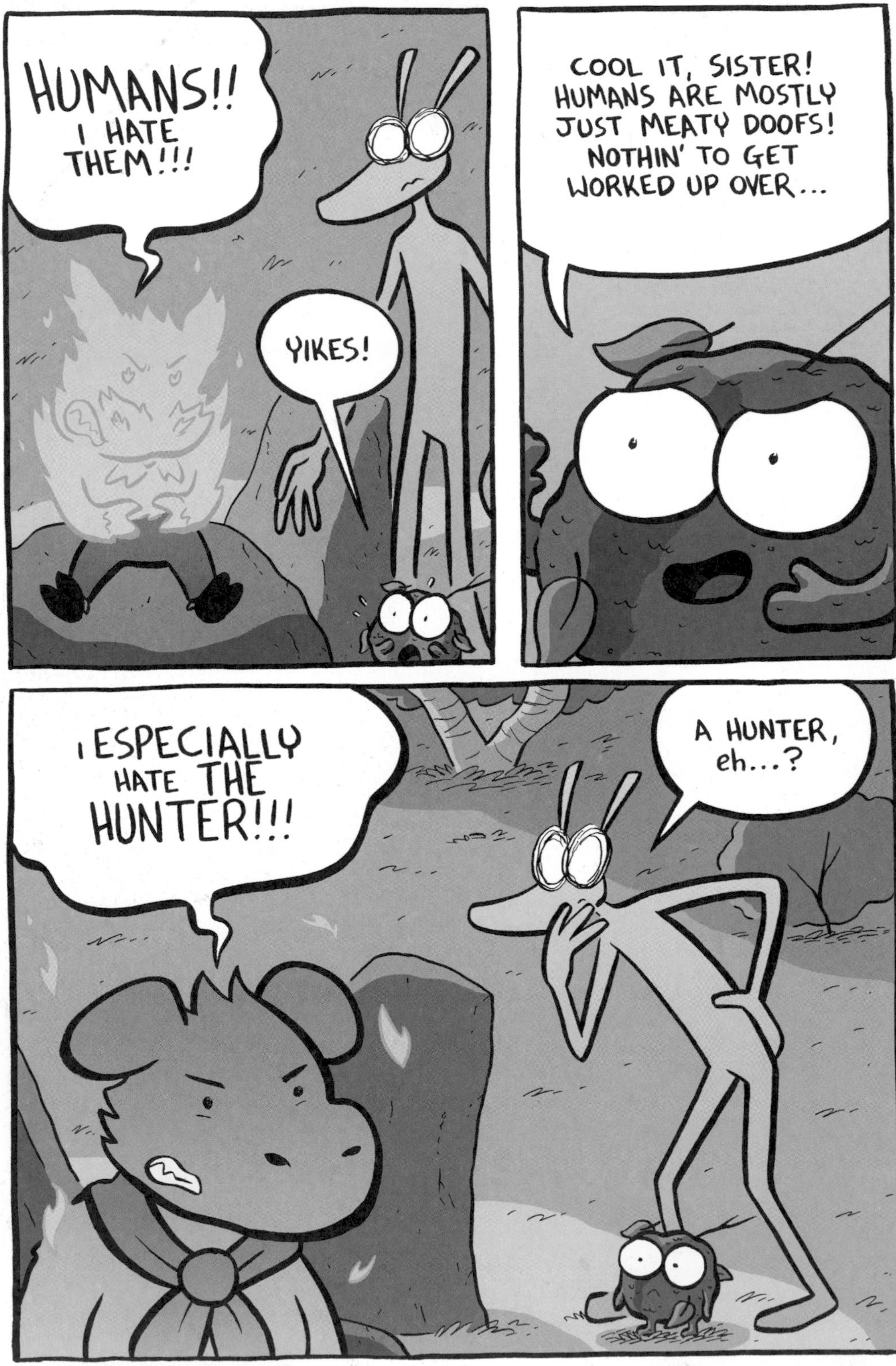
HUMANS!! I HATE THEM!!!
YIKES!
COOL IT, SISTER! HUMANS ARE MOSTLY JUST MEATY DOOFS! NOTHIN' TO GET WORKED UP OVER...
I ESPECIALLY HATE THE HUNTER!!!
A HUNTER, eh...?

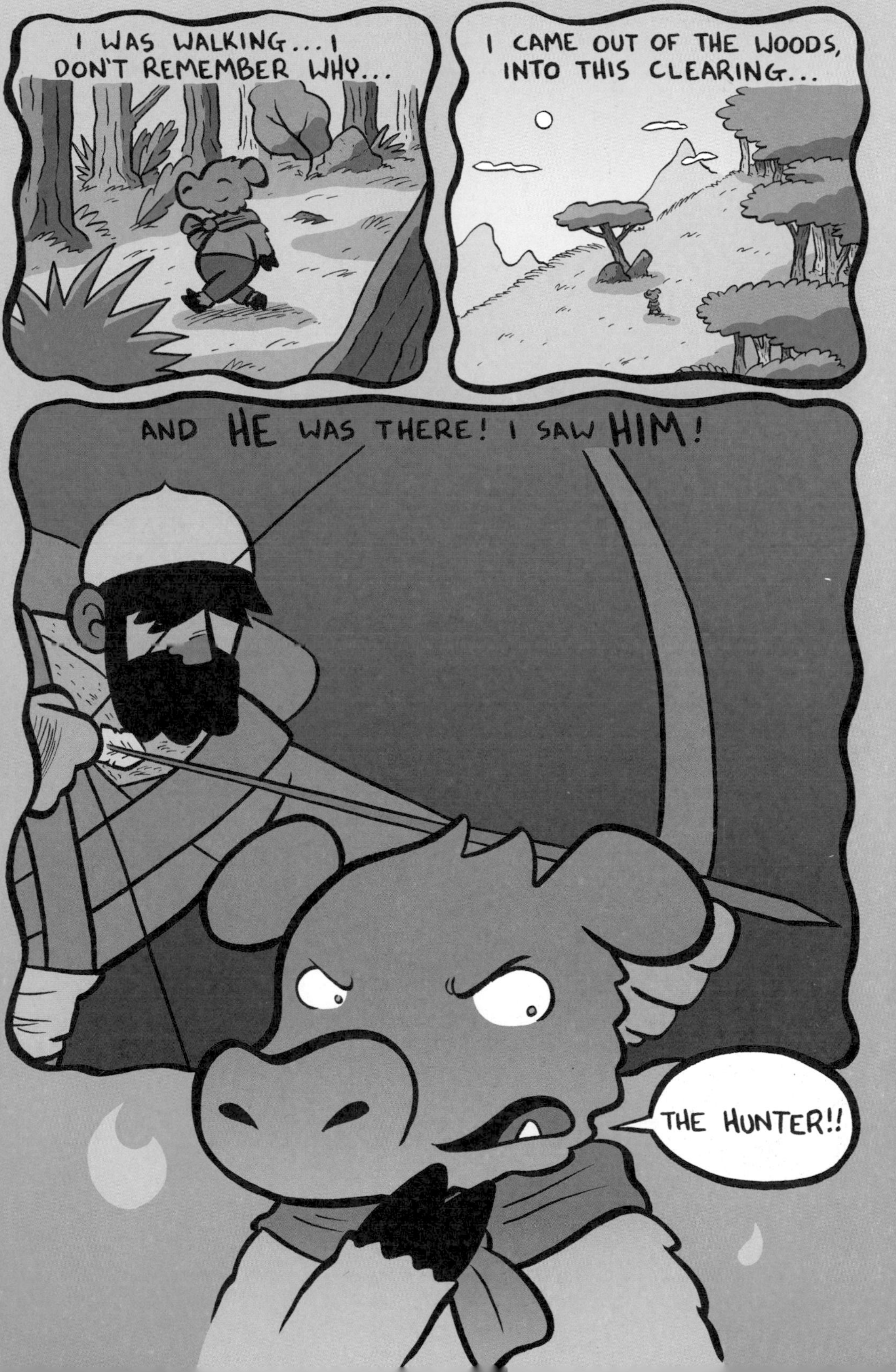
I WAS WALKING... I DON'T REMEMBER WHY...
I CAME OUT OF THE WOODS, INTO THIS CLEARING...
AND HE WAS THERE! I SAW HIM!
THE HUNTER!!

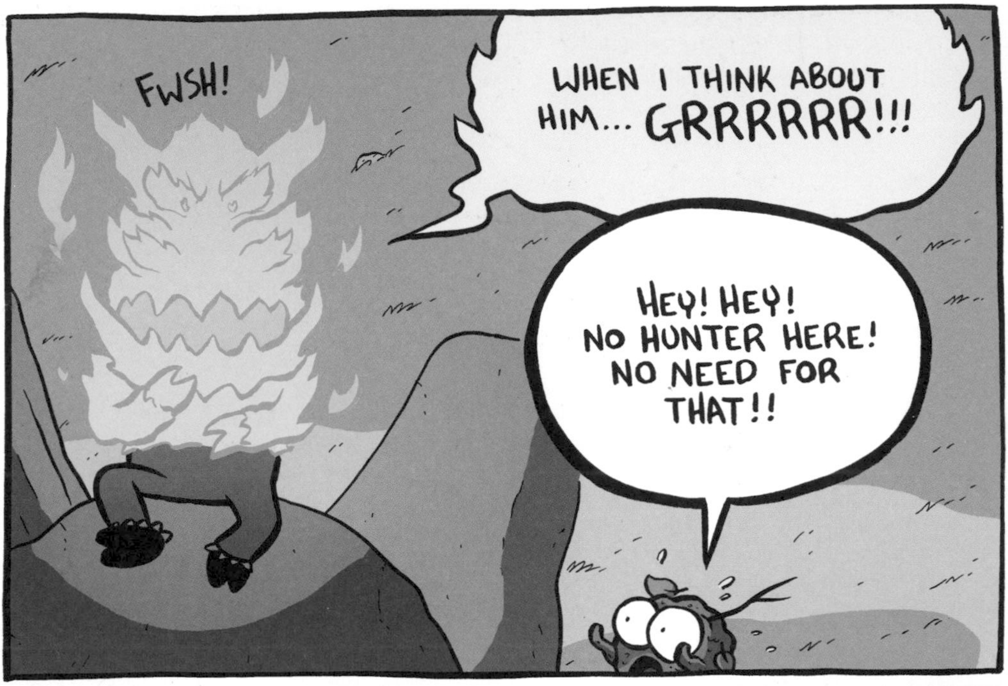
FWSH!
WHEN I THINK ABOUT HIM... GRRRRRR!!!
HEY! HEY! NO HUNTER HERE! NO NEED FOR THAT!!

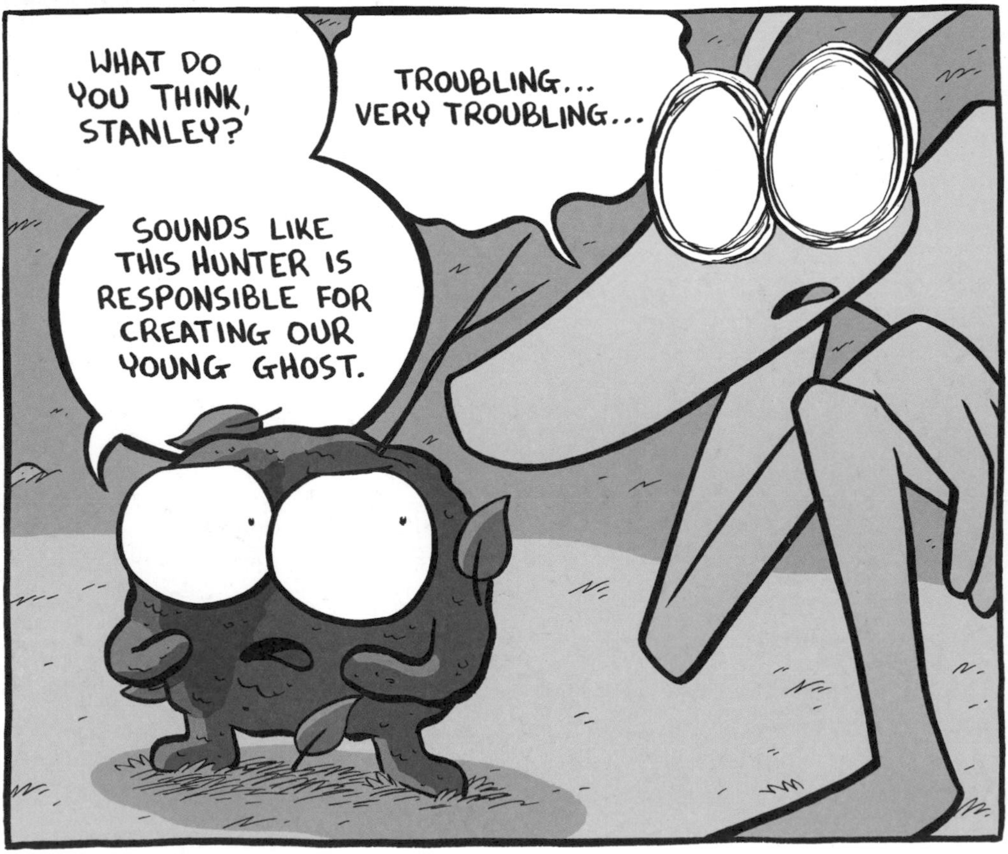
WHAT DO YOU THINK, STANLEY?
TROUBLING... VERY TROUBLING...
SOUNDS LIKE THIS HUNTER IS RESPONSIBLE FOR CREATING OUR YOUNG GHOST.

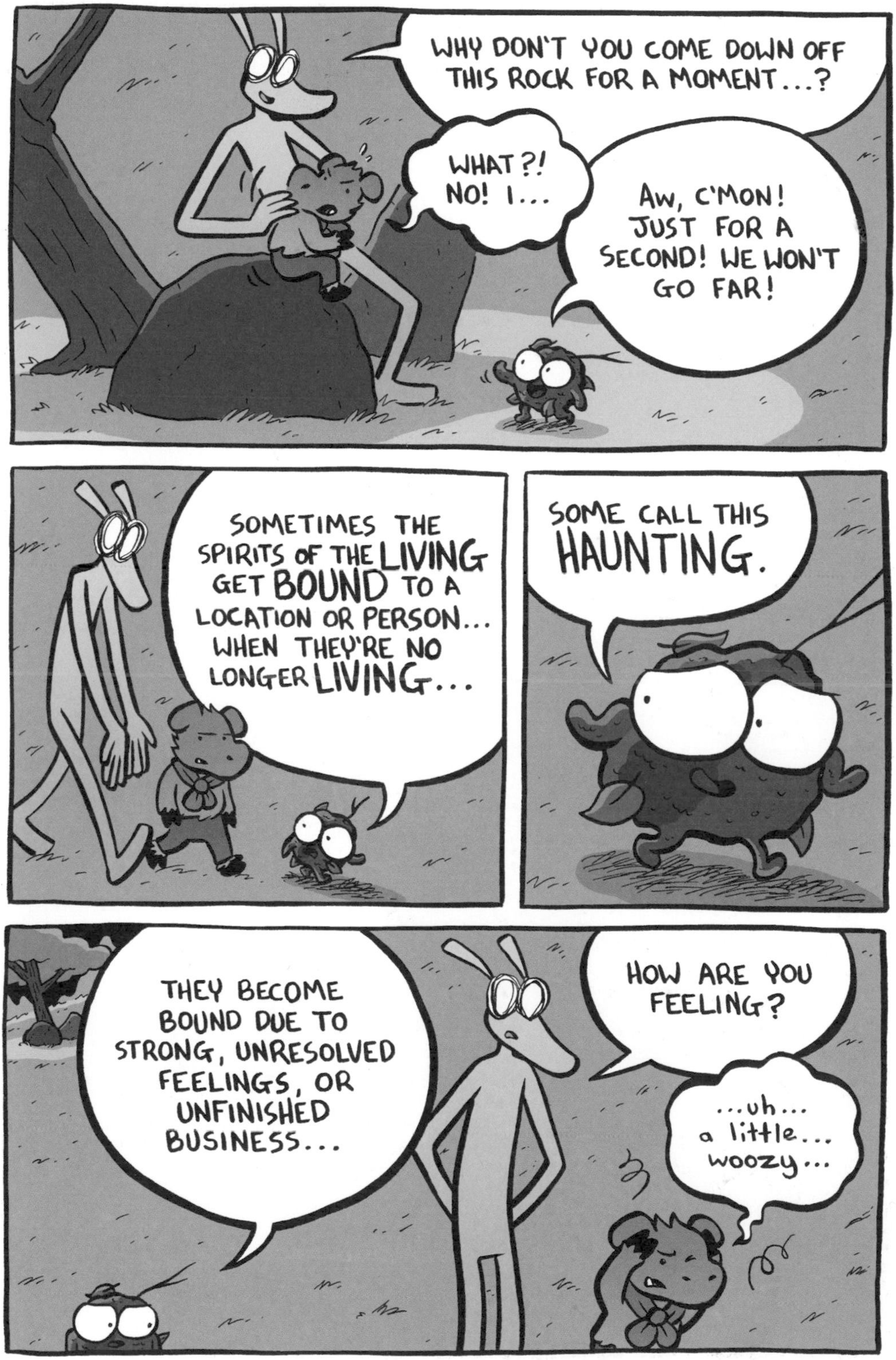
WHY DON'T YOU COME DOWN OFF THIS ROCK FOR A MOMENT...?
WHAT?! NO! I...
AW, C'MON! JUST FOR A SECOND! WE WON'T GO FAR!
SOMETIMES THE SPIRITS OF THE LIVING GET BOUND TO A LOCATION OR PERSON... WHEN THEY'RE NO LONGER LIVING...
SOME CALL THIS HAUNTING.
THEY BECOME BOUND DUE TO STRONG, UNRESOLVED FEELINGS, OR UNFINISHED BUSINESS...
HOW ARE YOU FEELING?
...uh... a little... woozy...

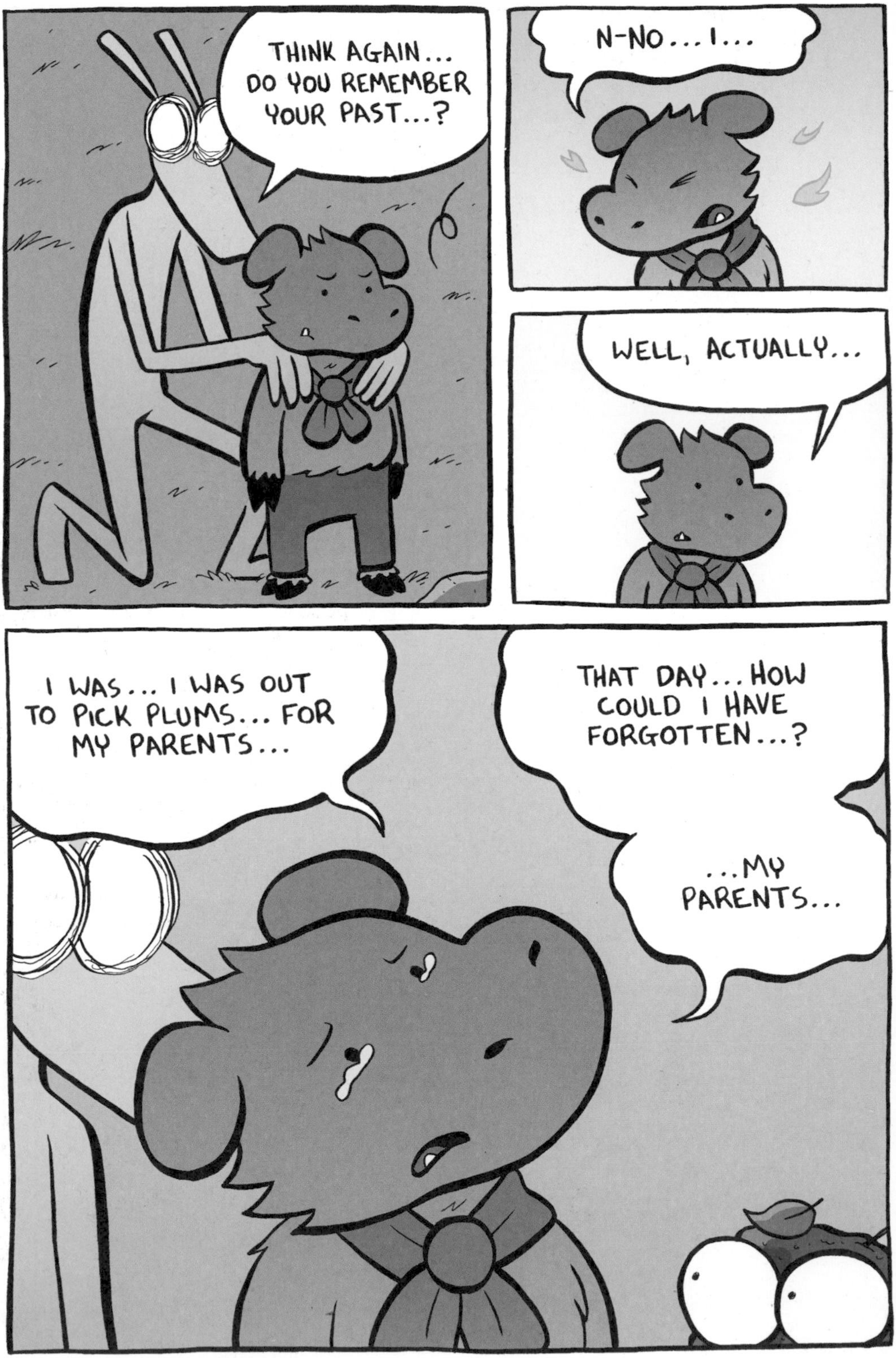
THINK AGAIN... DO YOU REMEMBER YOUR PAST...?
N-NO... I...
WELL, ACTUALLY...
I WAS... I WAS OUT TO PICK PLUMS... FOR MY PARENTS...
THAT DAY... HOW COULD I HAVE FORGOTTEN...?
...MY PARENTS...

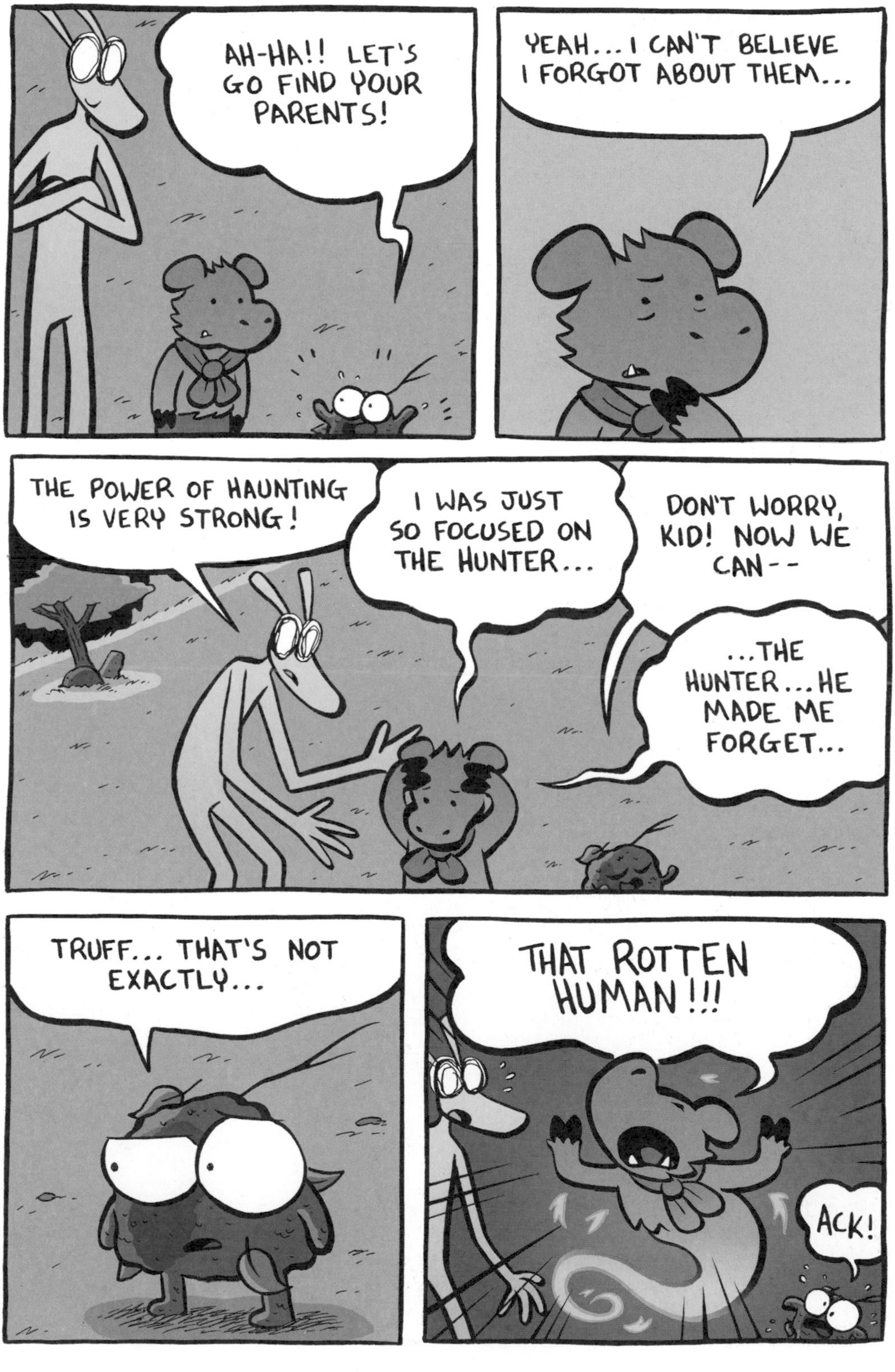
AH-HA!! LET'S GO FIND YOUR PARENTS!
YEAH... I CAN'T BELIEVE I FORGOT ABOUT THEM...
THE POWER OF HAUNTING IS VERY STRONG!
I WAS JUST SO FOCUSED ON THE HUNTER...
DON'T WORRY, KID! NOW WE CAN--
...THE HUNTER...HE MADE ME FORGET...
TRUFF... THAT'S NOT EXACTLY...
THAT ROTTEN HUMAN!!!
ACK!

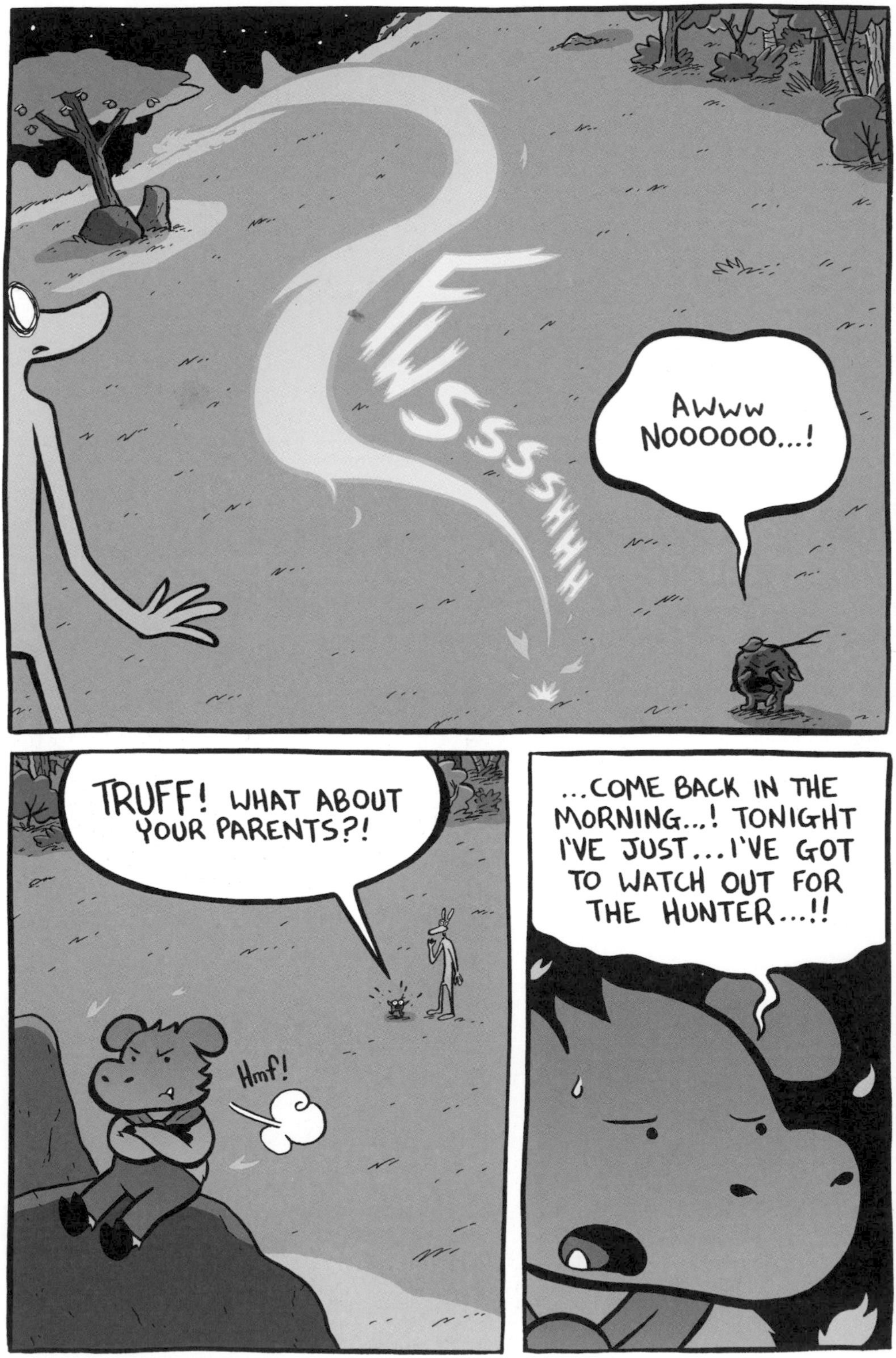
FWSSSSHHHH
AWWW NOOOOOO...!
TRUFF! WHAT ABOUT YOUR PARENTS?!
Hmf!
...COME BACK IN THE MORNING...! TONIGHT I'VE JUST...I'VE GOT TO WATCH OUT FOR THE HUNTER...!!

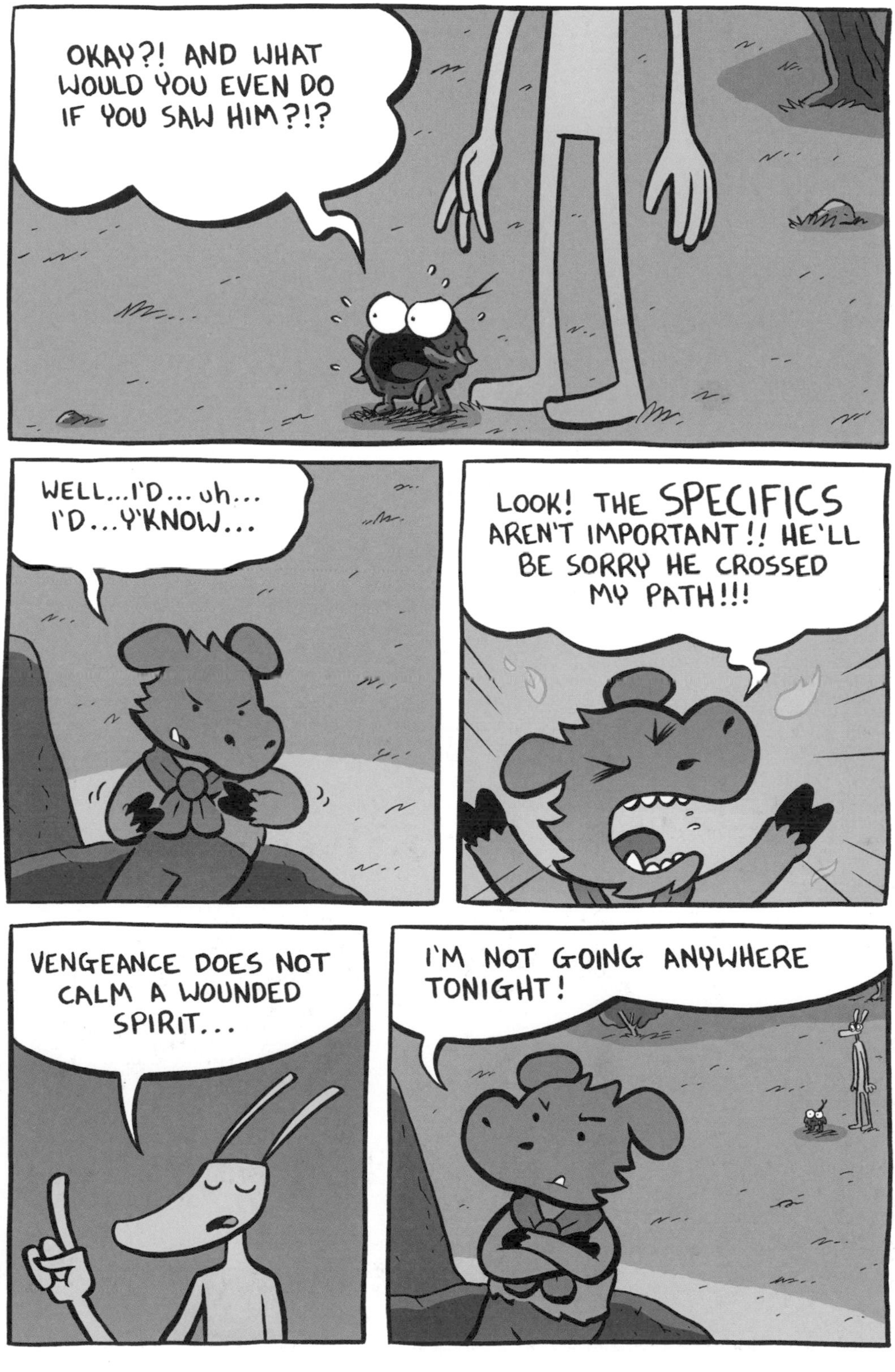
OKAY?! AND WHAT WOULD YOU EVEN DO IF YOU SAW HIM?!?
WELL...I'D... uh... I'D...Y'KNOW...
LOOK! THE SPECIFICS AREN'T IMPORTANT!! HE'LL BE SORRY HE CROSSED MY PATH!!!
VENGEANCE DOES NOT CALM A WOUNDED SPIRIT...
I'M NOT GOING ANYWHERE TONIGHT!

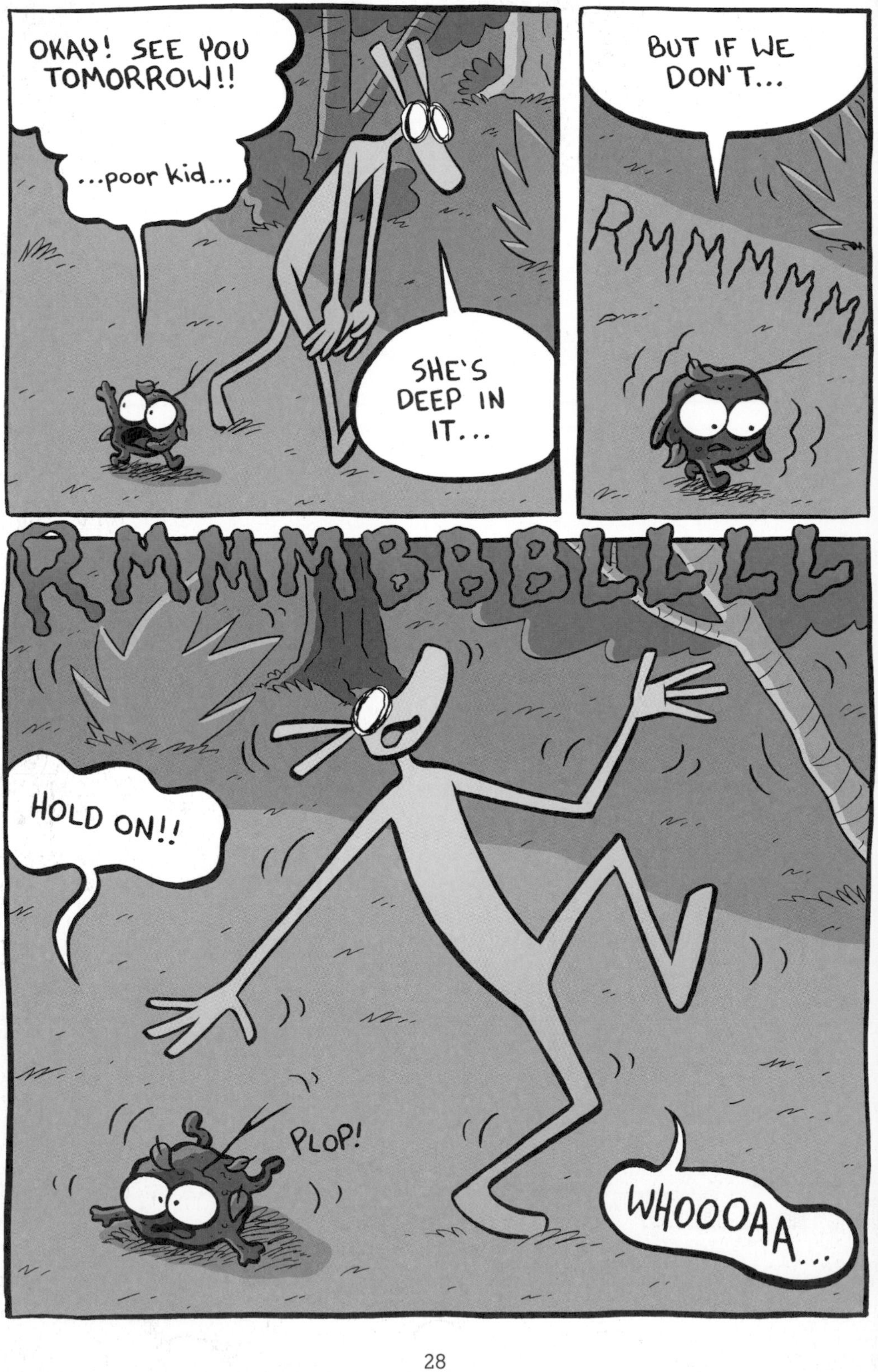
OKAY! SEE YOU TOMORROW!!
...poor kid...
SHE'S DEEP IN IT...
BUT IF WE DON'T...
RMMMMMM
RMMMBBBLLLL
HOLD ON!!
PLOP!
WHOOOAA...

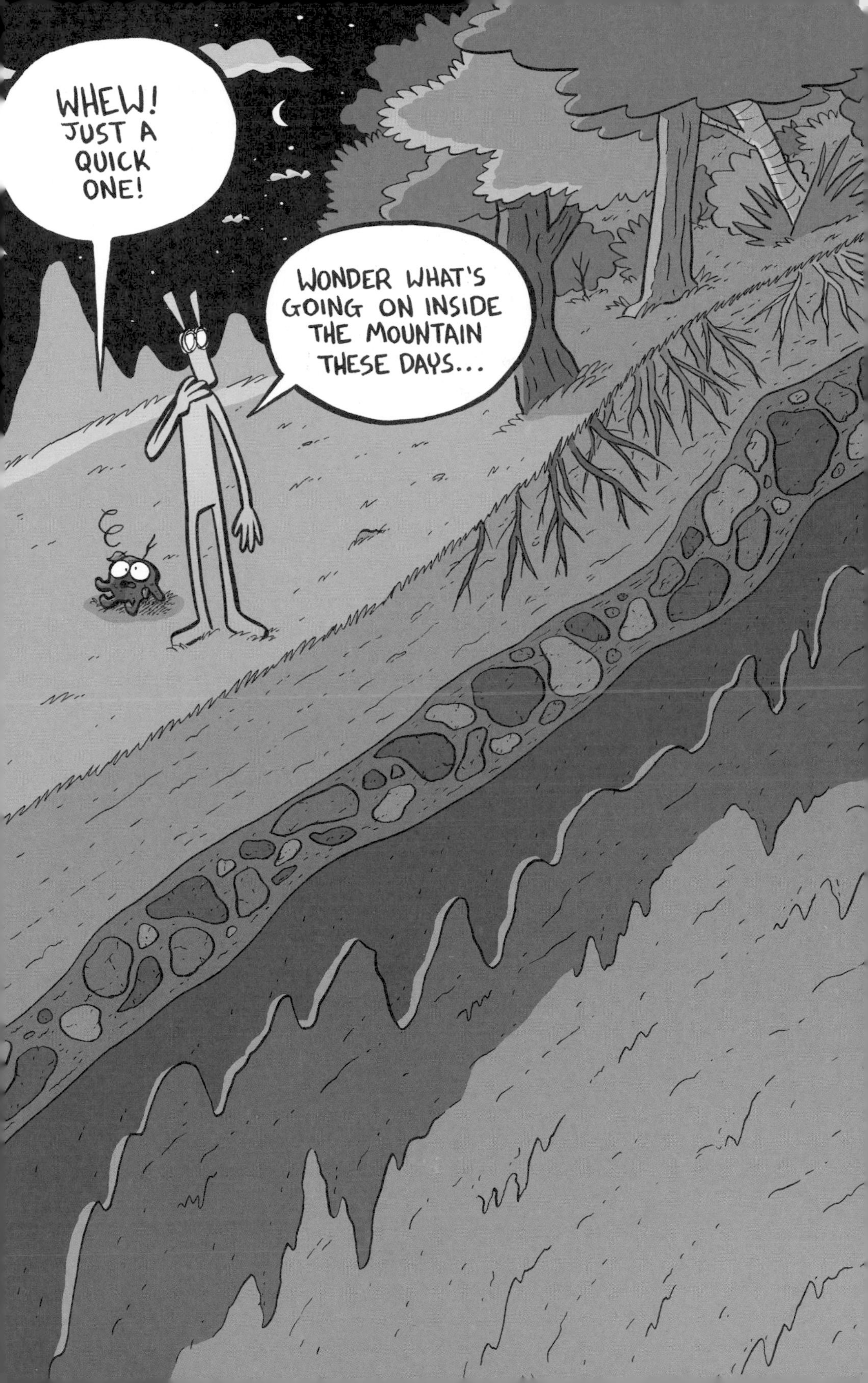
WHEW! JUST A QUICK ONE!
WONDER WHAT'S GOING ON INSIDE THE MOUNTAIN THESE DAYS...

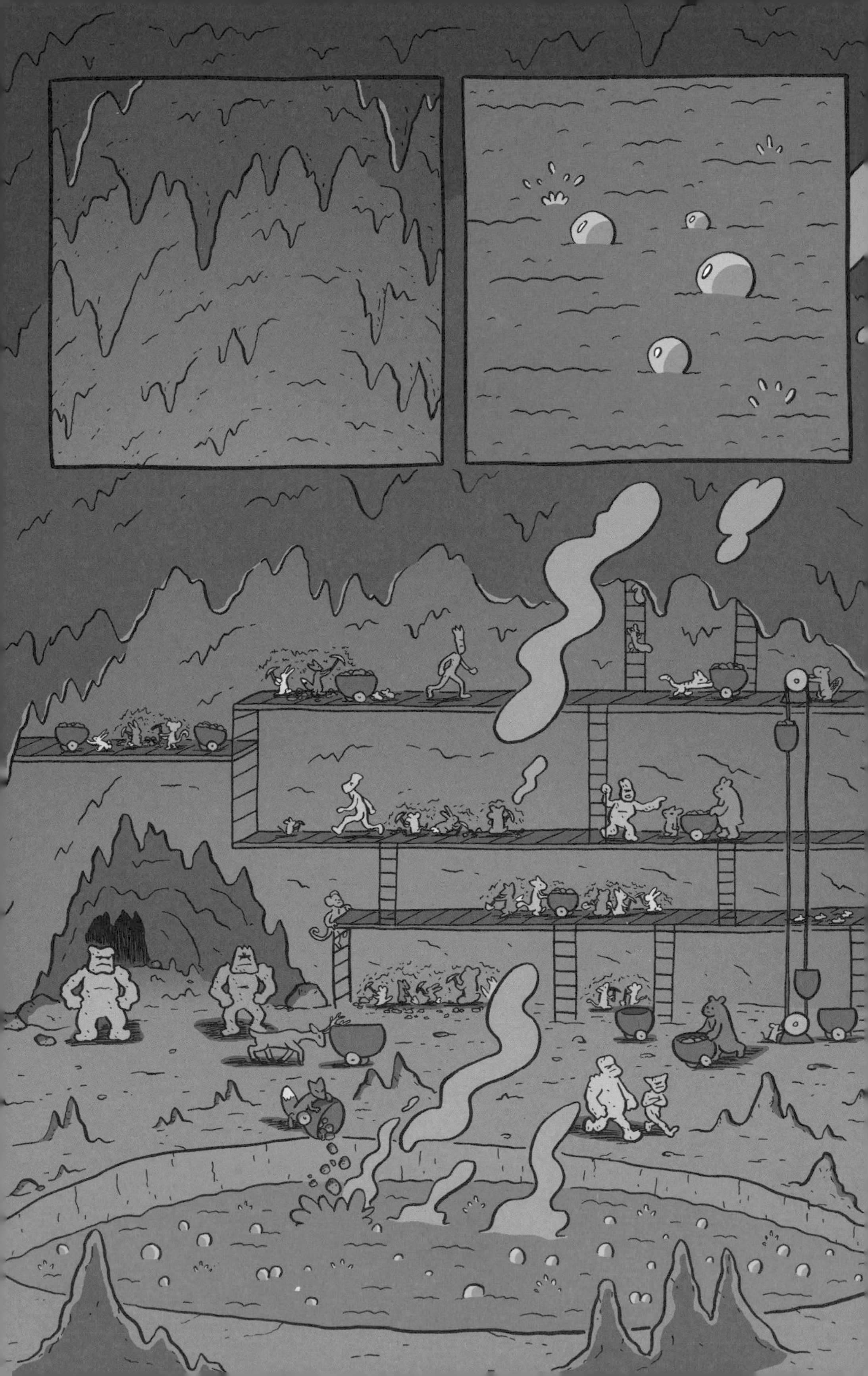

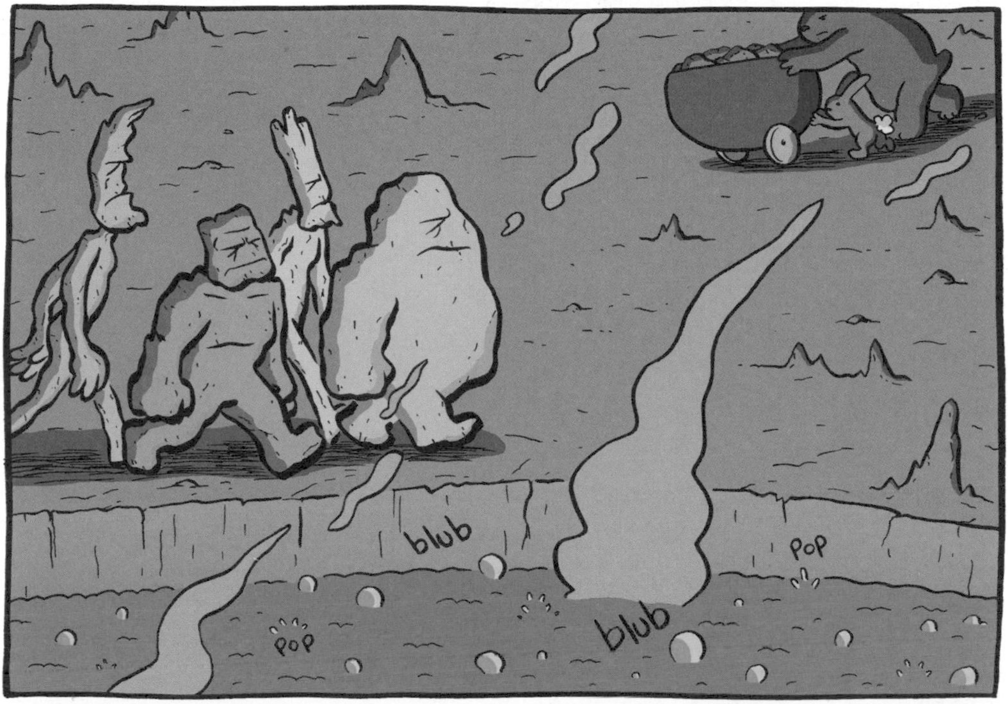
blub
POP
POP
blub

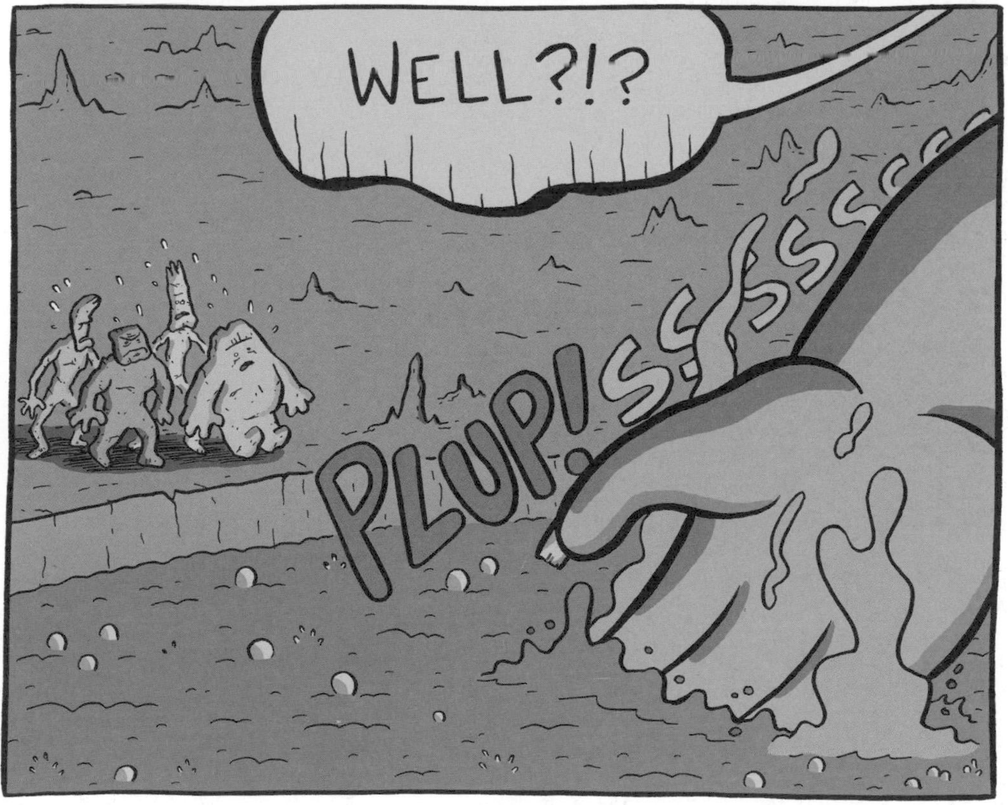
WELL?!?
PLUP!
SSSSSSSSS

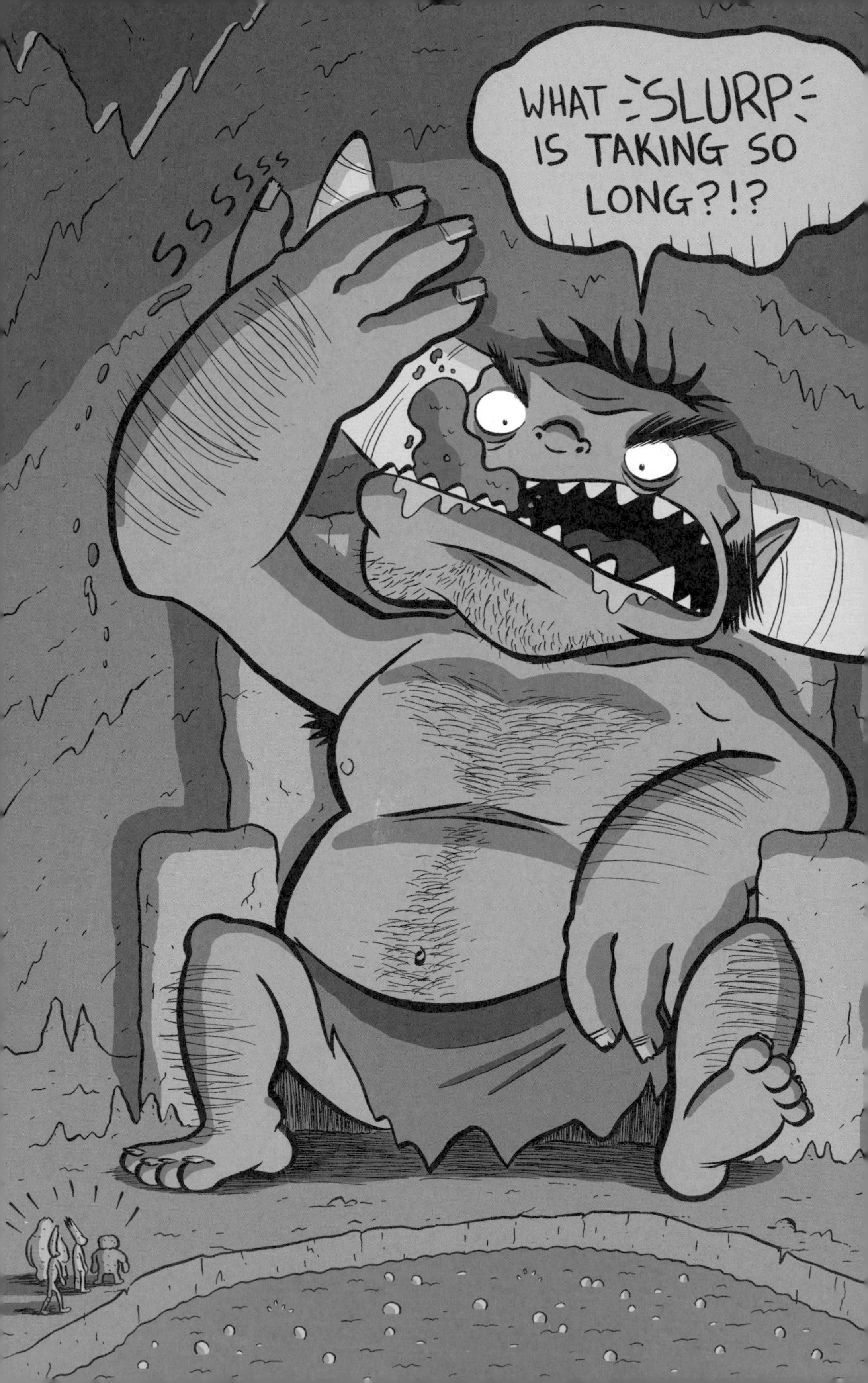
WHAT SLURP IS TAKING SO LONG?!?
SSSSSSS

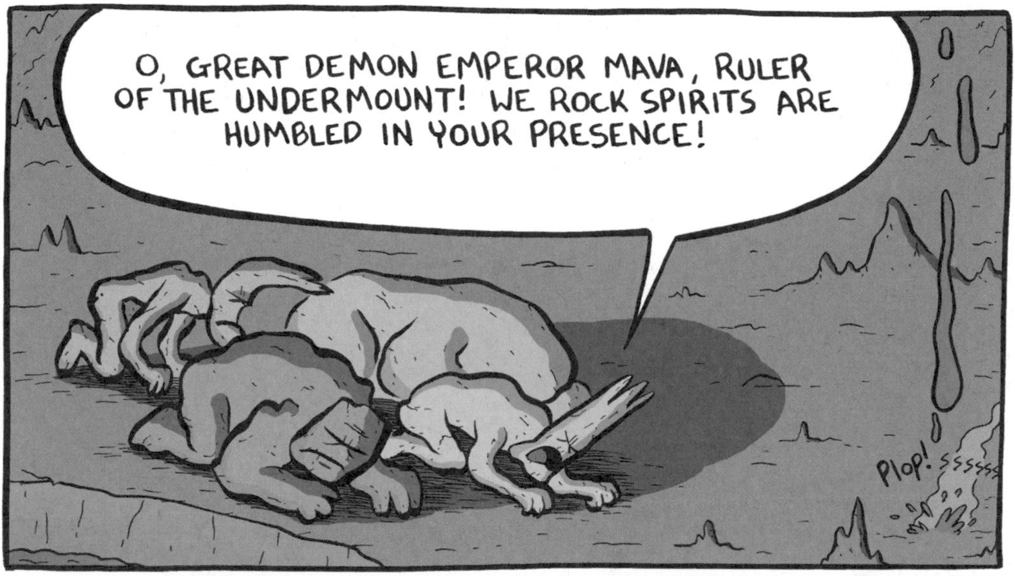
O, GREAT DEMON EMPEROR MAVA, RULER OF THE UNDERMOUNT! WE ROCK SPIRITS ARE HUMBLED IN YOUR PRESENCE!
PLOP! SSSSSS

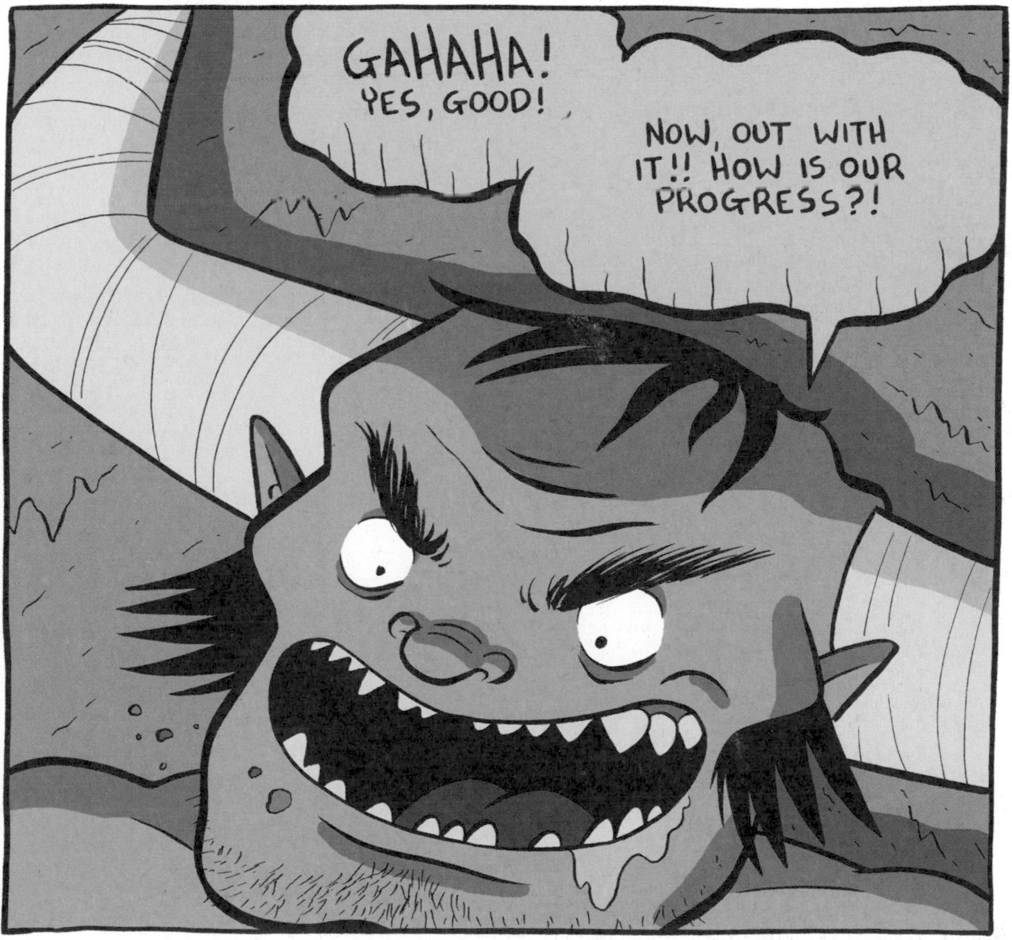
GAHAHA! YES, GOOD!
NOW, OUT WITH IT!! HOW IS OUR PROGRESS?!

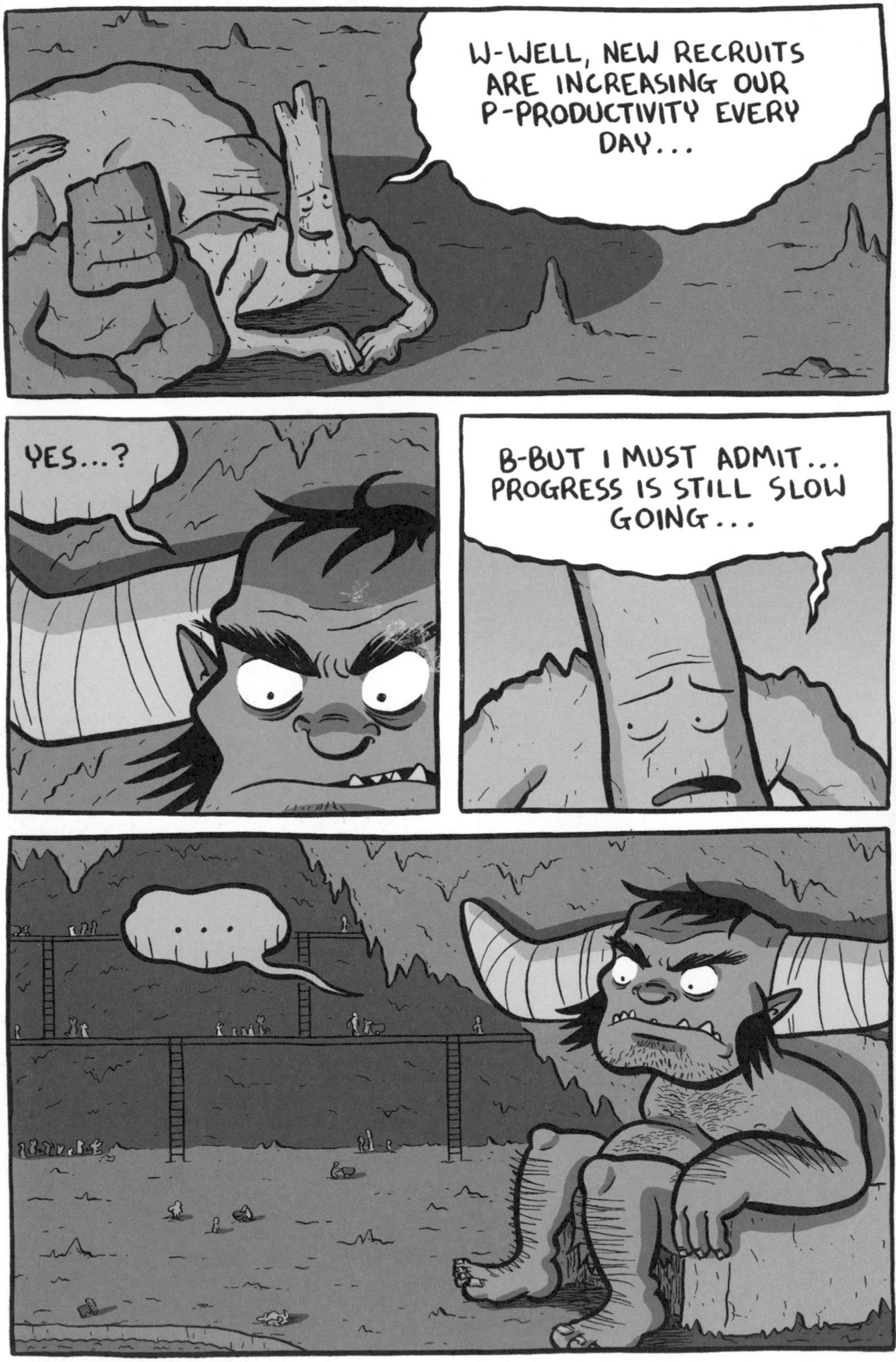
W-WELL, NEW RECRUITS ARE INCREASING OUR P-PRODUCTIVITY EVERY DAY...
YES...?
B-BUT I MUST ADMIT... PROGRESS IS STILL SLOW GOING...
...

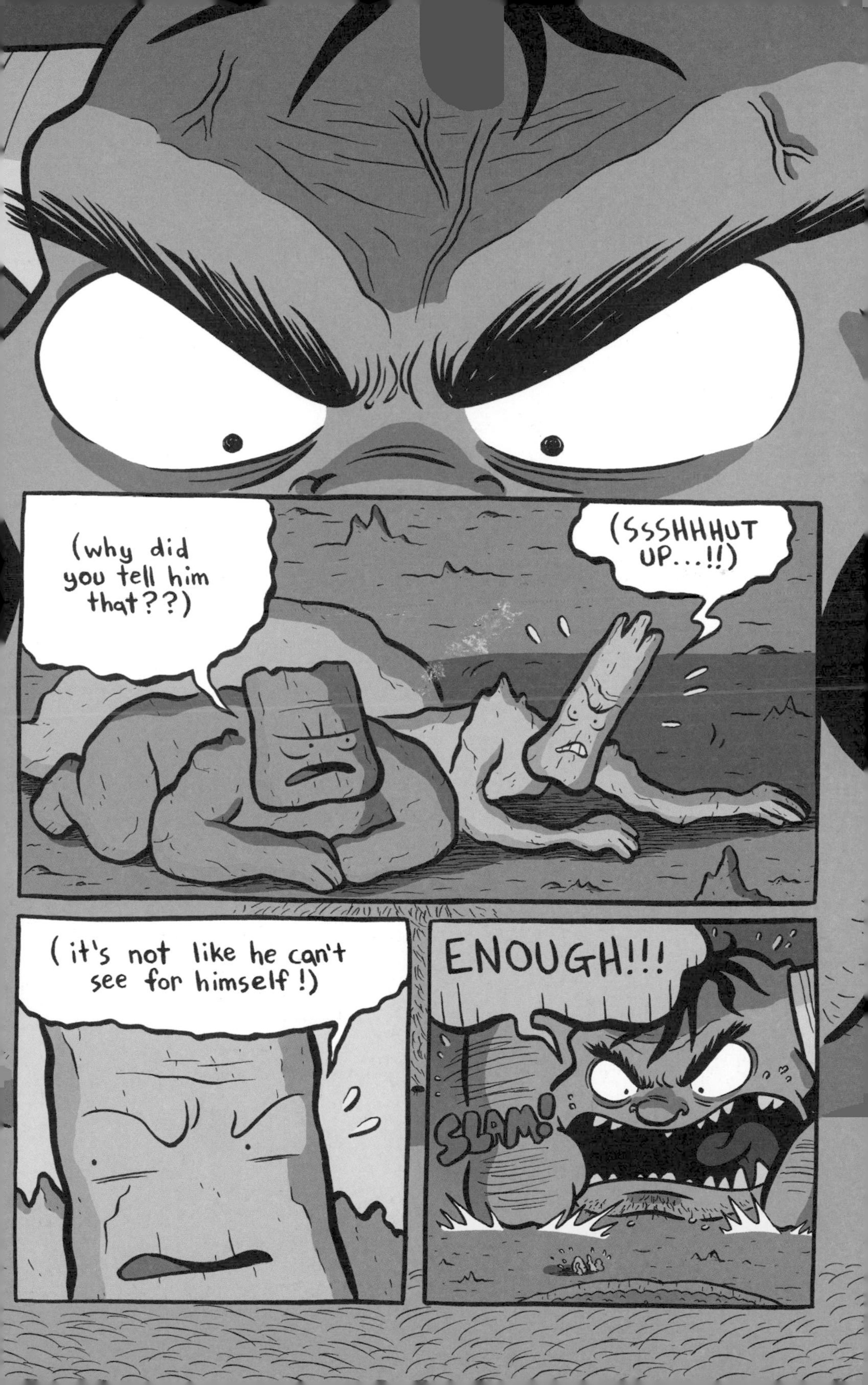
(why did you tell him that??)
(SSSHHHUT UP...!!)
(it's not like he can't see for himself !)
ENOUGH!!!
SLAM!

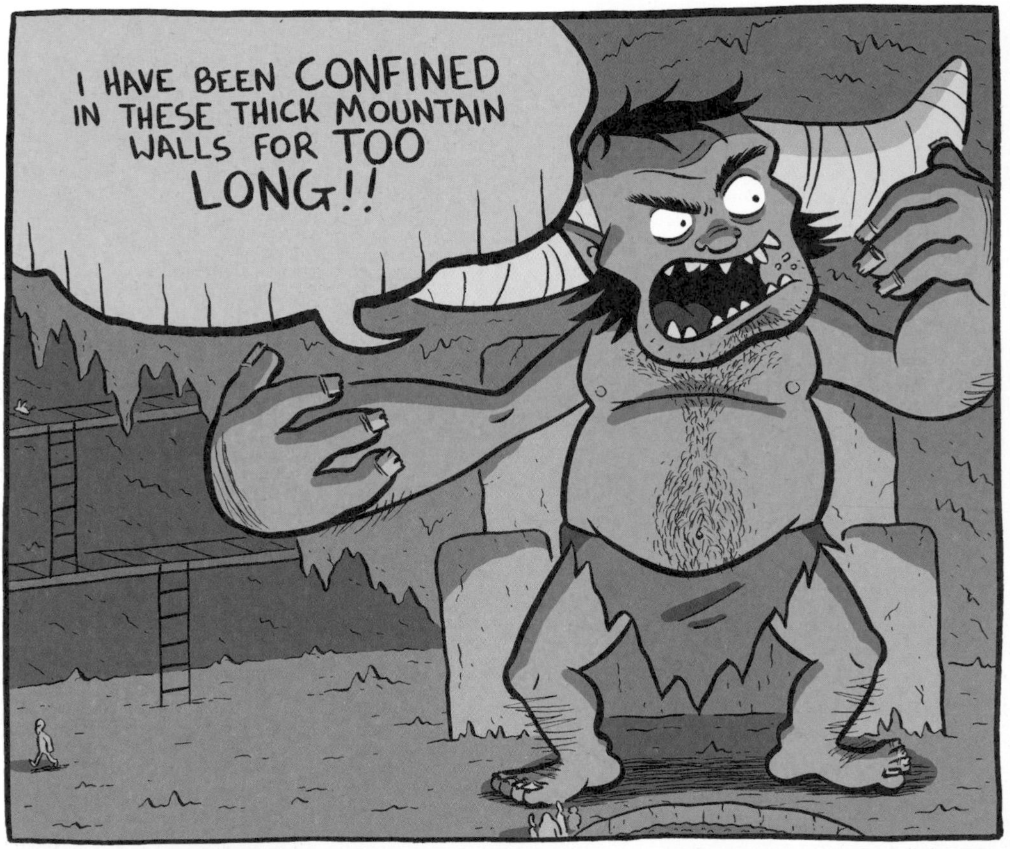
I HAVE BEEN CONFINED IN THESE THICK MOUNTAIN WALLS FOR TOO LONG!!

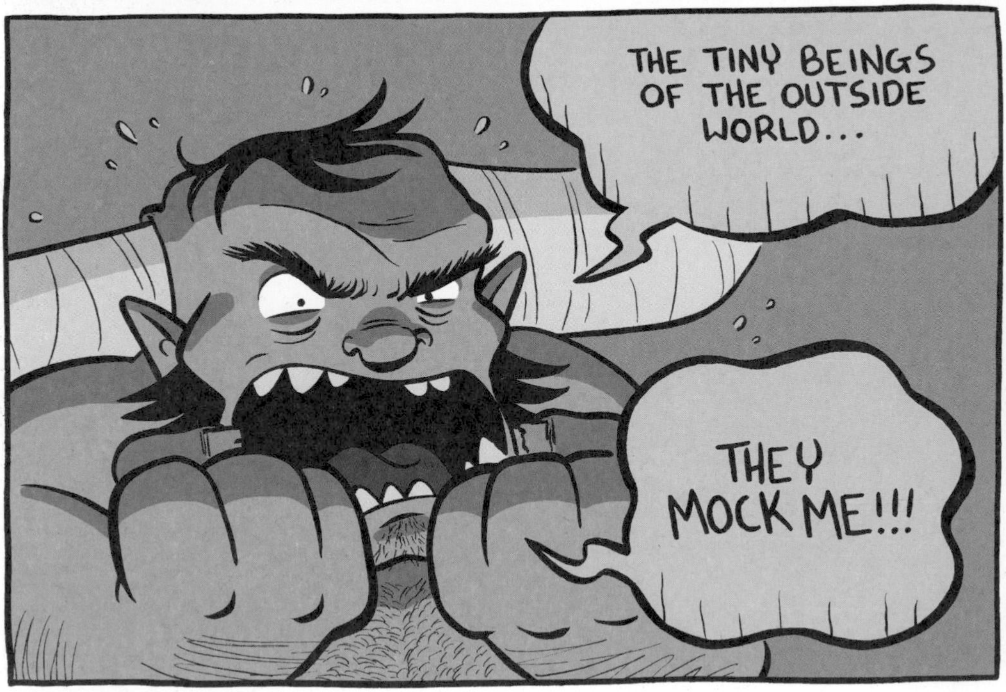
THE TINY BEINGS OF THE OUTSIDE WORLD...
THEY MOCK ME!!!

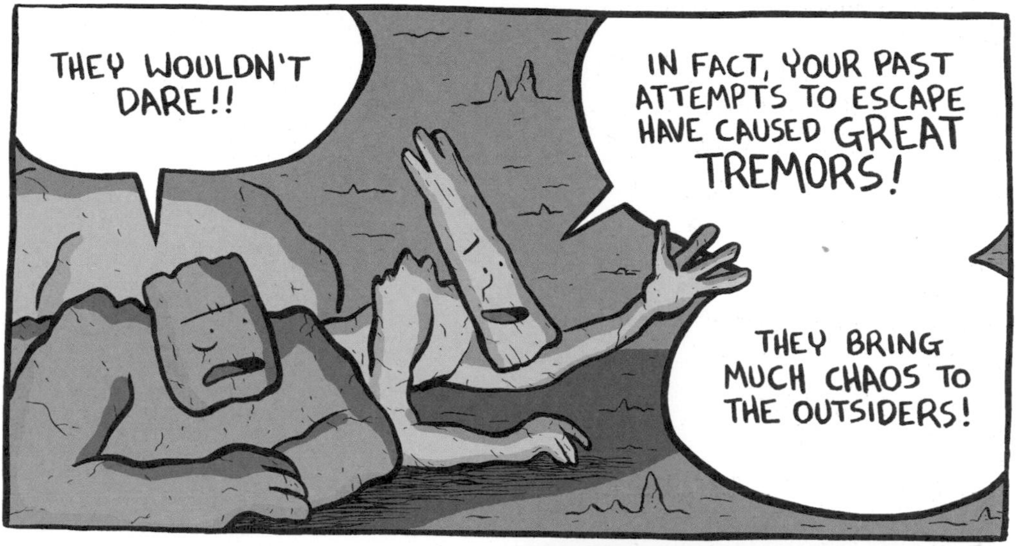
THEY WOULDN'T DARE!!
IN FACT, YOUR PAST ATTEMPTS TO ESCAPE HAVE CAUSED GREAT TREMORS!
THEY BRING MUCH CHAOS TO THE OUTSIDERS!

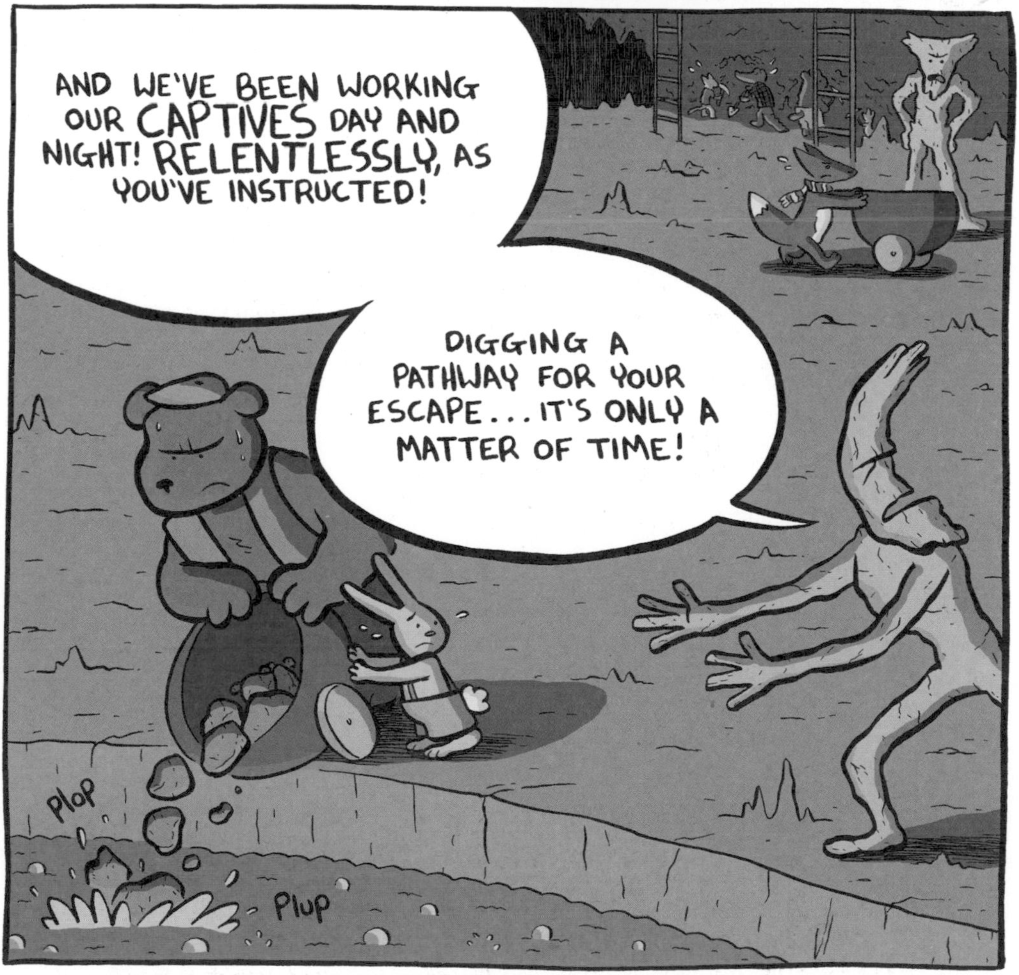
AND WE'VE BEEN WORKING OUR CAPTIVES DAY AND NIGHT! RELENTLESSLY, AS YOU'VE INSTRUCTED!
DIGGING A PATHWAY FOR YOUR ESCAPE... IT'S ONLY A MATTER OF TIME!
PLOP
PLUP

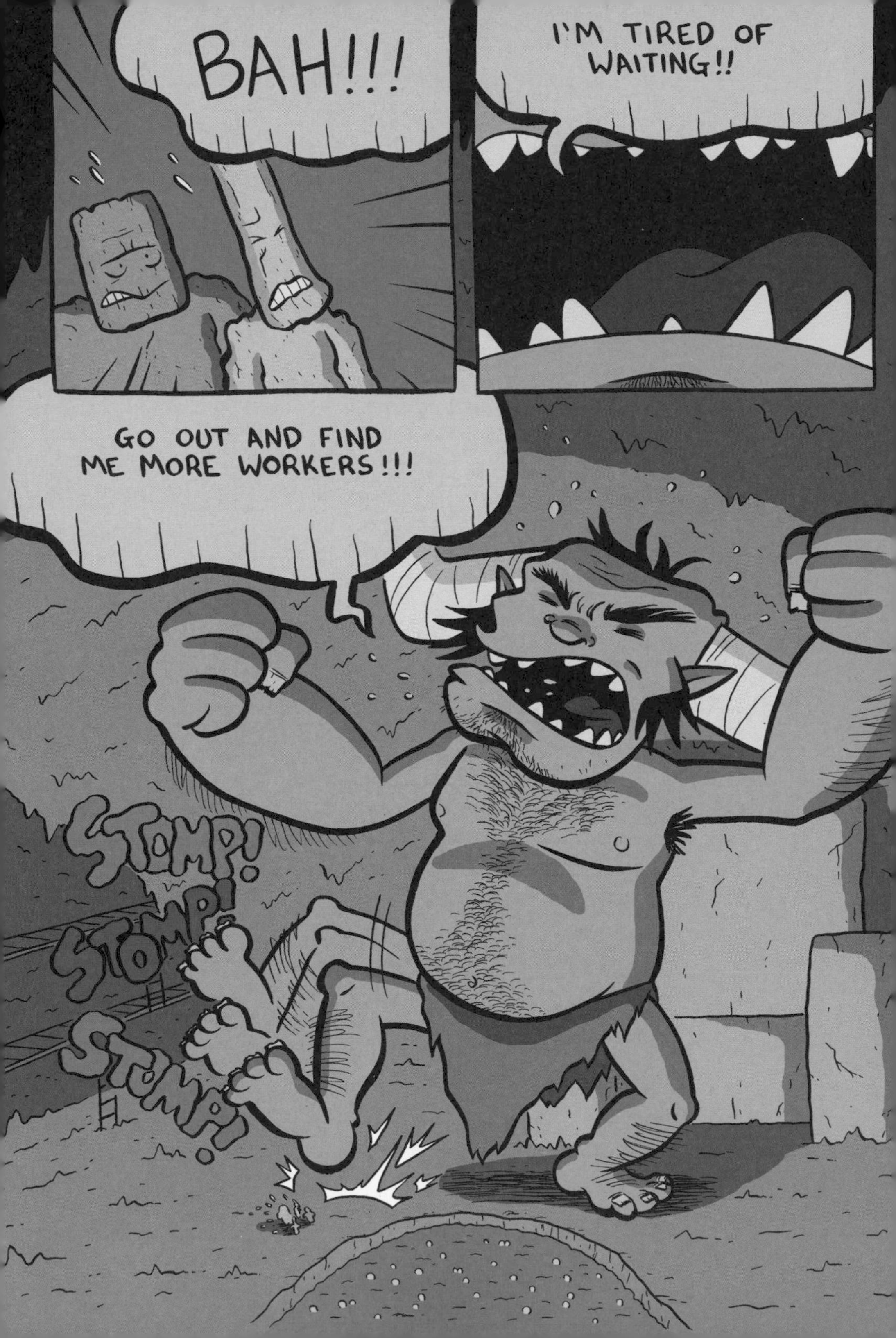
BAH!!!
I'M TIRED OF WAITING!!
GO OUT AND FIND ME MORE WORKERS!!!
STOMP!
STOMP!
STOMP!

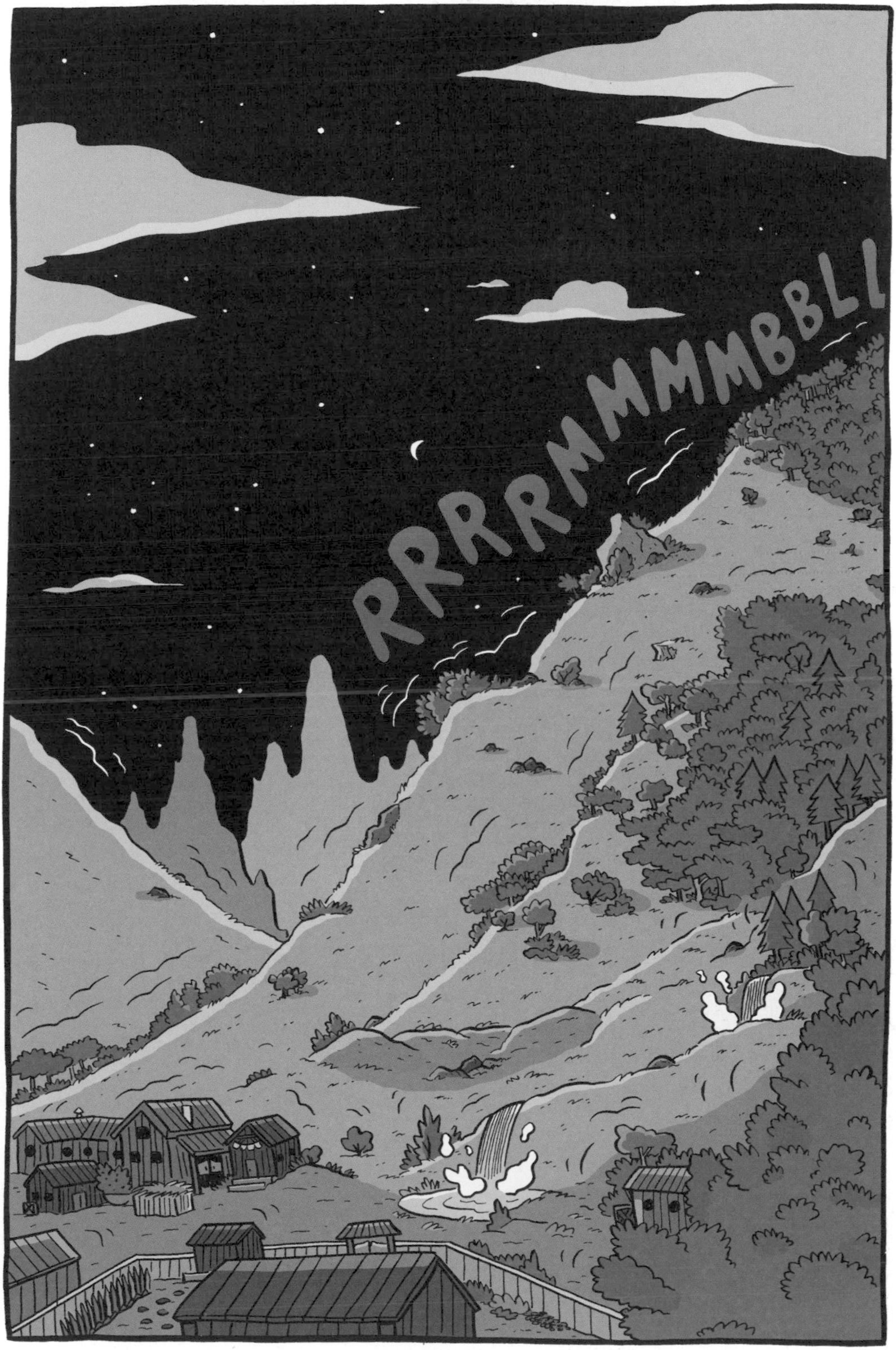
RRRRMMMMBBLL

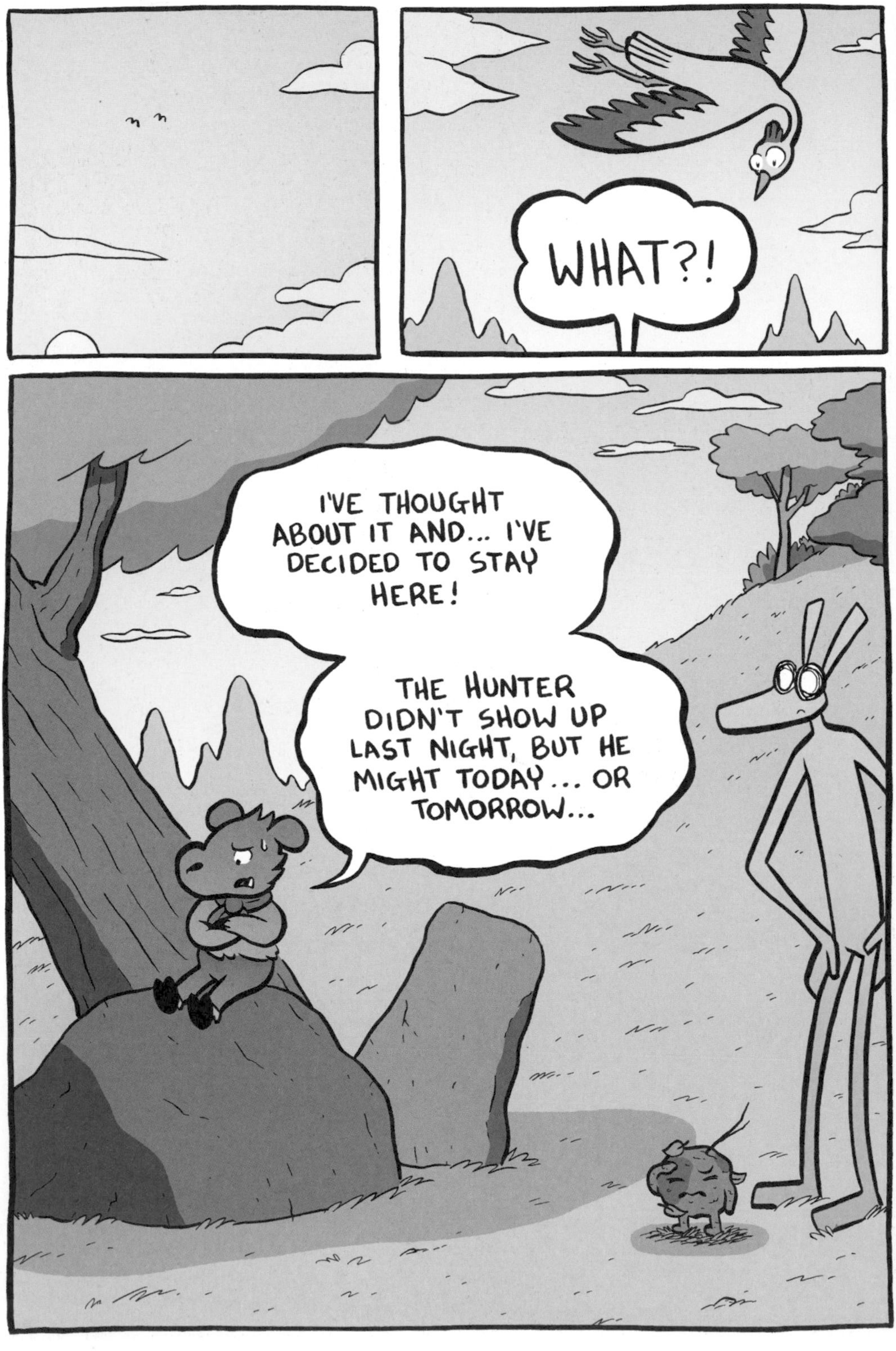
WHAT?!
I'VE THOUGHT ABOUT IT AND... I'VE DECIDED TO STAY HERE!
THE HUNTER DIDN'T SHOW UP LAST NIGHT, BUT HE MIGHT TODAY... OR TOMORROW...

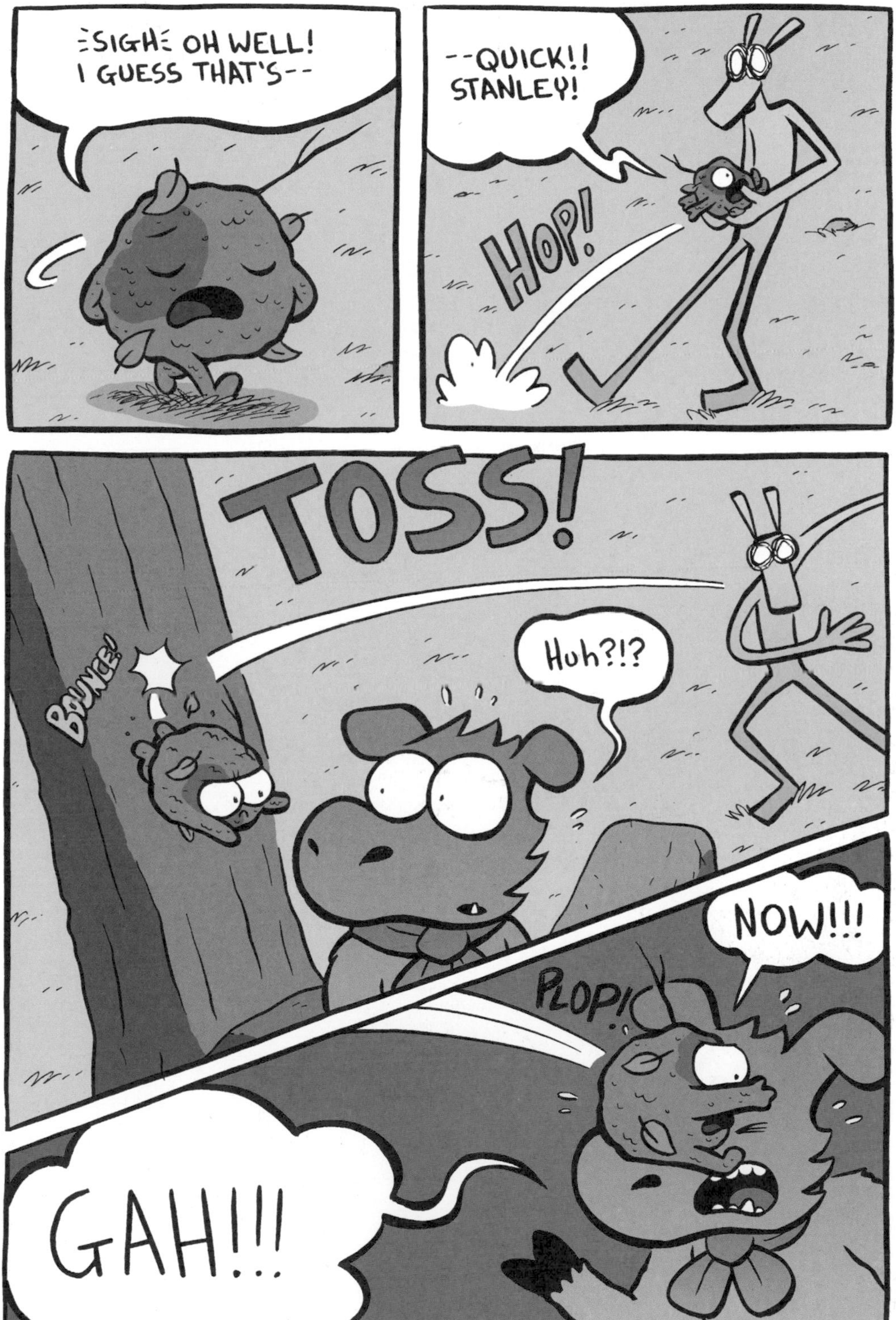

SIGH OH WELL! I GUESS THAT'S--
--QUICK!! STANLEY!
HOP!
TOSS!
BOUNCE!
Huh?!?
NOW!!!
PLOP!
GAH!!!...

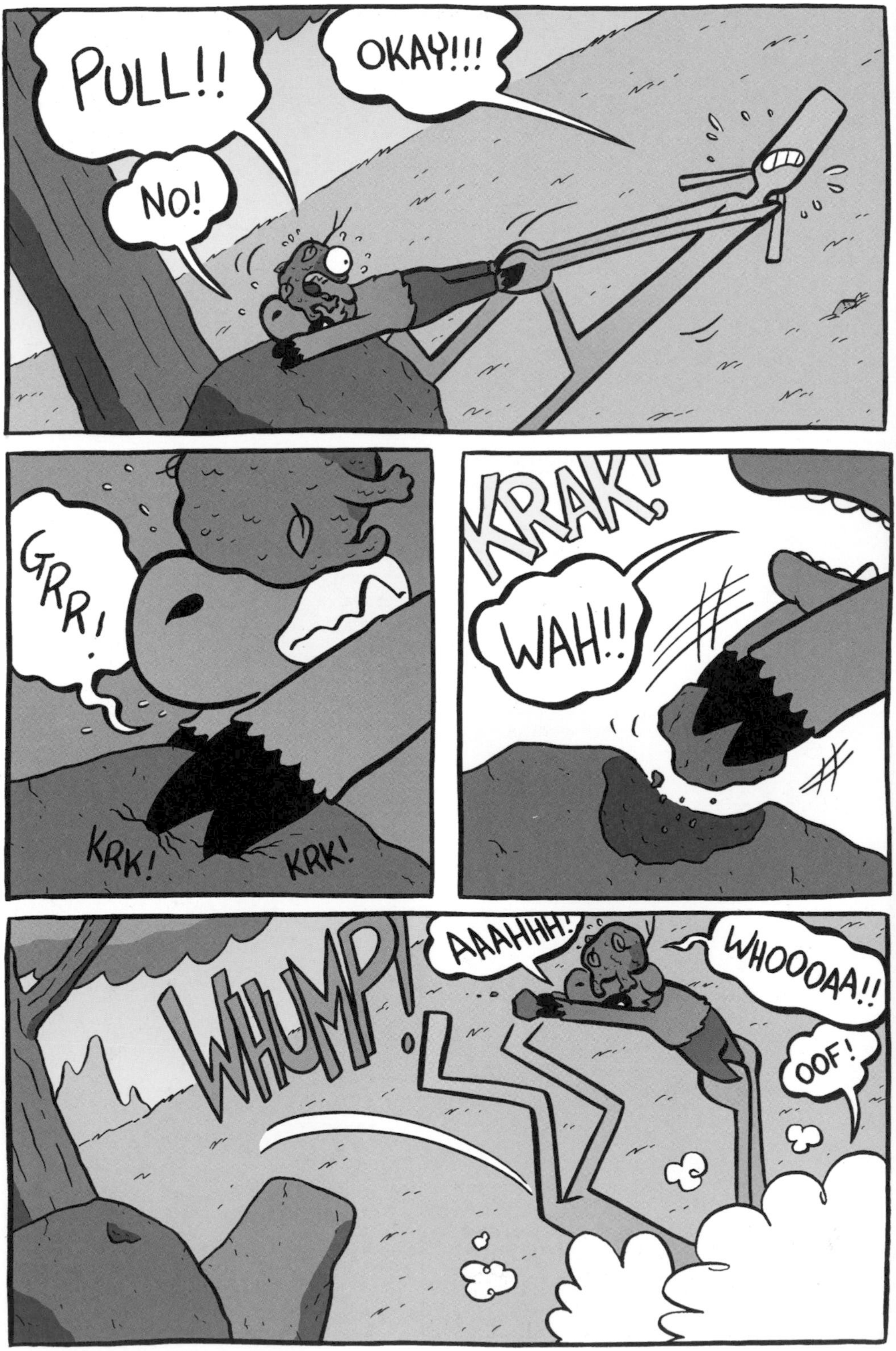
PULL!!
OKAY!!!
NO!
GRRR!
KRK!
KRK!
KRAK!
WAH!!
WHUMP!
AAAHHH!
WHOOOAA!!
OOF!

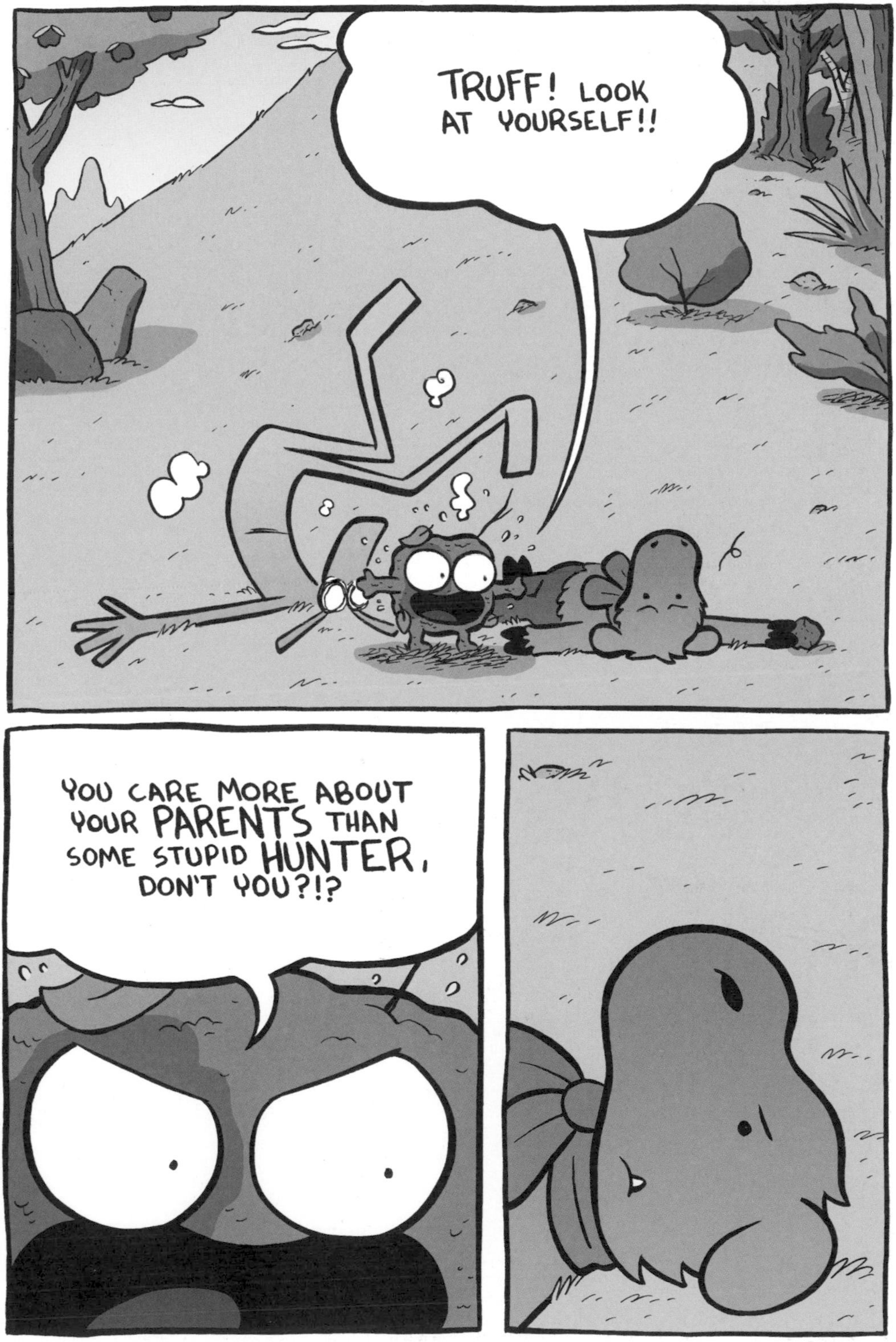
TRUFF! LOOK AT YOURSELF!!
YOU CARE MORE ABOUT YOUR PARENTS THAN SOME STUPID HUNTER, DON'T YOU?!?

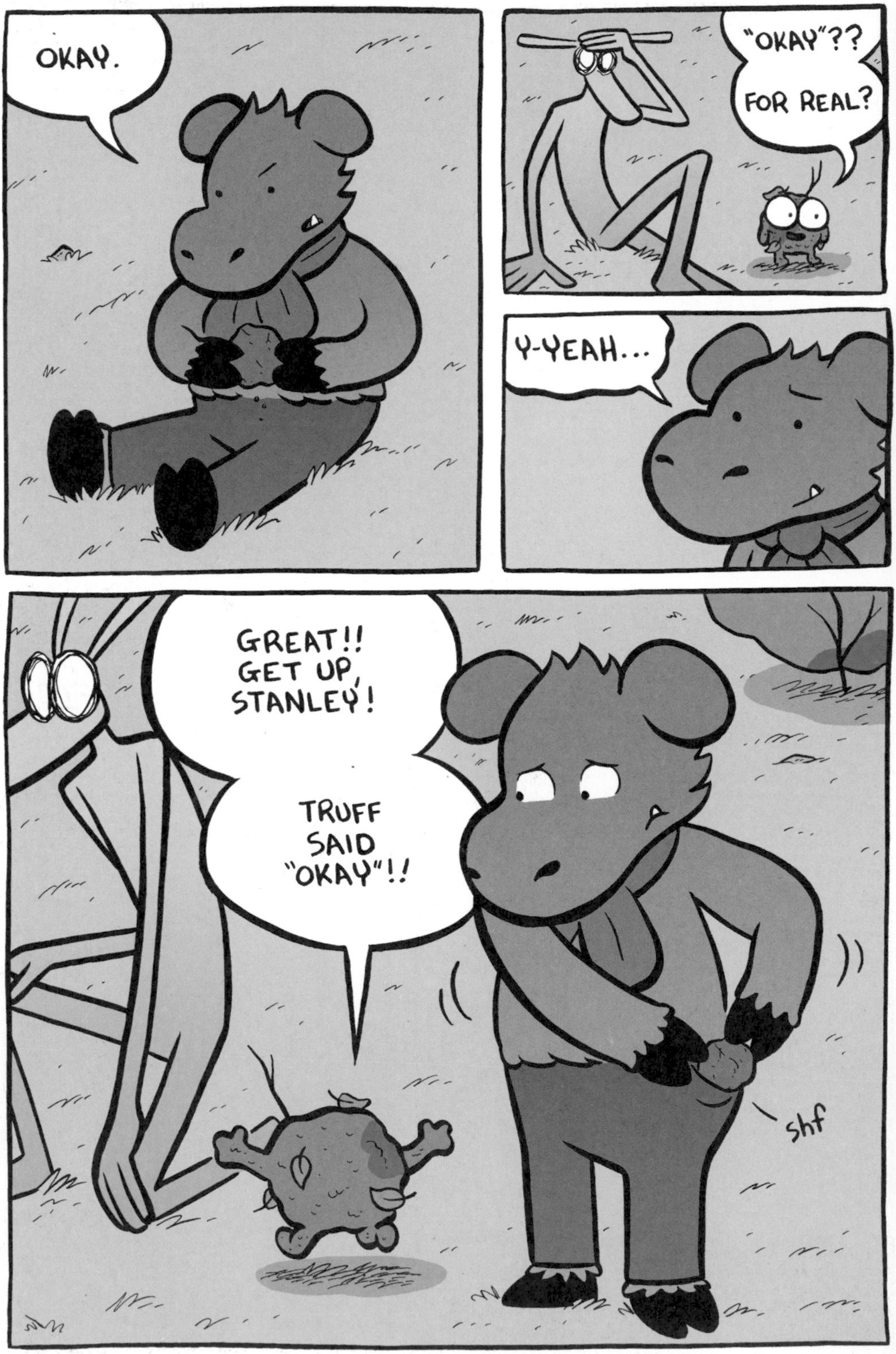
OKAY.
"OKAY"??
FOR REAL?
Y-YEAH...
GREAT!! GET UP, STANLEY!
TRUFF SAID "OKAY"!!
shf

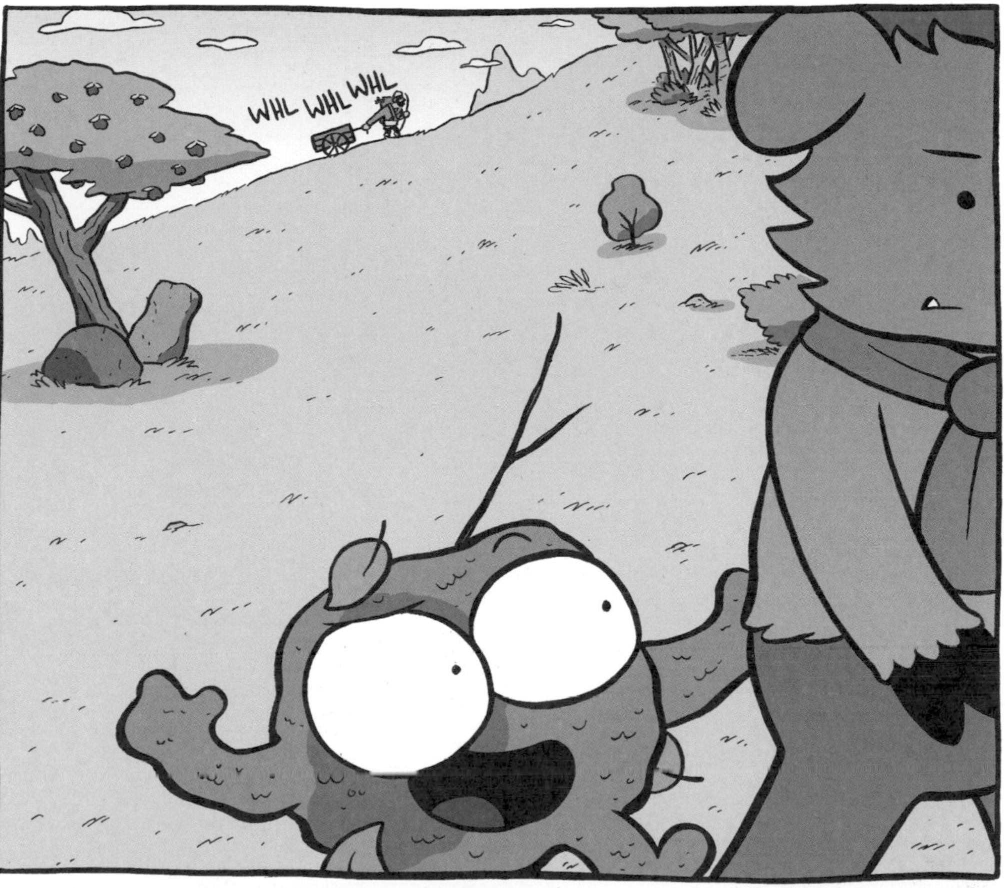
WHL WHL WHL

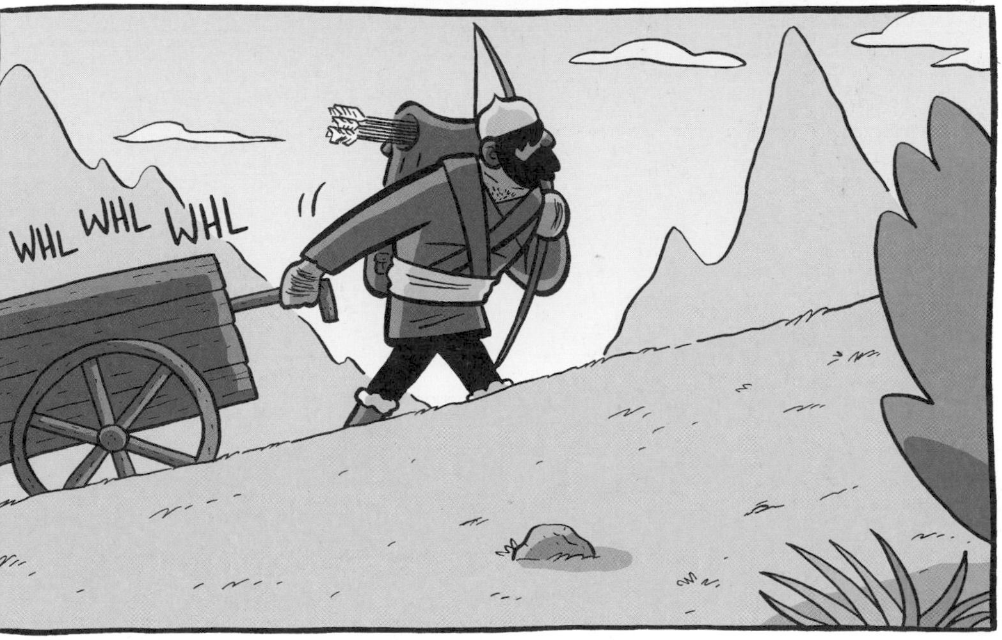
WHL WHL WHL

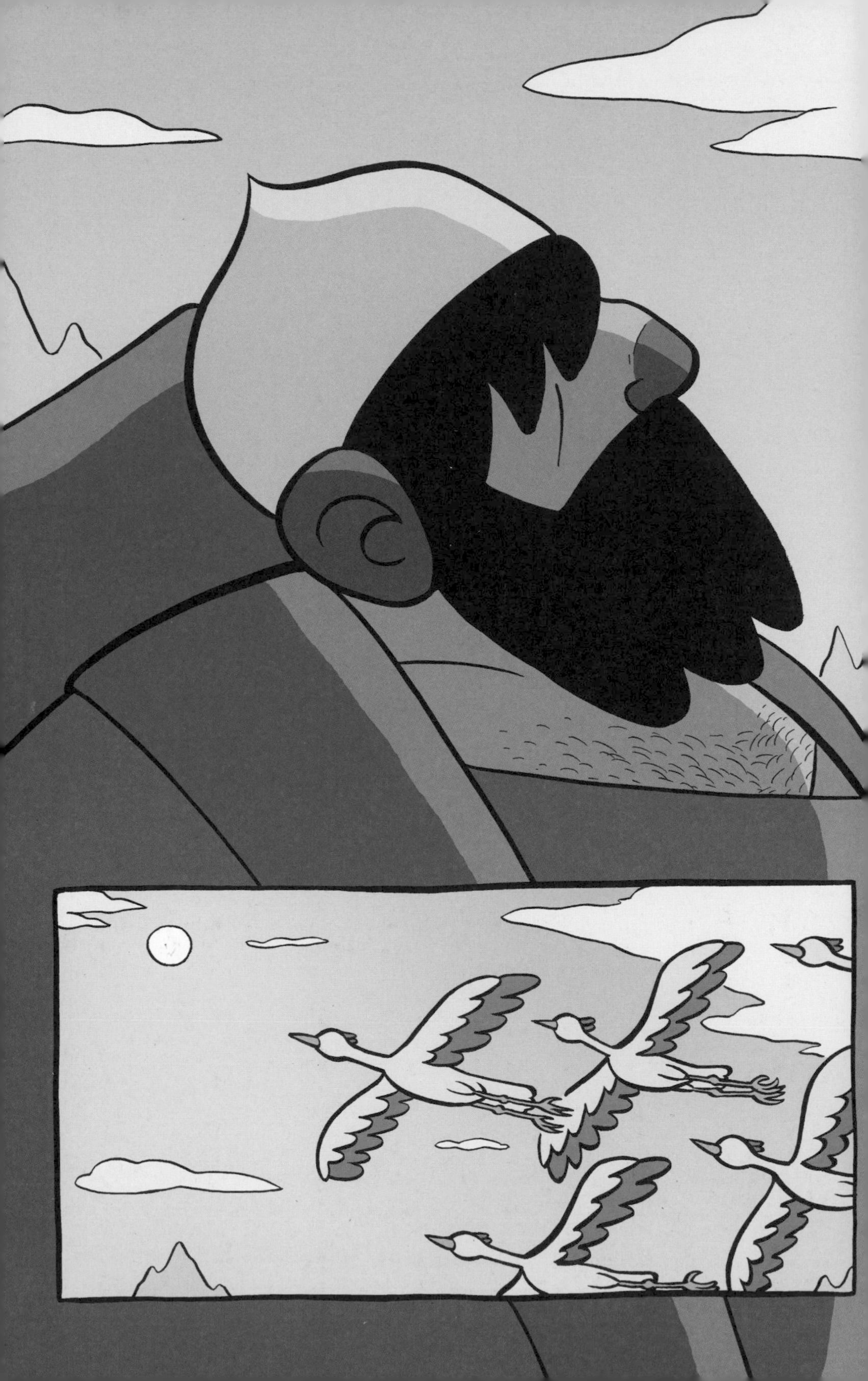

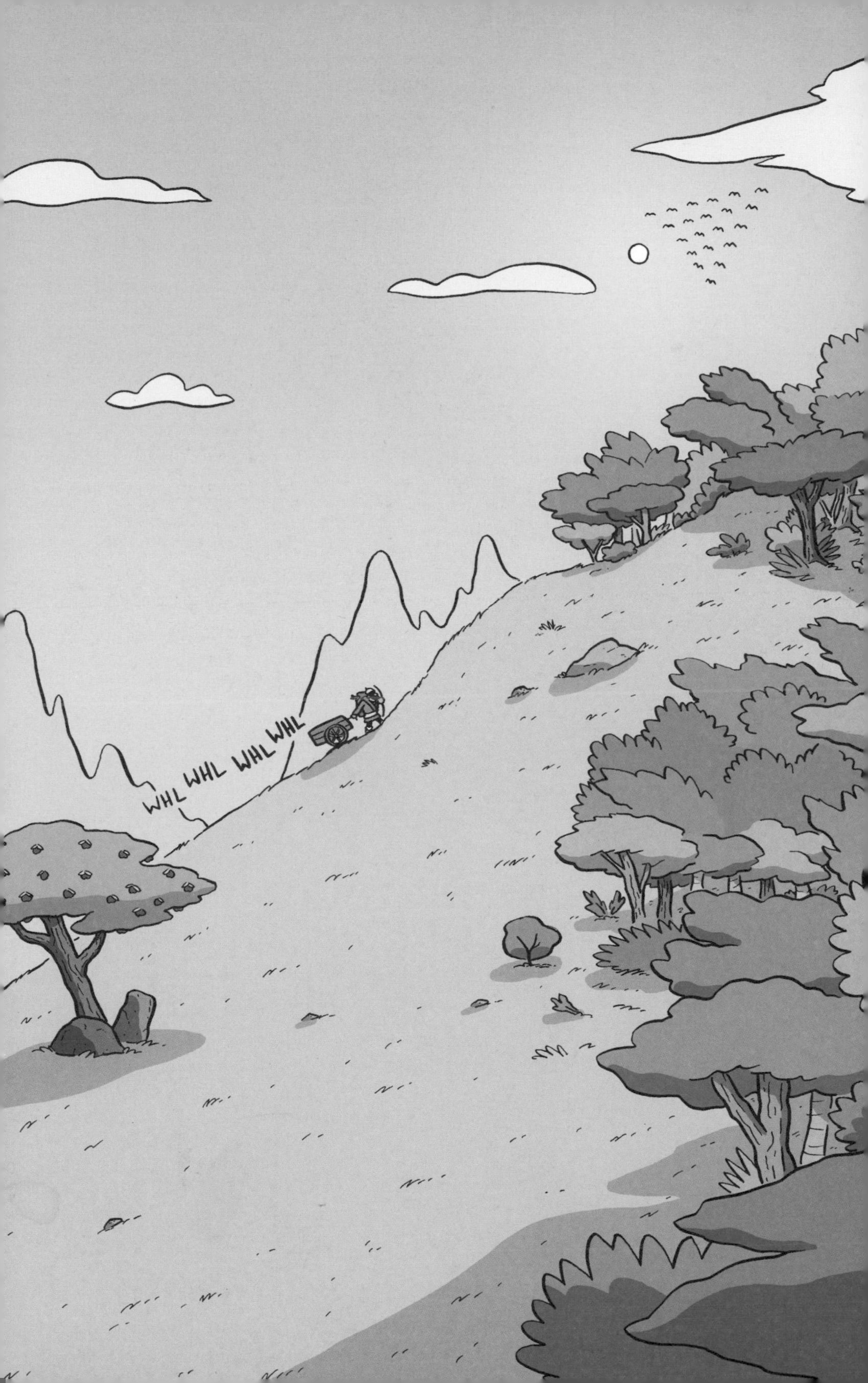
WHL WHL WHL WHL

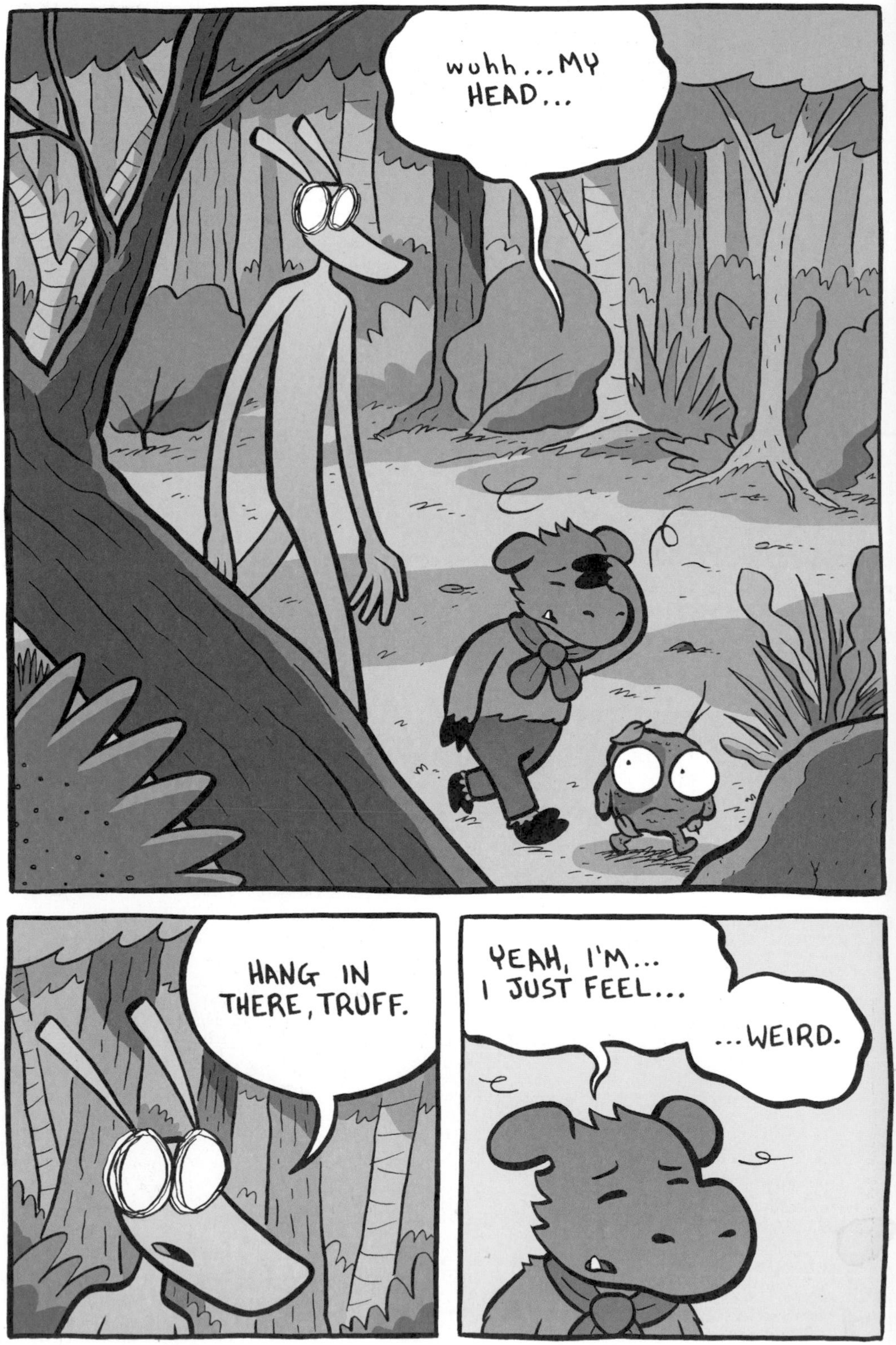
wuhh...MY HEAD...
HANG IN THERE, TRUFF.
YEAH, I'M... I JUST FEEL...
...WEIRD.

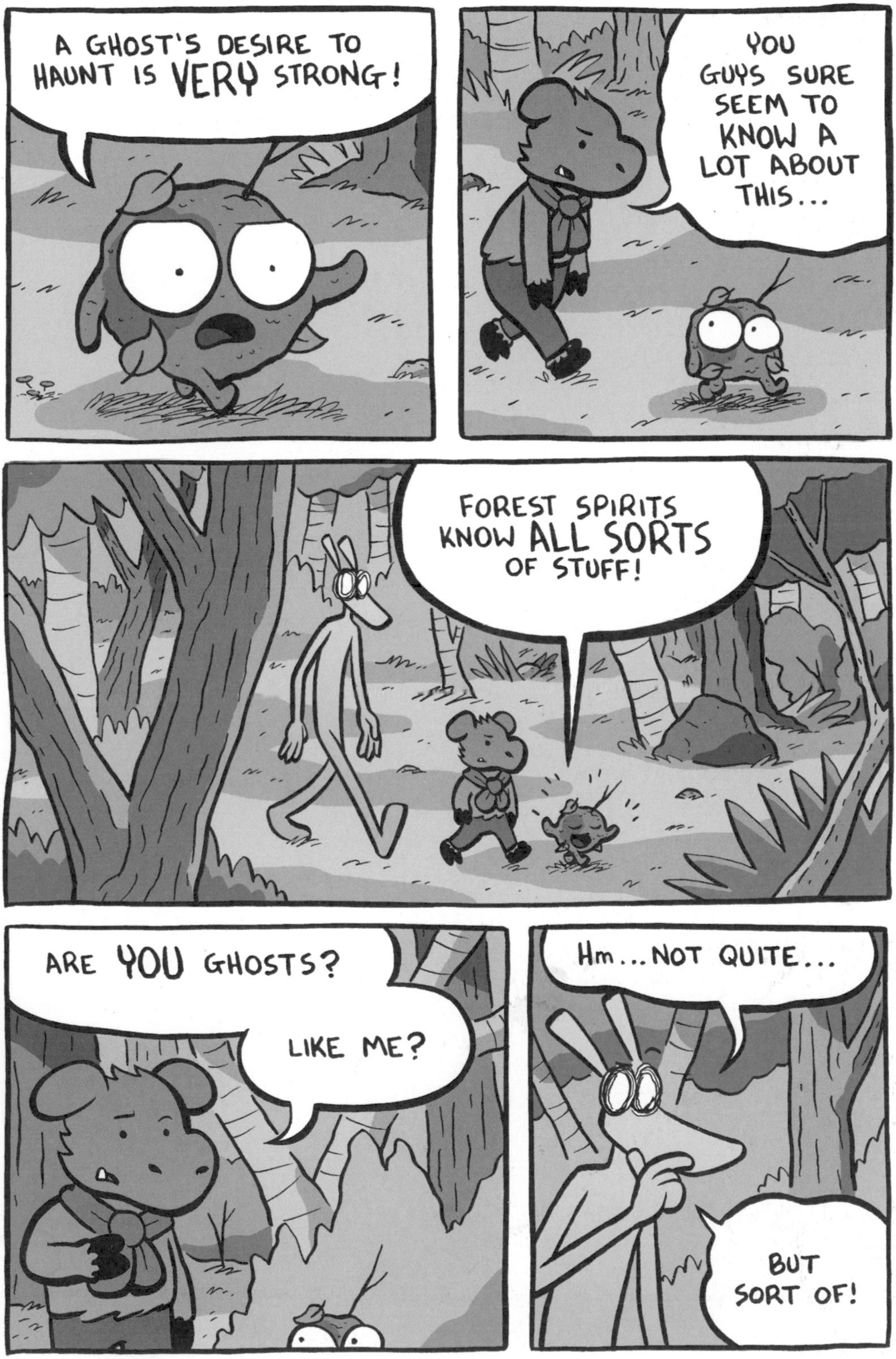

A GHOST'S DESIRE TO HAUNT IS VERY STRONG!
YOU GUYS SURE SEEM TO KNOW A LOT ABOUT THIS...
FOREST SPIRITS KNOW ALL SORTS OF STUFF!
ARE YOU GHOSTS?
LIKE ME?
Hm... NOT QUITE...
BUT SORT OF!

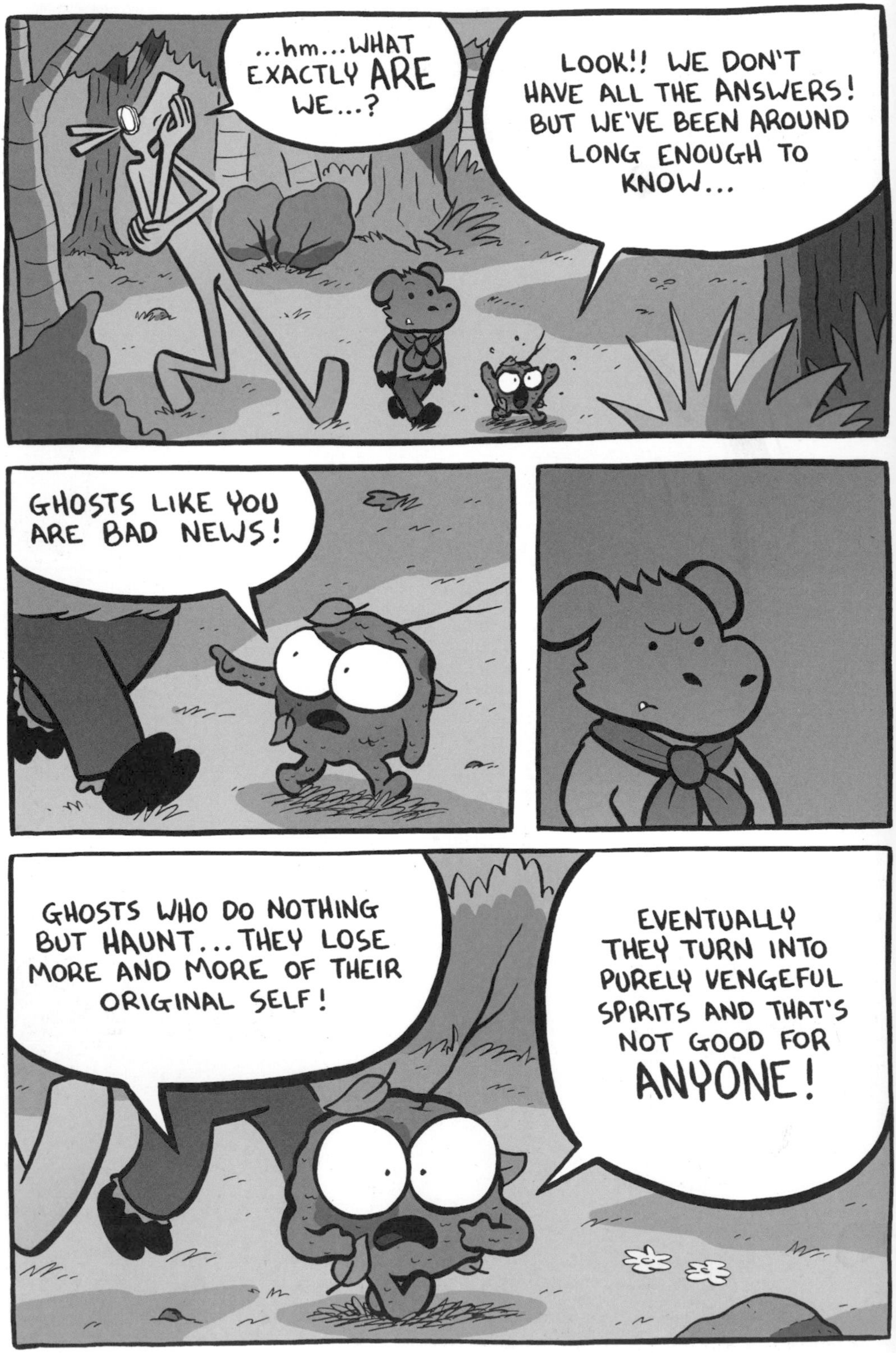
...hm...WHAT EXACTLY ARE WE...?
LOOK!! WE DON'T HAVE ALL THE ANSWERS! BUT WE'VE BEEN AROUND LONG ENOUGH TO KNOW...
GHOSTS LIKE YOU ARE BAD NEWS!
GHOSTS WHO DO NOTHING BUT HAUNT... THEY LOSE MORE AND MORE OF THEIR ORIGINAL SELF!
EVENTUALLY THEY TURN INTO PURELY VENGEFUL SPIRITS AND THAT'S NOT GOOD FOR ANYONE!

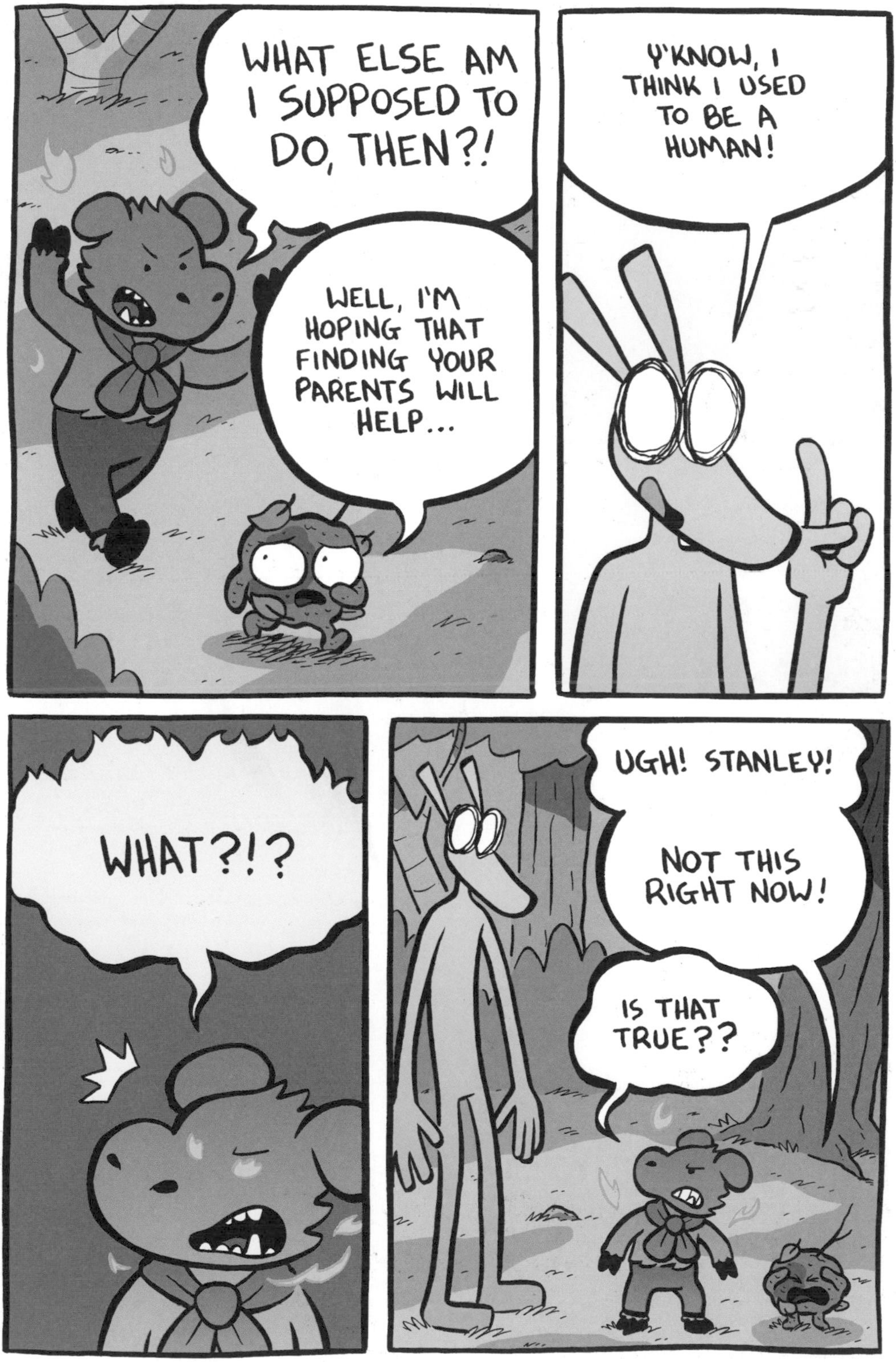
WHAT ELSE AM I SUPPOSED TO DO, THEN?!
WELL, I'M HOPING THAT FINDING YOUR PARENTS WILL HELP...
Y'KNOW, I THINK I USED TO BE A HUMAN!
WHAT?!?
UGH! STANLEY!
NOT THIS RIGHT NOW!
IS THAT TRUE??

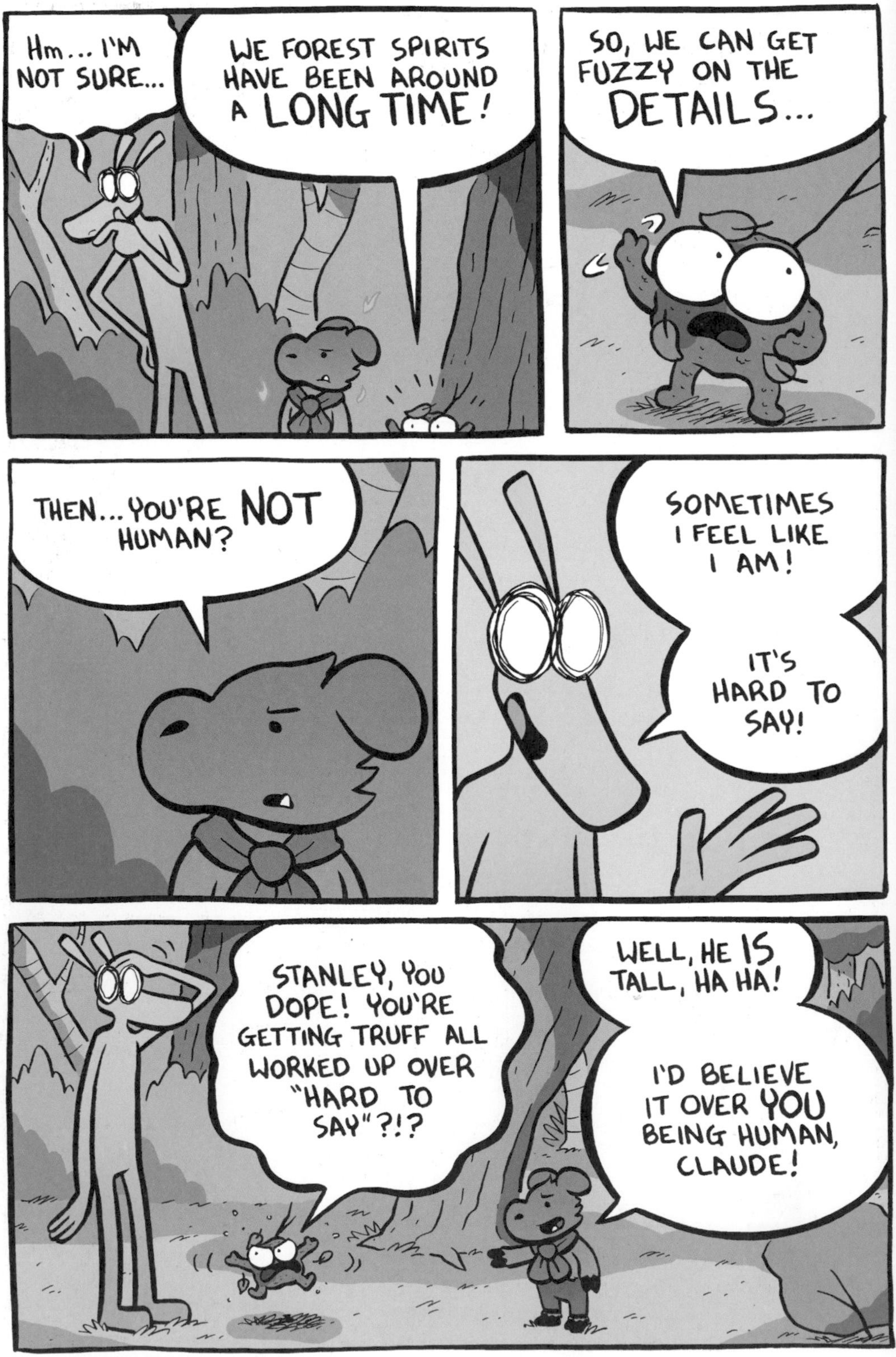
Hm... I'M NOT SURE...
WE FOREST SPIRITS HAVE BEEN AROUND A LONG TIME!
SO, WE CAN GET FUZZY ON THE DETAILS...
THEN... YOU'RE NOT HUMAN?
SOMETIMES I FEEL LIKE I AM!
IT'S HARD TO SAY!
STANLEY, YOU DOPE! YOU'RE GETTING TRUFF ALL WORKED UP OVER "HARD TO SAY"?!?
WELL, HE IS TALL, HA HA!
I'D BELIEVE IT OVER YOU BEING HUMAN, CLAUDE!

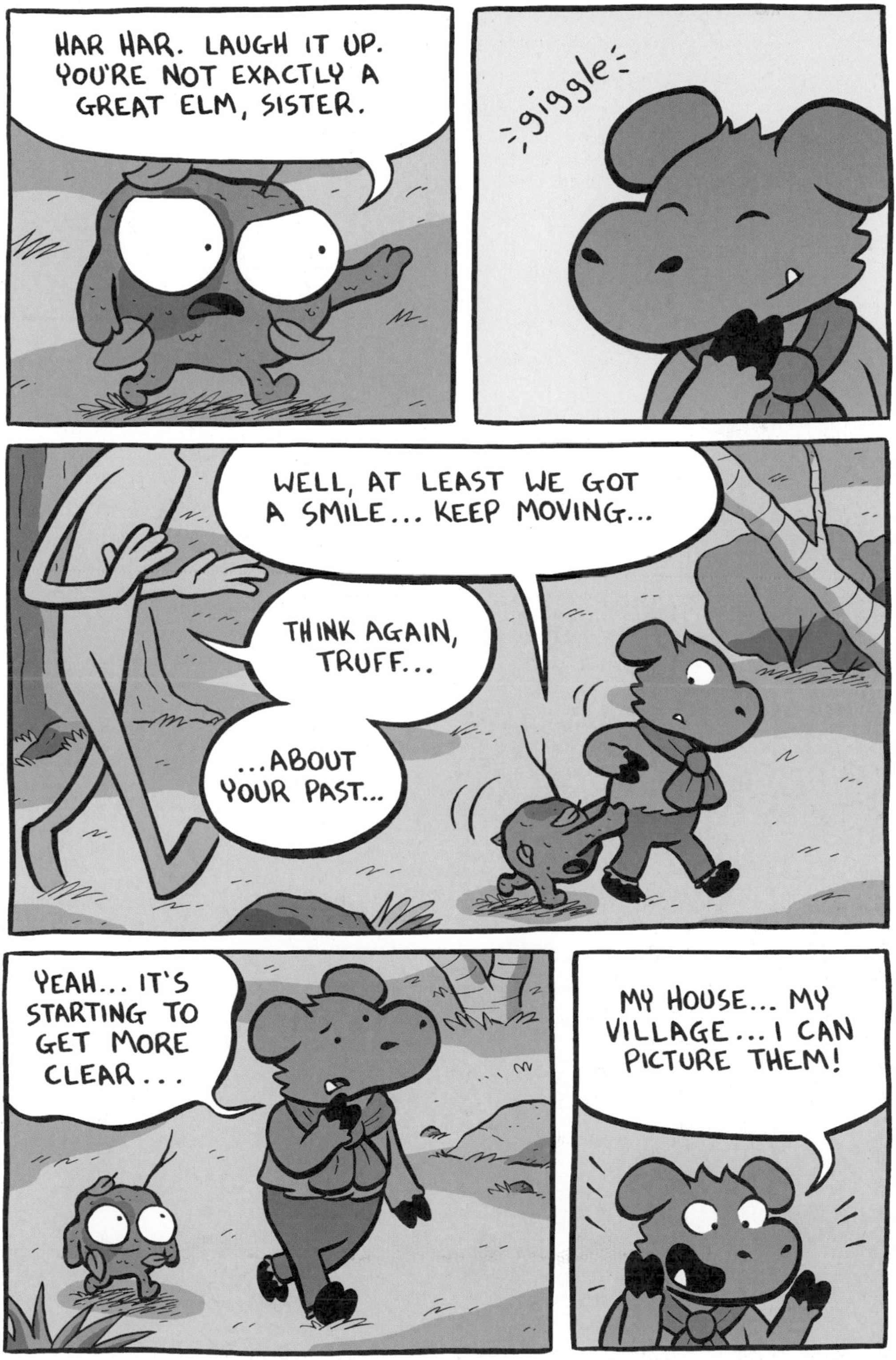
HAR HAR. LAUGH IT UP. YOU'RE NOT EXACTLY A GREAT ELM, SISTER.
giggle
WELL, AT LEAST WE GOT A SMILE... KEEP MOVING...
THINK AGAIN, TRUFF...
...ABOUT YOUR PAST...
YEAH... IT'S STARTING TO GET MORE CLEAR...
MY HOUSE... MY VILLAGE... I CAN PICTURE THEM!

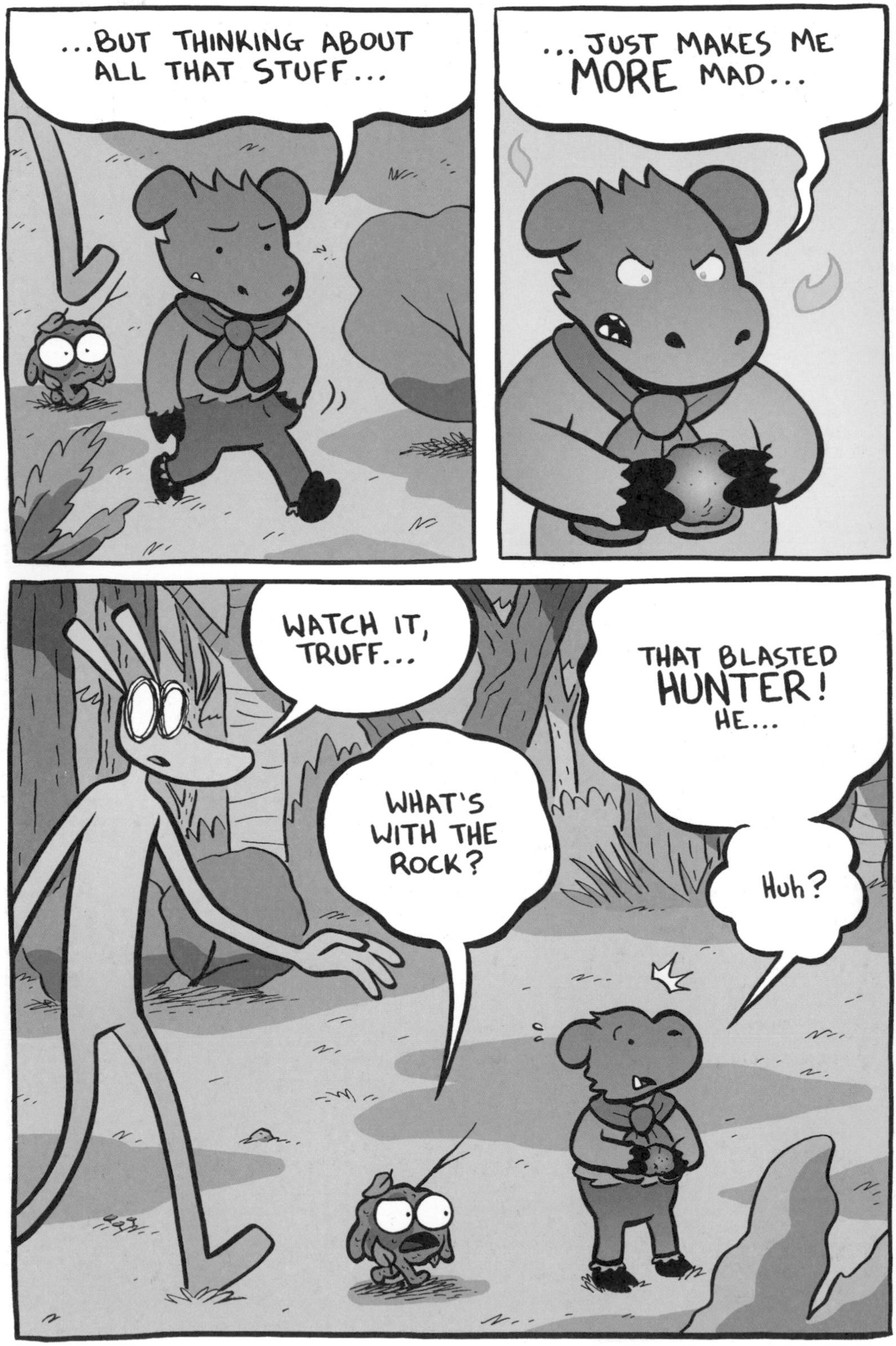
...BUT THINKING ABOUT ALL THAT STUFF...
...JUST MAKES ME MORE MAD...
WATCH IT, TRUFF...
WHAT'S WITH THE ROCK?
THAT BLASTED HUNTER! HE...
Huh?

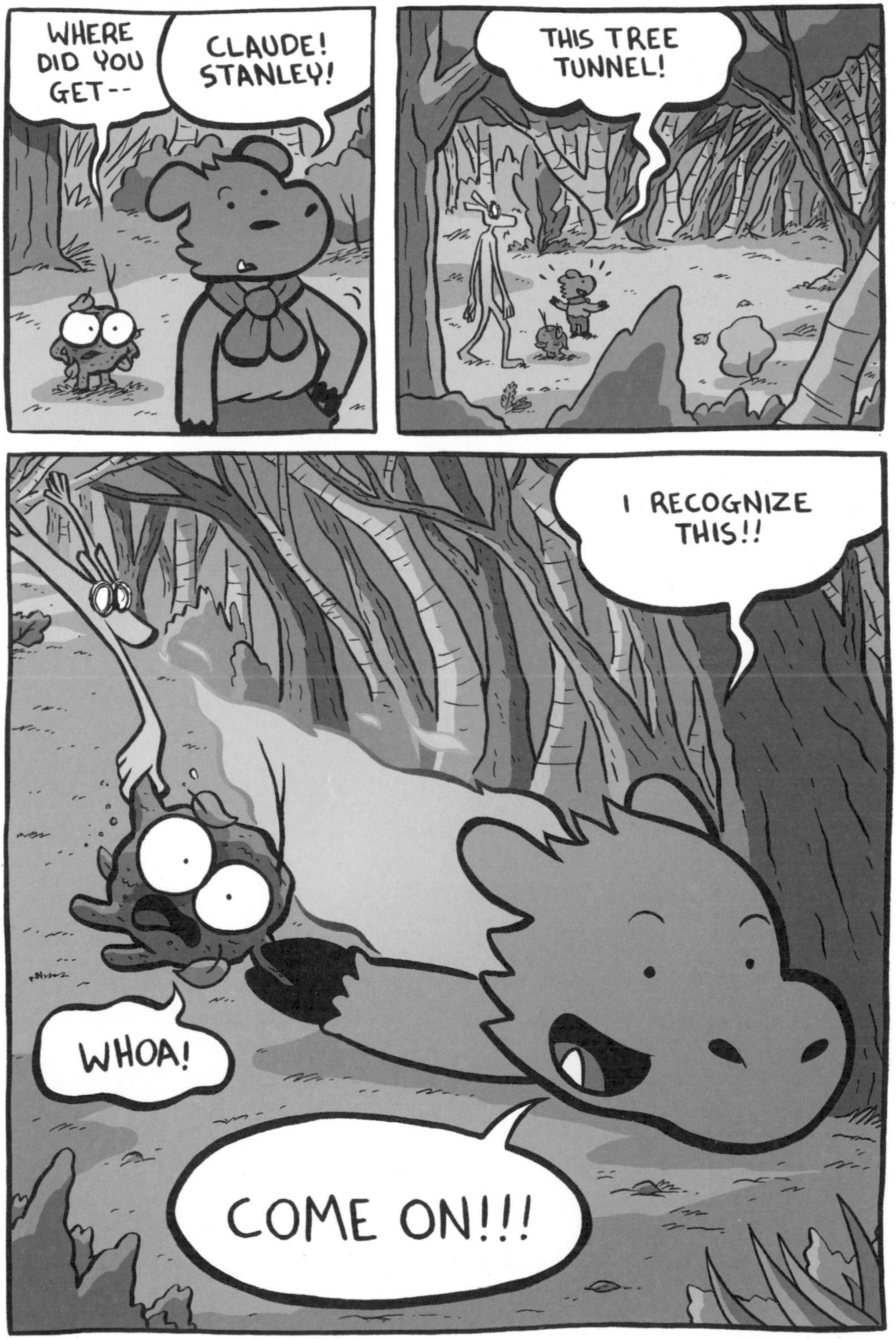
WHERE DID YOU GET--
CLAUDE! STANLEY!
THIS TREE TUNNEL!
I RECOGNIZE THIS!!
WHOA!
COME ON!!!

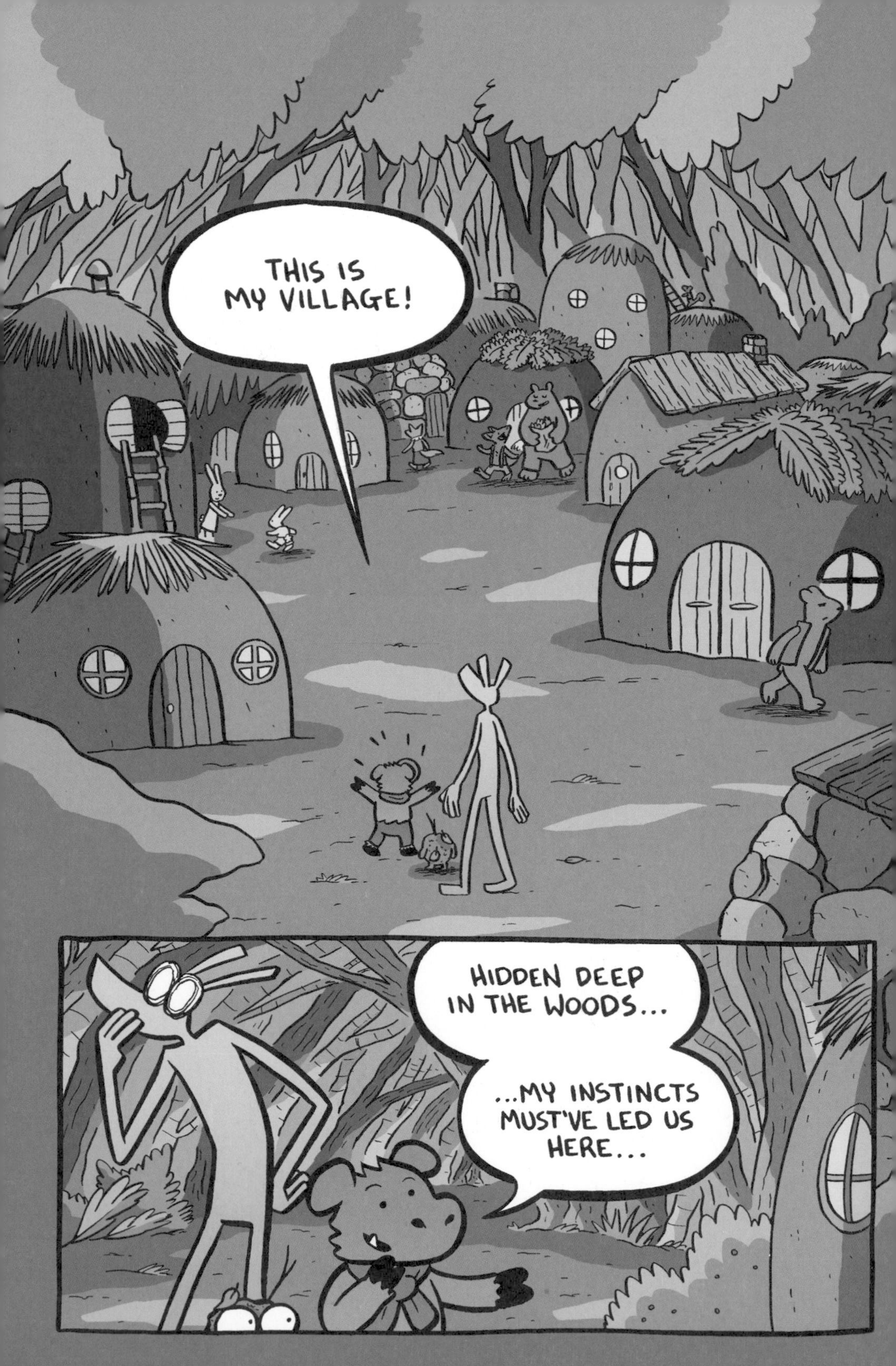
THIS IS MY VILLAGE!
HIDDEN DEEP IN THE WOODS...
...MY INSTINCTS MUST'VE LED US HERE...

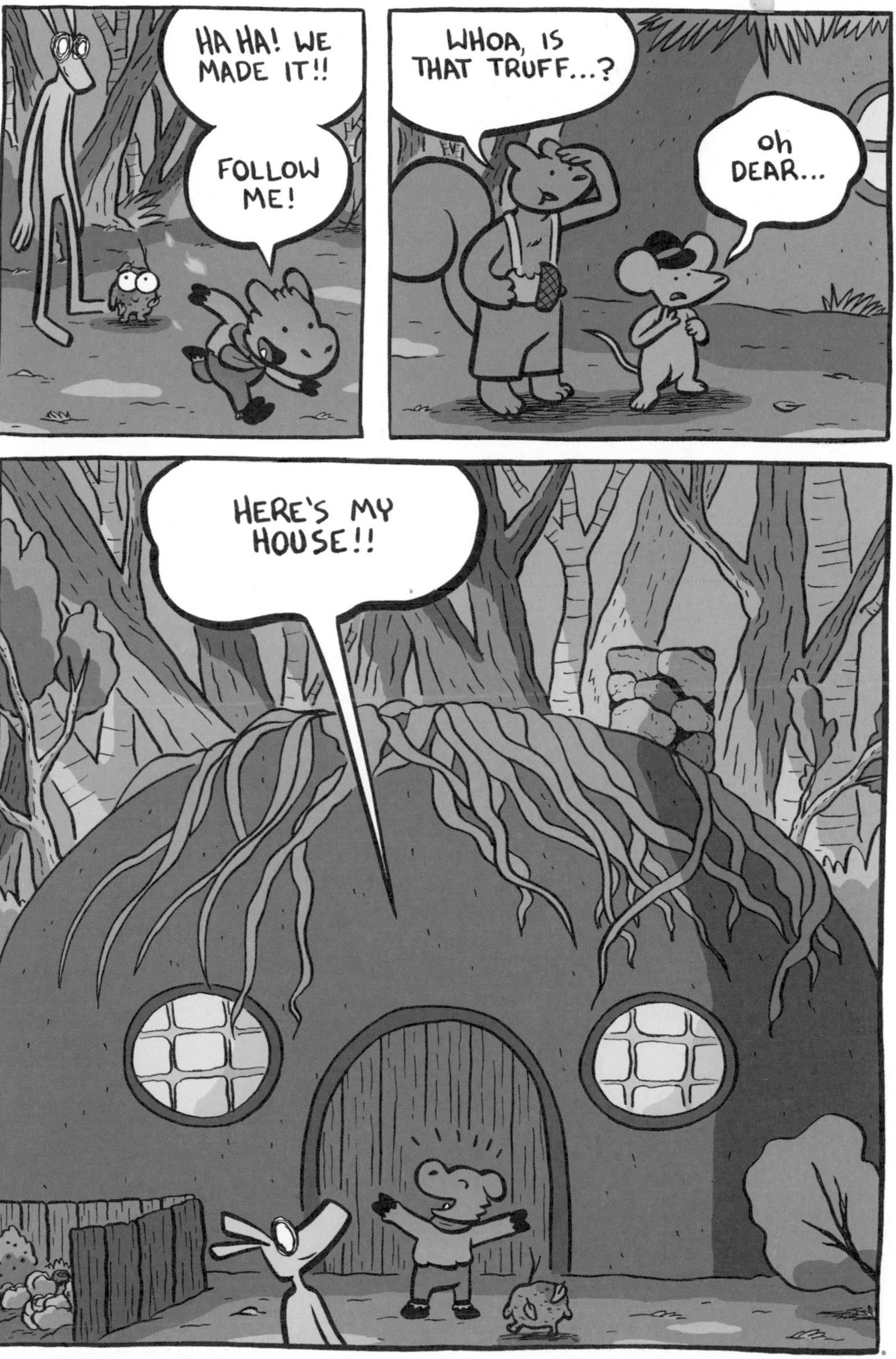
HA HA! WE MADE IT!!
FOLLOW ME!
WHOA, IS THAT TRUFF...?
oh DEAR...
HERE'S MY HOUSE!!

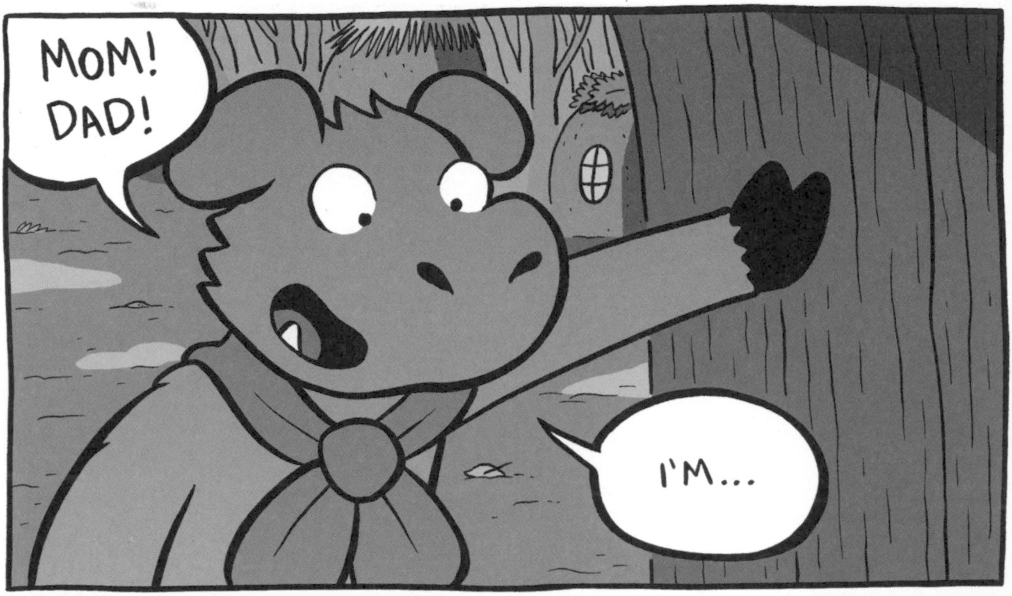
MOM! DAD!
I'M...

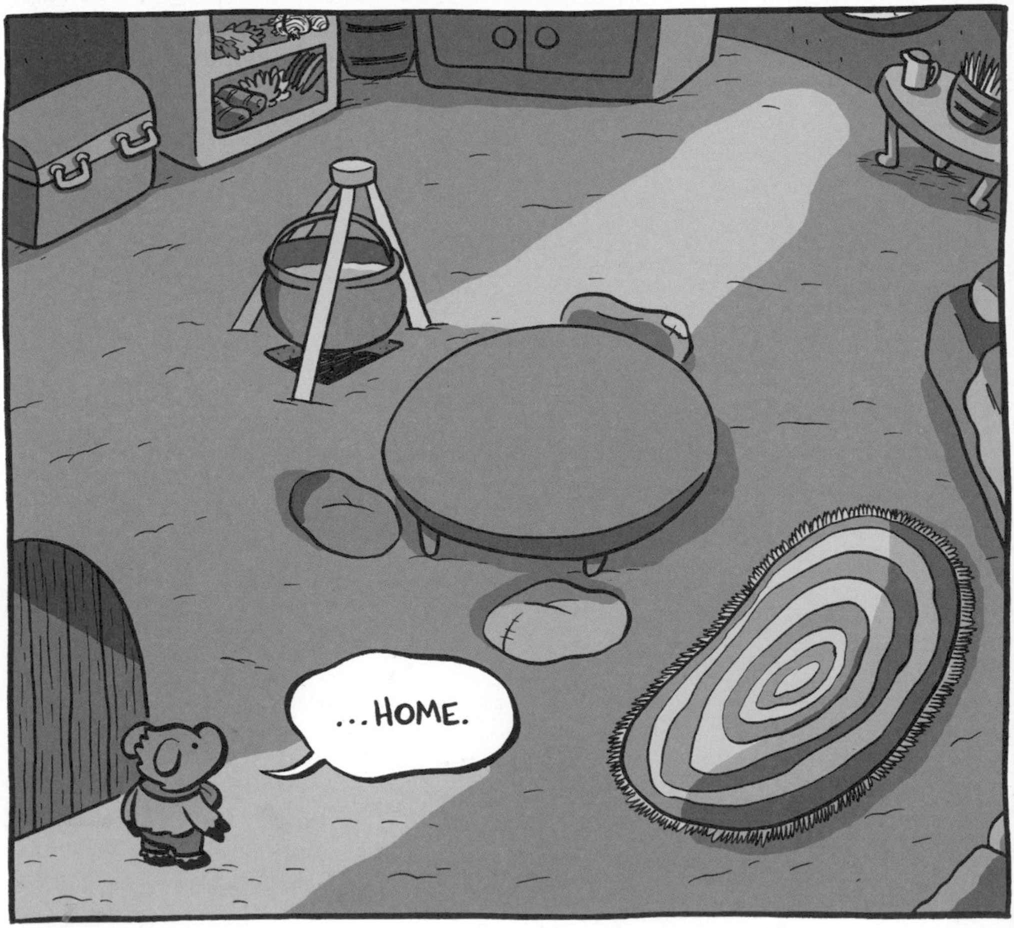
...HOME.

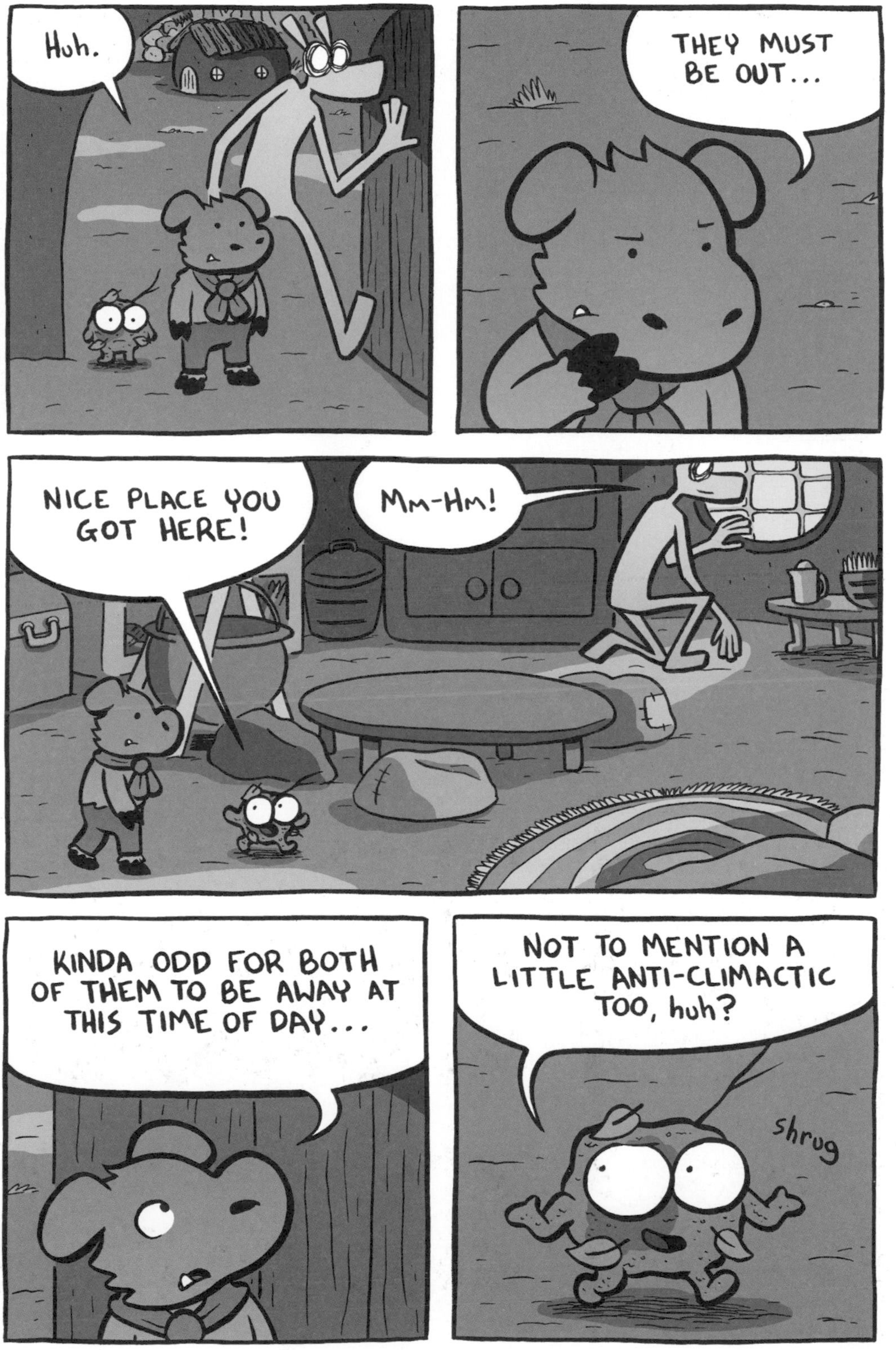
Huh.
THEY MUST BE OUT...
NICE PLACE YOU GOT HERE!
Mm-Hm!
KINDA ODD FOR BOTH OF THEM TO BE AWAY AT THIS TIME OF DAY...
NOT TO MENTION A LITTLE ANTI-CLIMACTIC TOO, huh?
shrug

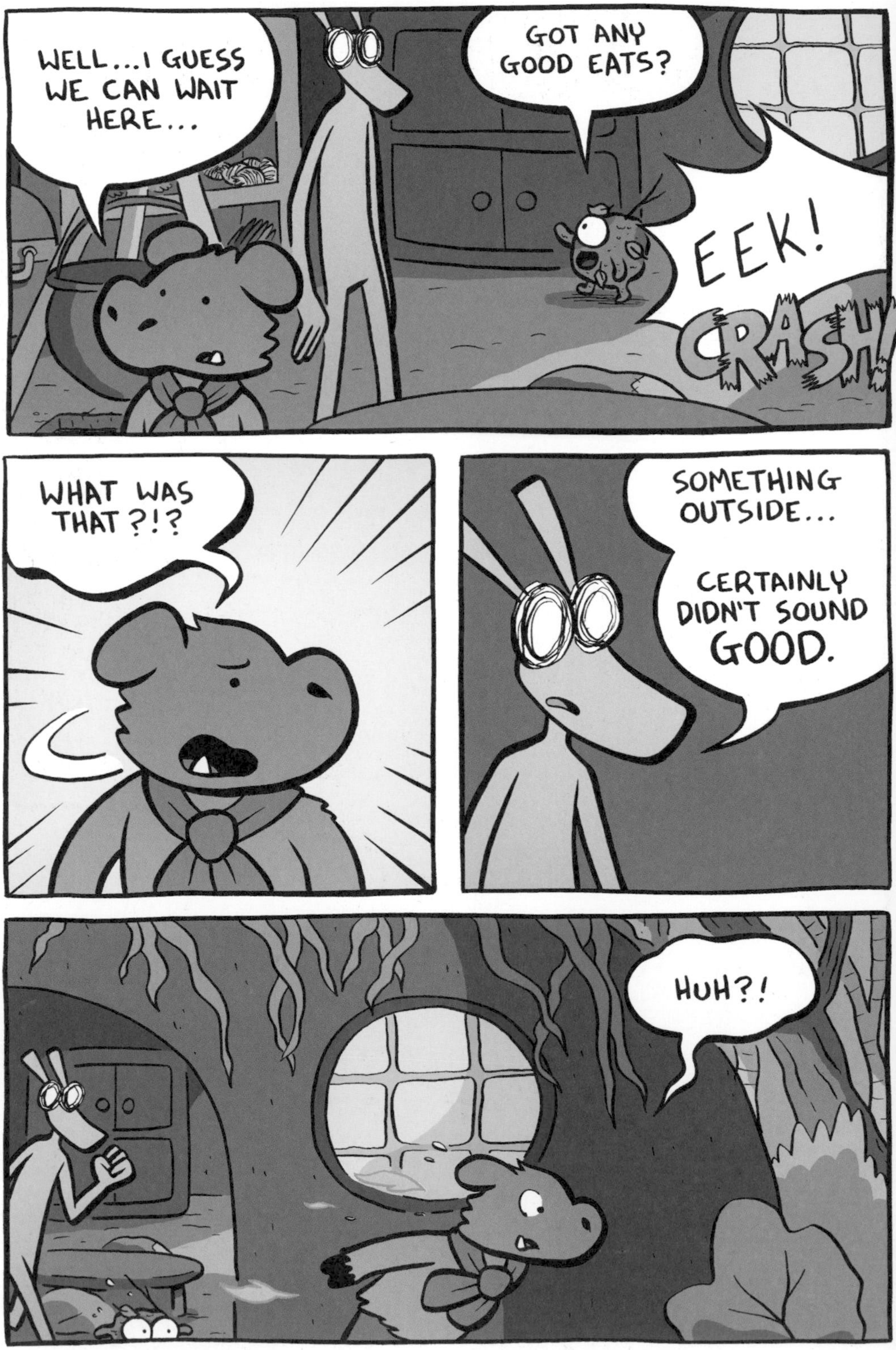
WELL...I GUESS WE CAN WAIT HERE...
GOT ANY GOOD EATS?
EEK!
CRASH!
WHAT WAS THAT?!?
SOMETHING OUTSIDE...
CERTAINLY DIDN'T SOUND GOOD.
HUH?!

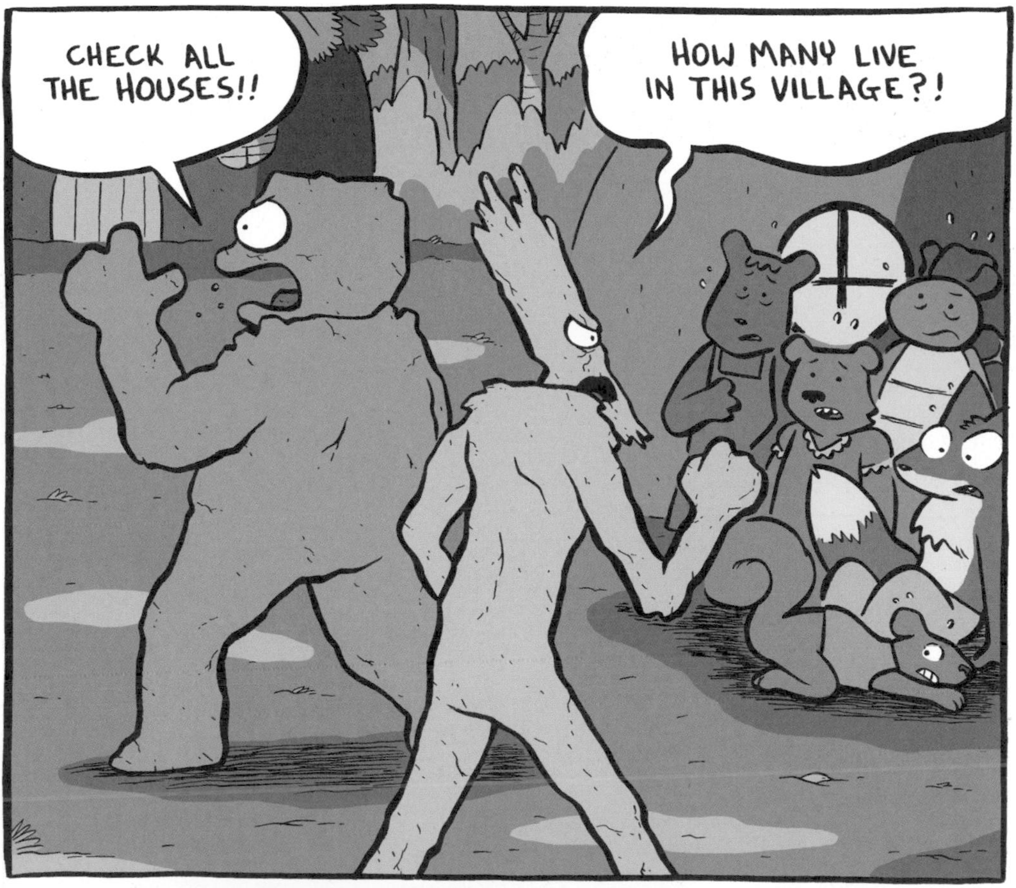
CHECK ALL THE HOUSES!!
HOW MANY LIVE IN THIS VILLAGE?!

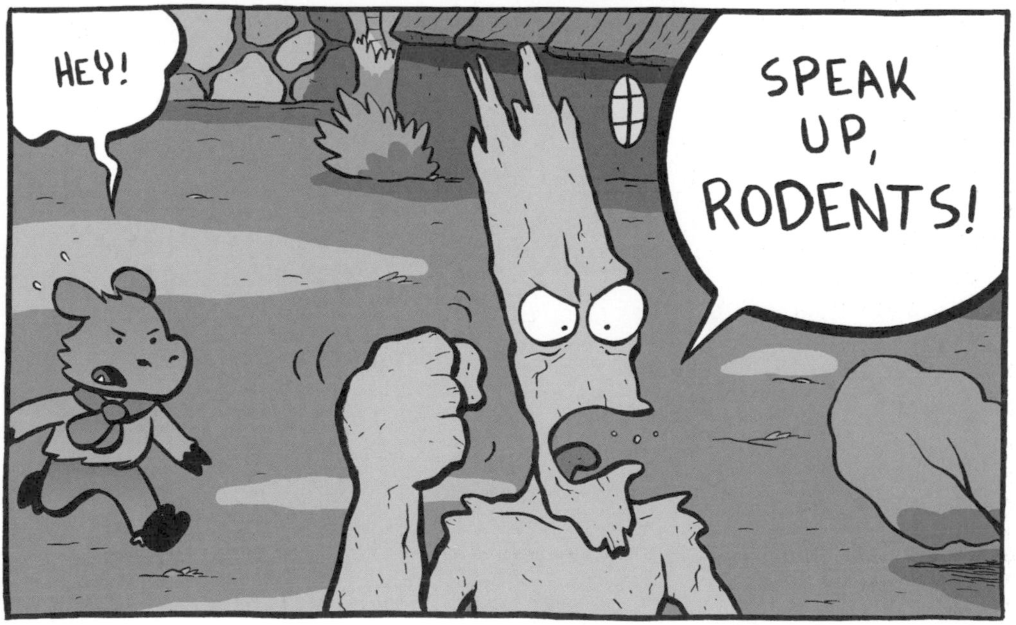
HEY!
SPEAK UP, RODENTS!

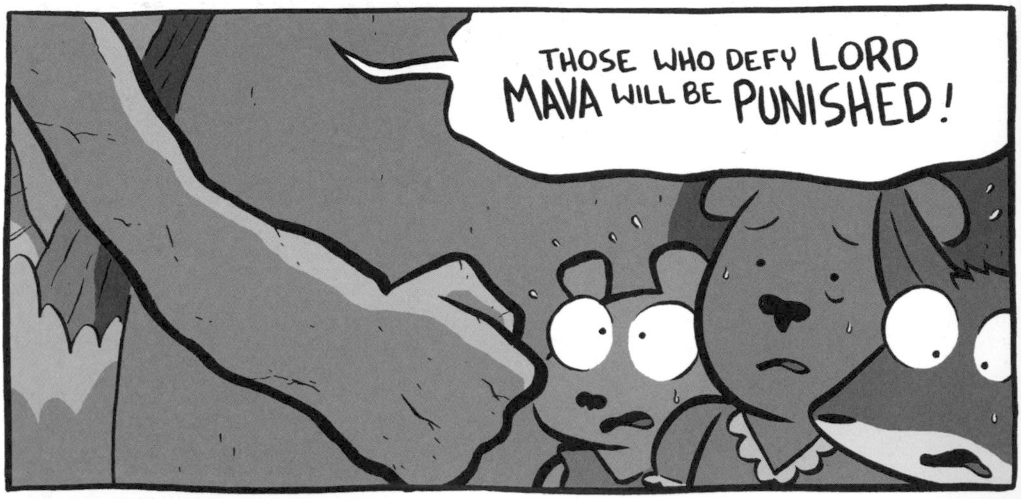
THOSE WHO DEFY LORD MAVA WILL BE PUNISHED!

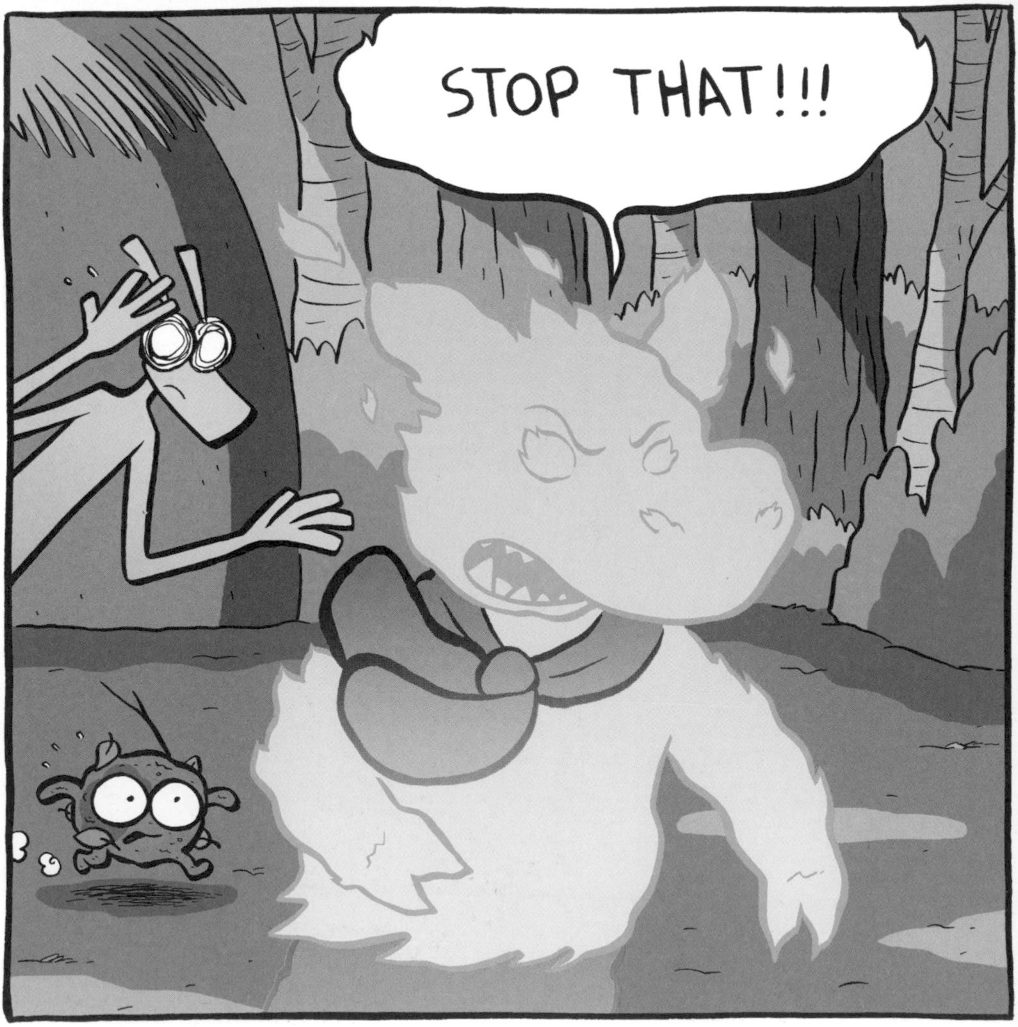
STOP THAT!!!

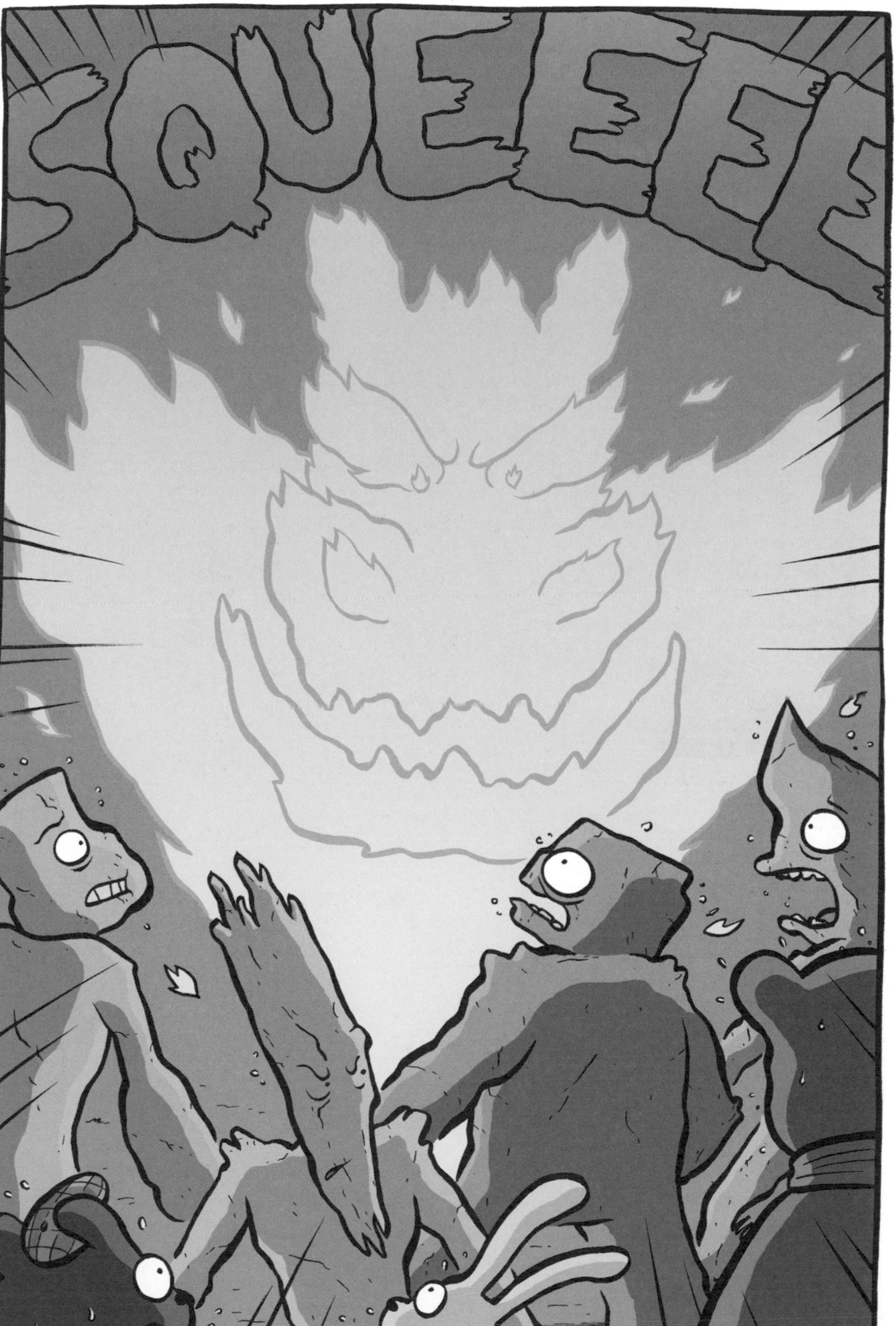
SQUEEEE

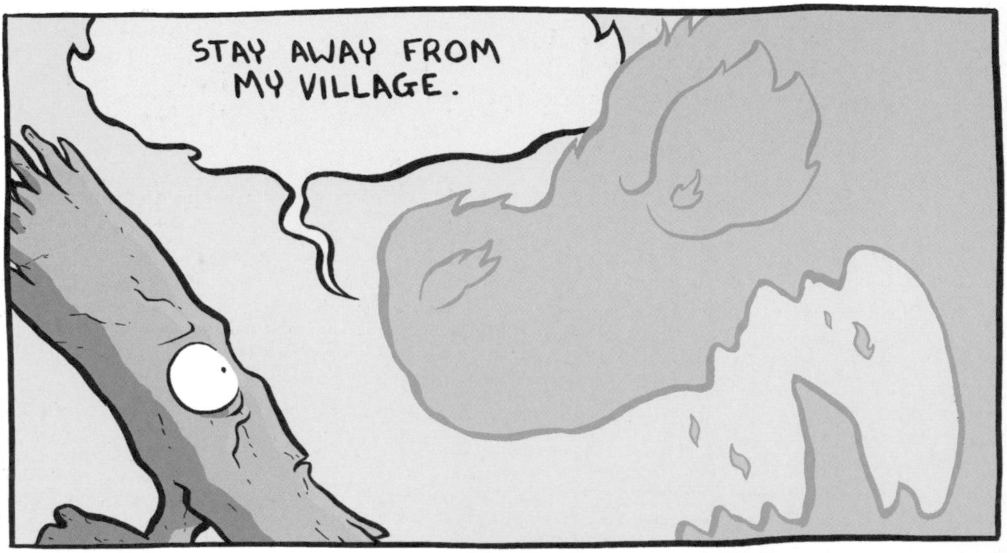
STAY AWAY FROM MY VILLAGE.

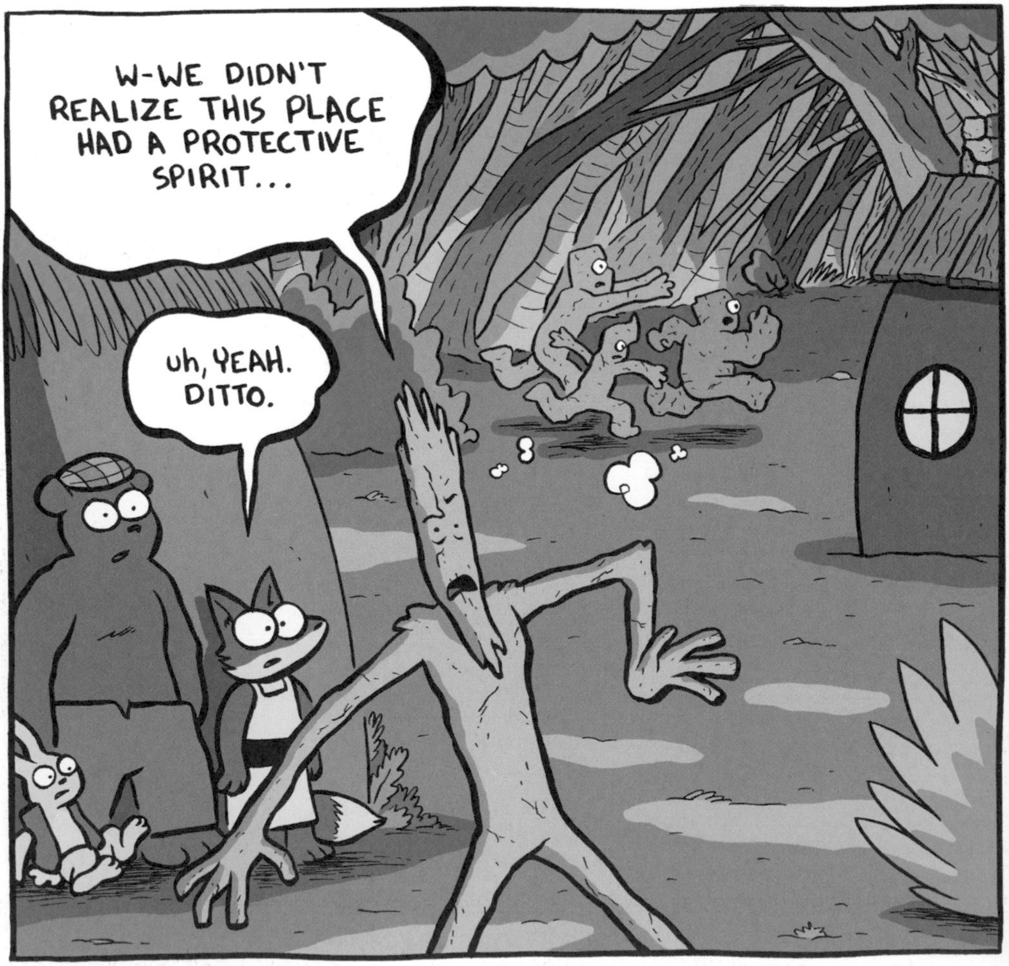
W-WE DIDN'T REALIZE THIS PLACE HAD A PROTECTIVE SPIRIT...
uh, YEAH. DITTO.

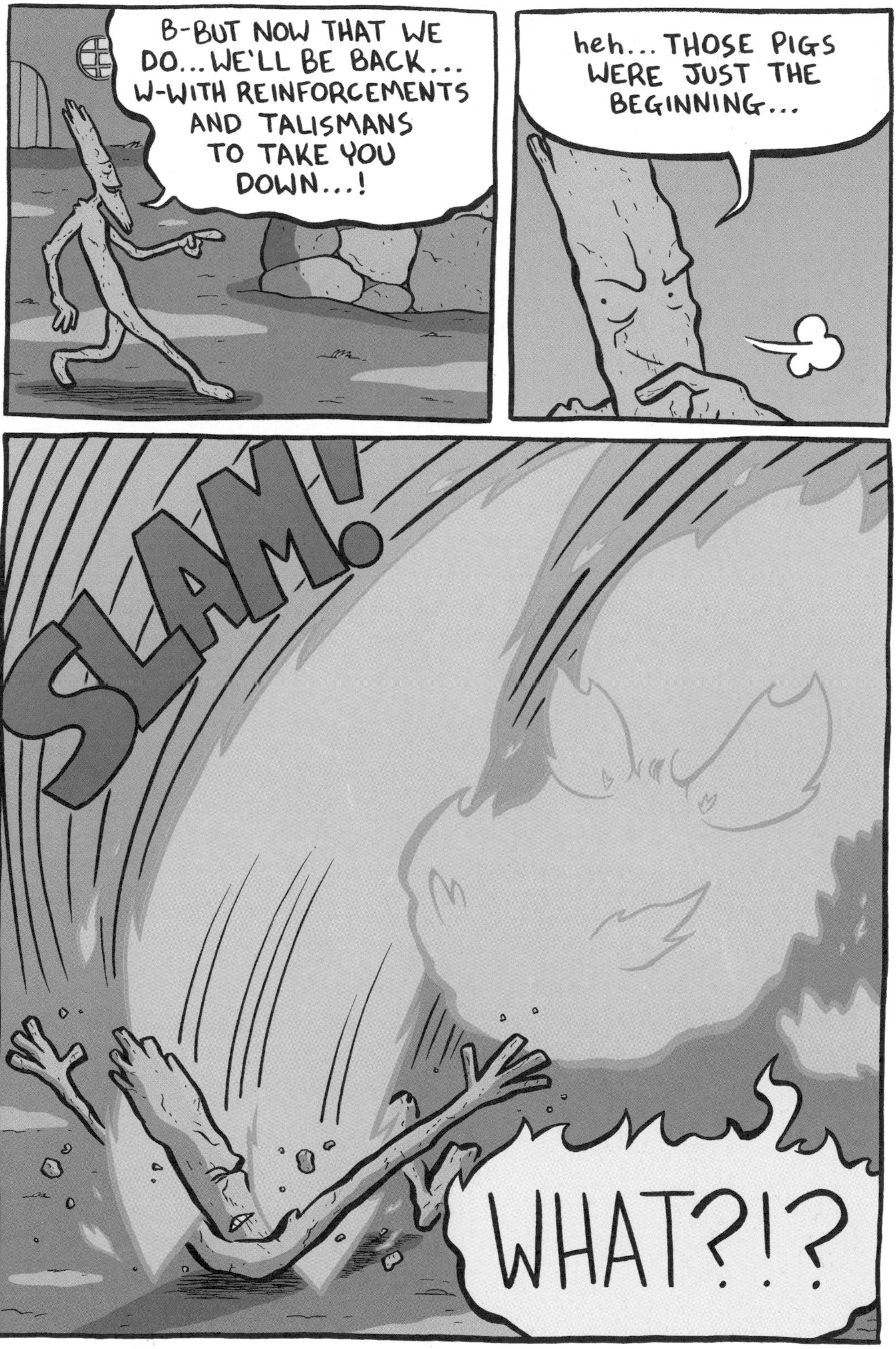
B-BUT NOW THAT WE DO... WE'LL BE BACK... W-WITH REINFORCEMENTS AND TALISMANS TO TAKE YOU DOWN...!
heh... THOSE PIGS WERE JUST THE BEGINNING...
SLAM!
WHAT?!?

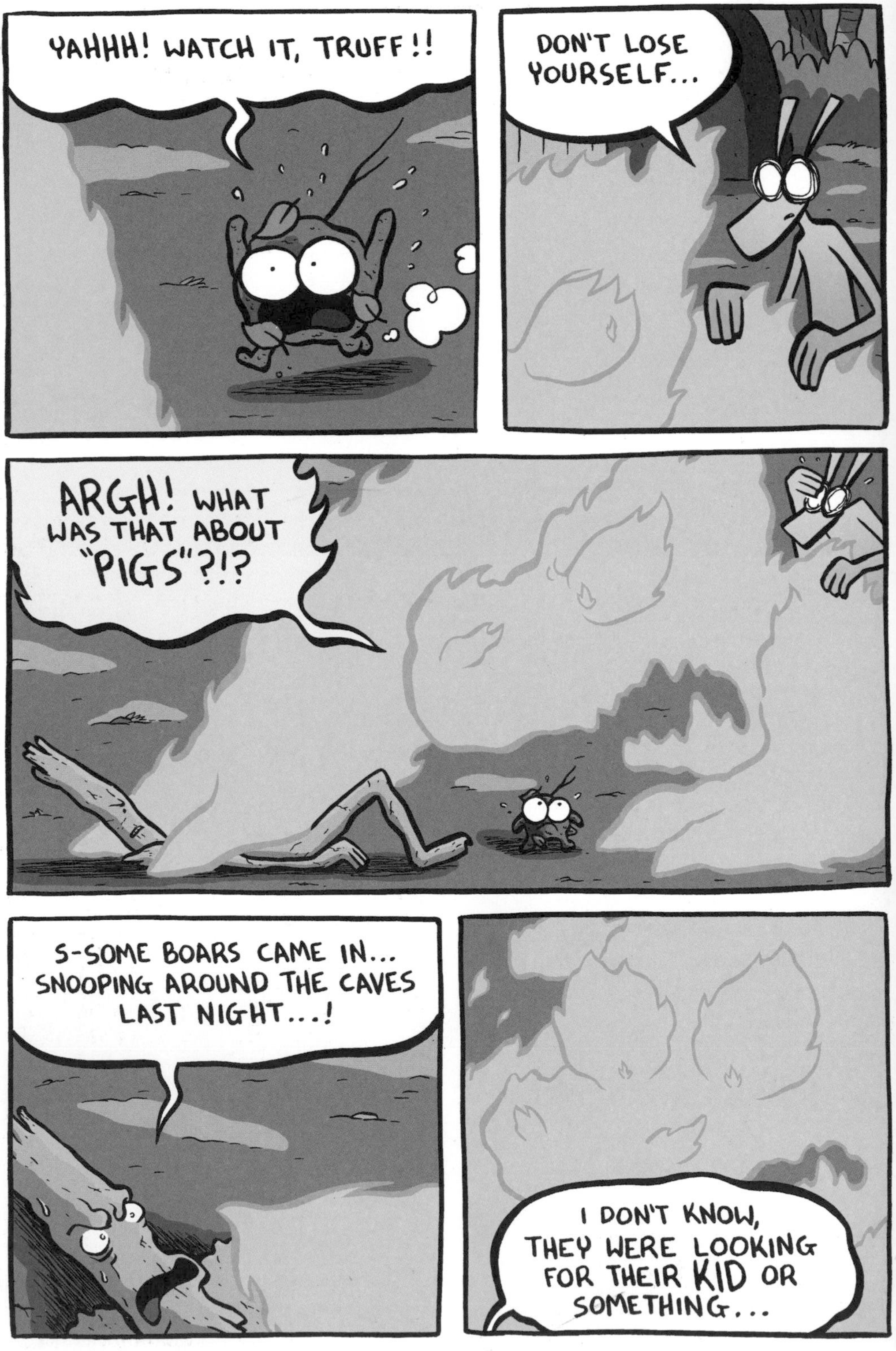
YAHHH! WATCH IT, TRUFF!!
DON'T LOSE YOURSELF...
ARGH! WHAT WAS THAT ABOUT "PIGS"?!?
S-SOME BOARS CAME IN... SNOOPING AROUND THE CAVES LAST NIGHT...!
I DON'T KNOW, THEY WERE LOOKING FOR THEIR KID OR SOMETHING...

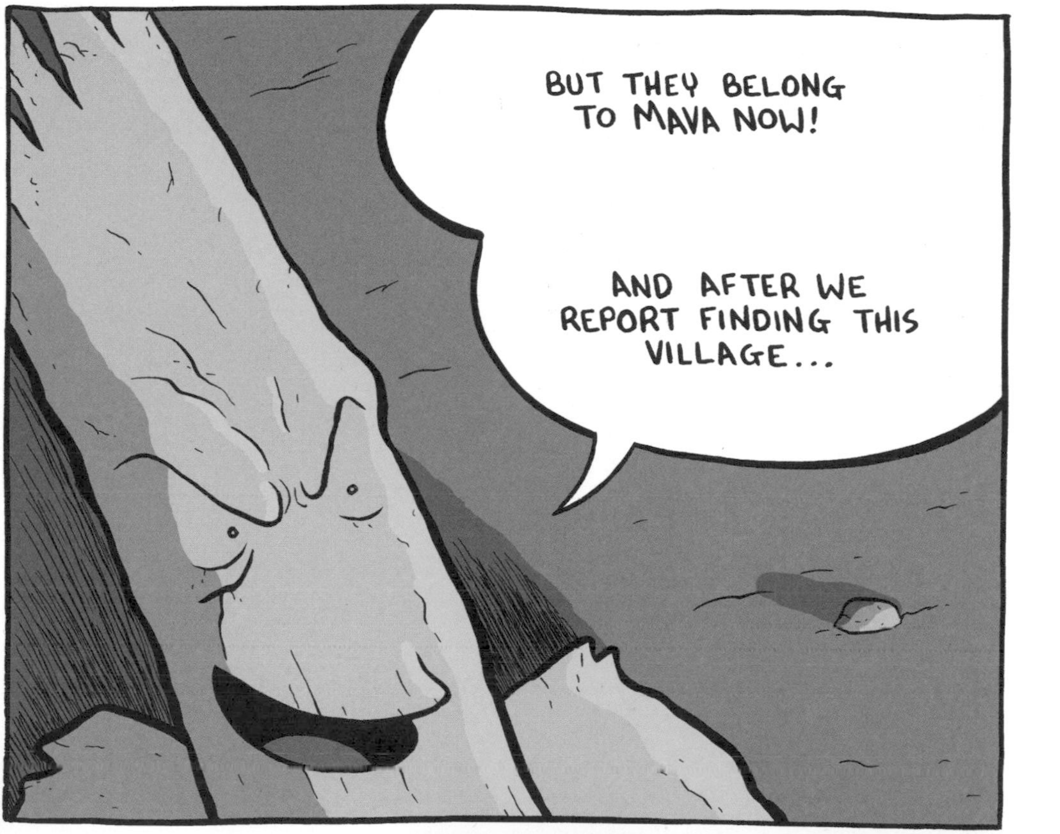
BUT THEY BELONG TO MAVA NOW!
AND AFTER WE REPORT FINDING THIS VILLAGE...

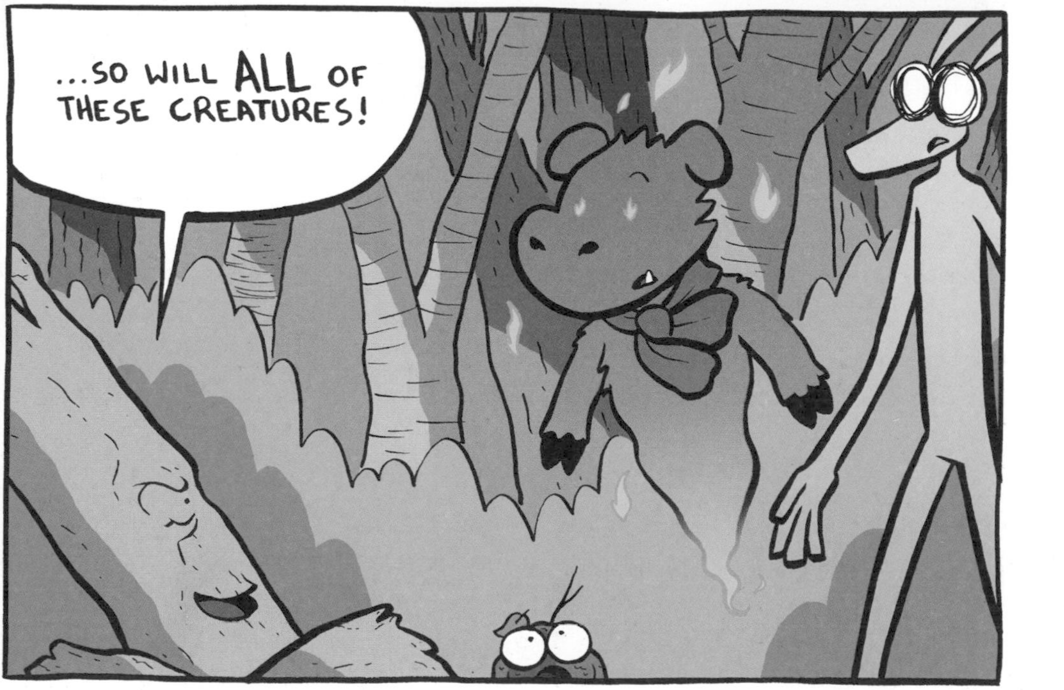
...SO WILL ALL OF THESE CREATURES!

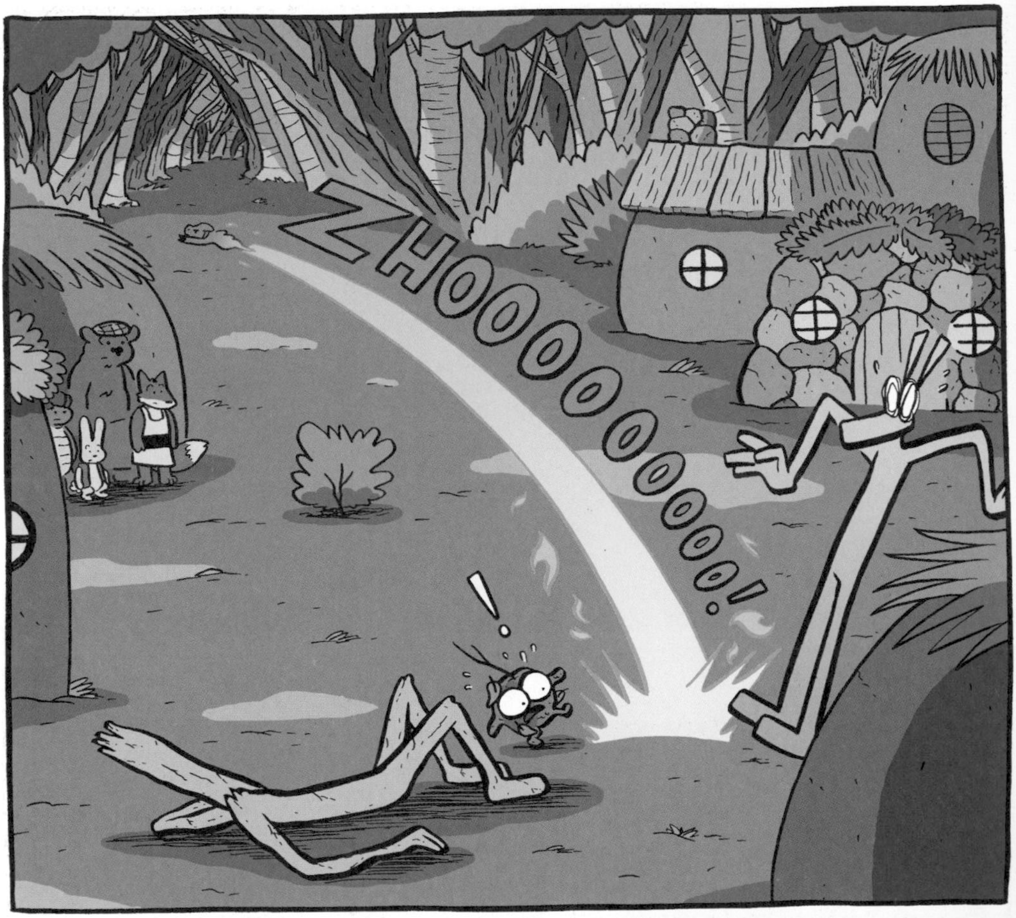
ZHOOOOOOOOOOO!
!

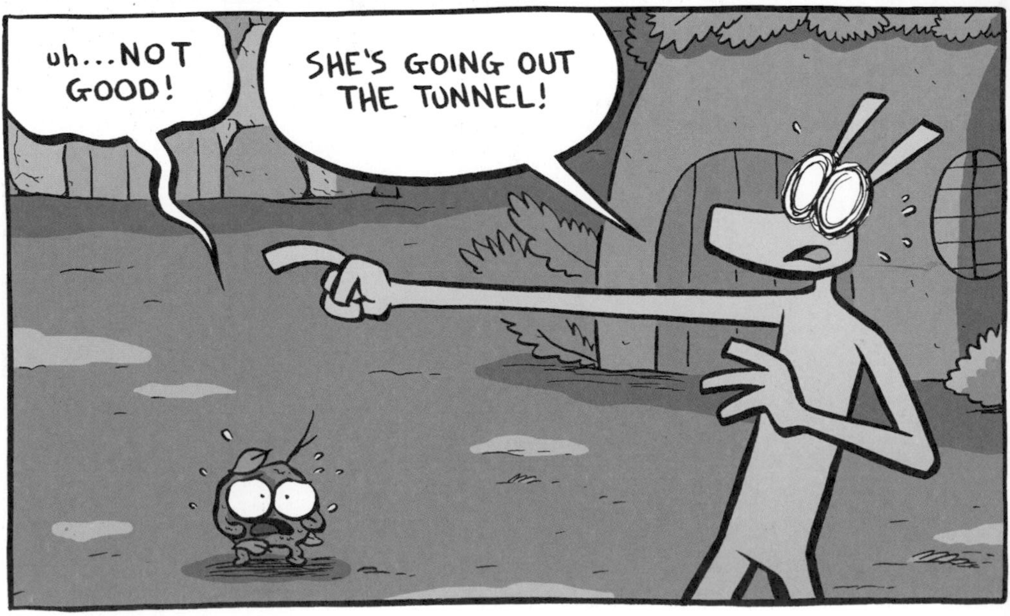
uh...NOT GOOD!
SHE'S GOING OUT THE TUNNEL!

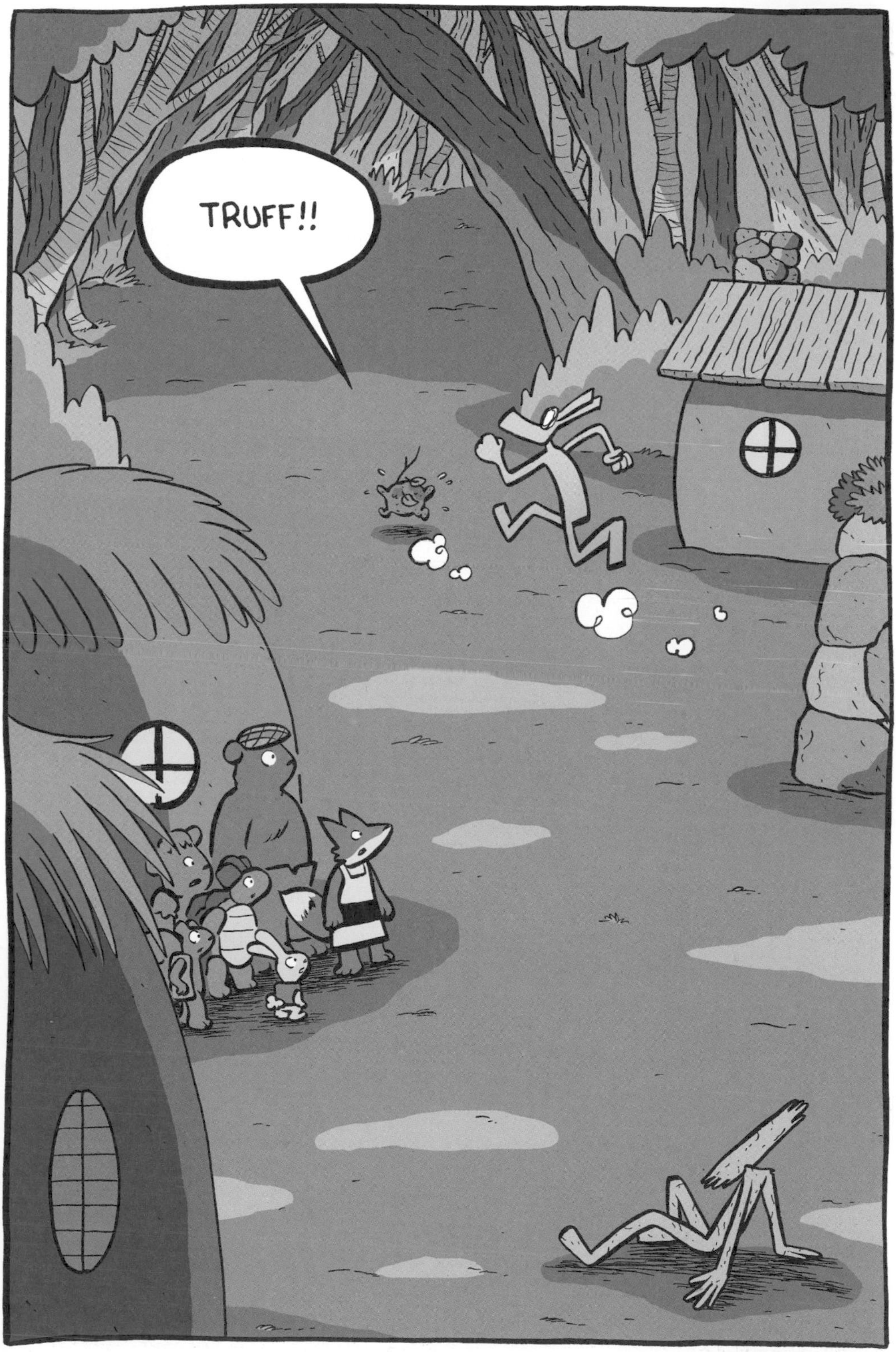
TRUFF!!

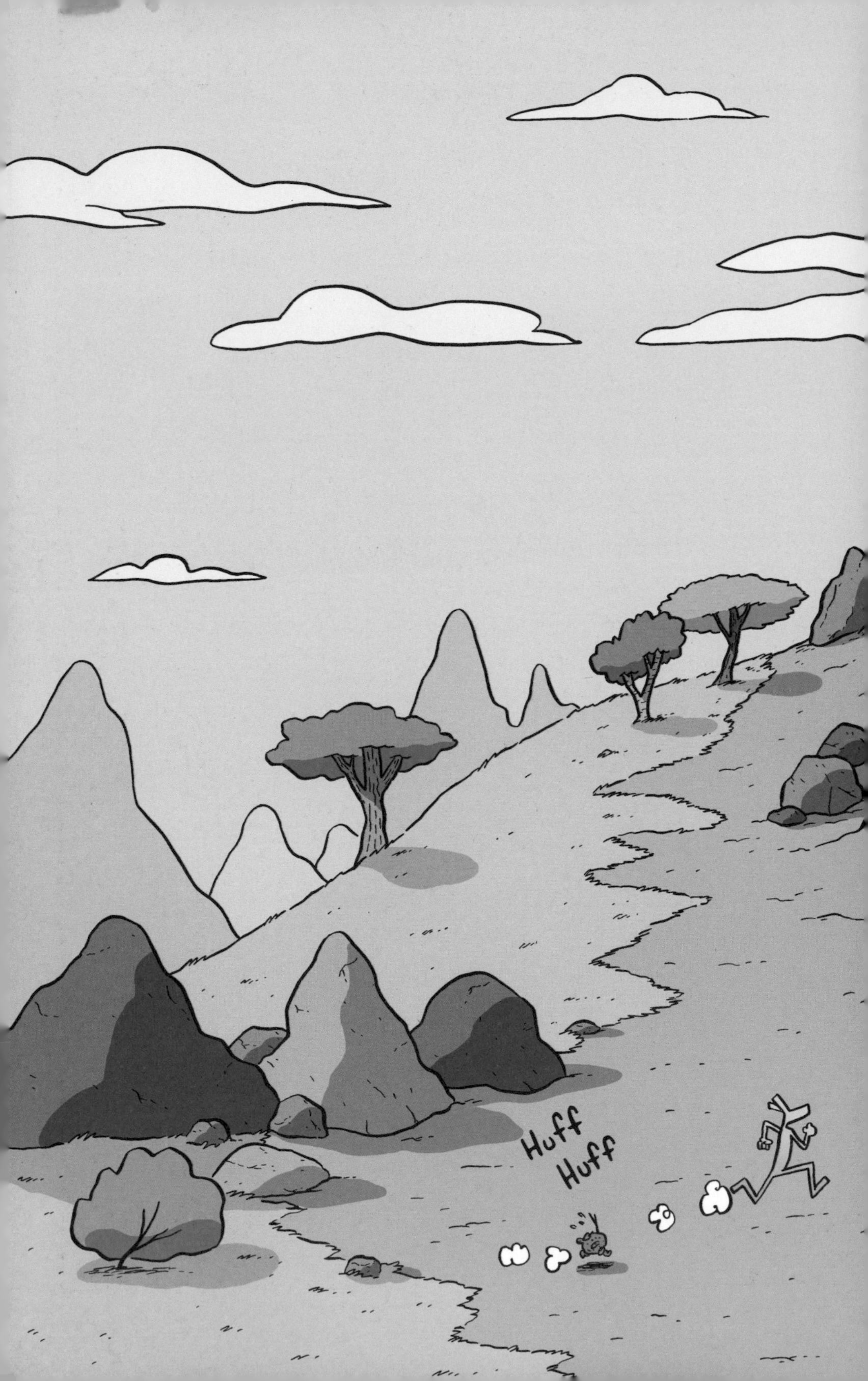
Huff
Huff

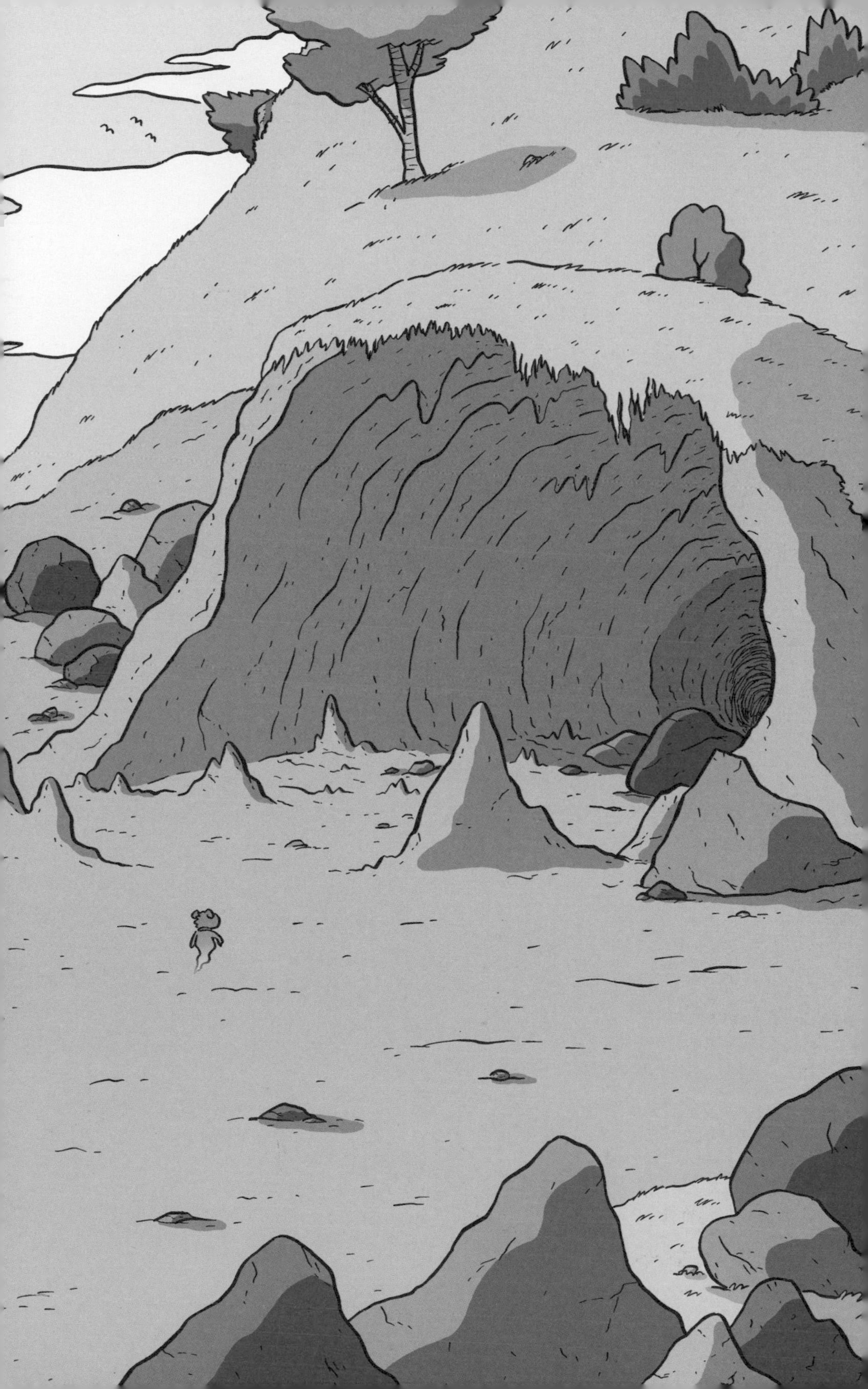

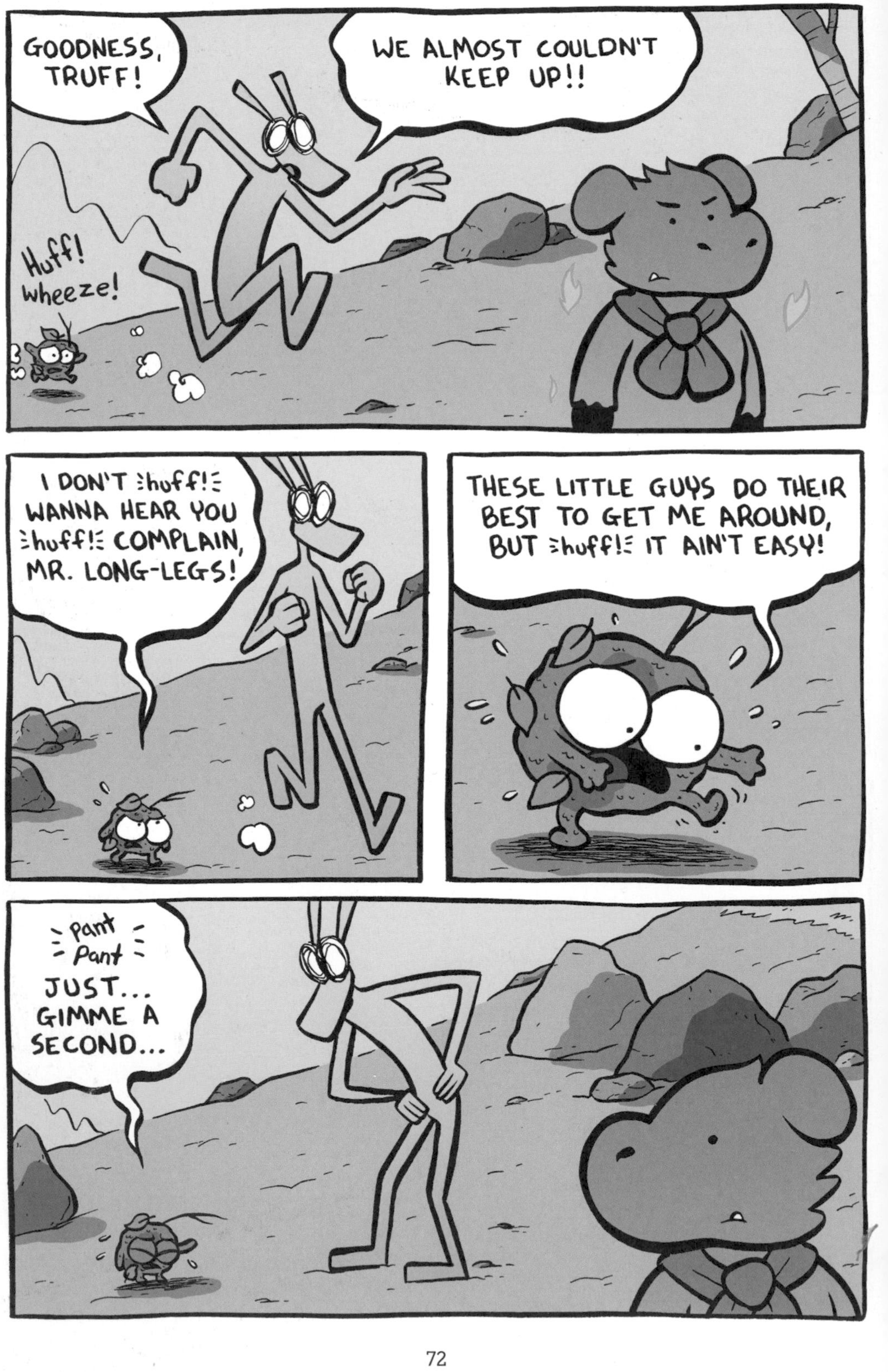
GOODNESS, TRUFF!
WE ALMOST COULDN'T KEEP UP!!
Huff! wheeze!
I DON'T huff! WANNA HEAR YOU huff! COMPLAIN, MR. LONG-LEGS!
THESE LITTLE GUYS DO THEIR BEST TO GET ME AROUND, BUT huff! IT AIN'T EASY!
Pant Pant JUST... GIMME A SECOND...

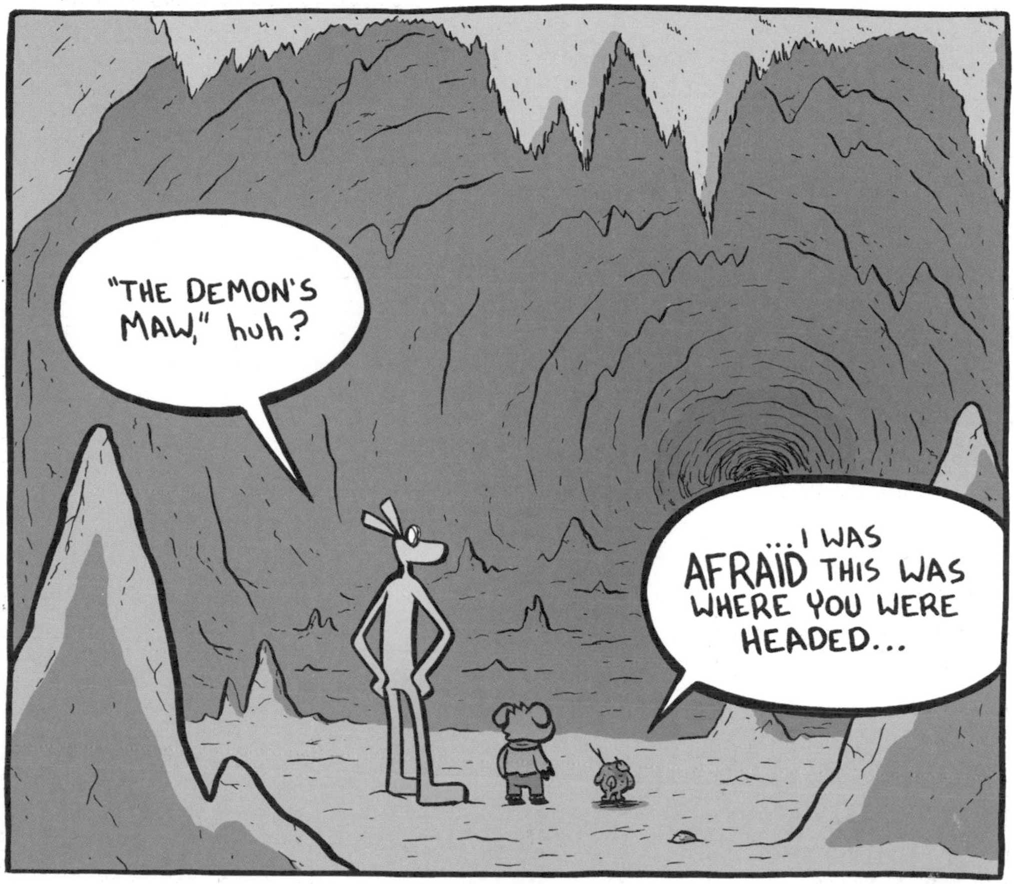
"THE DEMON'S MAW," huh?
...I WAS AFRAID THIS WAS WHERE YOU WERE HEADED...

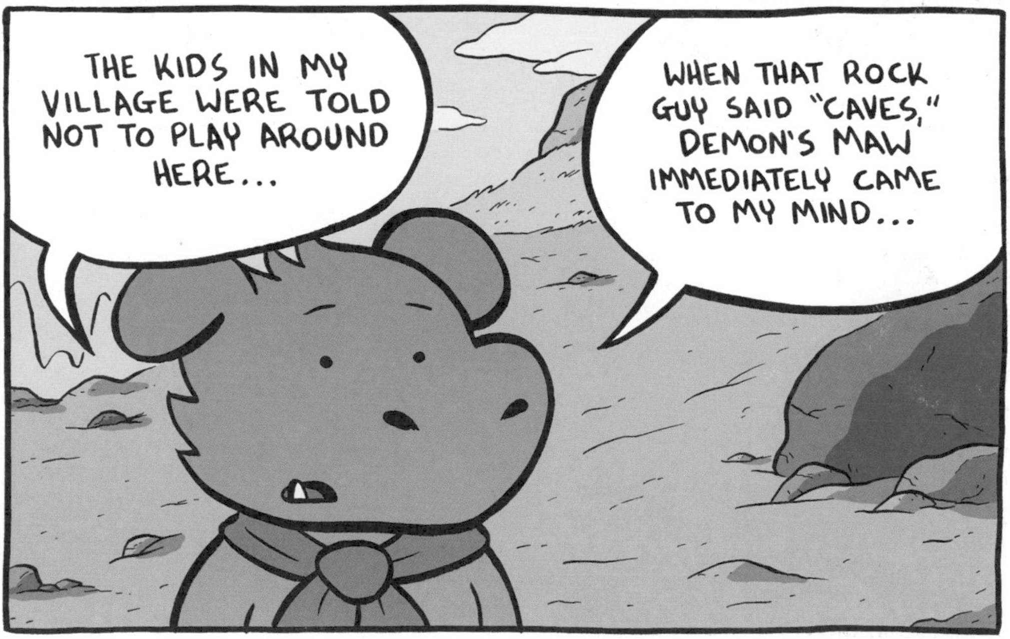
THE KIDS IN MY VILLAGE WERE TOLD NOT TO PLAY AROUND HERE...
WHEN THAT ROCK GUY SAID "CAVES," DEMON'S MAW IMMEDIATELY CAME TO MY MIND...

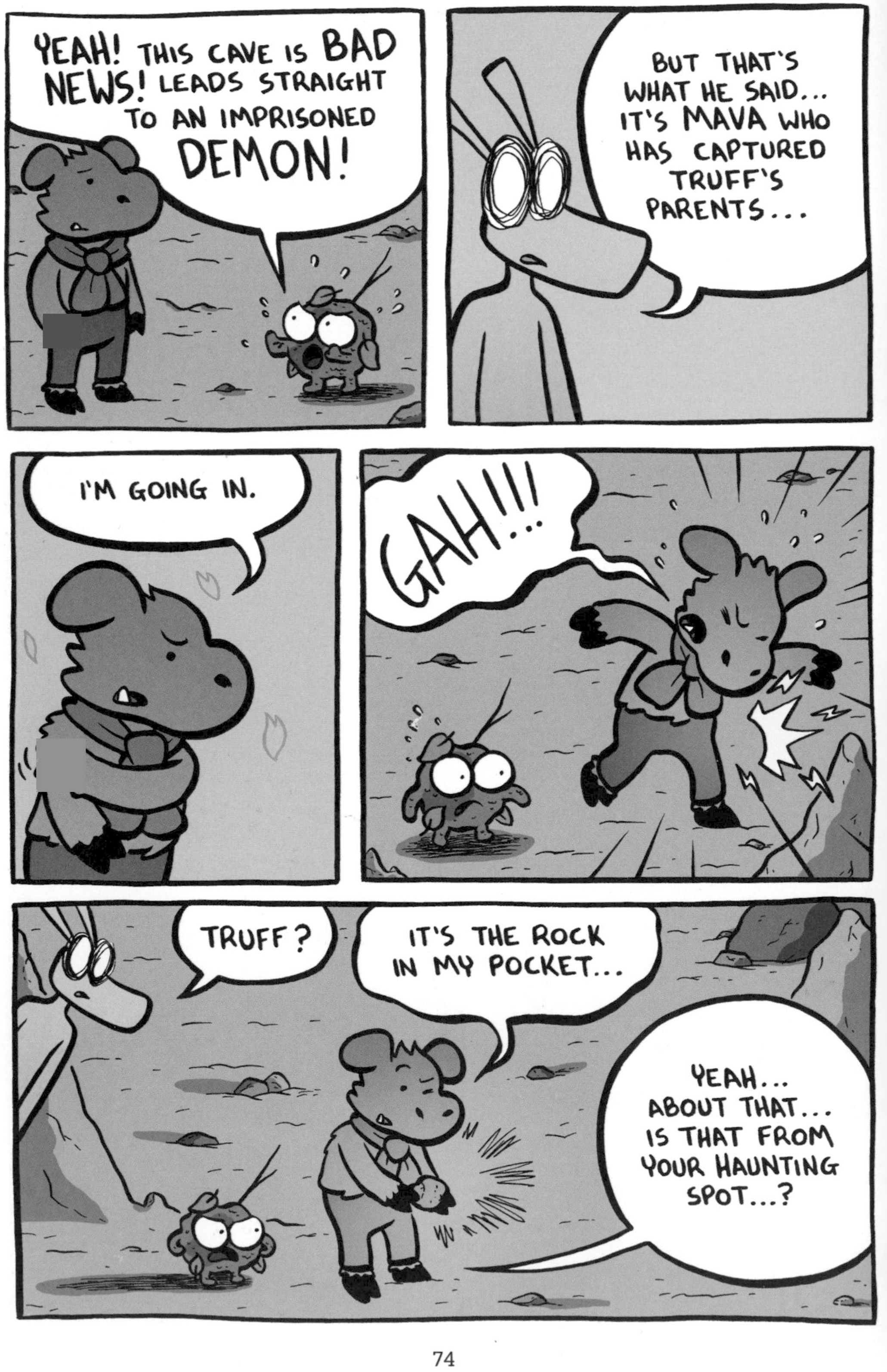
YEAH! THIS CAVE IS BAD NEWS! LEADS STRAIGHT TO AN IMPRISONED DEMON!
BUT THAT'S WHAT HE SAID... IT'S MAVA WHO HAS CAPTURED TRUFF'S PARENTS...
I'M GOING IN.
GAH!!!...
TRUFF?
IT'S THE ROCK IN MY POCKET...
YEAH... ABOUT THAT... IS THAT FROM YOUR HAUNTING SPOT...?

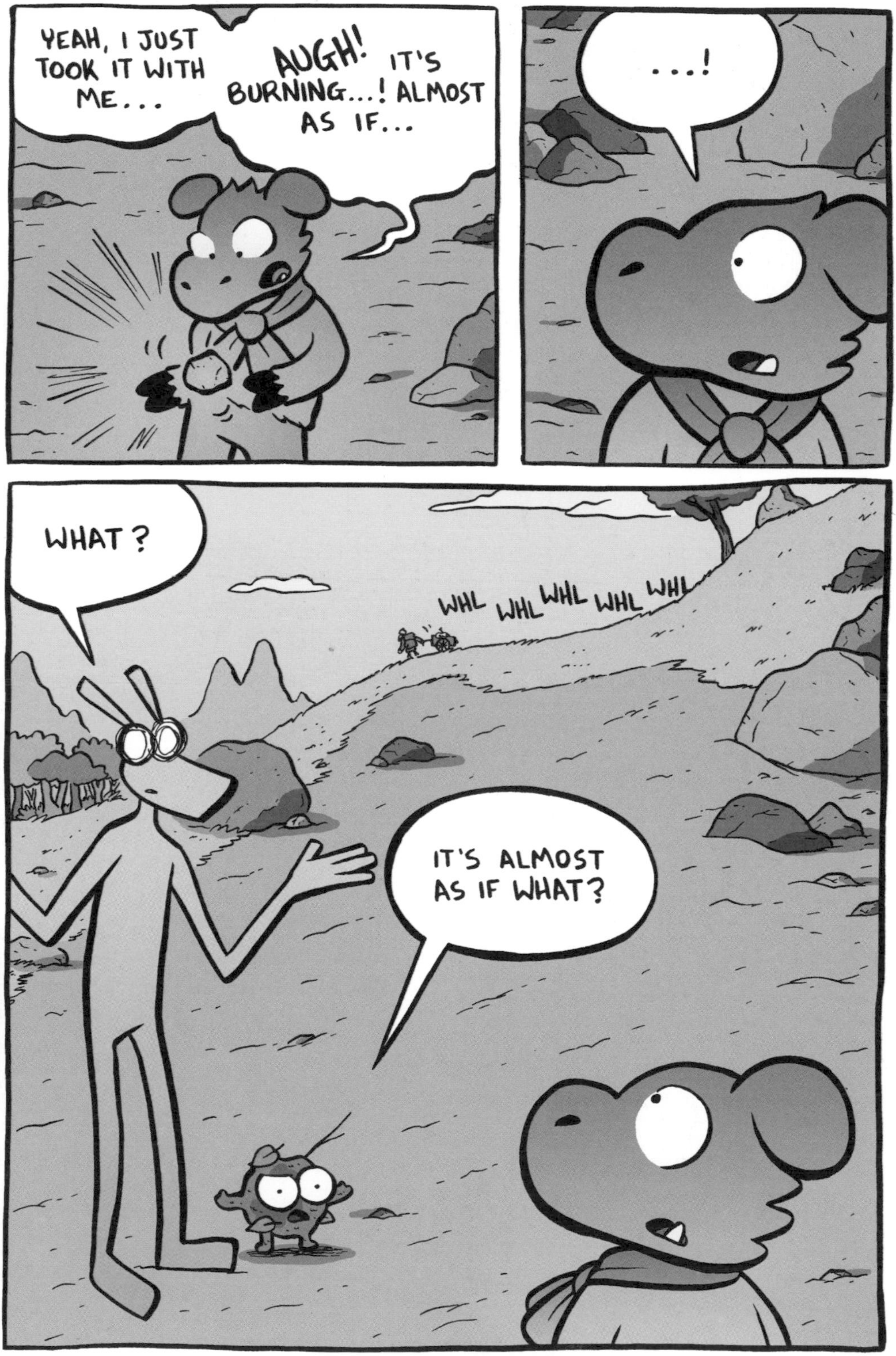
YEAH, I JUST TOOK IT WITH ME...
AUGH! BURNING...!
IT'S ALMOST AS IF...
...!
WHAT?
WHL WHL WHL WHL WHL
IT'S ALMOST AS IF WHAT?

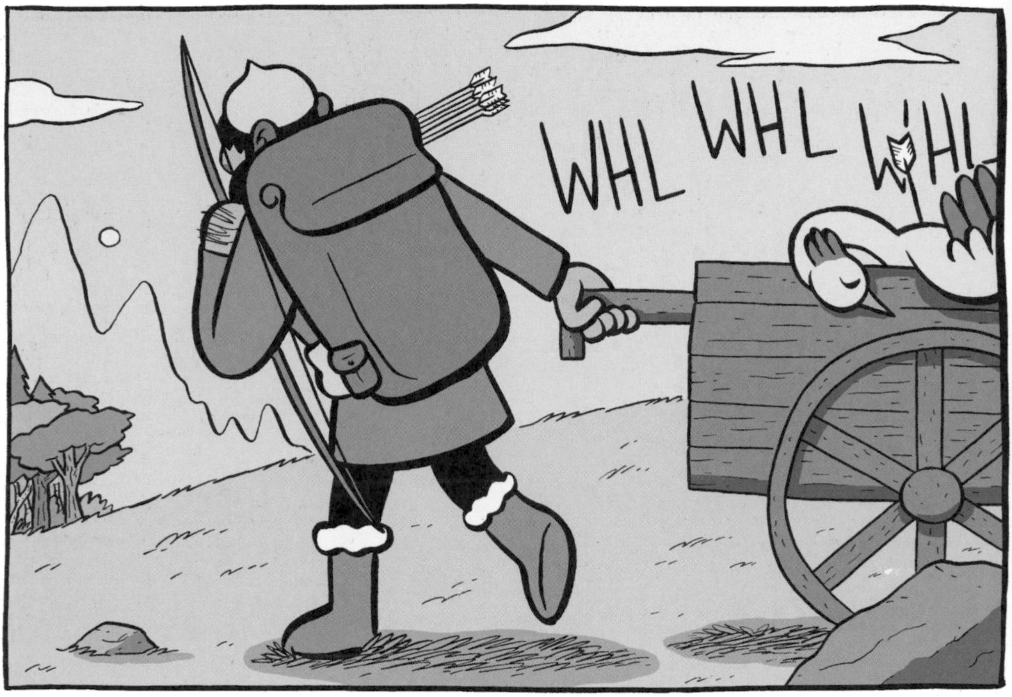
WHL WHL WHL

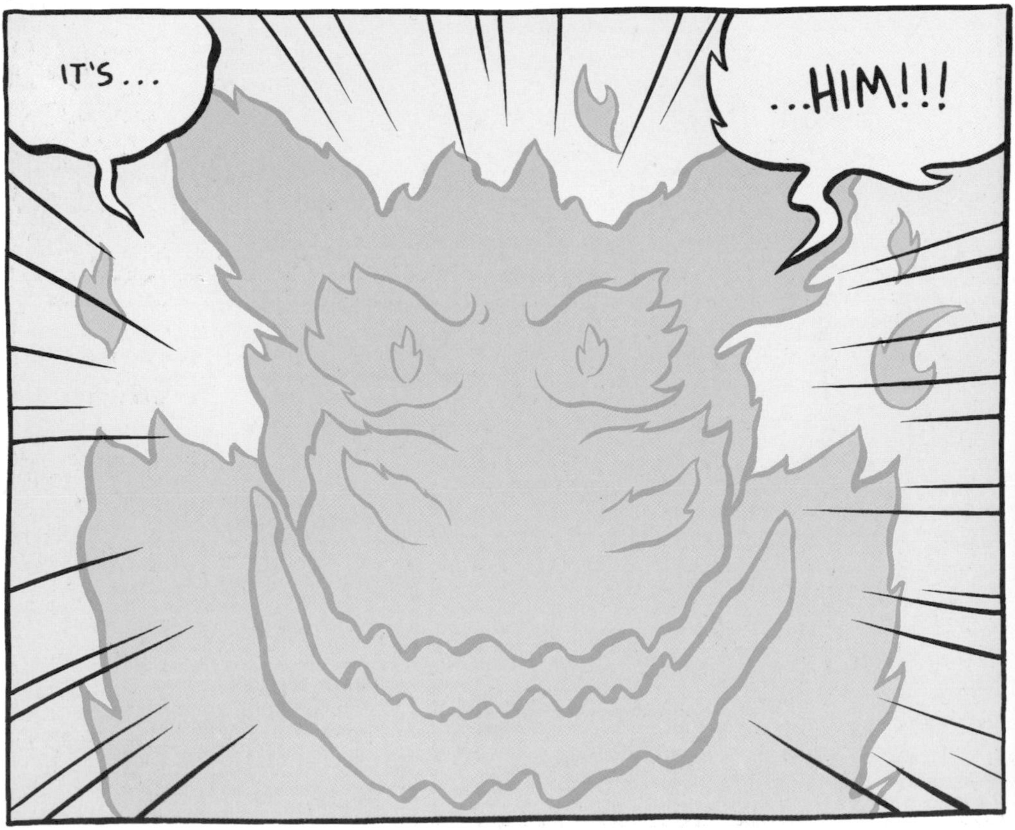
IT'S...
...HIM!!!

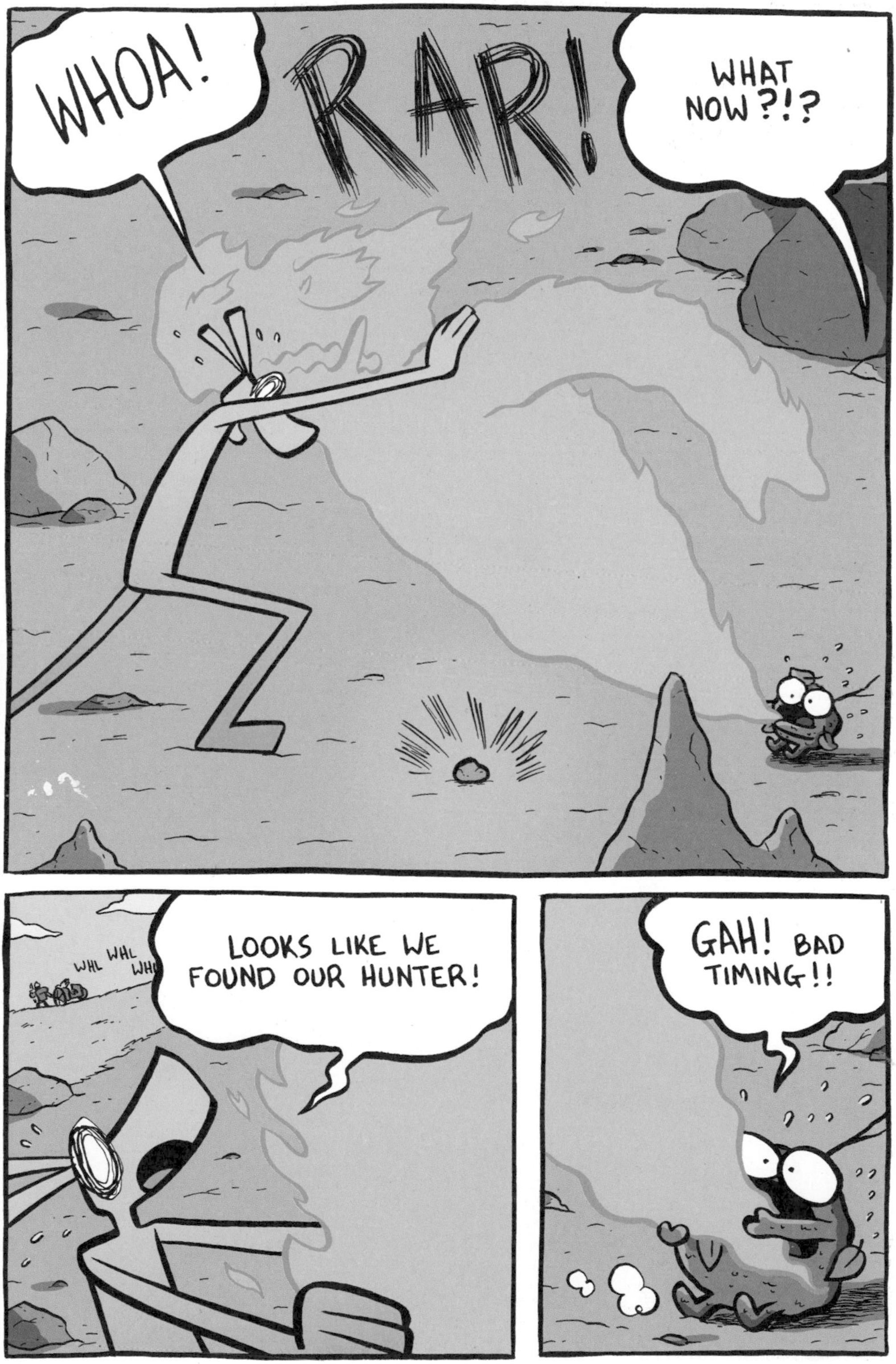
WHOA!
RAR!
WHAT NOW?!?
WHL WHL WHL
LOOKS LIKE WE FOUND OUR HUNTER!
GAH! BAD TIMING!!

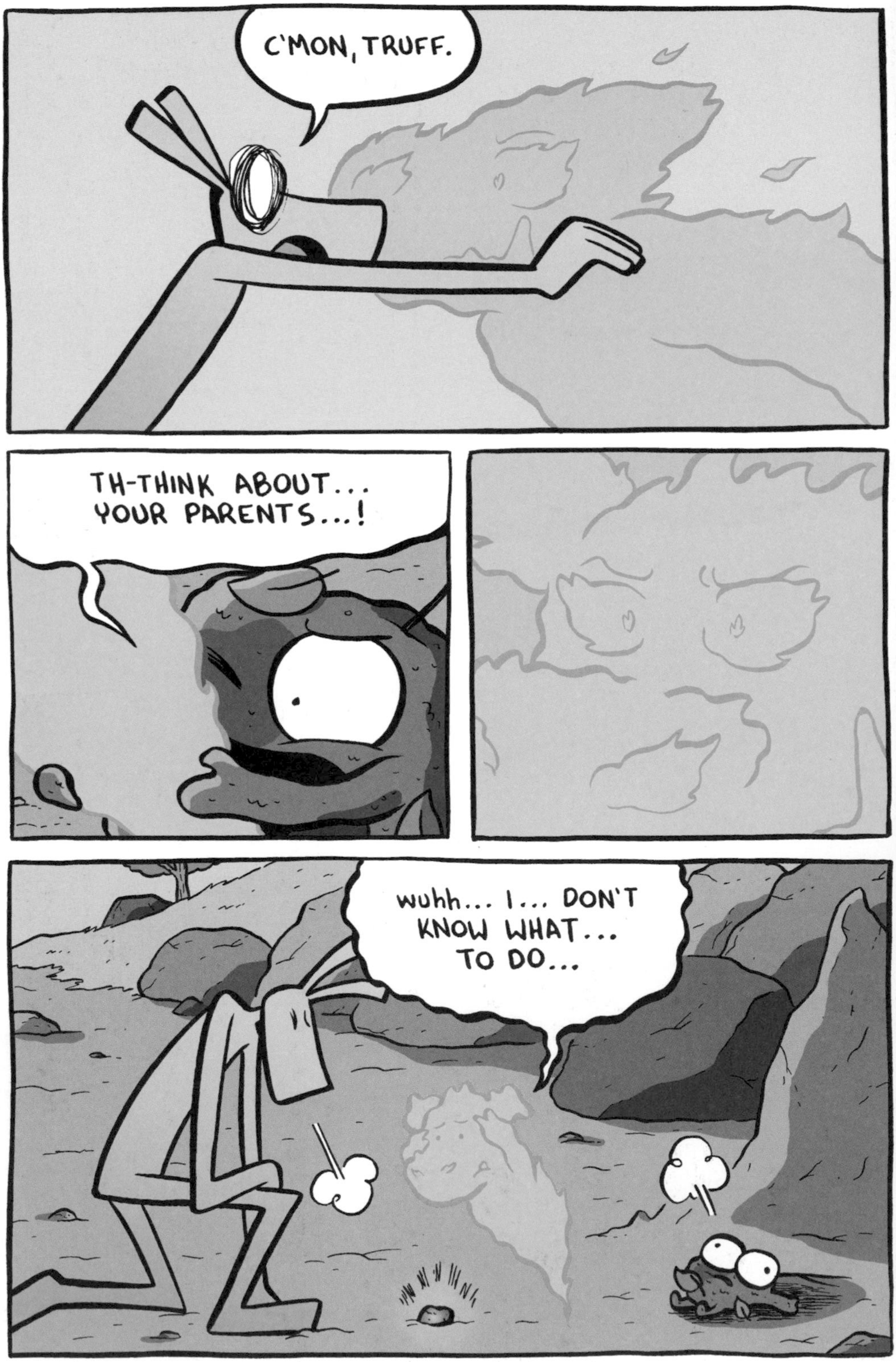
C'MON, TRUFF.
TH-THINK ABOUT... YOUR PARENTS...!
wuhh... I... DON'T KNOW WHAT... TO DO...

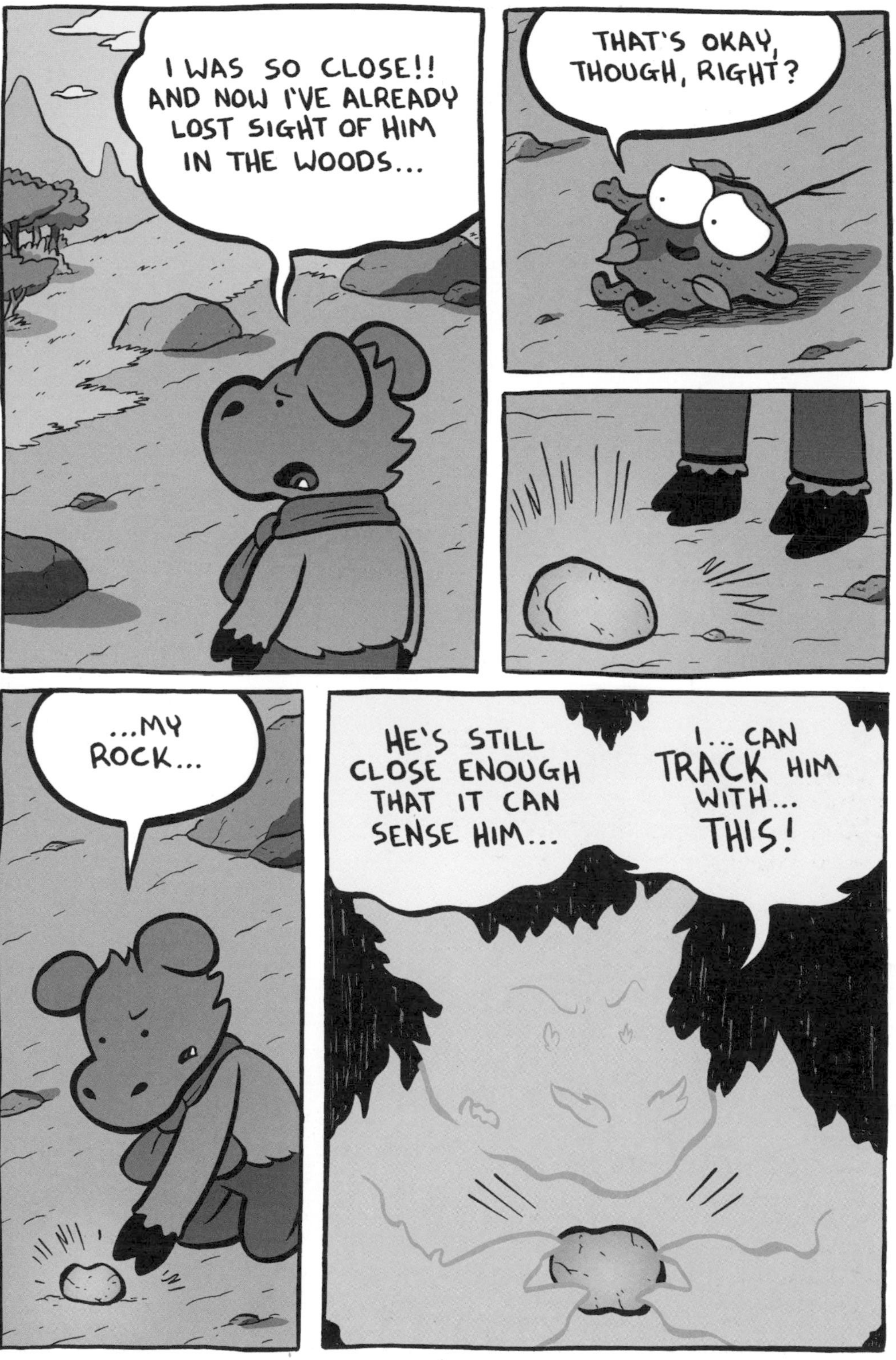
I WAS SO CLOSE!! AND NOW I'VE ALREADY LOST SIGHT OF HIM IN THE WOODS...
THAT'S OKAY, THOUGH, RIGHT?
...MY ROCK...
HE'S STILL CLOSE ENOUGH THAT IT CAN SENSE HIM...
I... CAN TRACK HIM WITH... THIS!

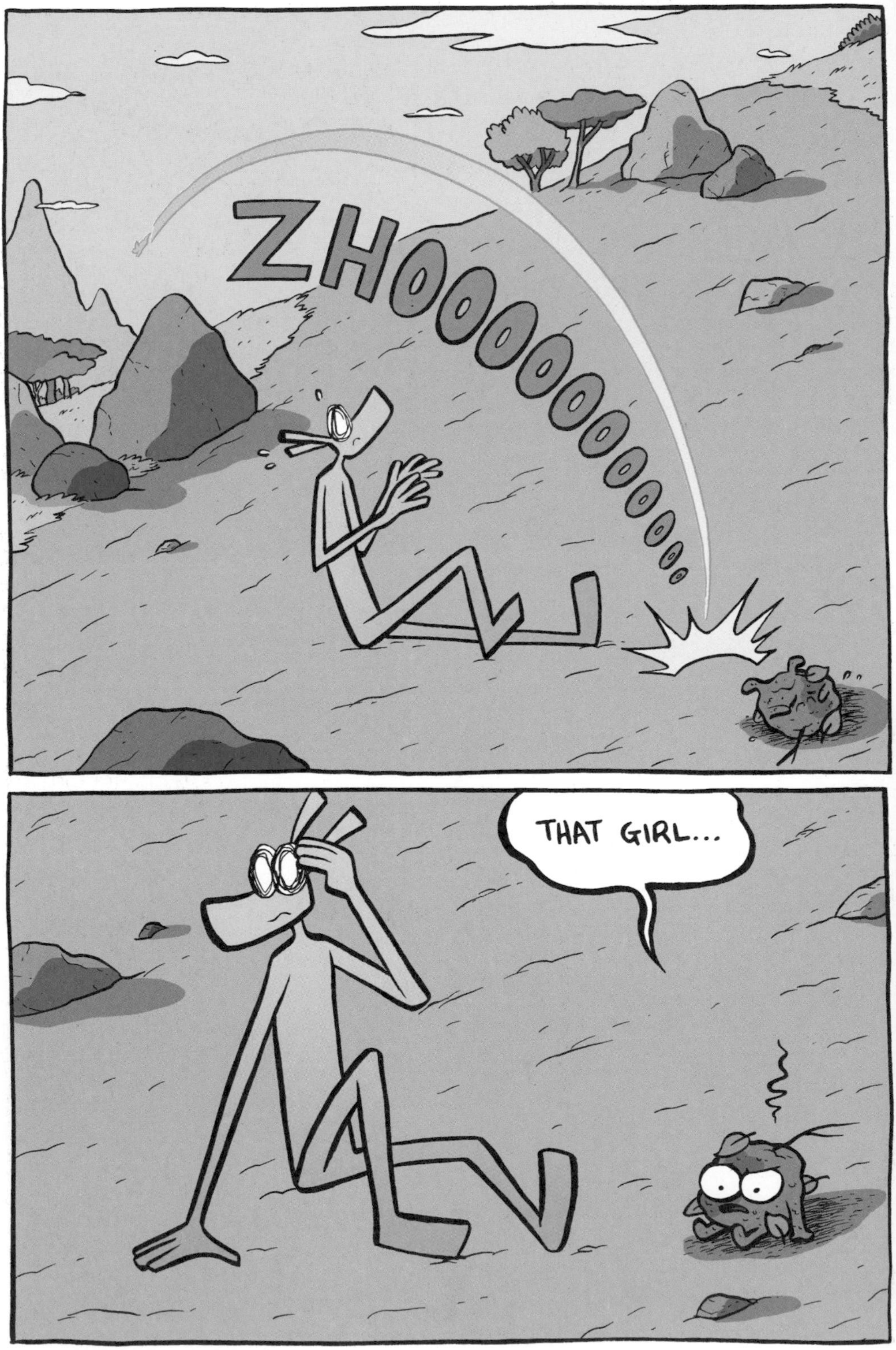
ZHOOOOOOOOOOO...
THAT GIRL...

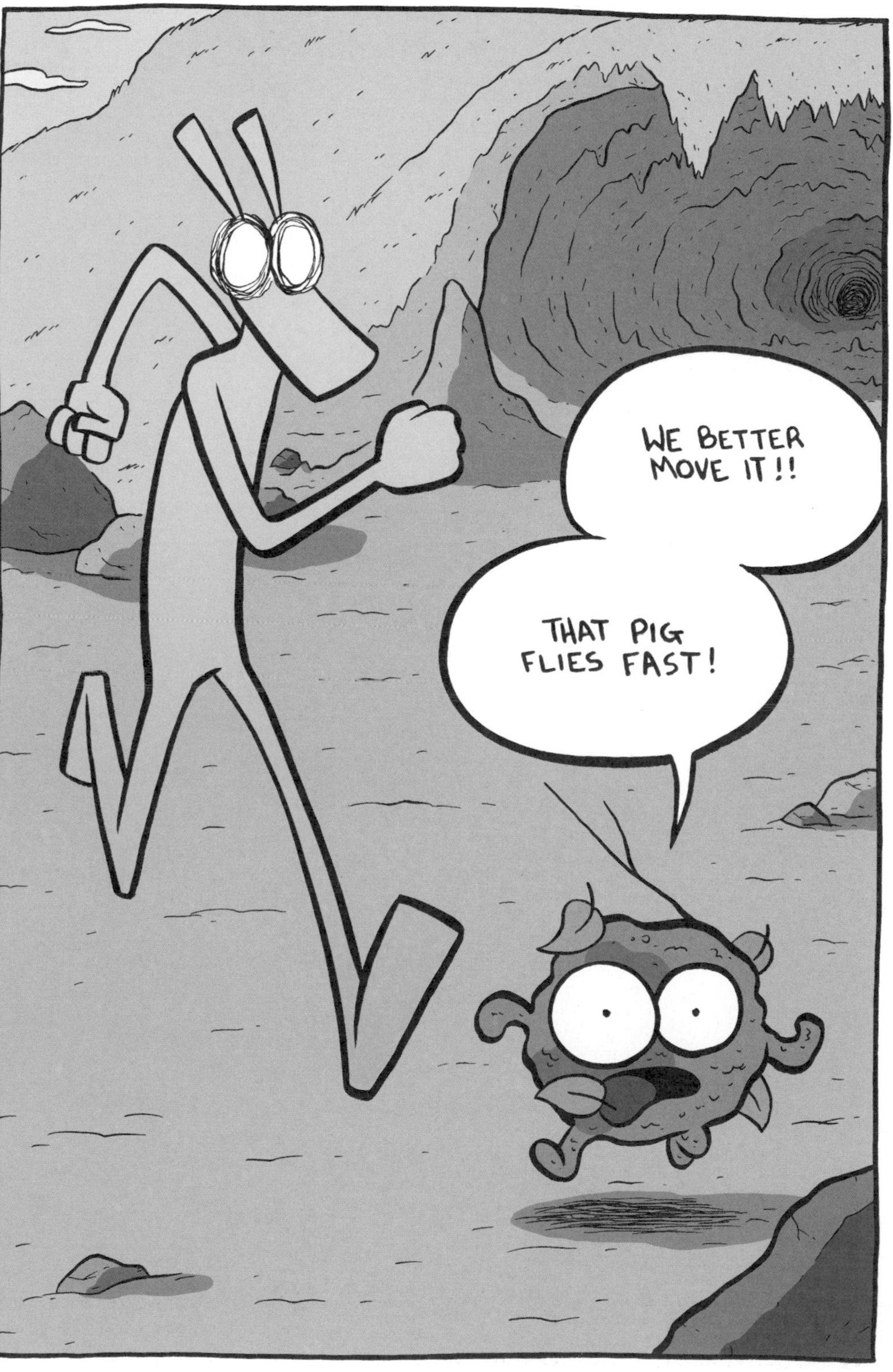
WE BETTER MOVE IT!!
THAT PIG FLIES FAST!

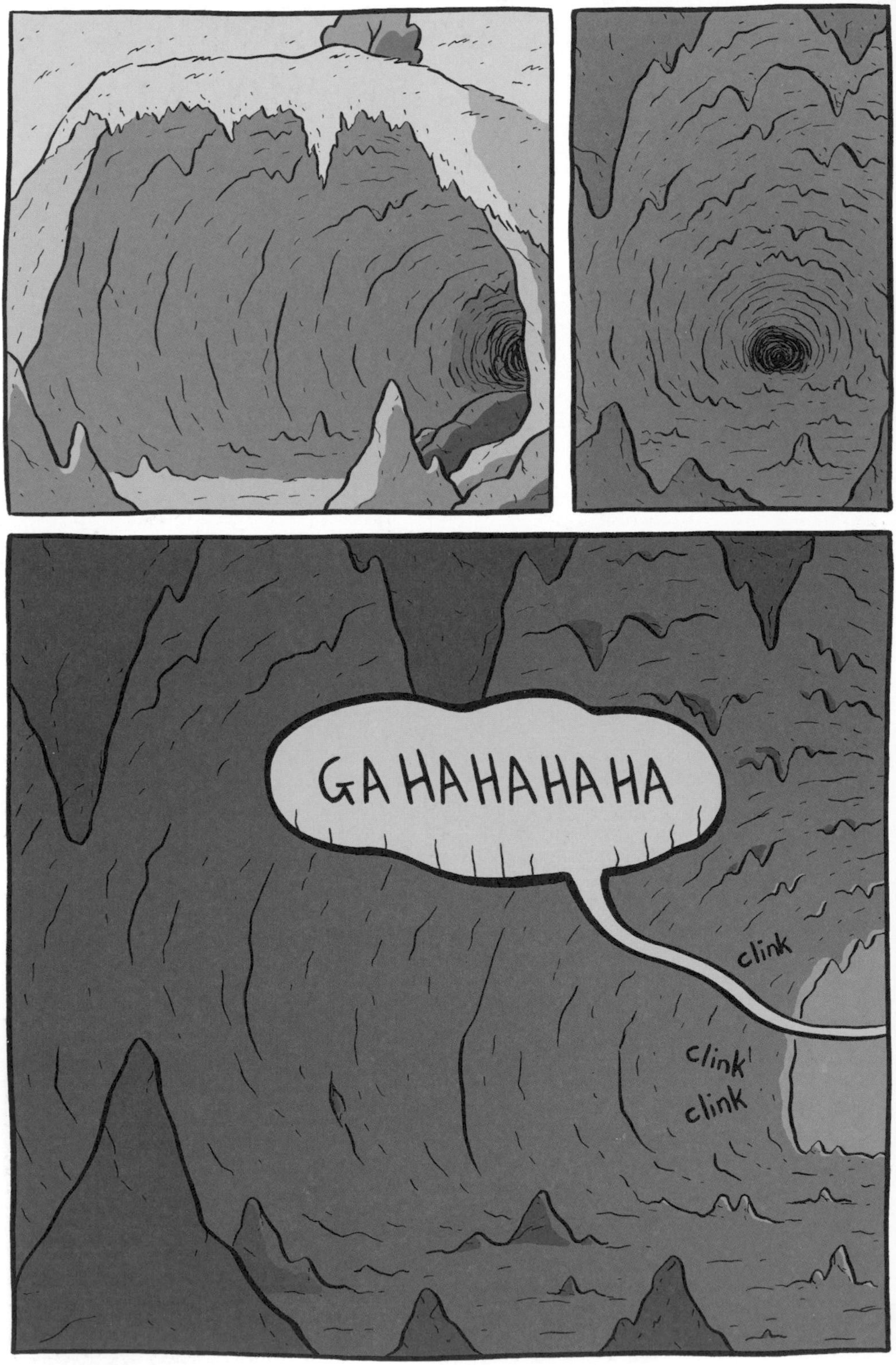
GAHAHAHAHA
clink
clink
clink

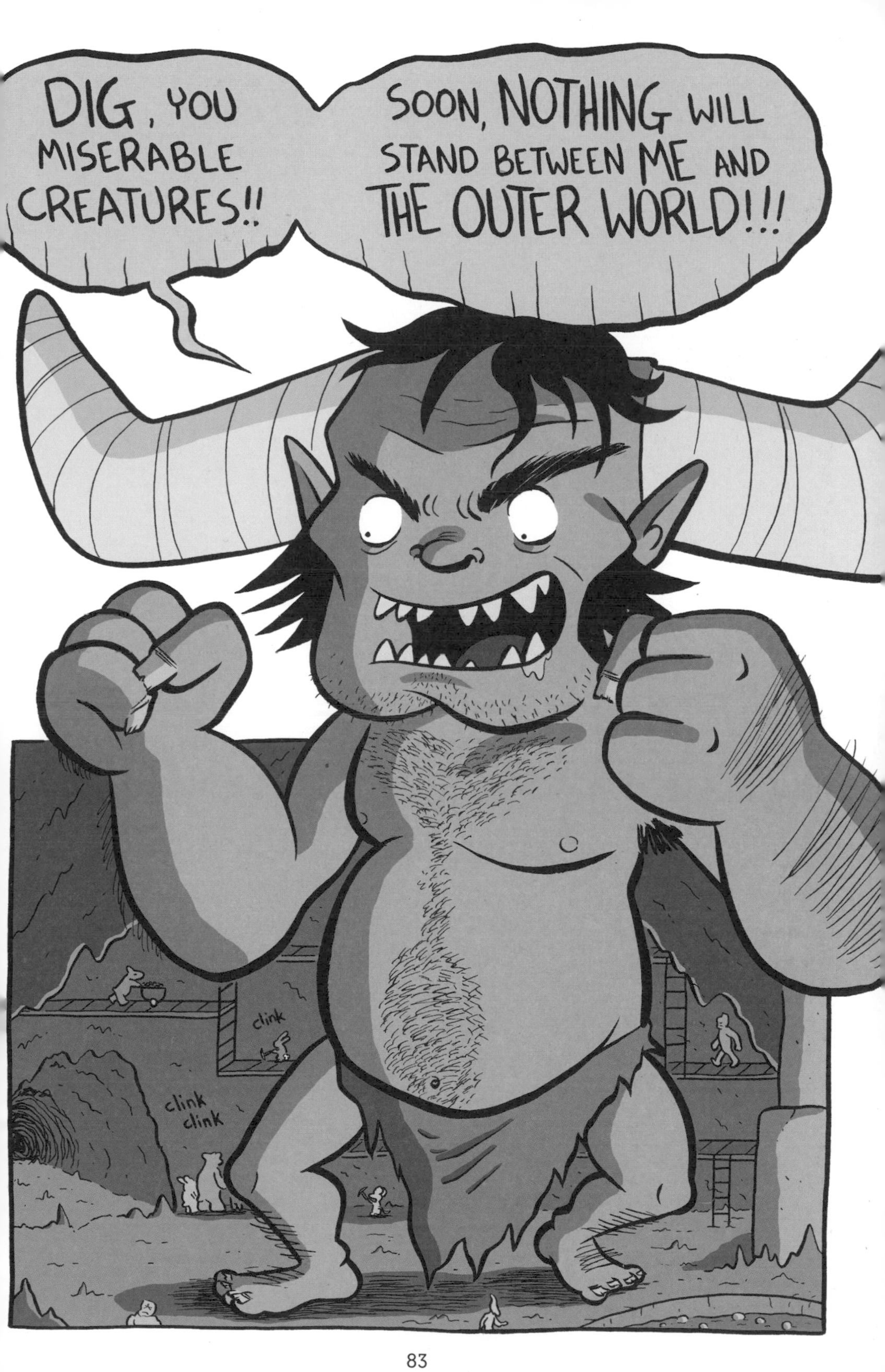
DIG, YOU MISERABLE CREATURES!!
SOON, NOTHING WILL STAND BETWEEN ME AND THE OUTER WORLD!!!
clink
clink clink

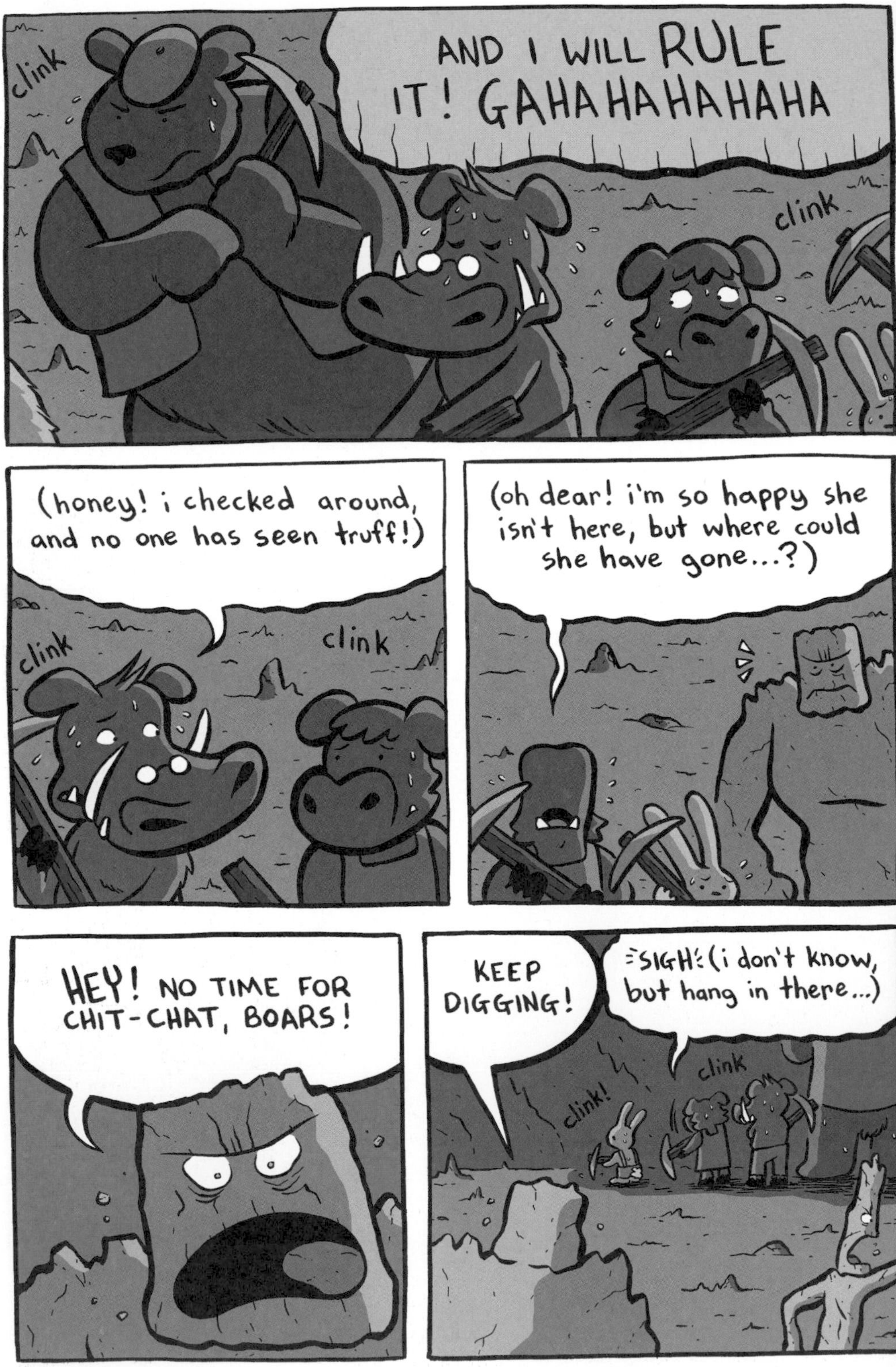
clink
AND I WILL RULE IT! GAHAHAHAHAHA
clink
(honey! i checked around, and no one has seen truff!)
clink
clink
(oh dear! i'm so happy she isn't here, but where could she have gone...?)
HEY! NO TIME FOR CHIT-CHAT, BOARS!
KEEP DIGGING!
SIGH (i don't know, but hang in there...)
clink
clink!

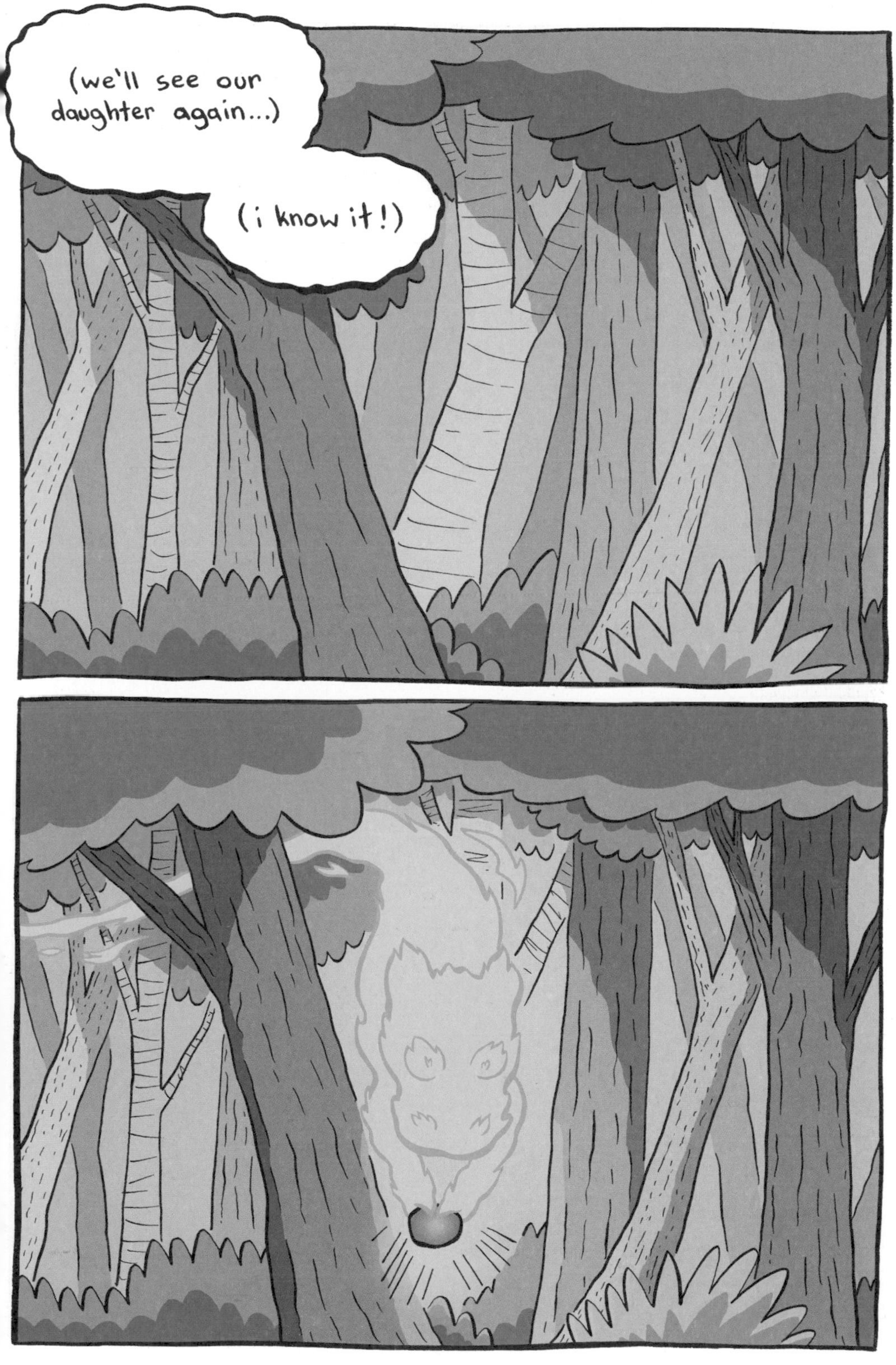
(we'll see our daughter again...)
(i know it!)

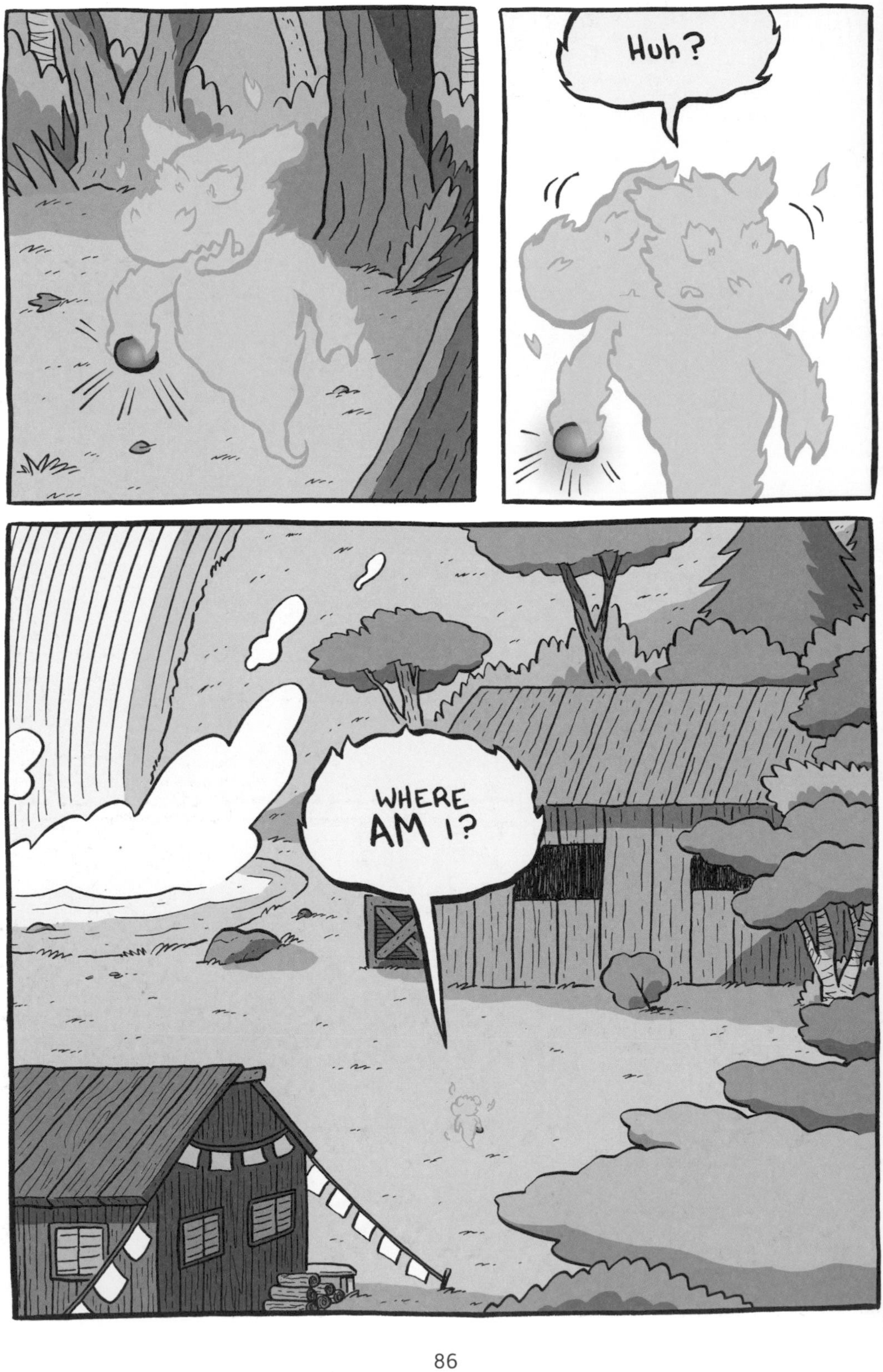
Huh?
WHERE AM I?

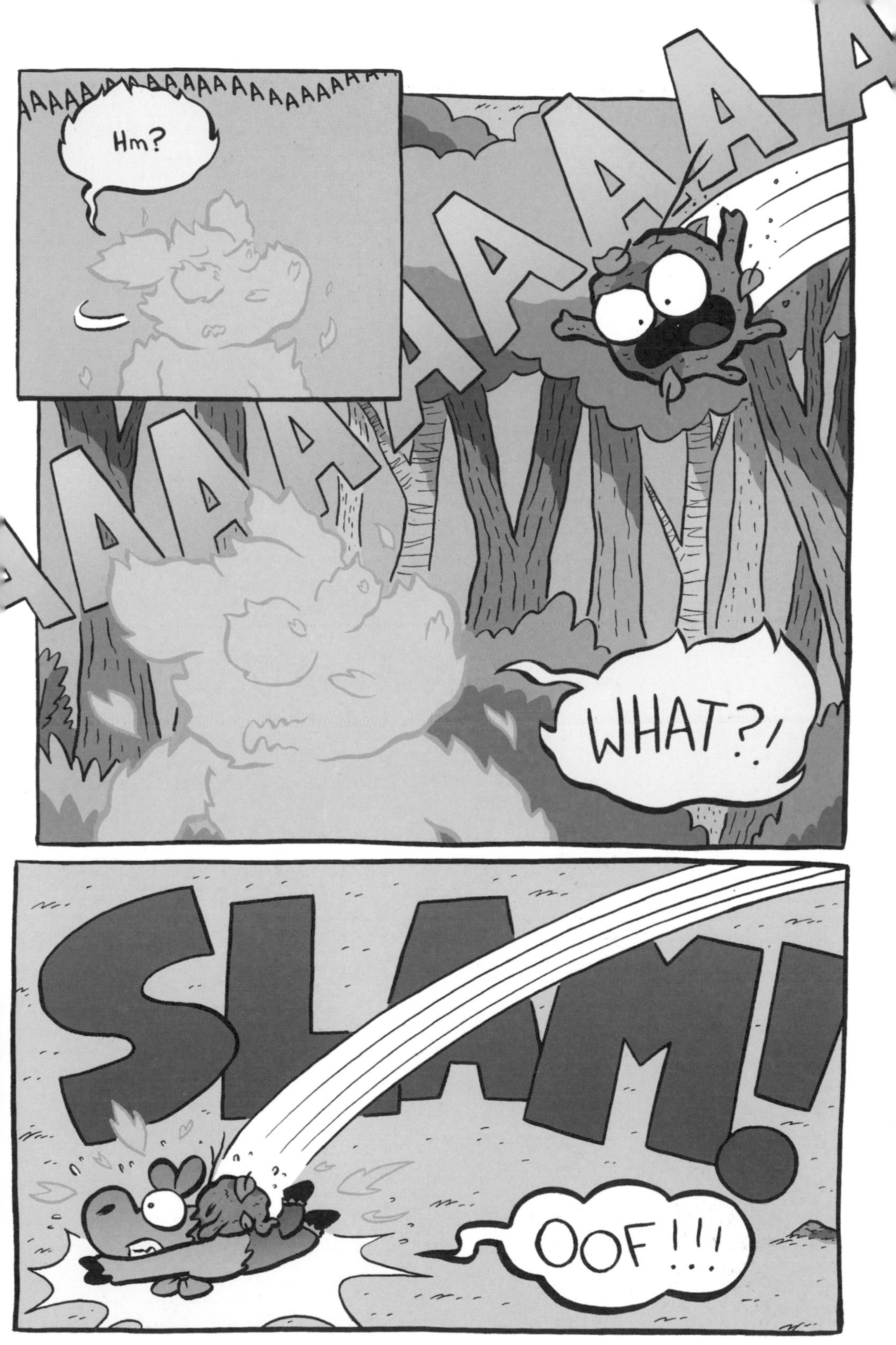
AAAAAAAAAAAAAAAAAAAA
Hm?
AAAAAAAAAA
WHAT?!
SLAM!
OOF!!!

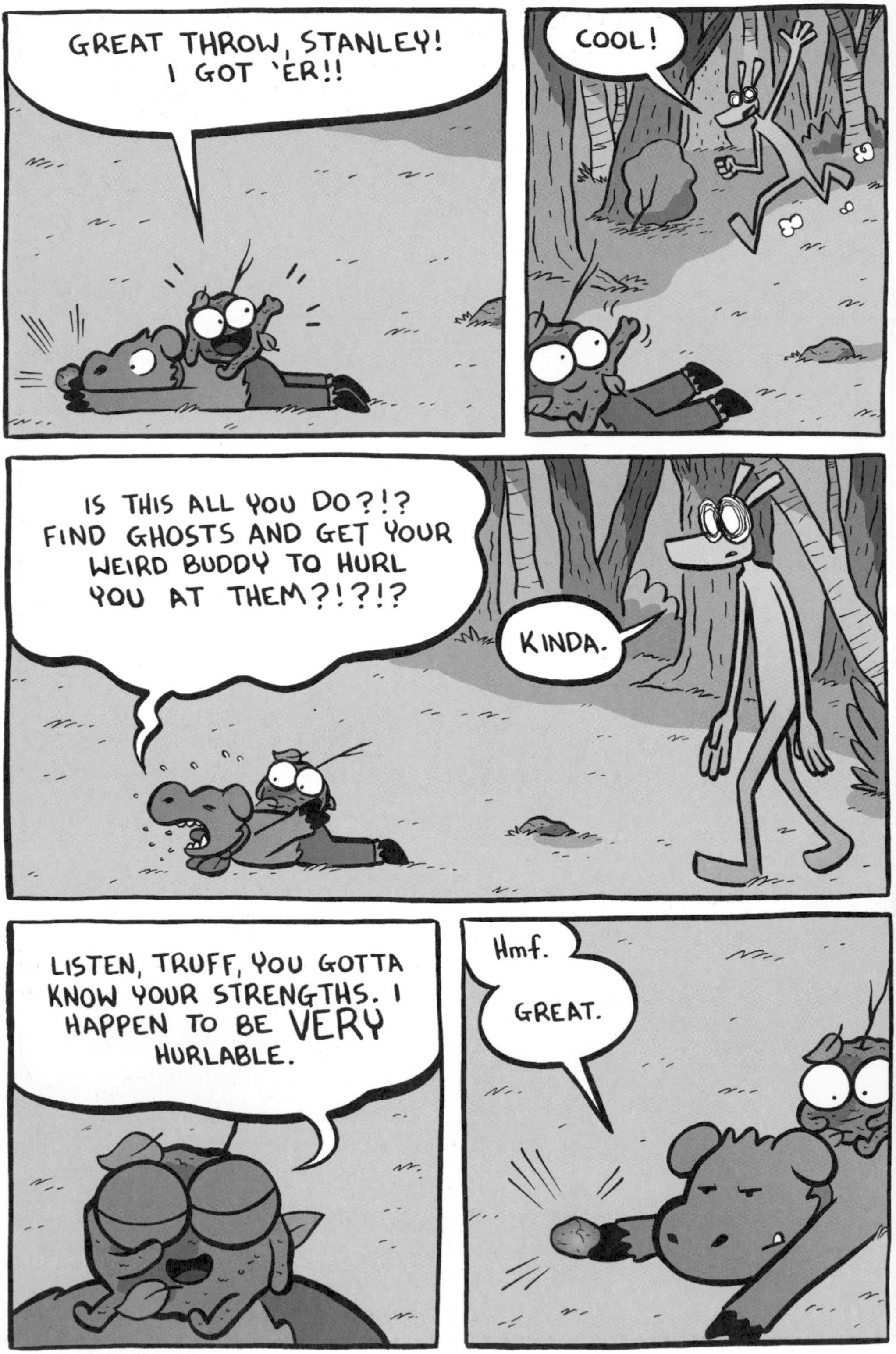
GREAT THROW, STANLEY! I GOT 'ER!!
COOL!
IS THIS ALL YOU DO?!? FIND GHOSTS AND GET YOUR WEIRD BUDDY TO HURL YOU AT THEM?!?!?
KINDA.
LISTEN, TRUFF, YOU GOTTA KNOW YOUR STRENGTHS. I HAPPEN TO BE VERY HURLABLE.
Hmf.
GREAT.

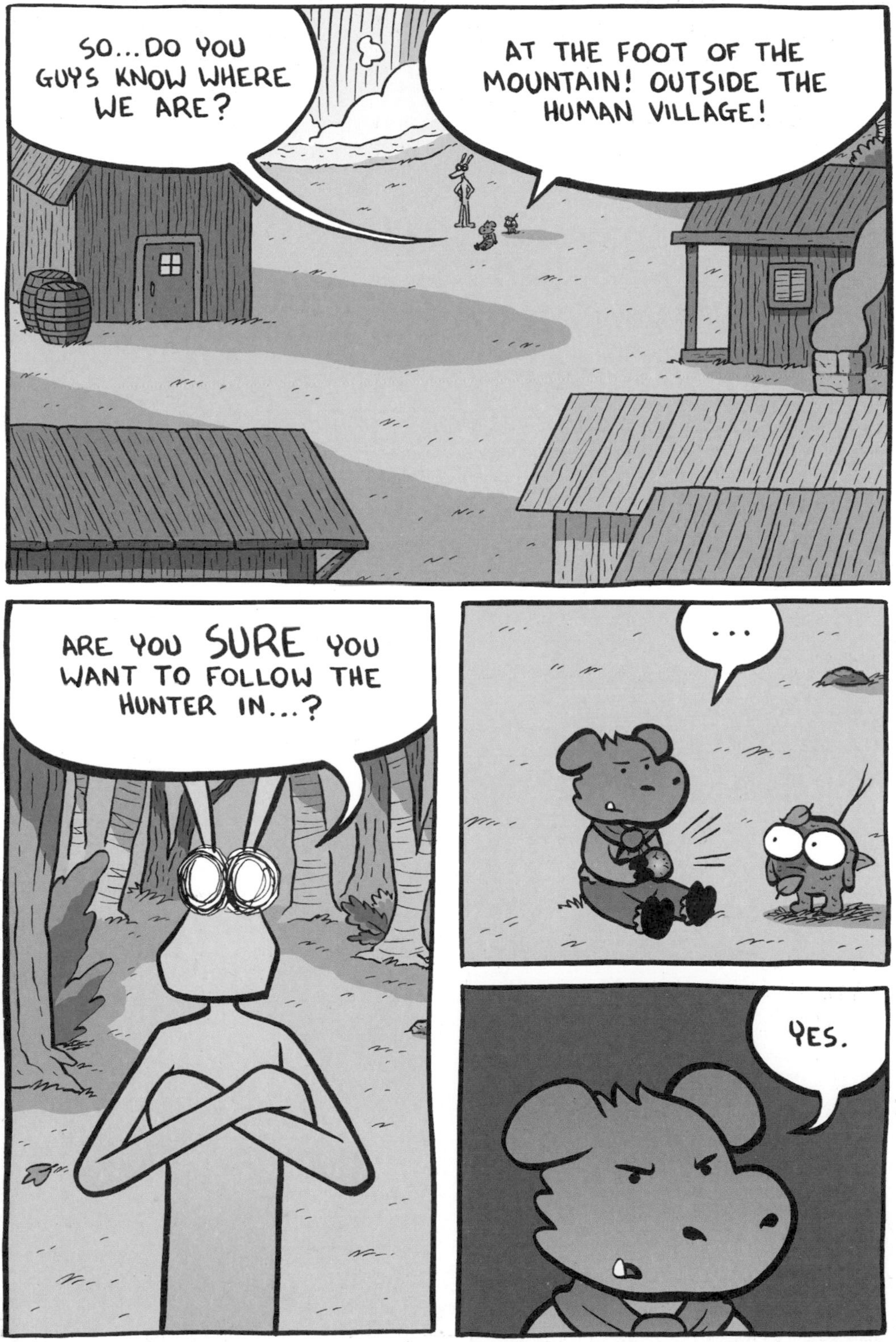
SO...DO YOU GUYS KNOW WHERE WE ARE?
AT THE FOOT OF THE MOUNTAIN! OUTSIDE THE HUMAN VILLAGE!
ARE YOU SURE YOU WANT TO FOLLOW THE HUNTER IN...?
...
YES.

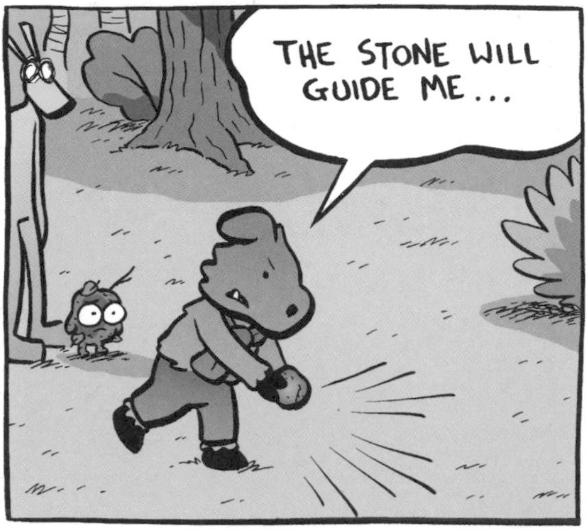
THE STONE WILL GUIDE ME...

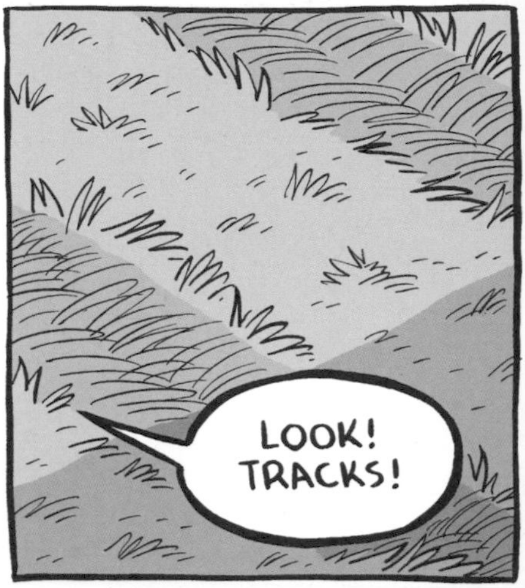
LOOK! TRACKS!

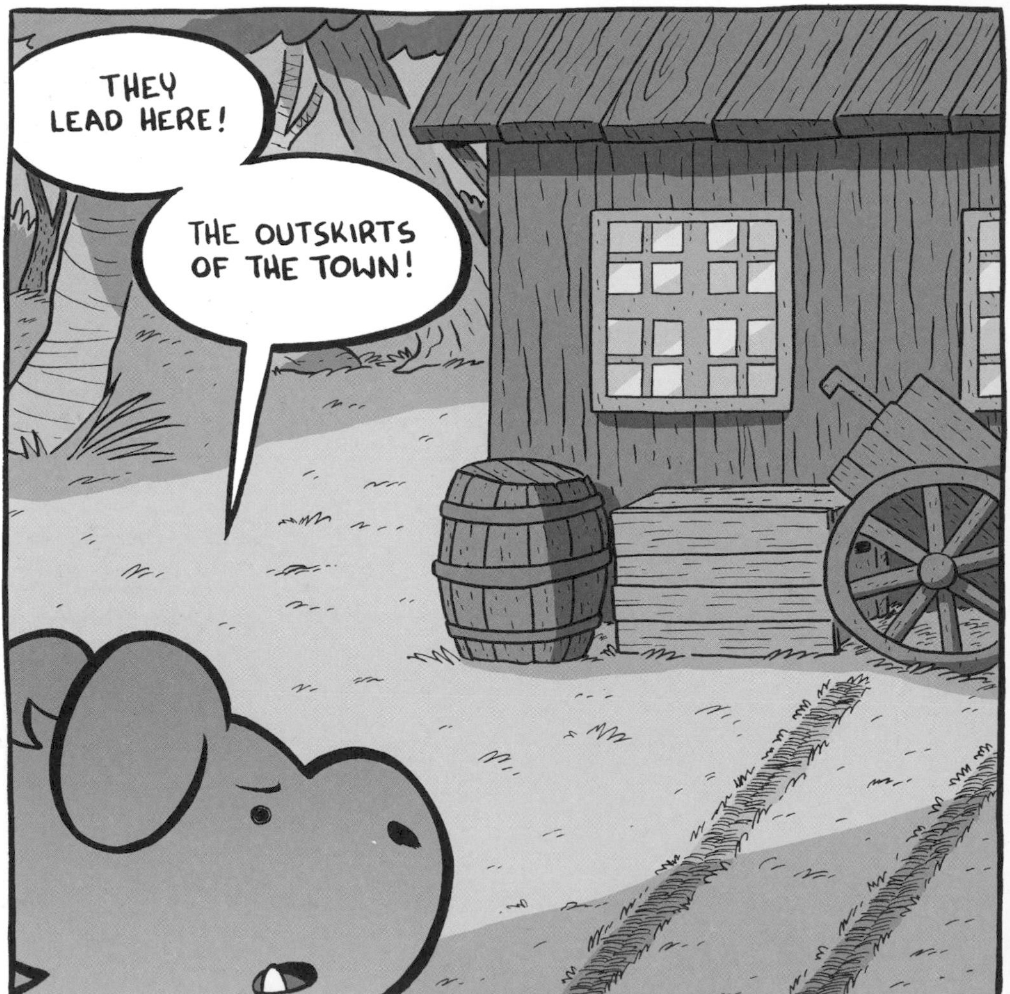
THEY LEAD HERE!
THE OUTSKIRTS OF THE TOWN!

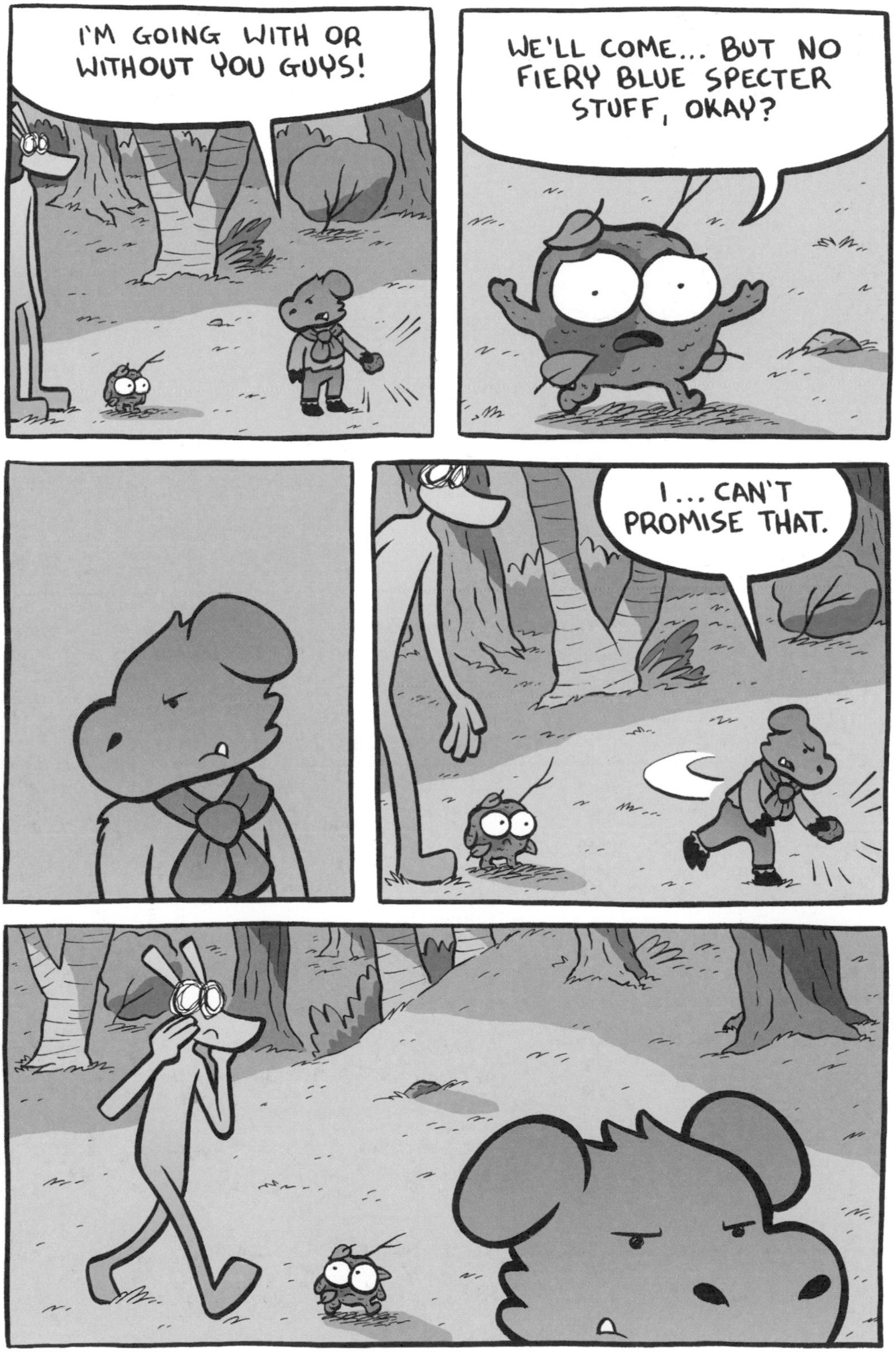
I'M GOING WITH OR WITHOUT YOU GUYS!
WE'LL COME... BUT NO FIERY BLUE SPECTER STUFF, OKAY?
I... CAN'T PROMISE THAT.

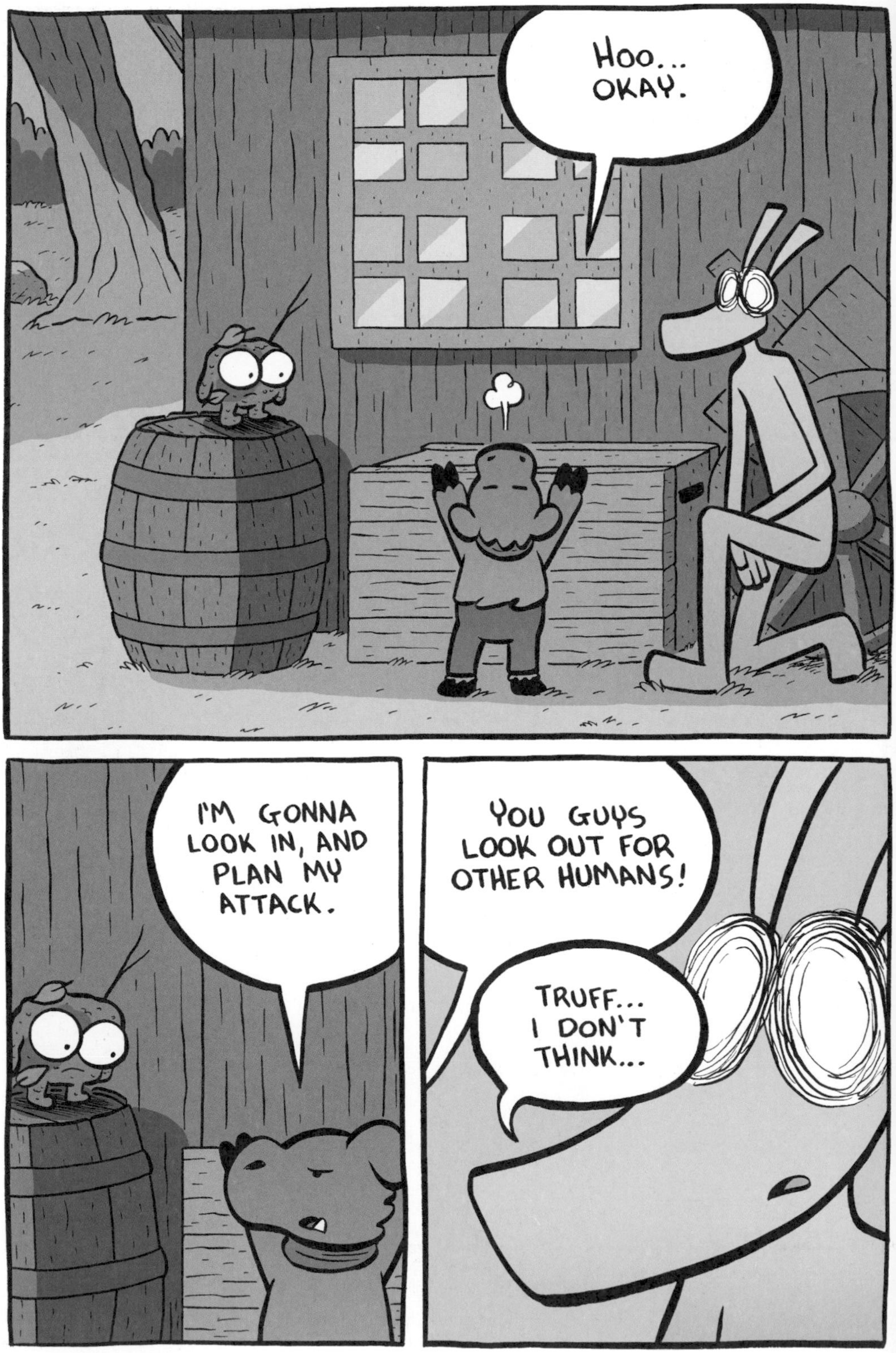
HOO... OKAY.
I'M GONNA LOOK IN, AND PLAN MY ATTACK.
YOU GUYS LOOK OUT FOR OTHER HUMANS!
TRUFF... I DON'T THINK...

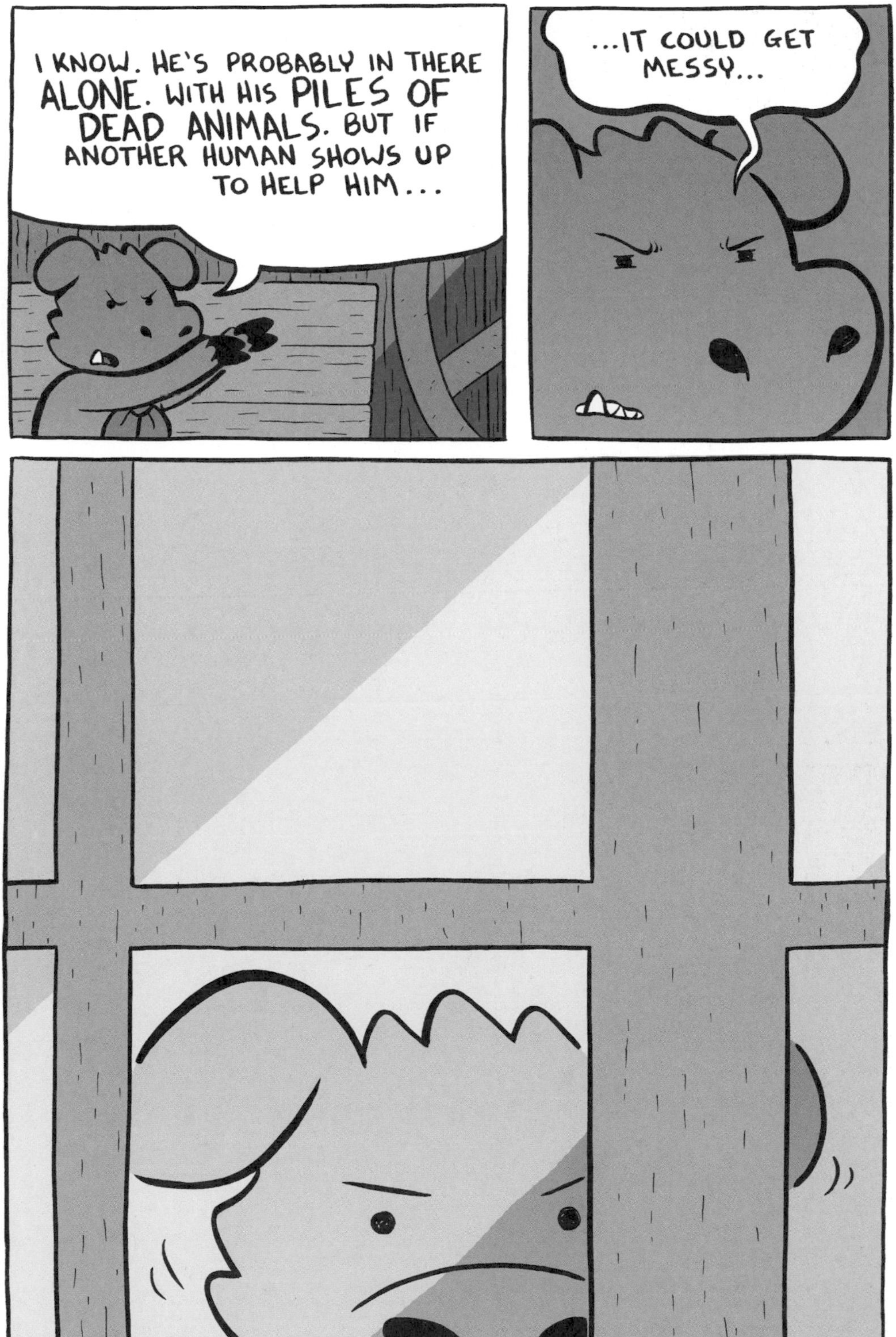
I KNOW. HE'S PROBABLY IN THERE ALONE. WITH HIS PILES OF DEAD ANIMALS. BUT IF ANOTHER HUMAN SHOWS UP TO HELP HIM...
...IT COULD GET MESSY...

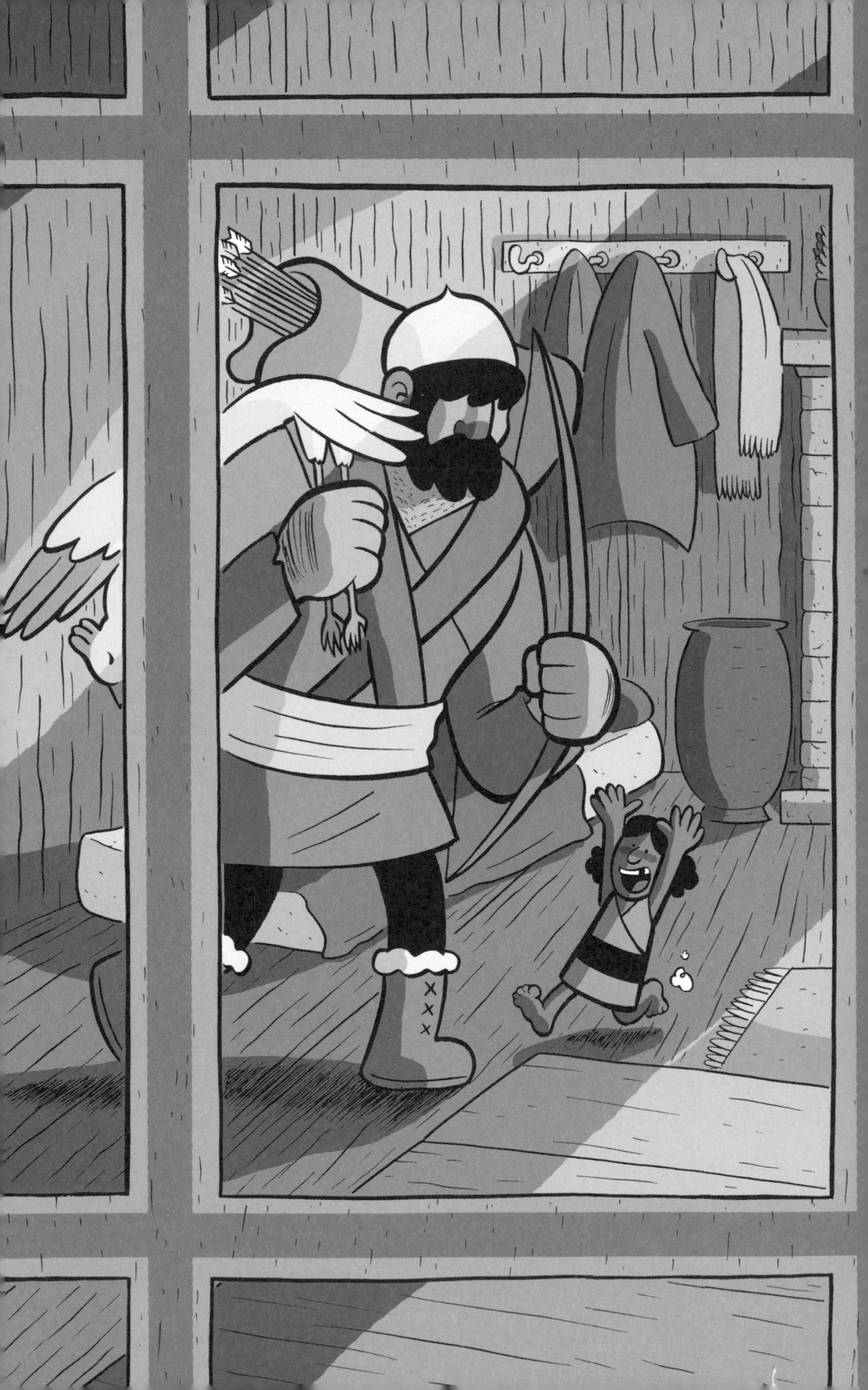

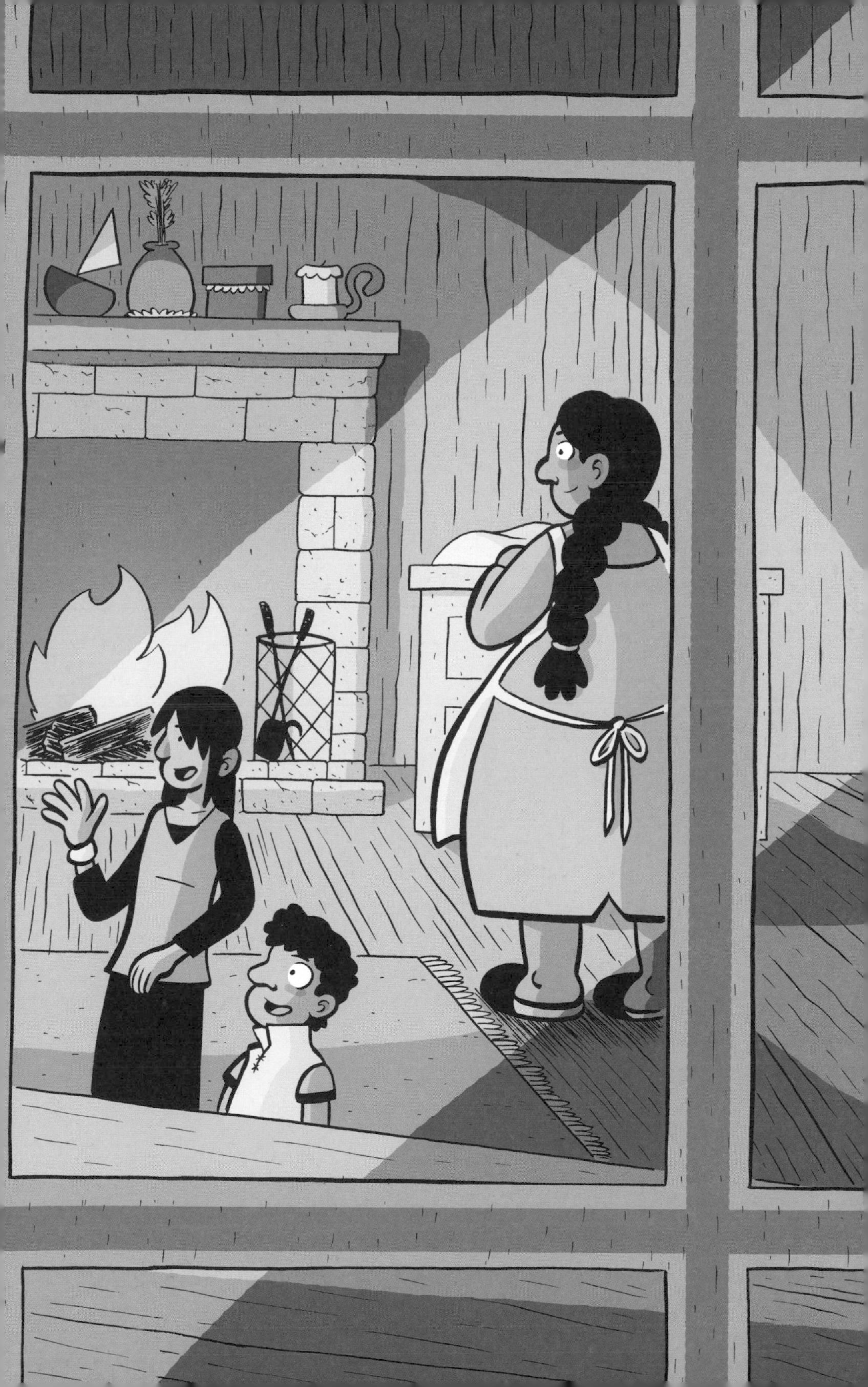

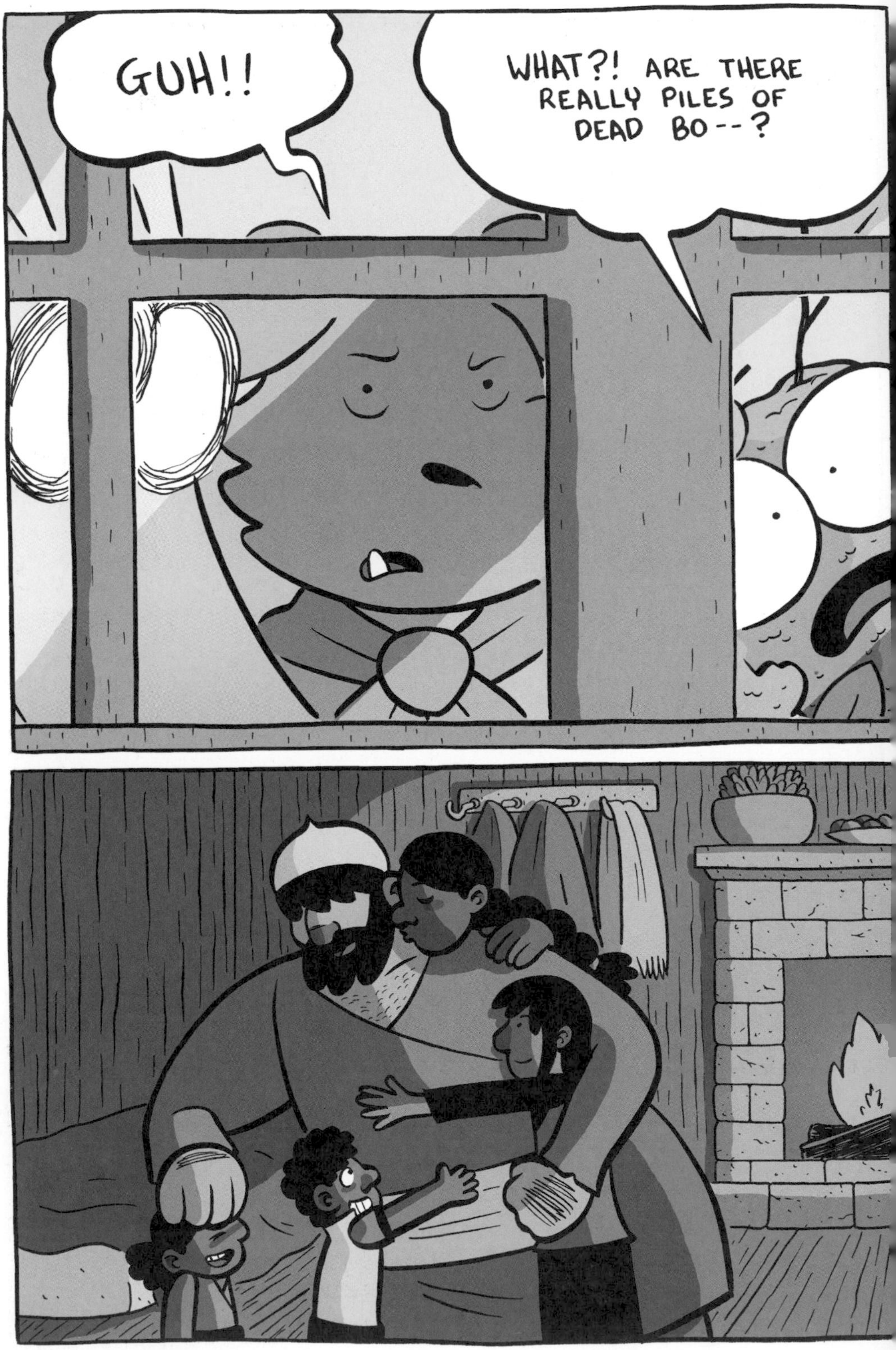
GUH!!
WHAT?! ARE THERE REALLY PILES OF DEAD BO--?

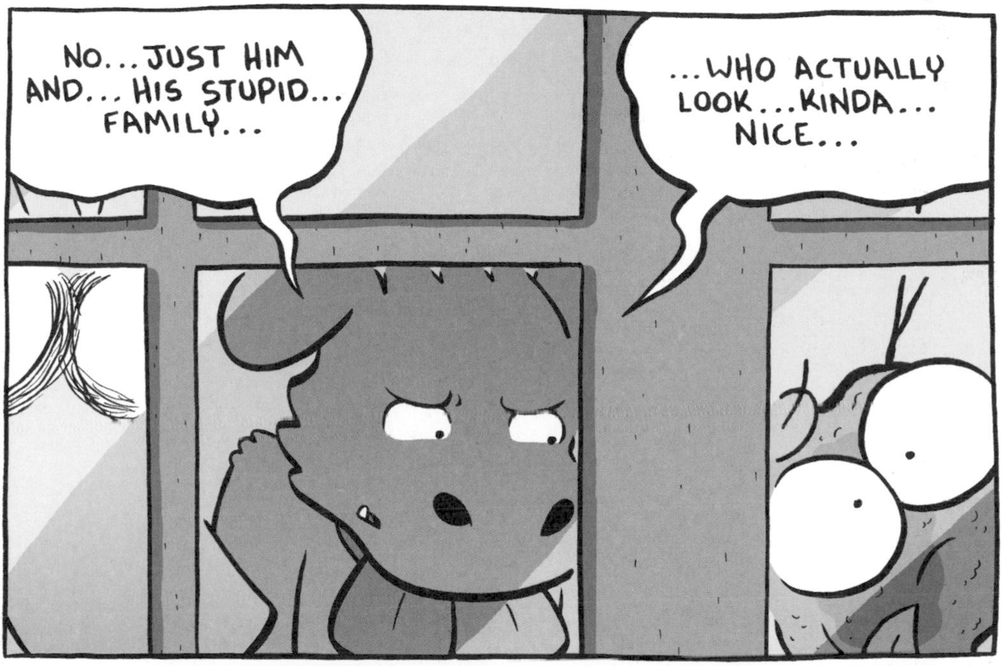
NO...JUST HIM AND... HIS STUPID... FAMILY...
...WHO ACTUALLY LOOK...KINDA... NICE...

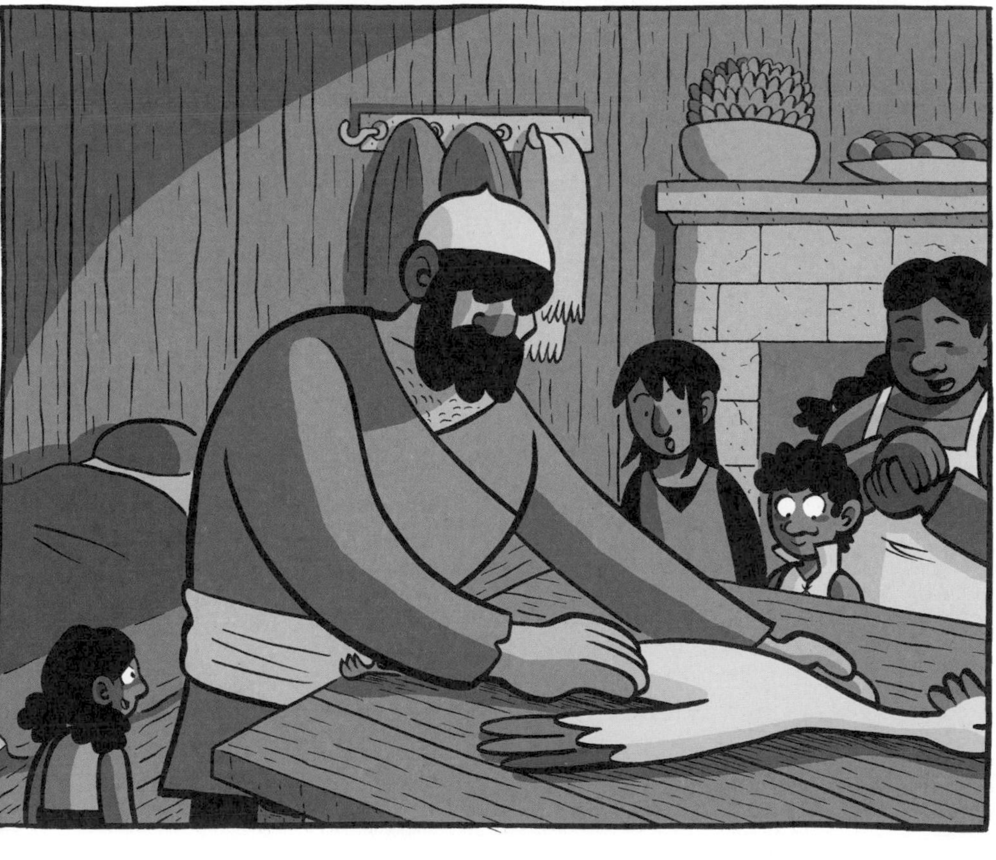

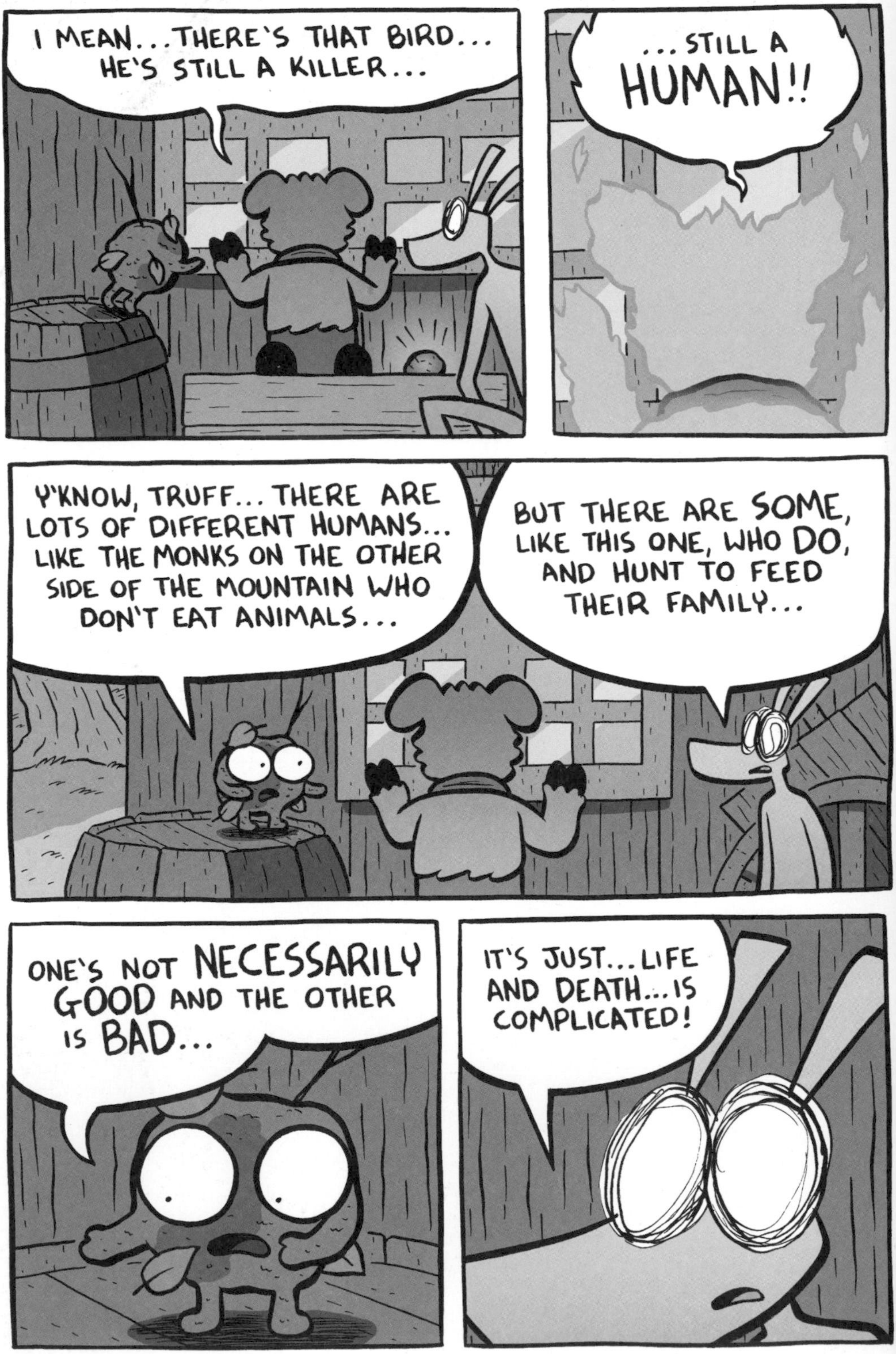
I MEAN... THERE'S THAT BIRD... HE'S STILL A KILLER...
...STILL A HUMAN!!
Y'KNOW, TRUFF... THERE ARE LOTS OF DIFFERENT HUMANS... LIKE THE MONKS ON THE OTHER SIDE OF THE MOUNTAIN WHO DON'T EAT ANIMALS...
BUT THERE ARE SOME, LIKE THIS ONE, WHO DO, AND HUNT TO FEED THEIR FAMILY...
ONE'S NOT NECESSARILY GOOD AND THE OTHER IS BAD...
IT'S JUST... LIFE AND DEATH... IS COMPLICATED!

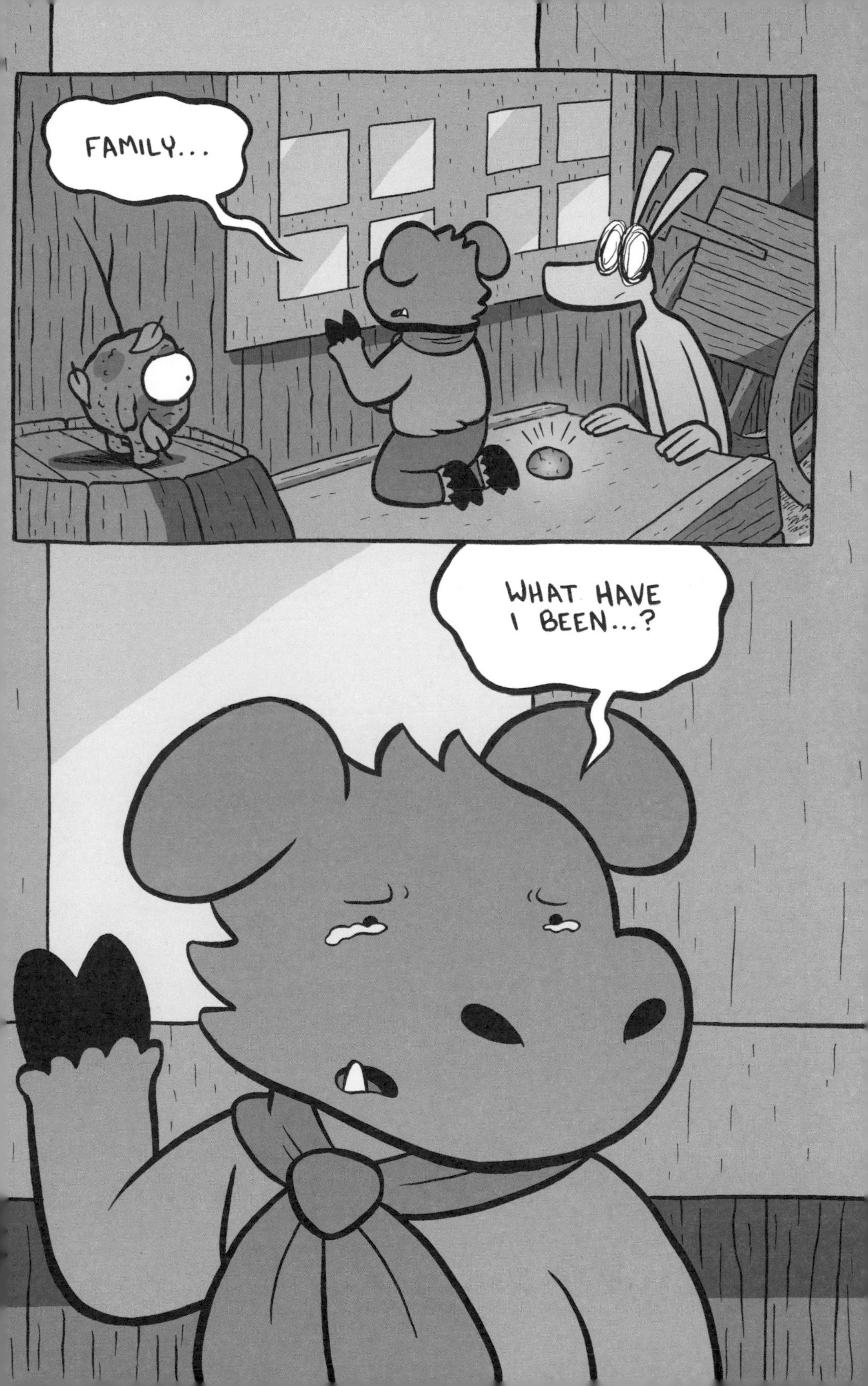
FAMILY...
WHAT HAVE I BEEN...?

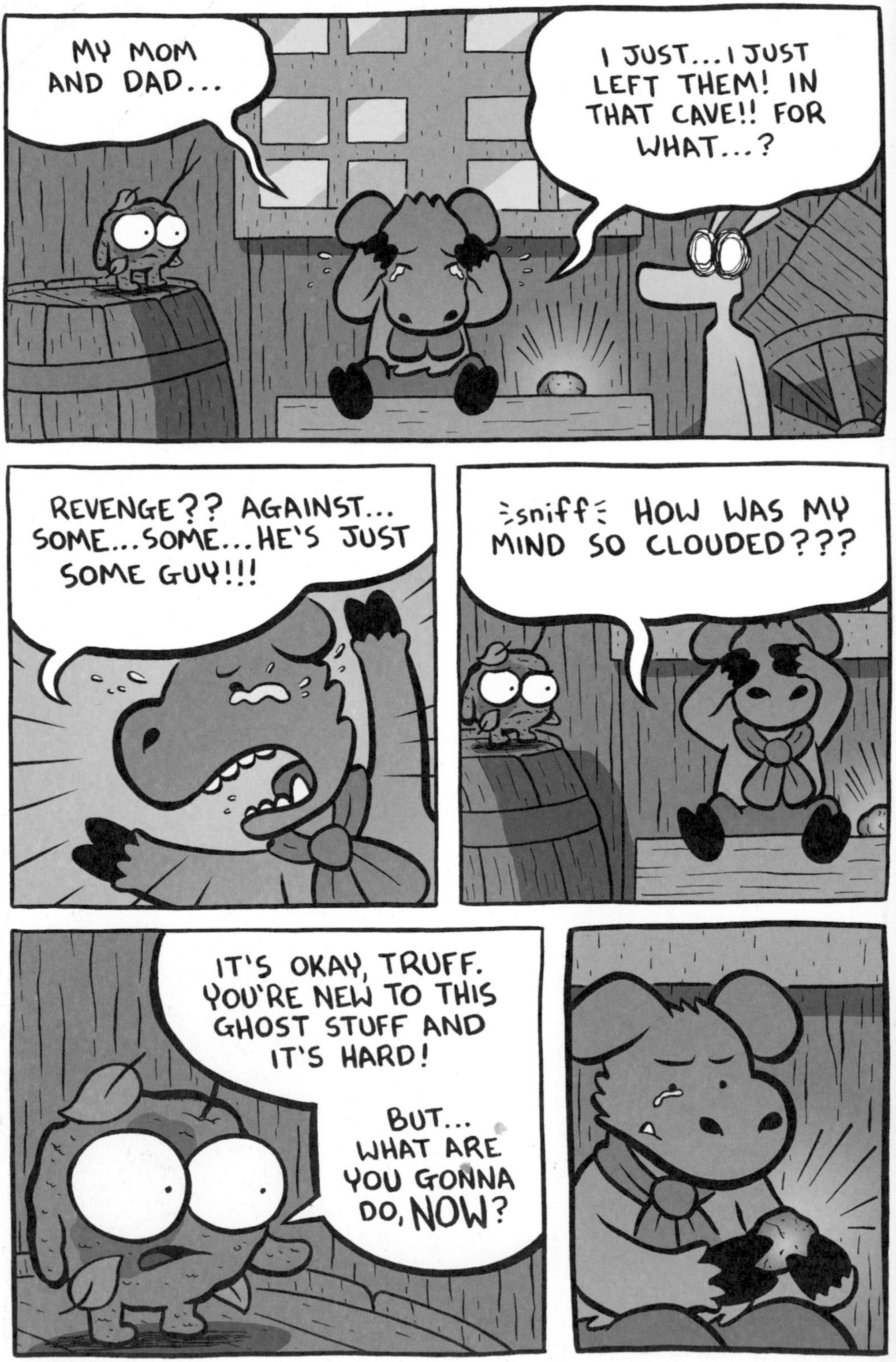
MY MOM AND DAD...
I JUST... I JUST LEFT THEM! IN THAT CAVE!! FOR WHAT...?
REVENGE?? AGAINST... SOME... SOME... HE'S JUST SOME GUY!!!
sniff HOW WAS MY MIND SO CLOUDED???
IT'S OKAY, TRUFF. YOU'RE NEW TO THIS GHOST STUFF AND IT'S HARD!
BUT... WHAT ARE YOU GONNA DO, NOW?

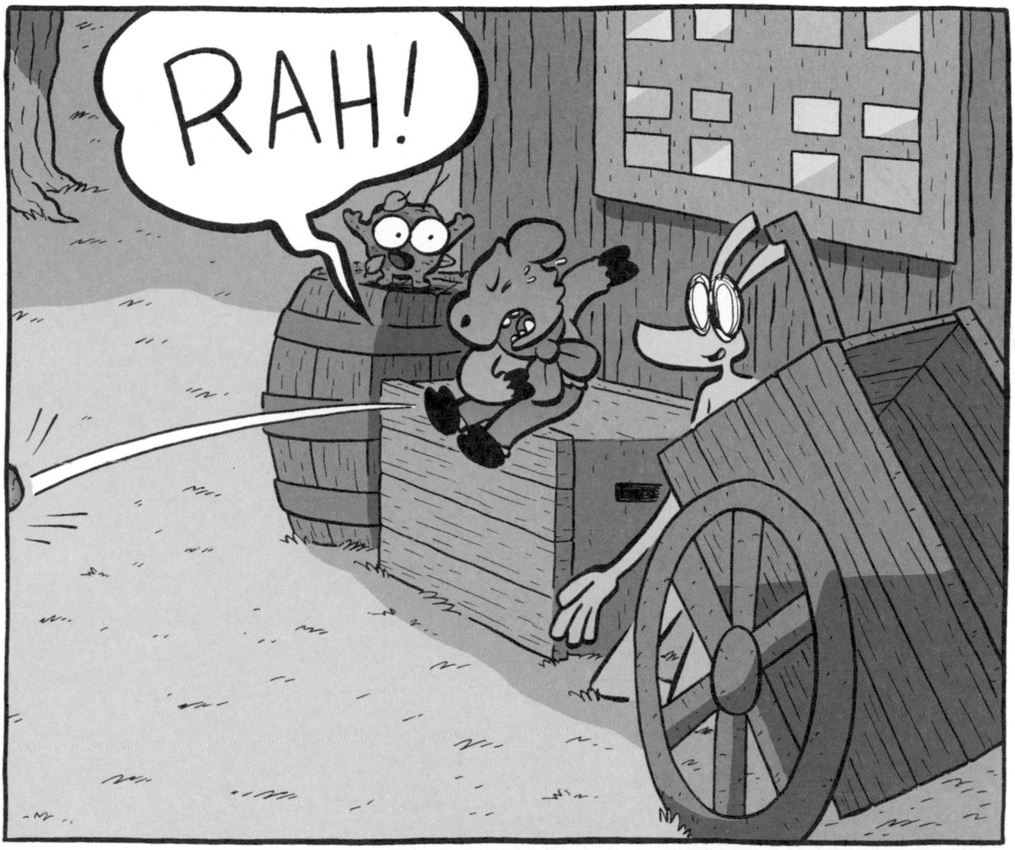
RAH!

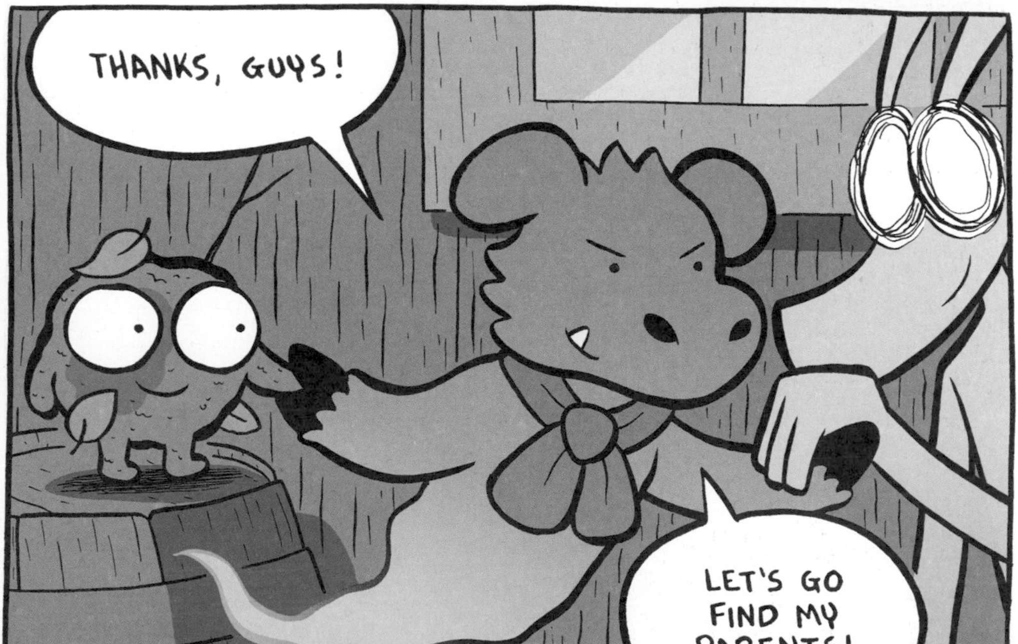
THANKS, GUYS!
LET'S GO FIND MY PARENTS!

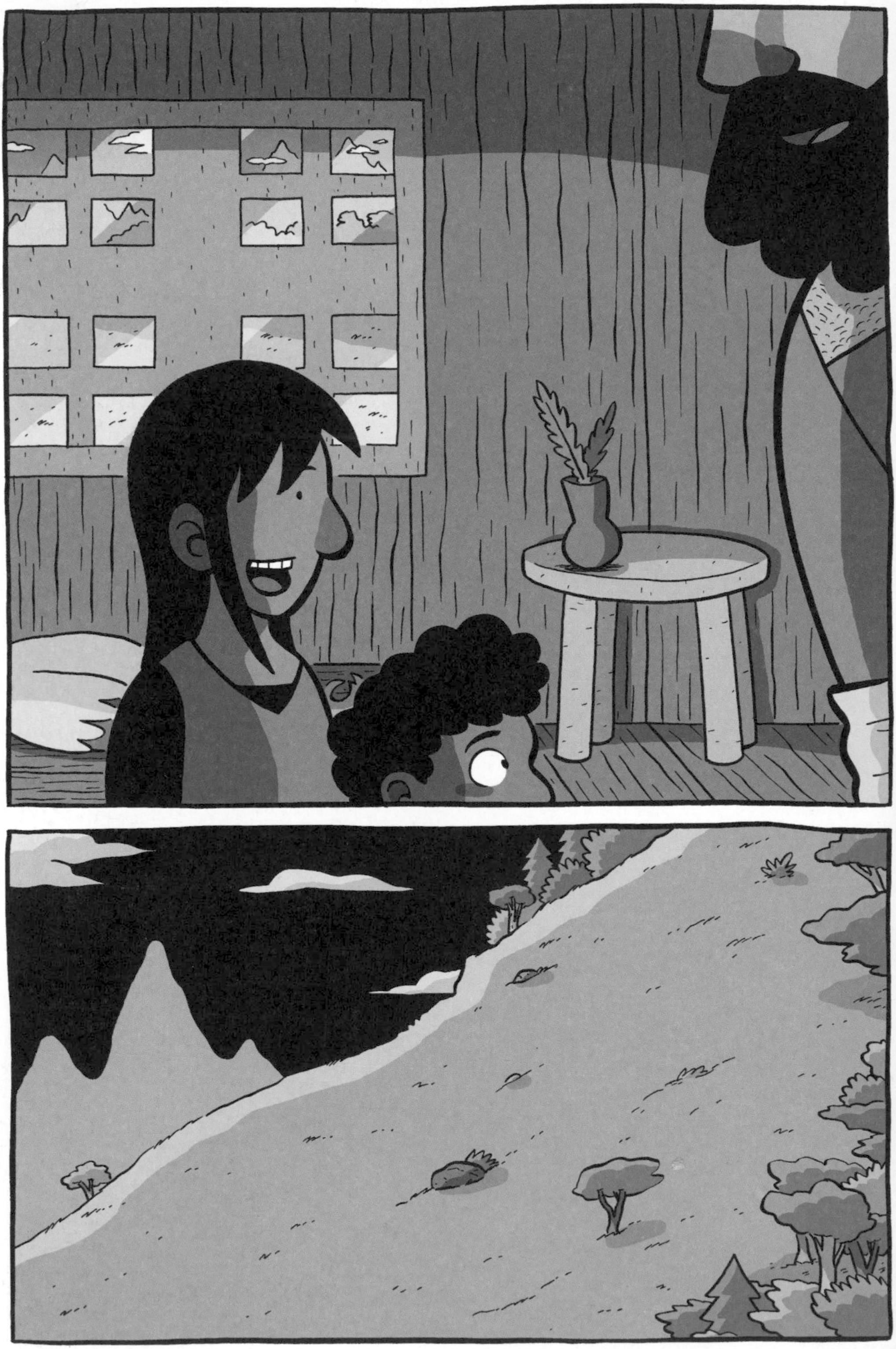

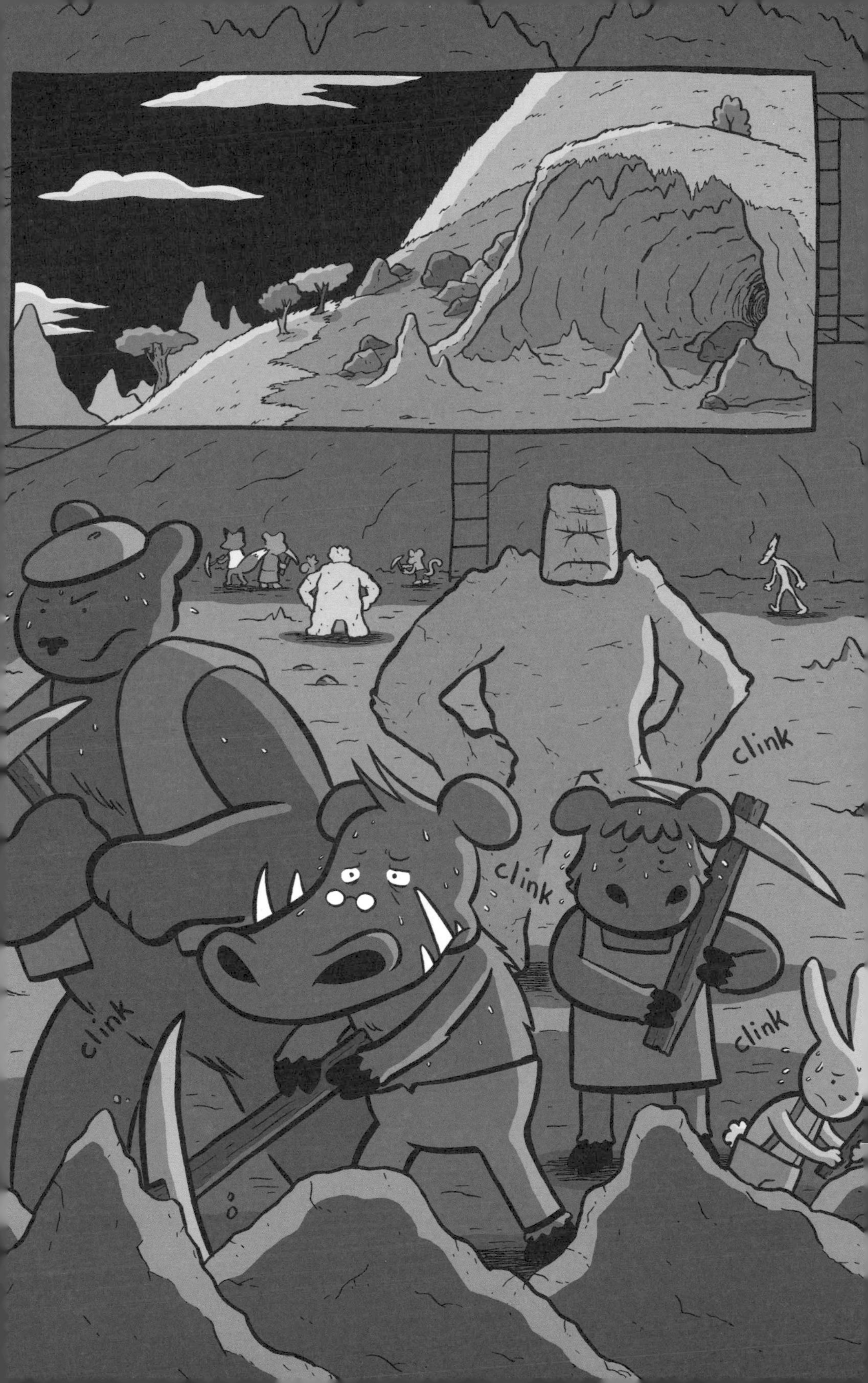
clink
clink
clink
clink

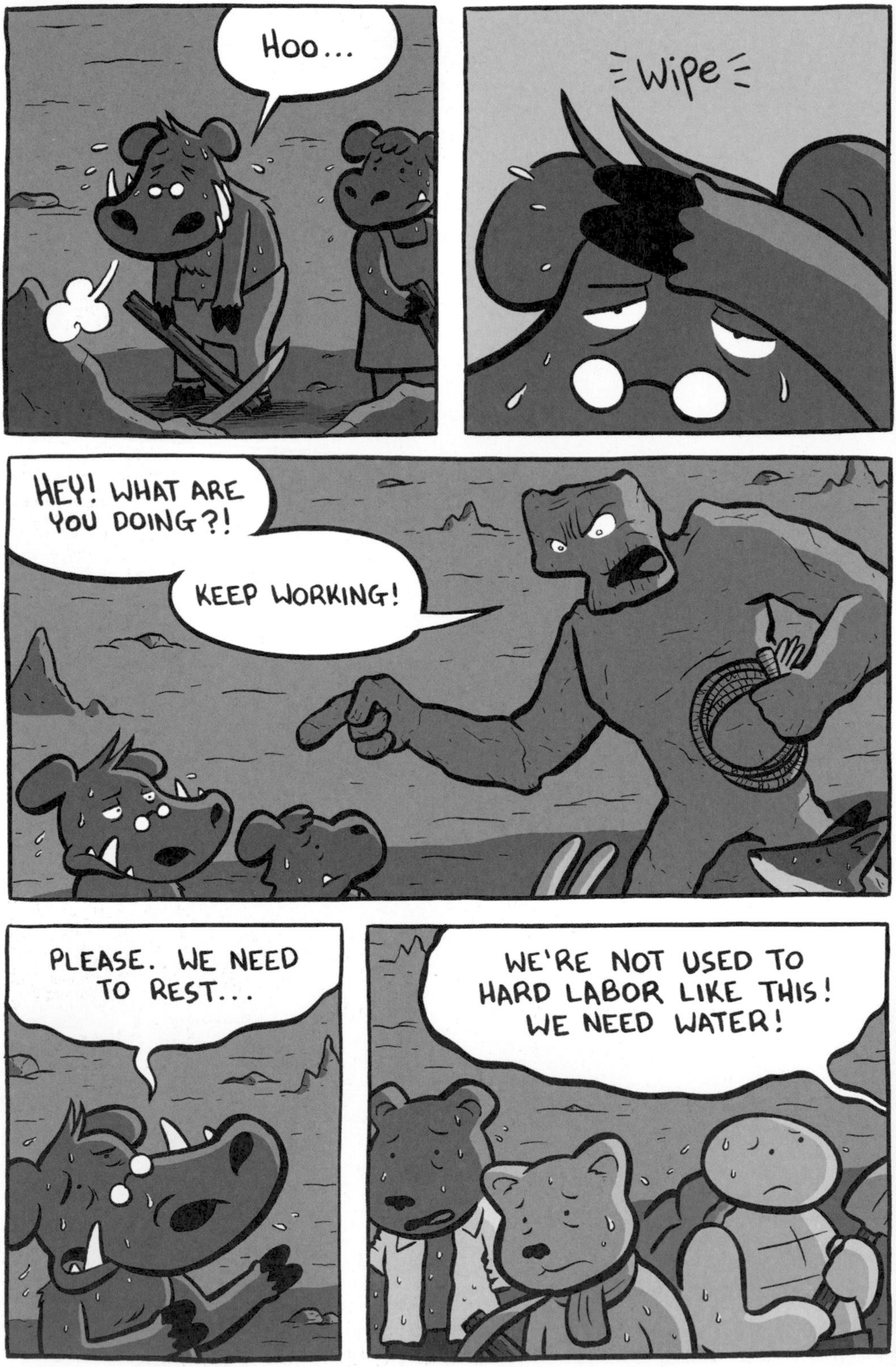
Hoo...
Wipe
HEY! WHAT ARE YOU DOING?!
KEEP WORKING!
PLEASE. WE NEED TO REST...
WE'RE NOT USED TO HARD LABOR LIKE THIS! WE NEED WATER!

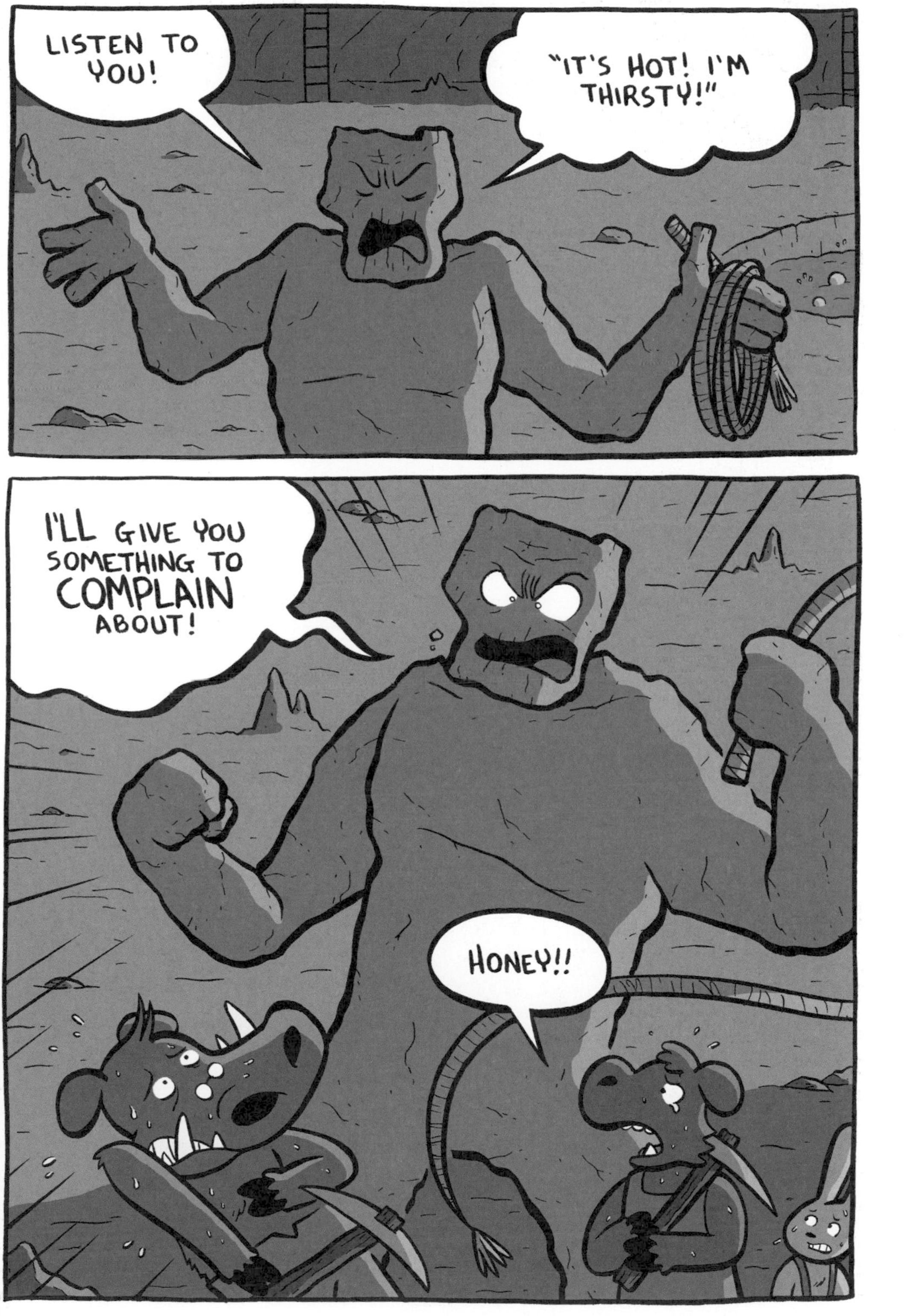
LISTEN TO YOU!
"IT'S HOT! I'M THIRSTY!"
I'LL GIVE YOU SOMETHING TO COMPLAIN ABOUT!
HONEY!!

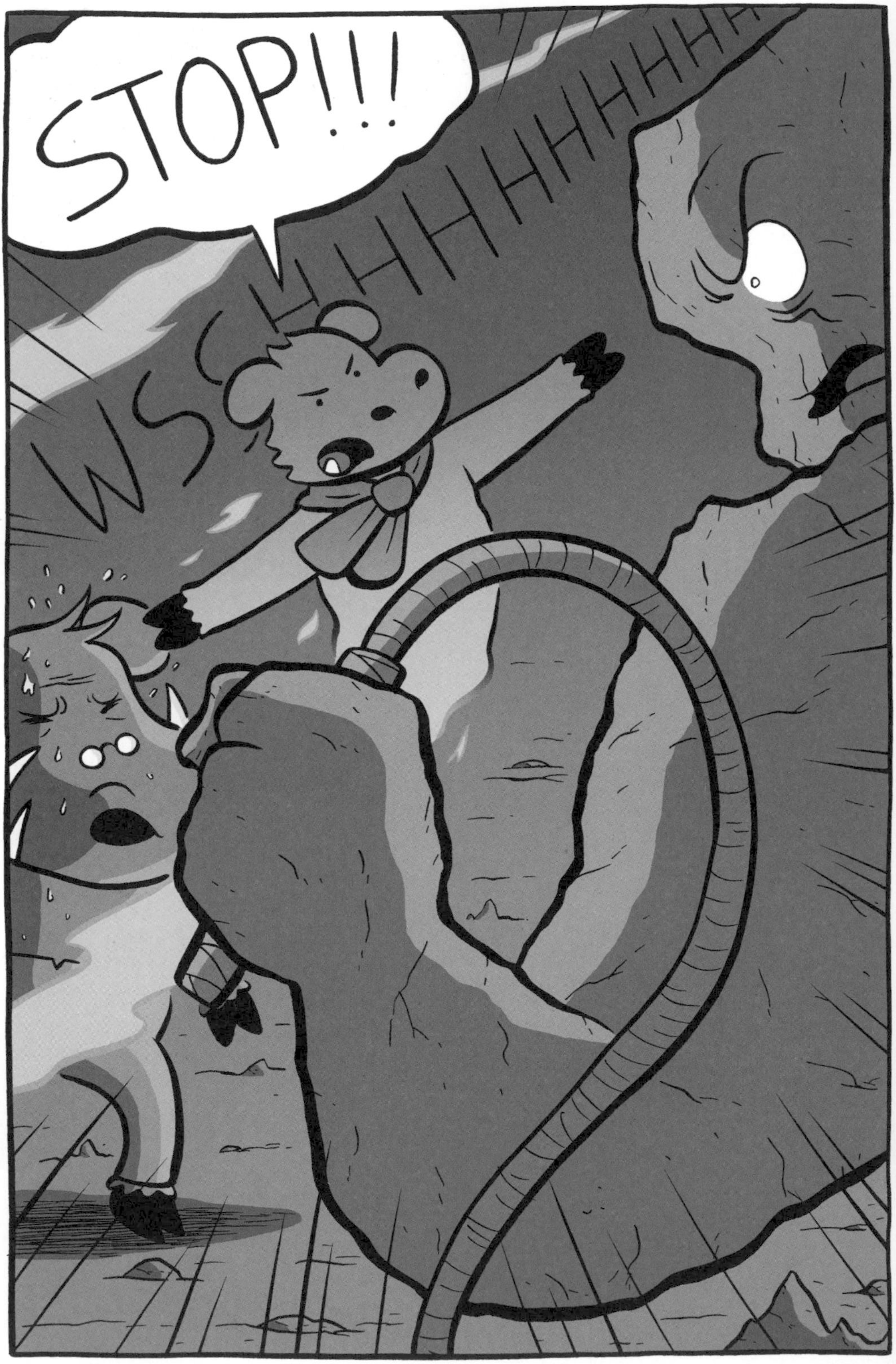
STOP!!!
WSSHHHHHHHHHHHH

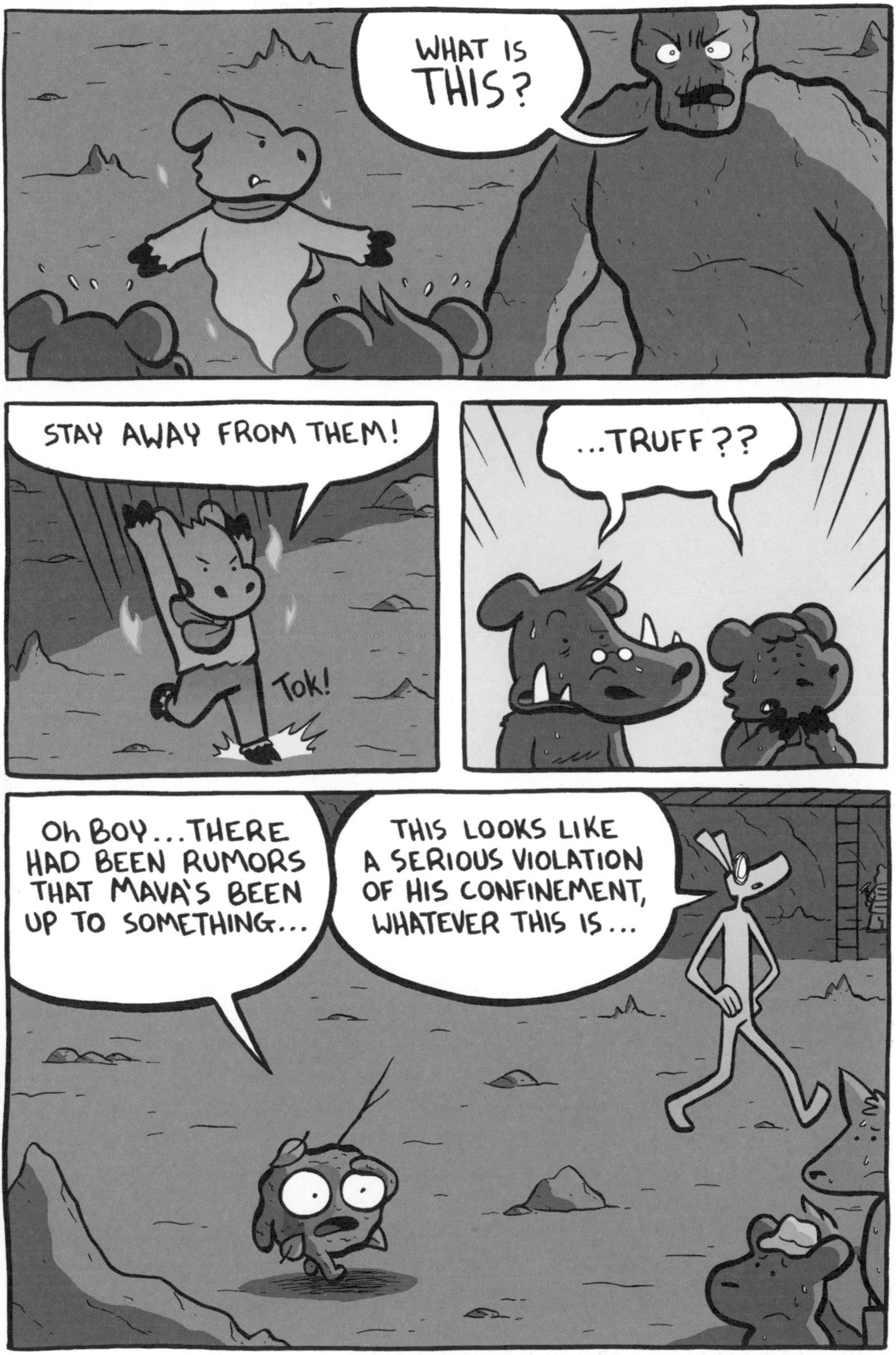
WHAT IS THIS?
STAY AWAY FROM THEM!
TOK!
...TRUFF??
Oh BOY... THERE HAD BEEN RUMORS THAT MAVA'S BEEN UP TO SOMETHING...
THIS LOOKS LIKE A SERIOUS VIOLATION OF HIS CONFINEMENT, WHATEVER THIS IS...

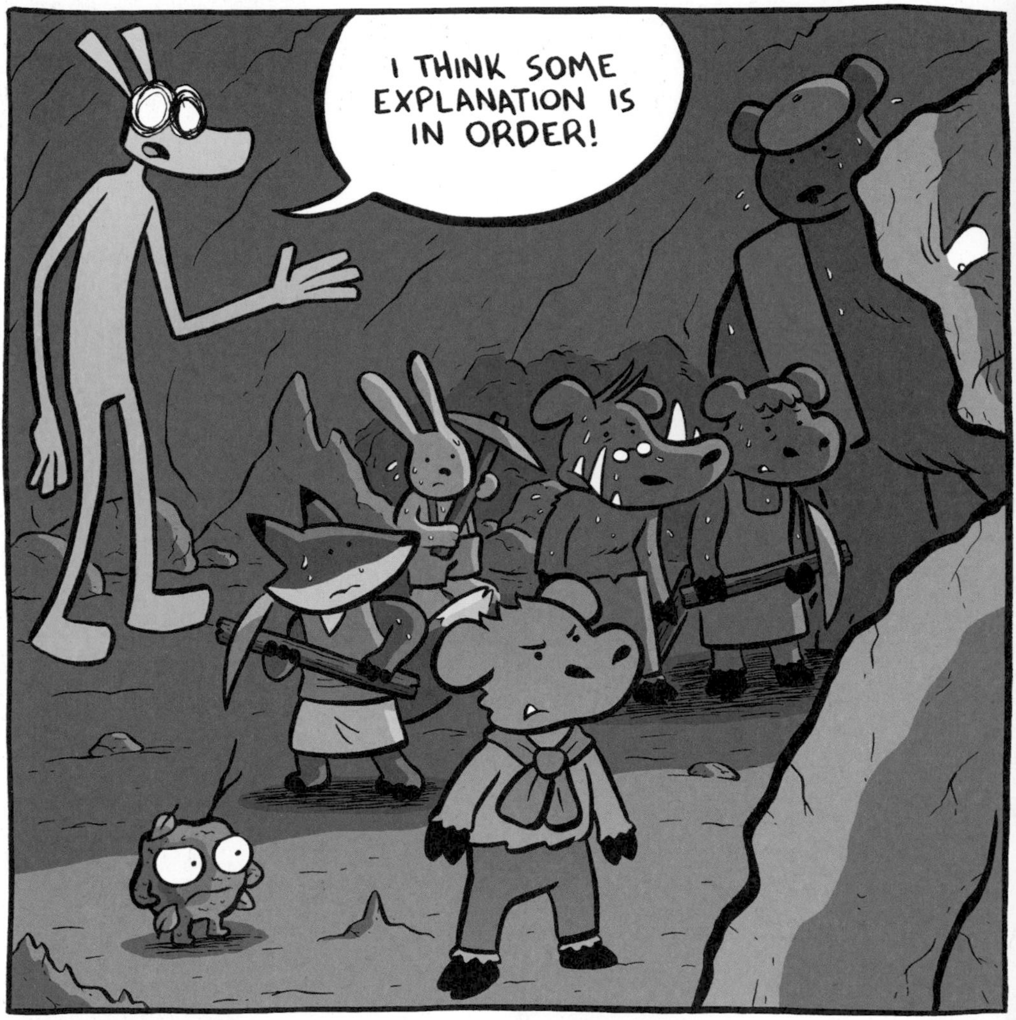
I THINK SOME EXPLANATION IS IN ORDER!
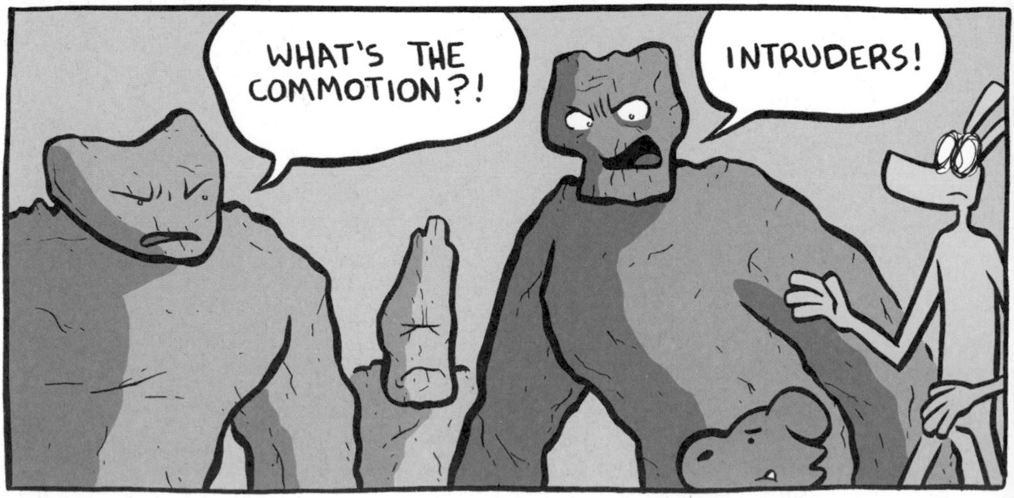
WHAT'S THE COMMOTION?!
INTRUDERS!

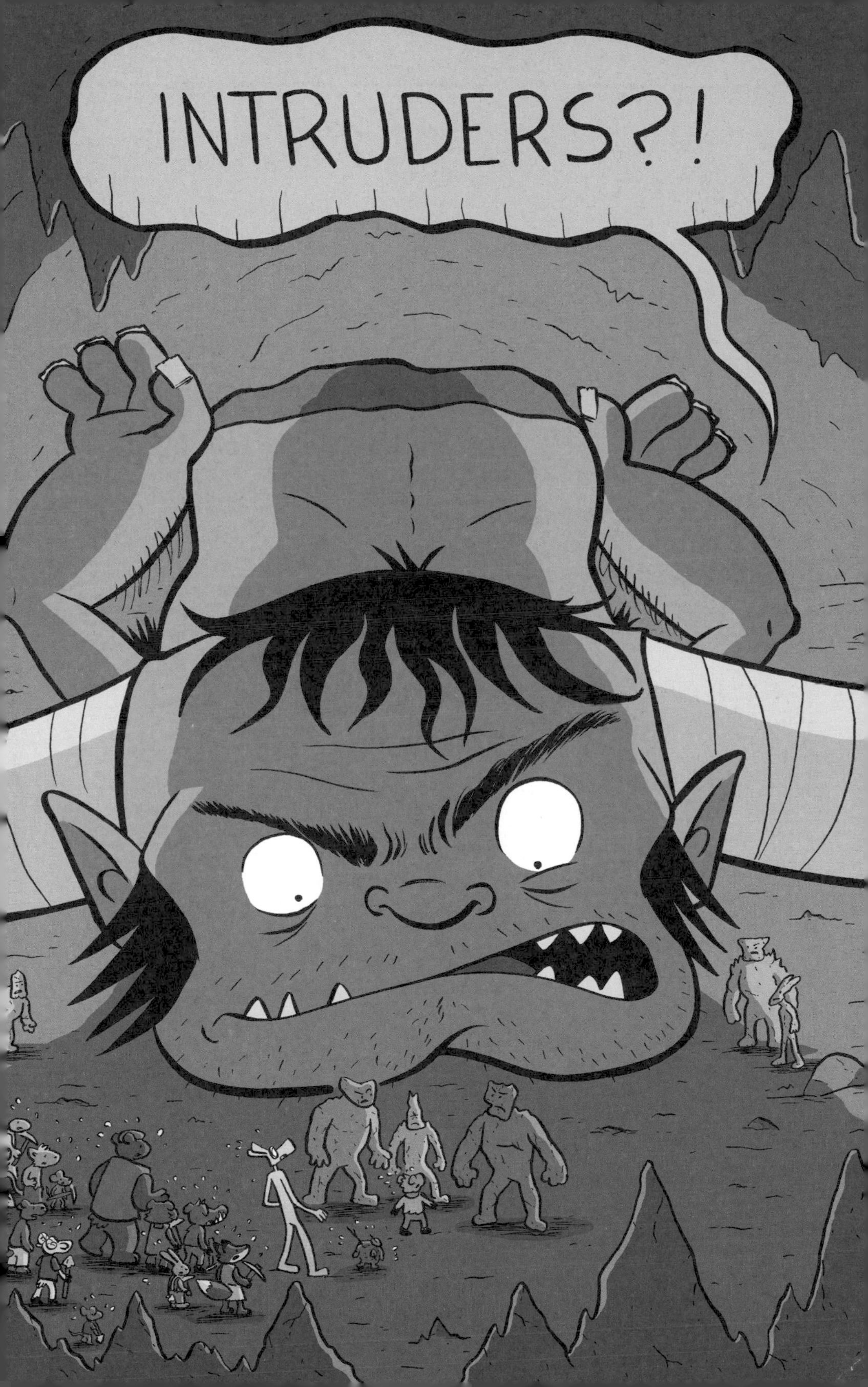
INTRUDERS?!

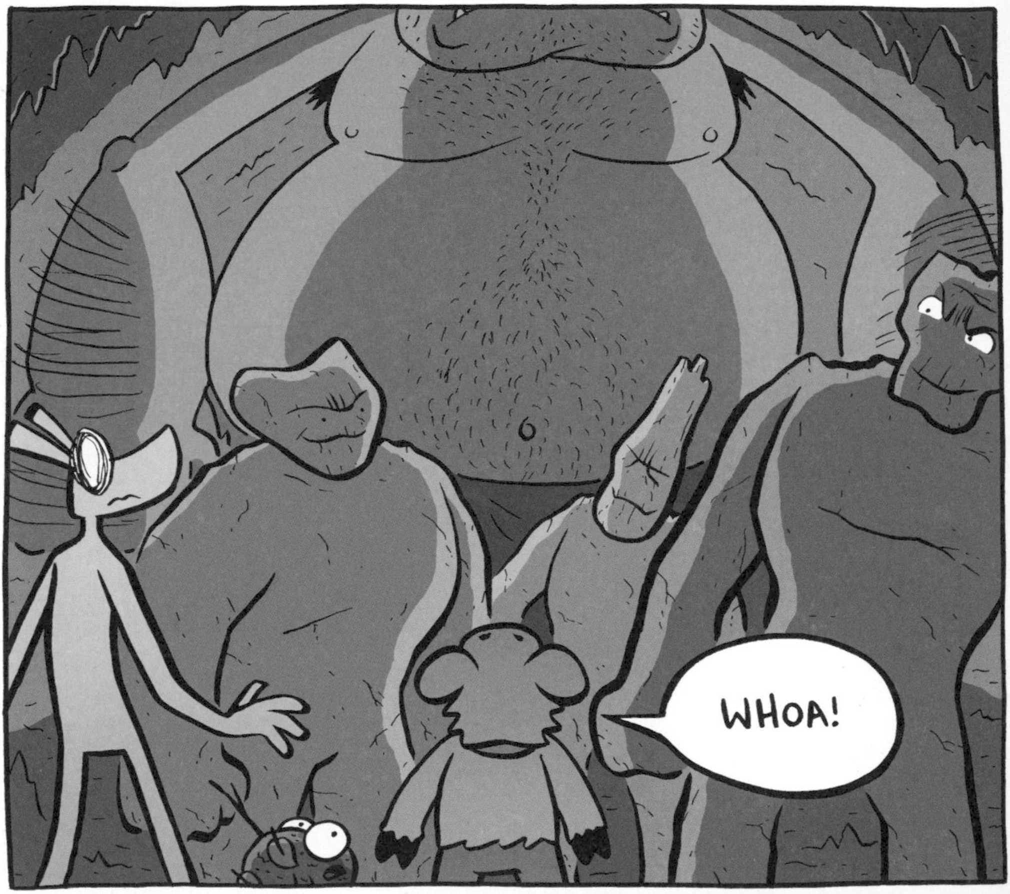
WHOA!

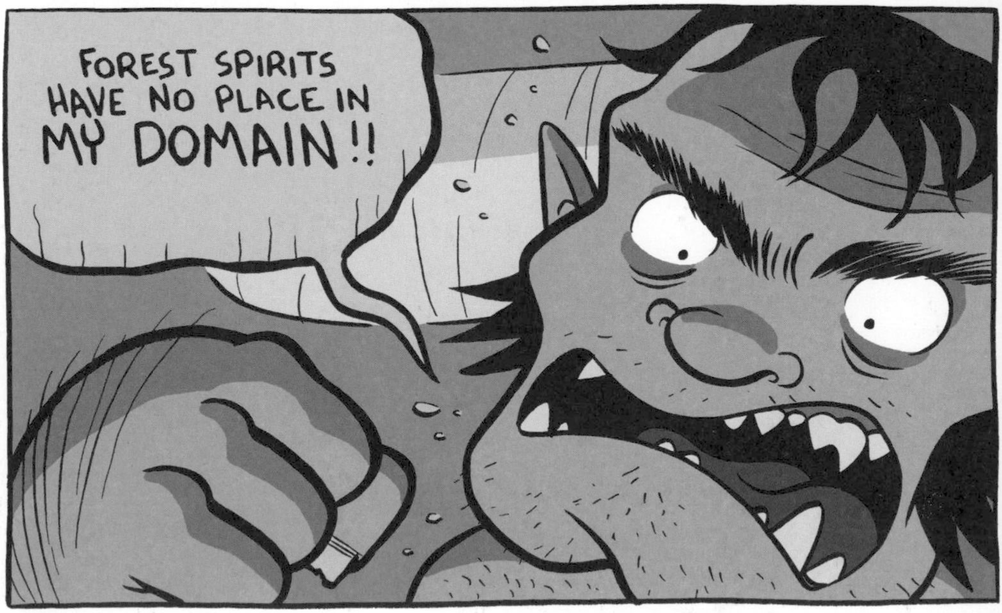
FOREST SPIRITS HAVE NO PLACE IN MY DOMAIN!!

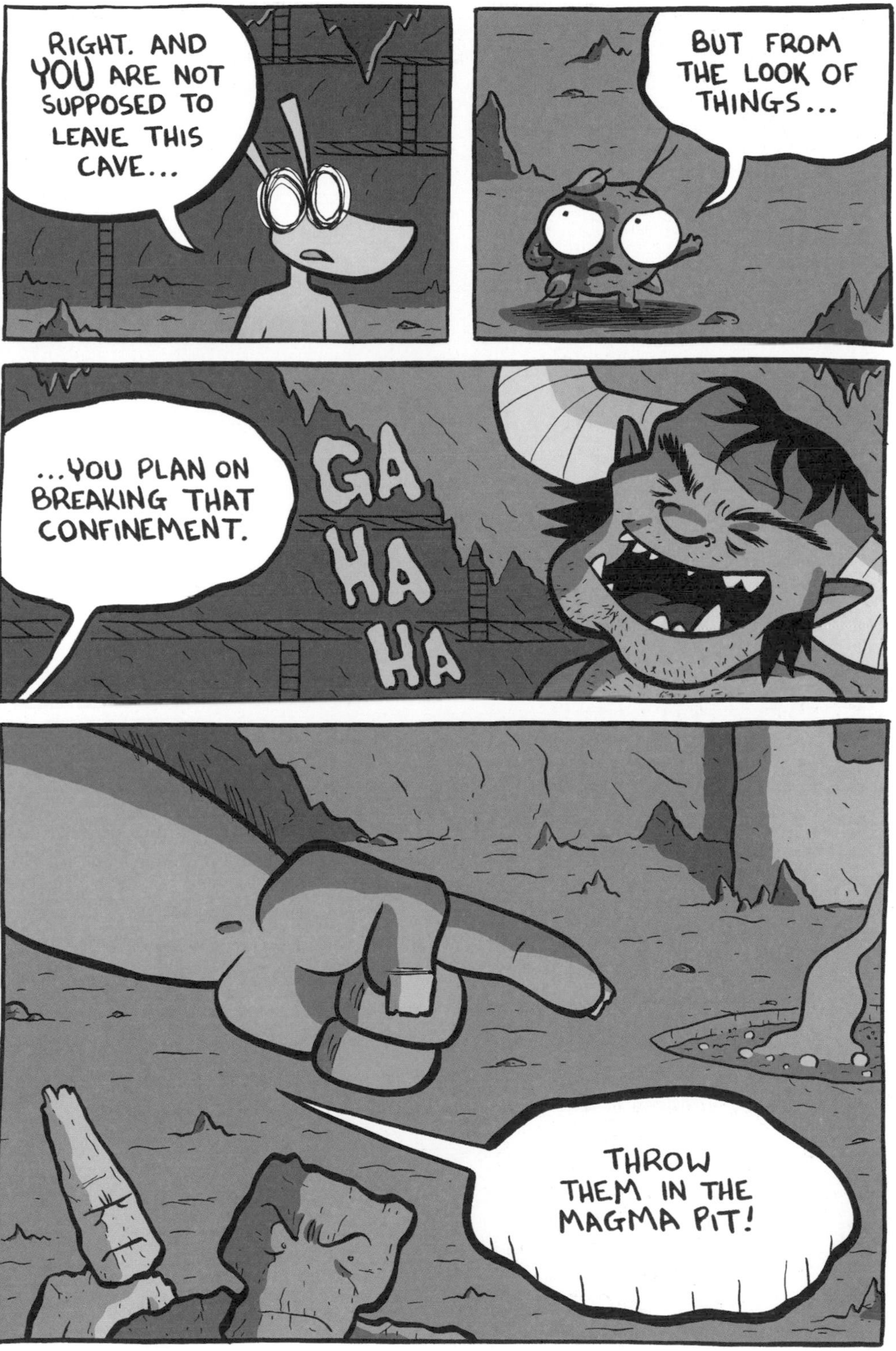
RIGHT. AND YOU ARE NOT SUPPOSED TO LEAVE THIS CAVE...
BUT FROM THE LOOK OF THINGS...
...YOU PLAN ON BREAKING THAT CONFINEMENT.
GA HA HA
THROW THEM IN THE MAGMA PIT!

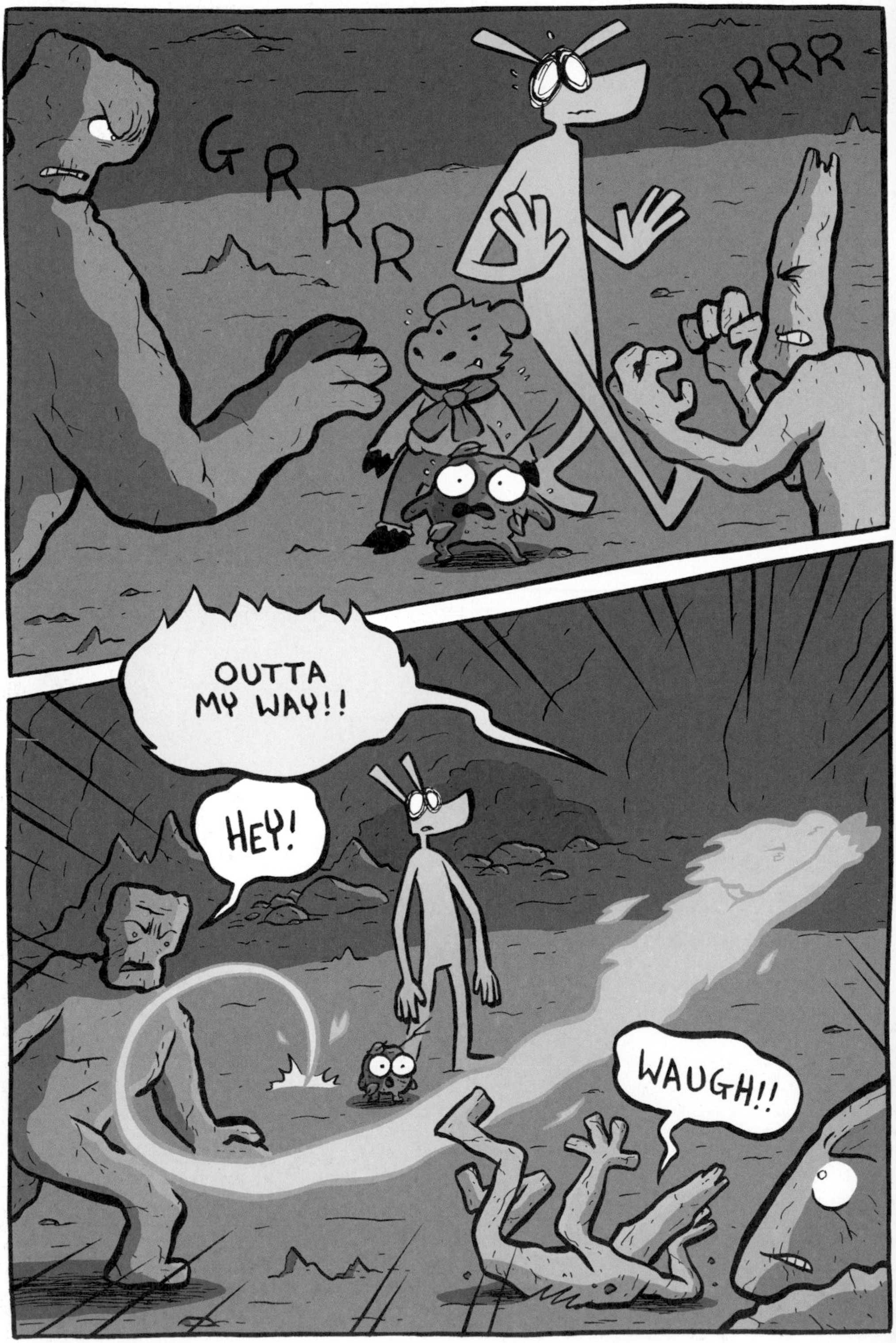
GRRRR
RRRR
OUTTA MY WAY!!
HEY!
WAUGH!!

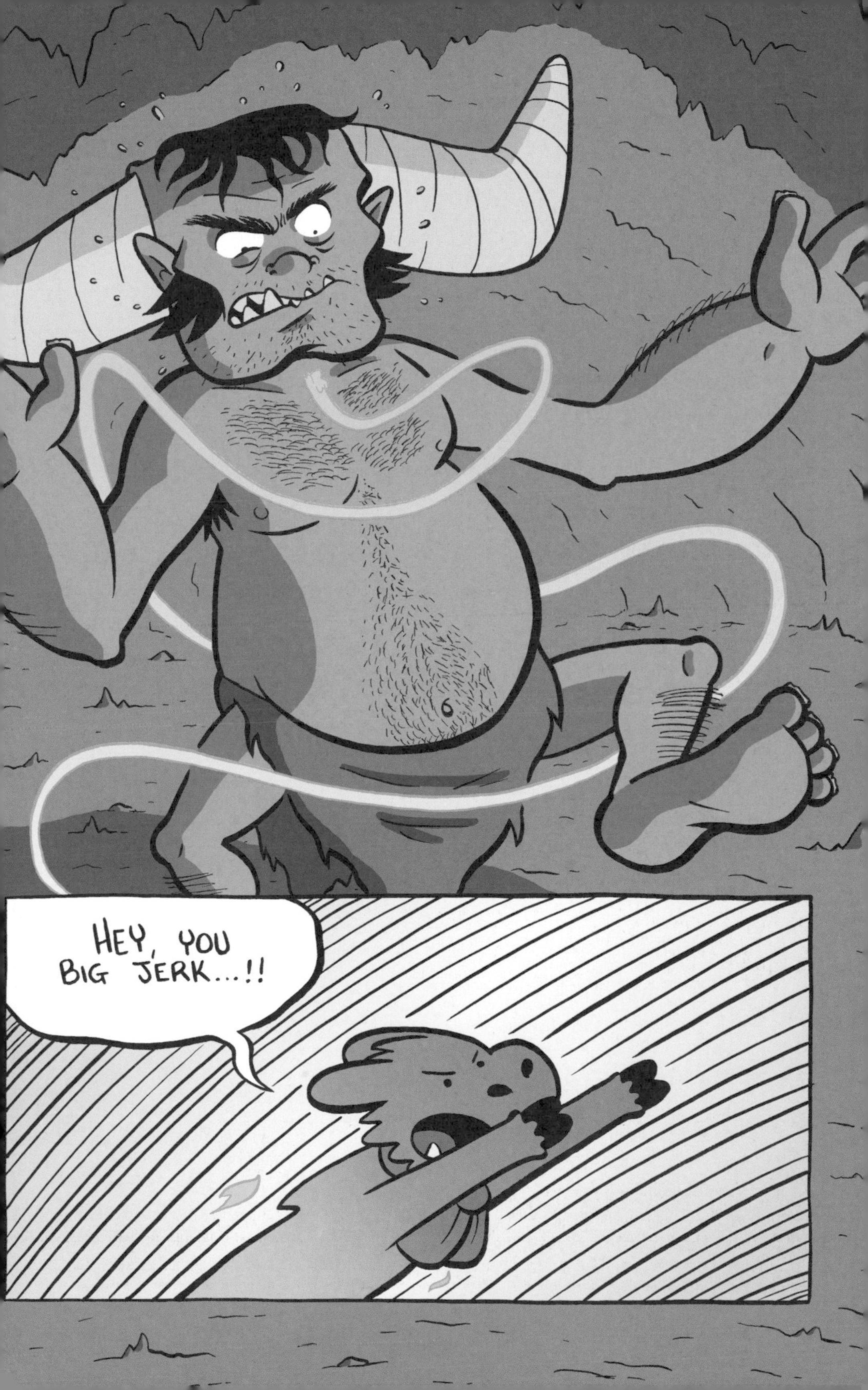
HEY, YOU
BIG JERK...!!

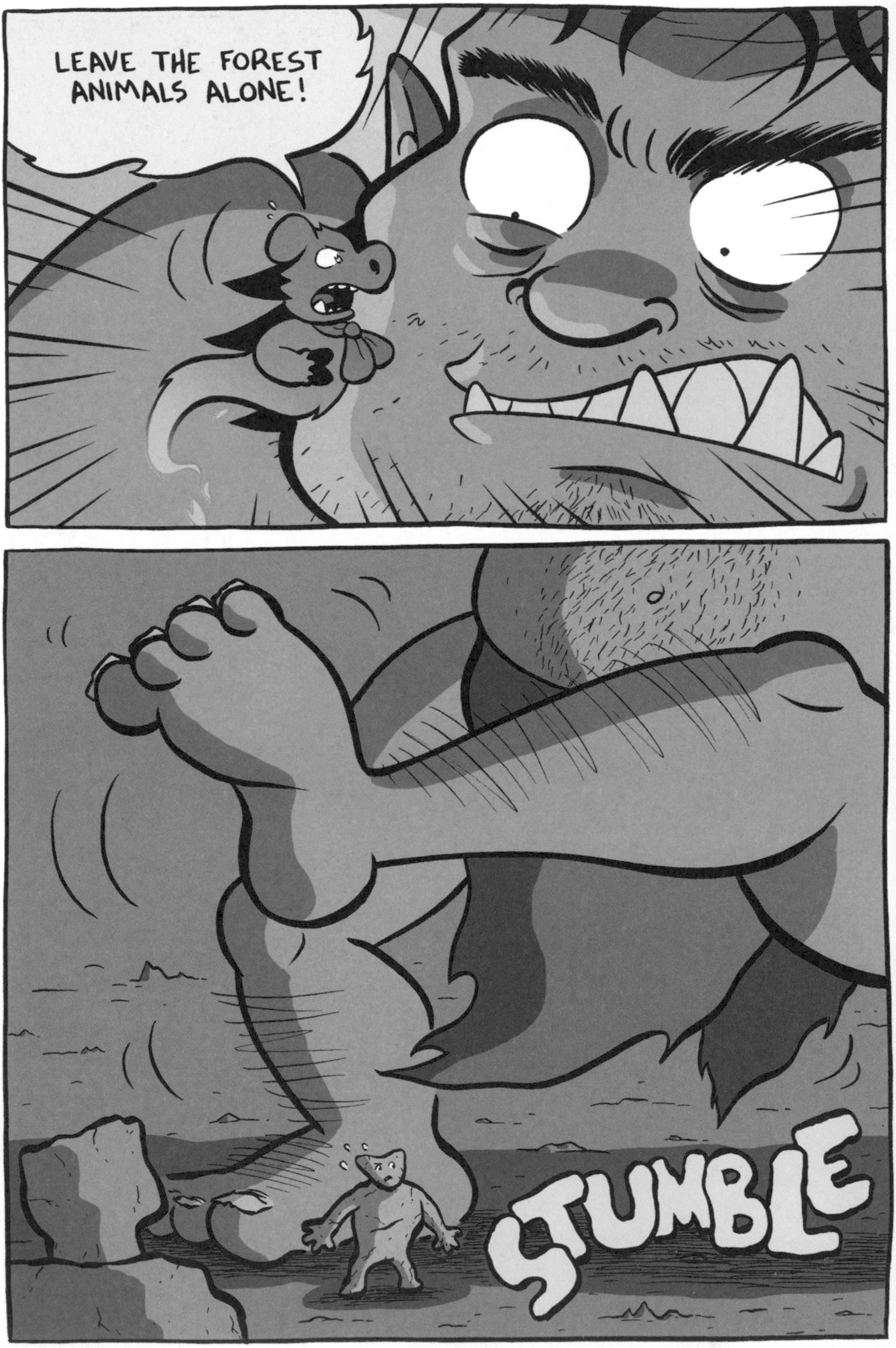
LEAVE THE FOREST ANIMALS ALONE!
STUMBLE

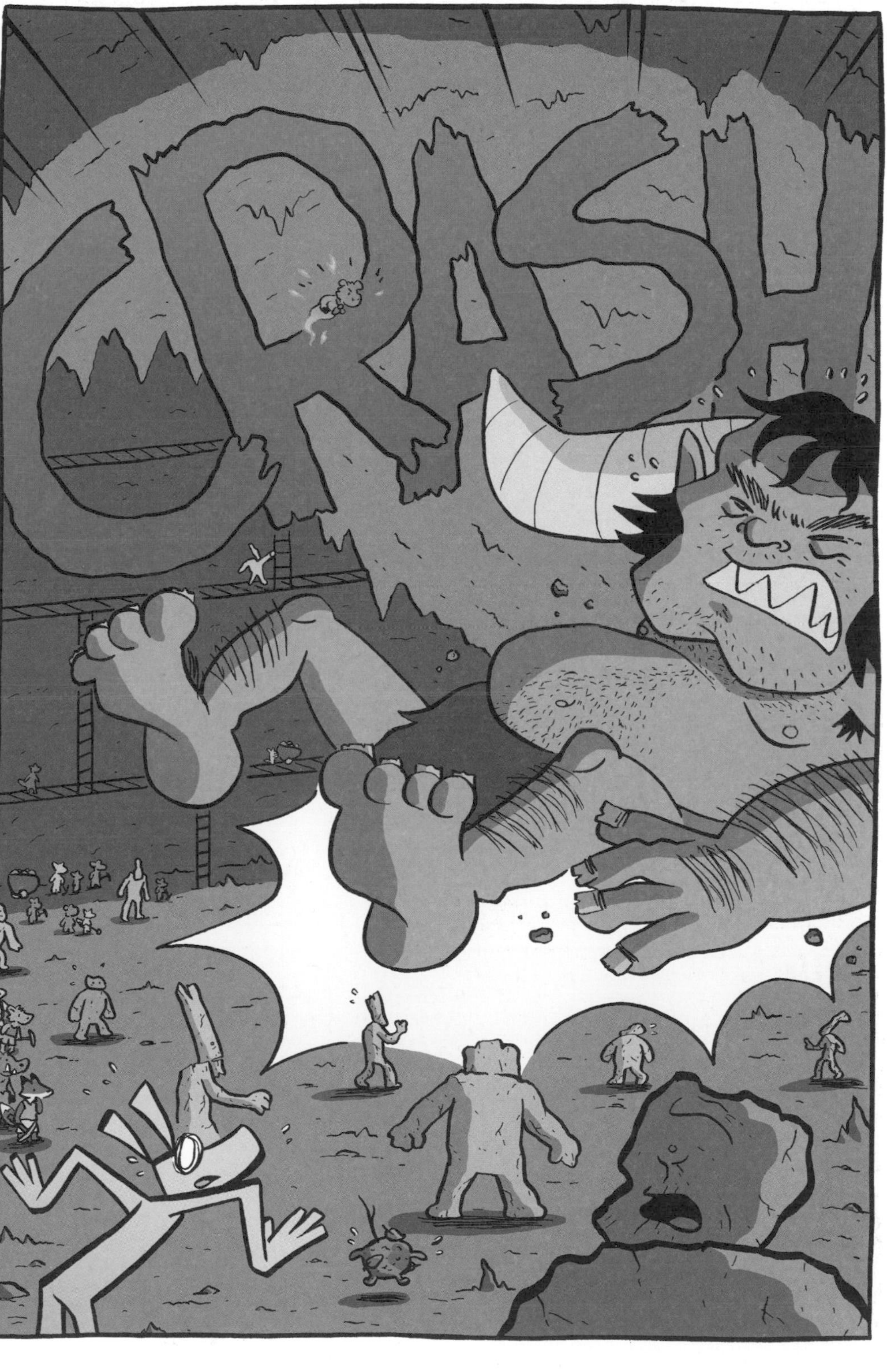
CRASH!

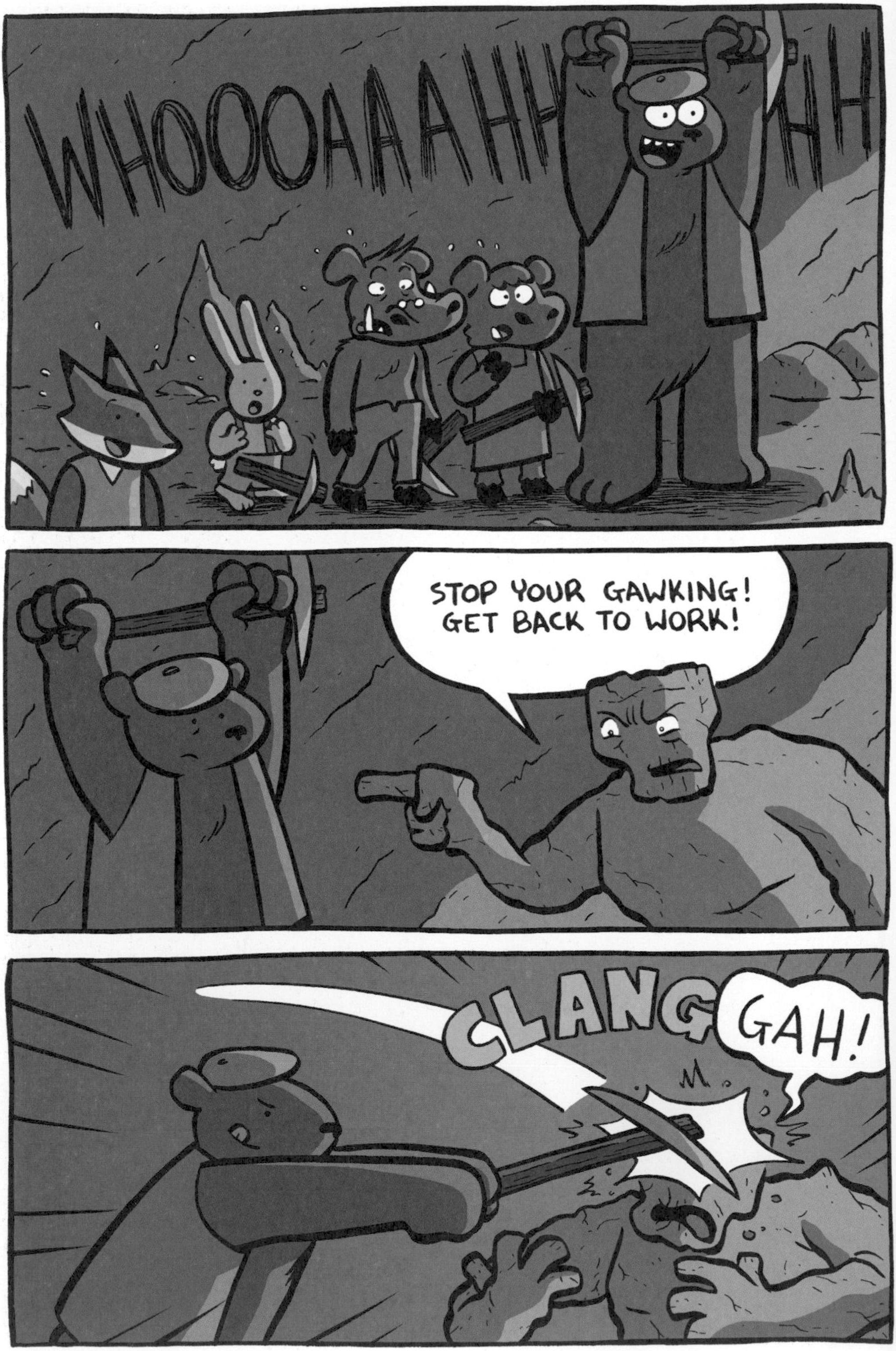
WHOOOAAAHHHH
STOP YOUR GAWKING! GET BACK TO WORK!
CLANG
GAH!

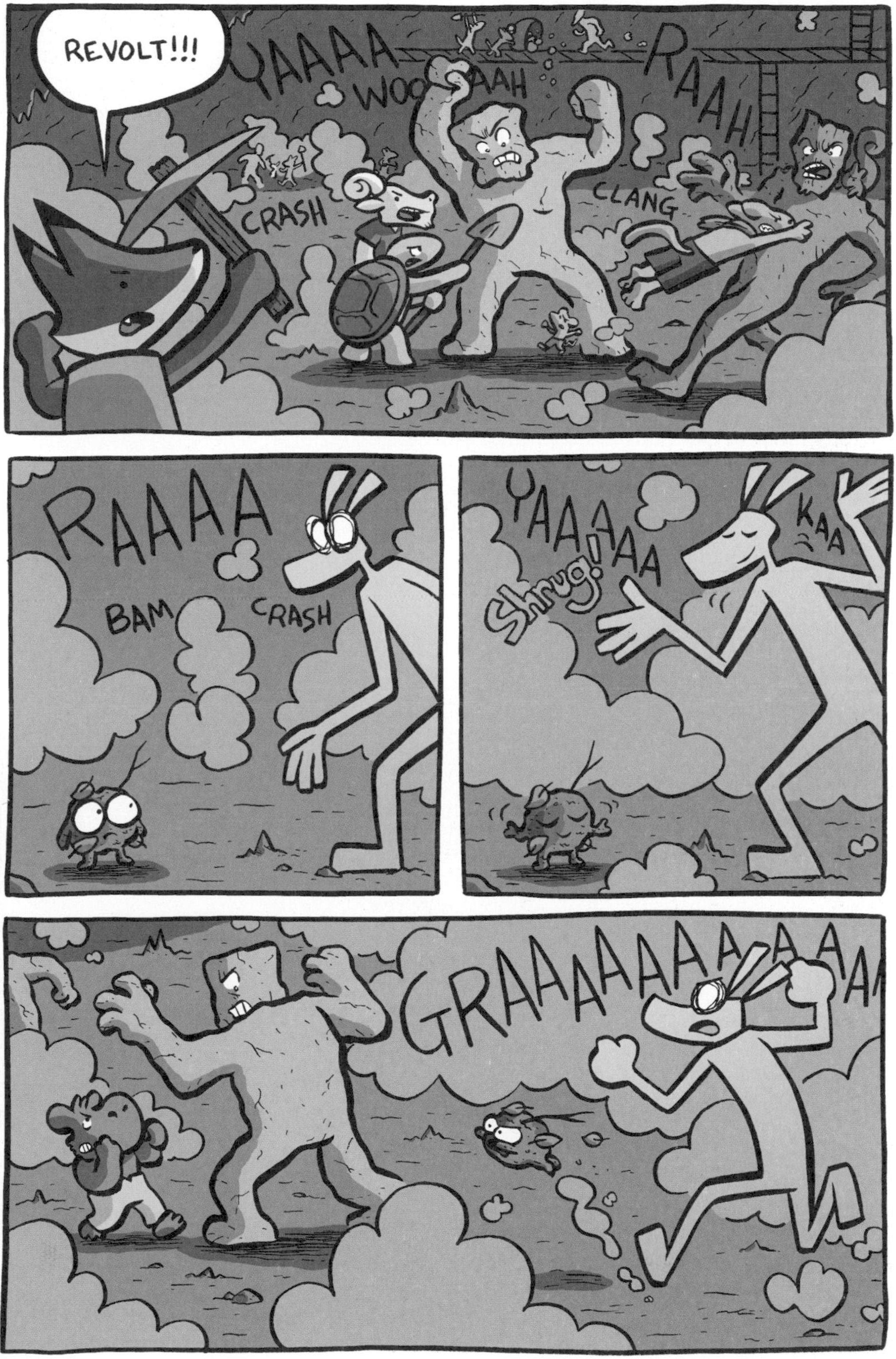
REVOLT!!!
YAAAA
WOO
AAH
RAAAH
CRASH
CLANG
RAAAA
BAM
CRASH
YAAAAAA
Shrug!
KAA
GRAAAAAAAAAA

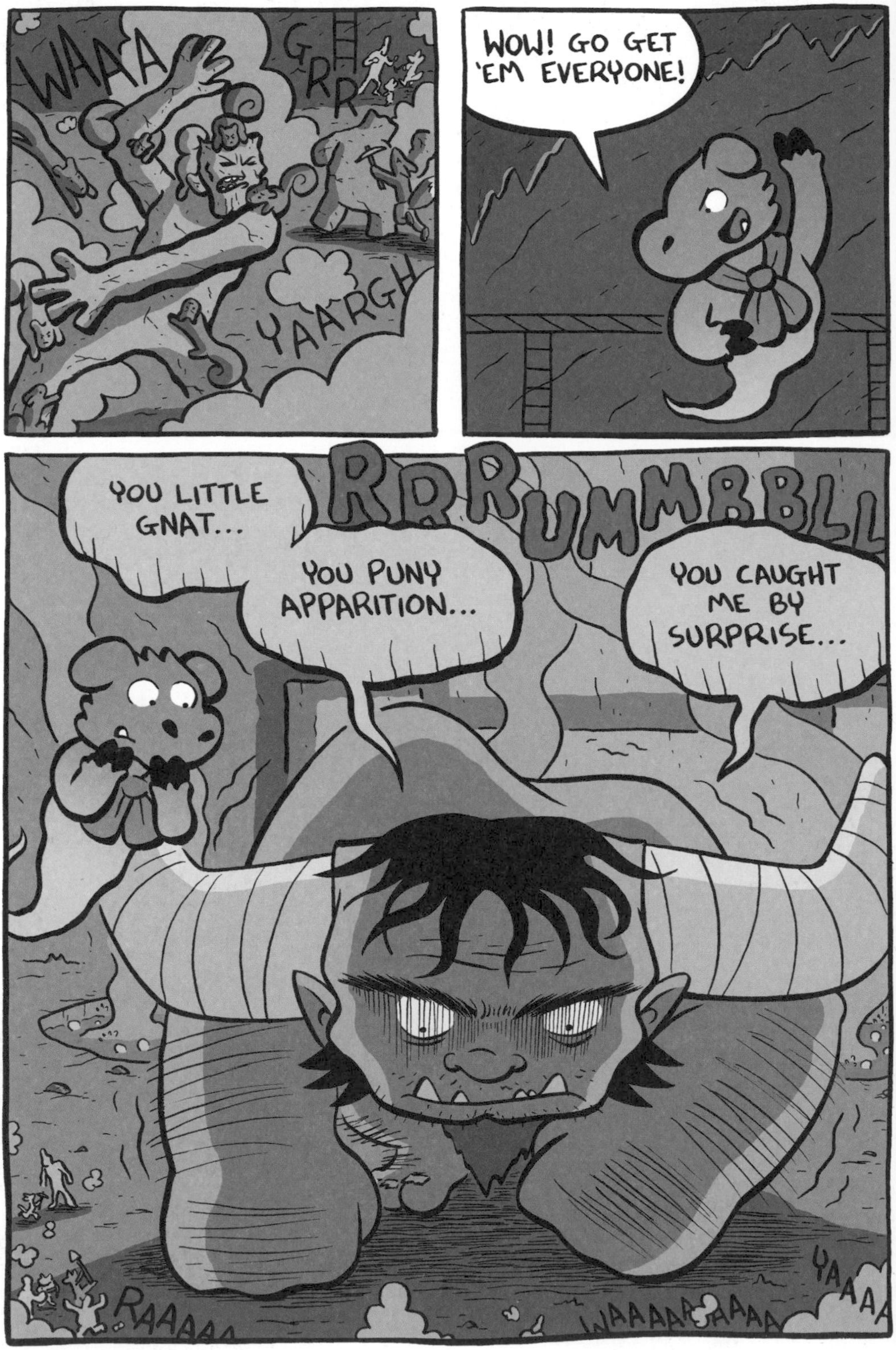
WAAA
GRRR
YAARGH
WOW! GO GET 'EM EVERYONE!
RRRUMMBBLL
YOU LITTLE GNAT...
YOU PUNY APPARITION...
YOU CAUGHT ME BY SURPRISE...
RAAAAA
WAAAAAAAAA
YAAAA

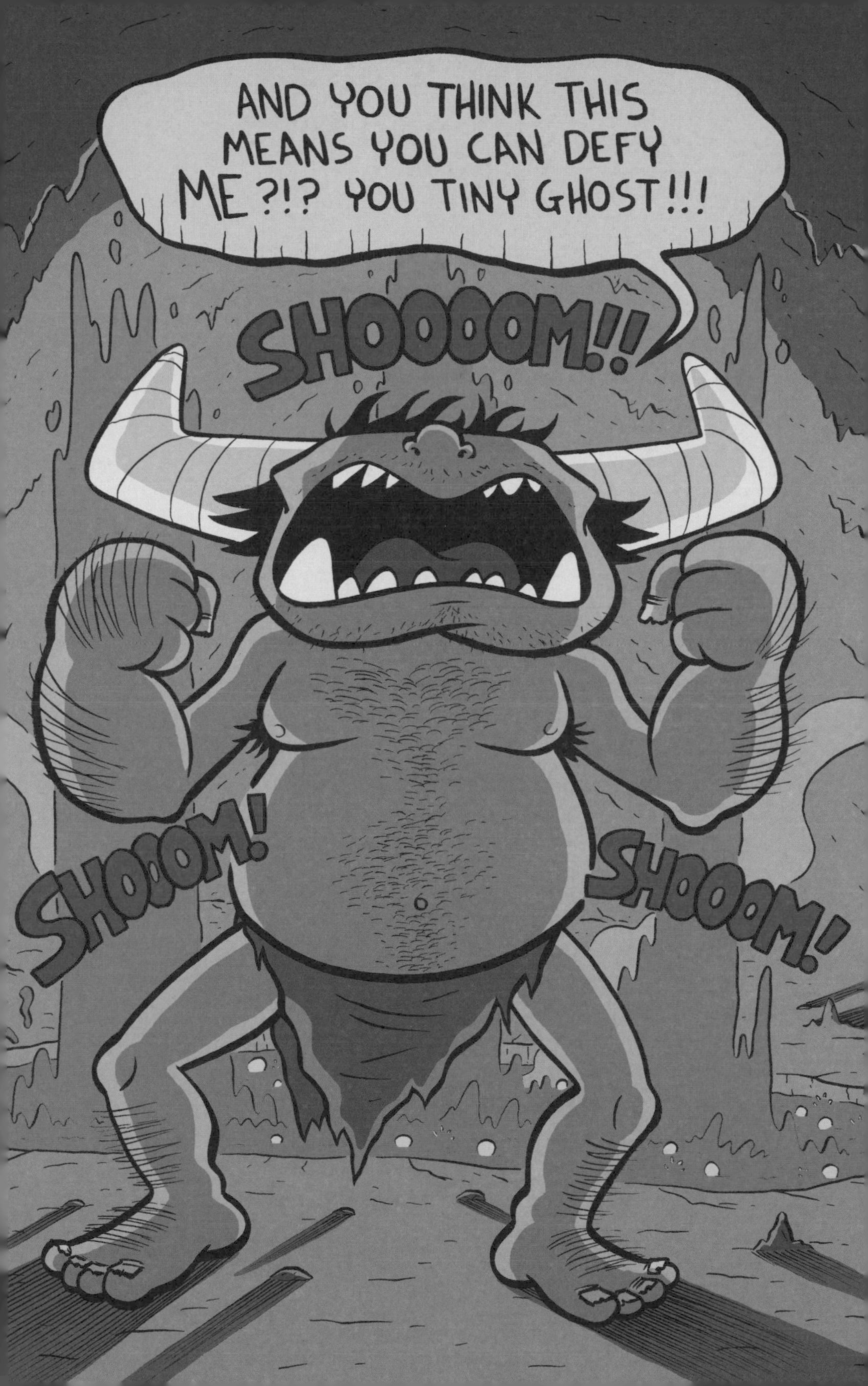
AND YOU THINK THIS MEANS YOU CAN DEFY ME?!? YOU TINY GHOST!!!
SHOOOOM!!!
SHOOOM!
SHOOOM!

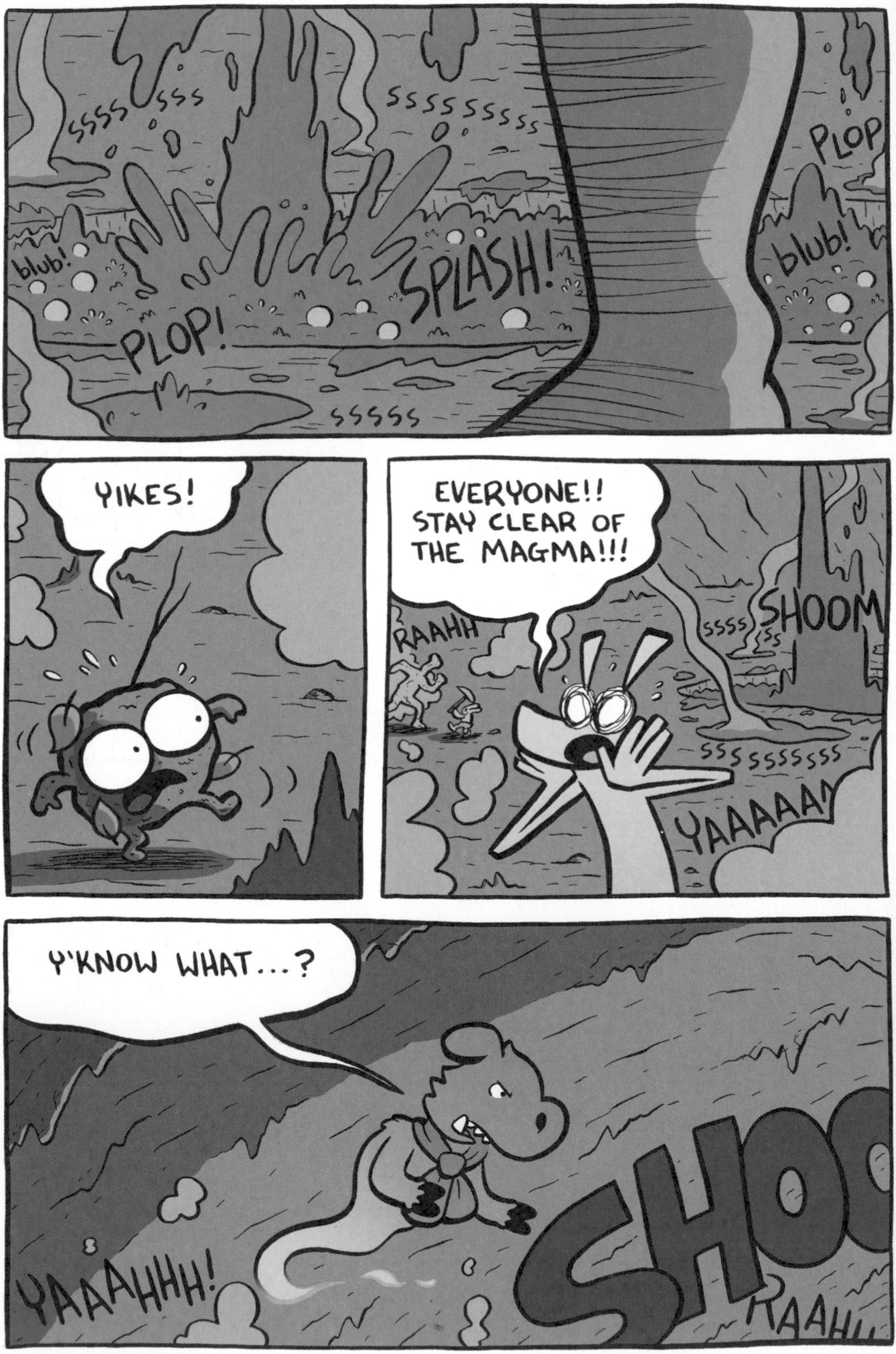
ssss sss
sssssssss
PLOP
blub!
blub!
PLOP!
SPLASH!
sssss
YIKES!
EVERYONE!! STAY CLEAR OF THE MAGMA!!!
RAAHH
ssss
SHOOM
sssssssss
YAAAAA
Y'KNOW WHAT...?
YAAAHHH!
SHOO
RAAH

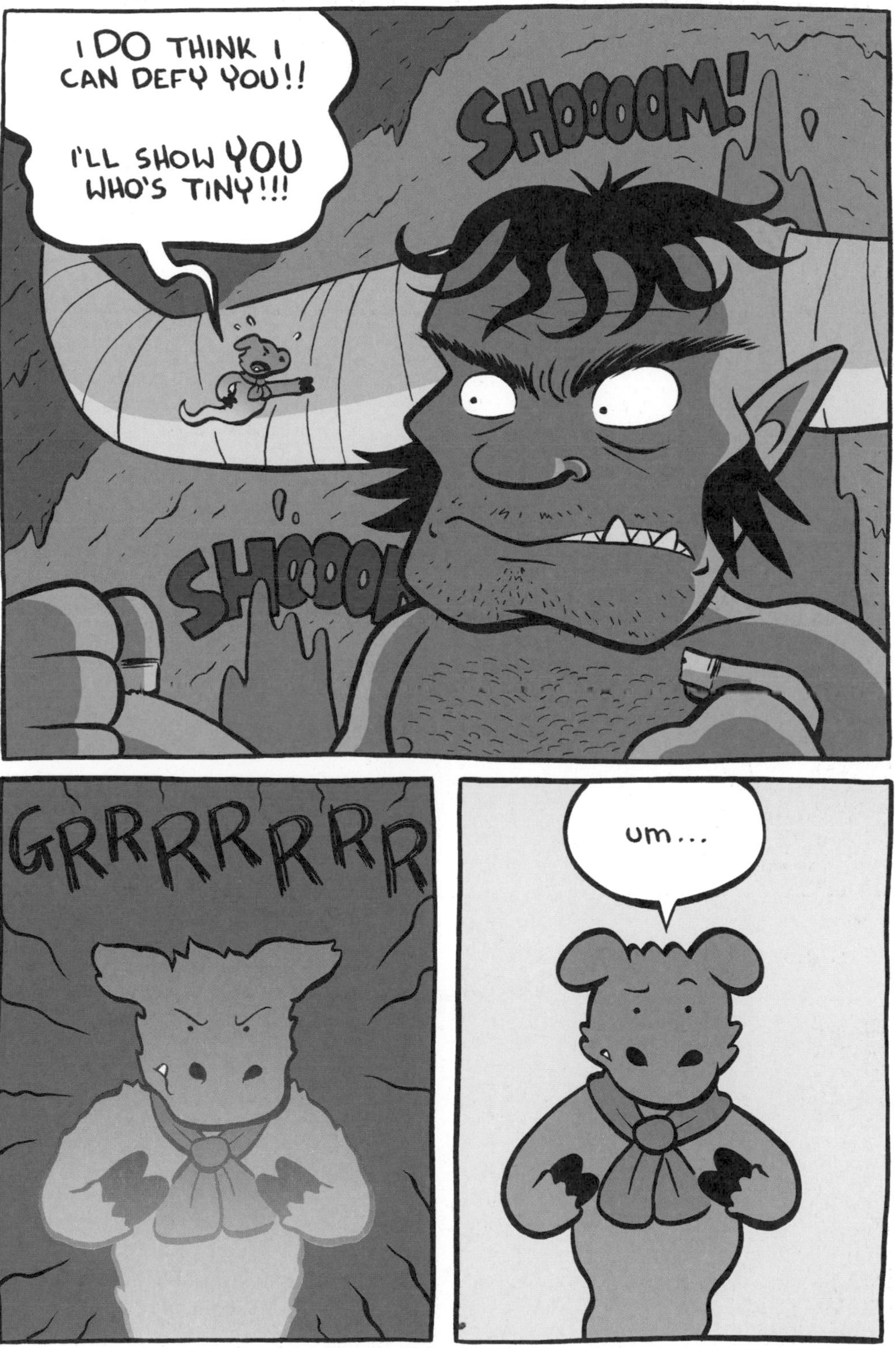
I DO THINK I CAN DEFY YOU!!
I'LL SHOW YOU WHO'S TINY!!!
SHOOOOM!
SHOOOO
GRRRRRRR
um...

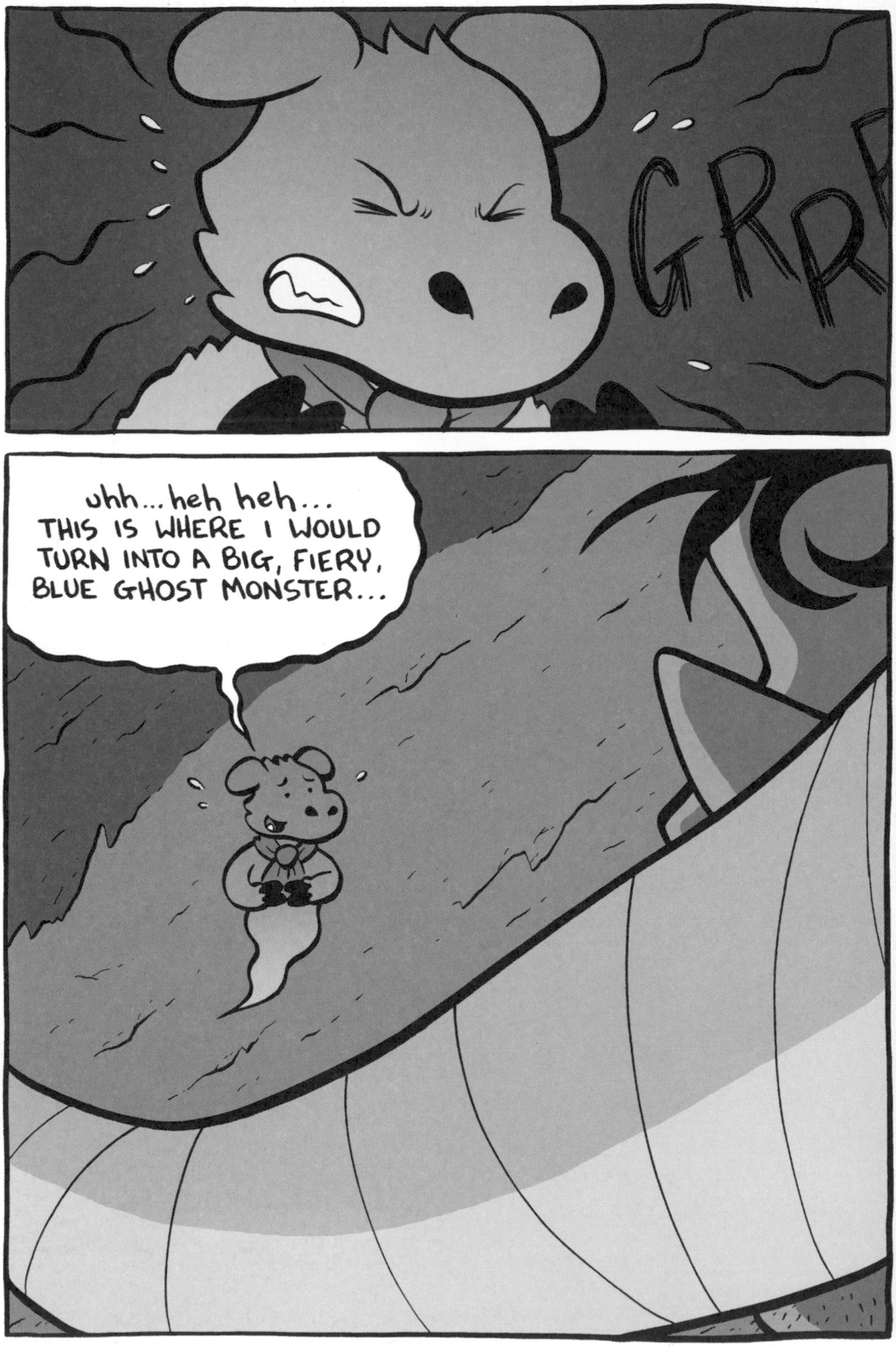
GRRR
uhh...heh heh...
THIS IS WHERE I WOULD
TURN INTO A BIG, FIERY,
BLUE GHOST MONSTER...

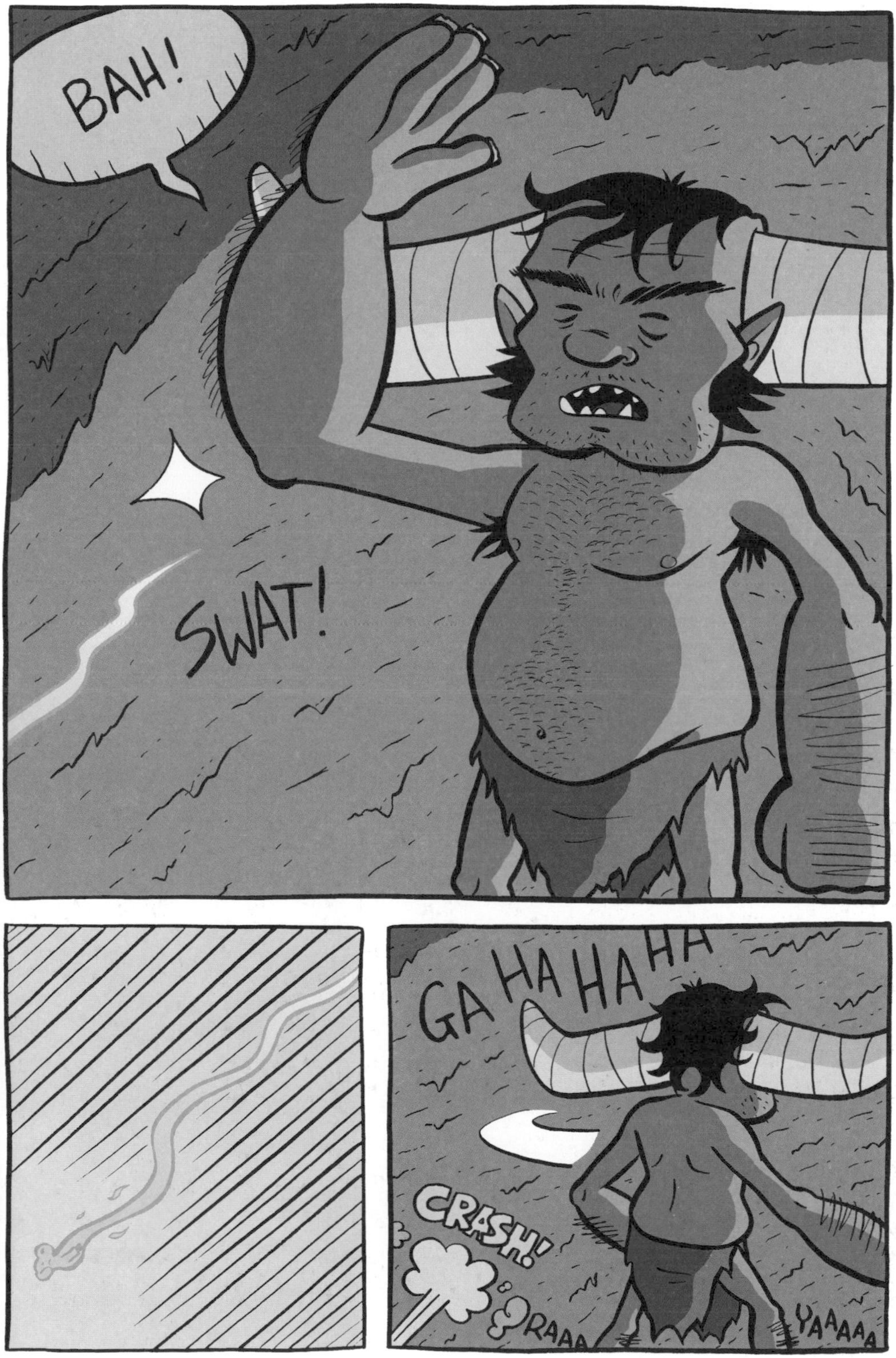
BAH!
SWAT!
GA HA HA HA HA
CRASH!
RAAA
YAAAAA

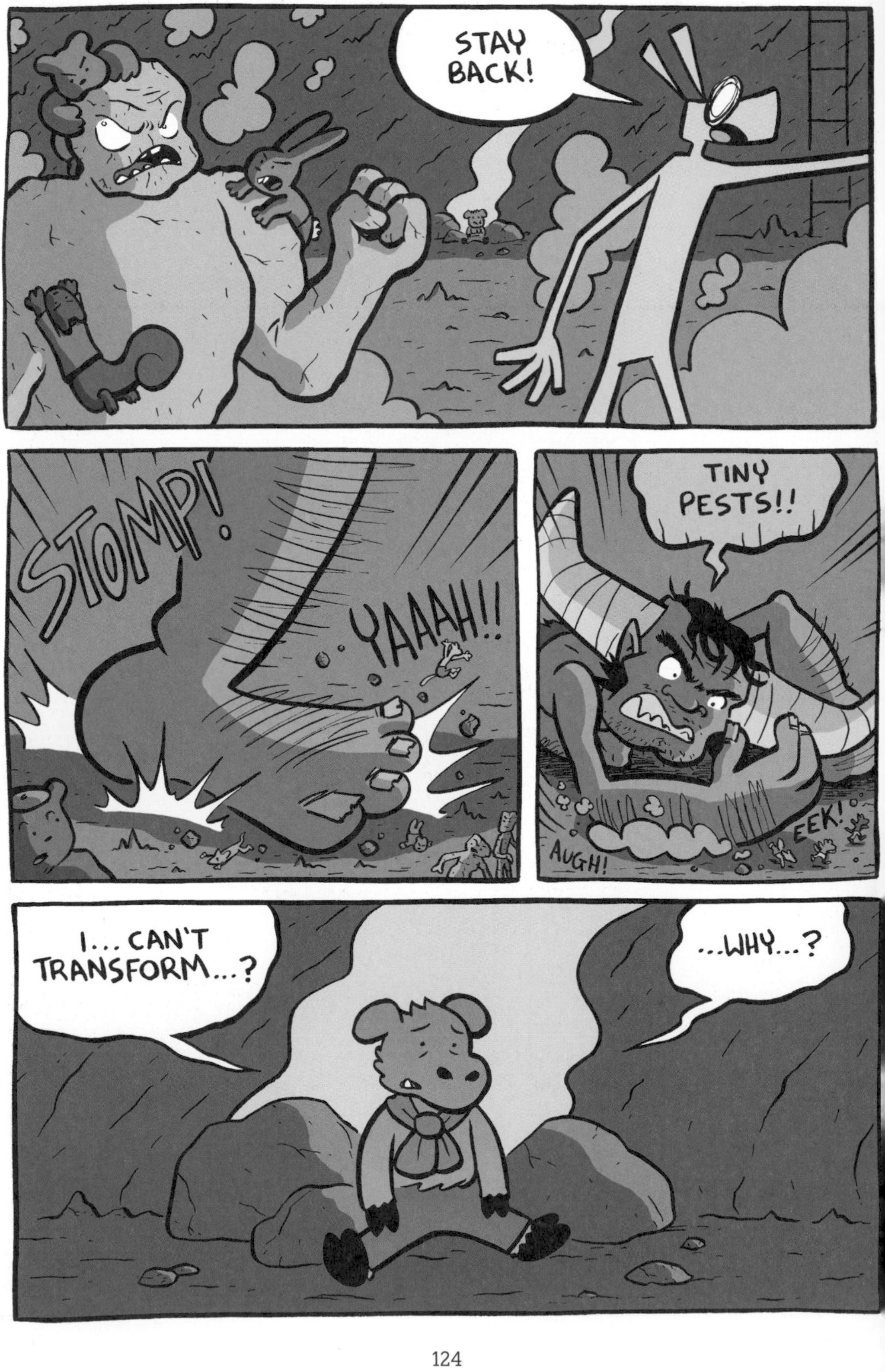
STAY BACK!
STOMP!
YAAAH!!
TINY PESTS!!
AUGH!
EEK!
I... CAN'T TRANSFORM...?
...WHY...?

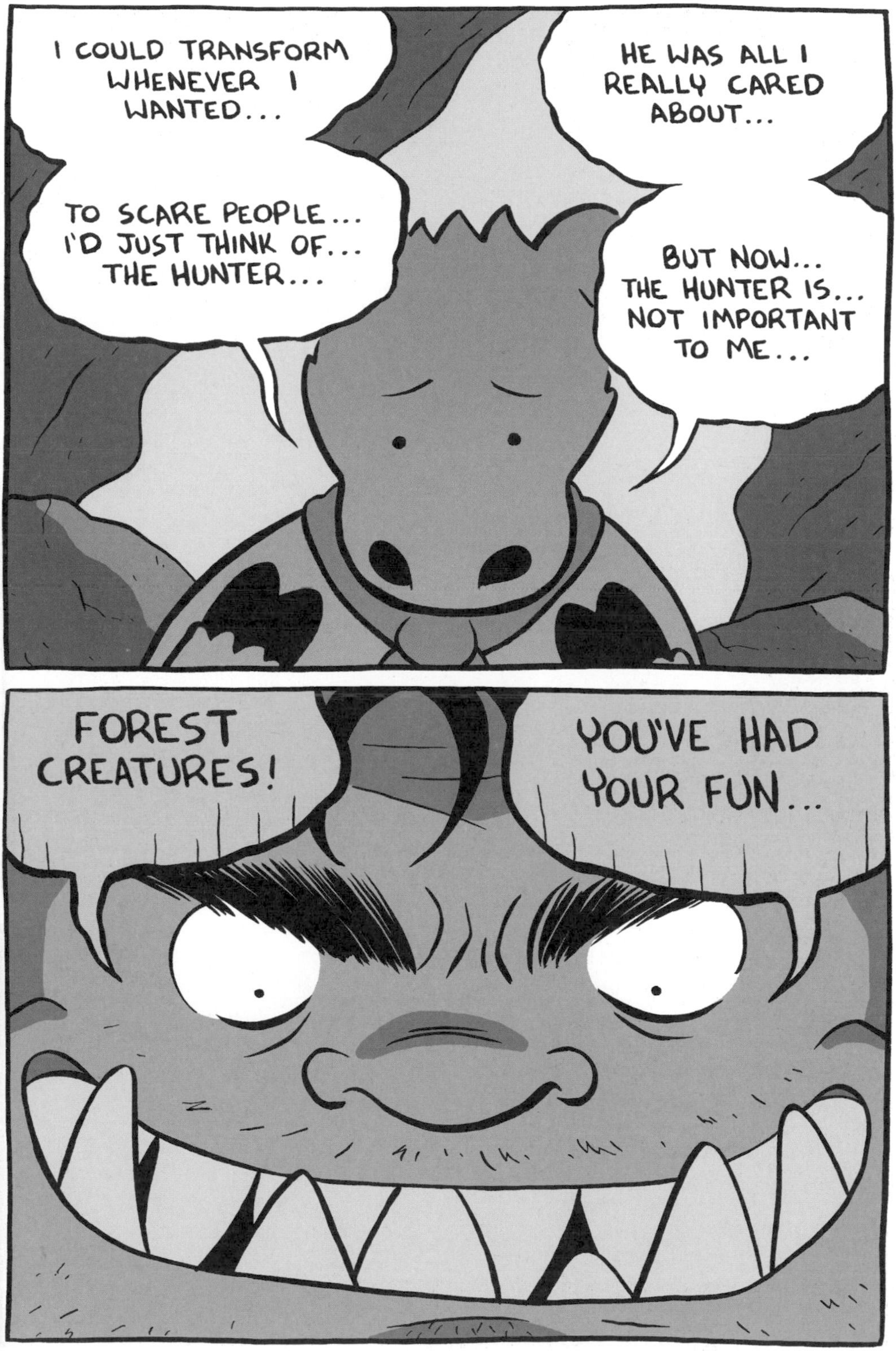
I COULD TRANSFORM WHENEVER I WANTED...
TO SCARE PEOPLE... I'D JUST THINK OF... THE HUNTER...
HE WAS ALL I REALLY CARED ABOUT...
BUT NOW... THE HUNTER IS... NOT IMPORTANT TO ME...
FOREST CREATURES!
YOU'VE HAD YOUR FUN...

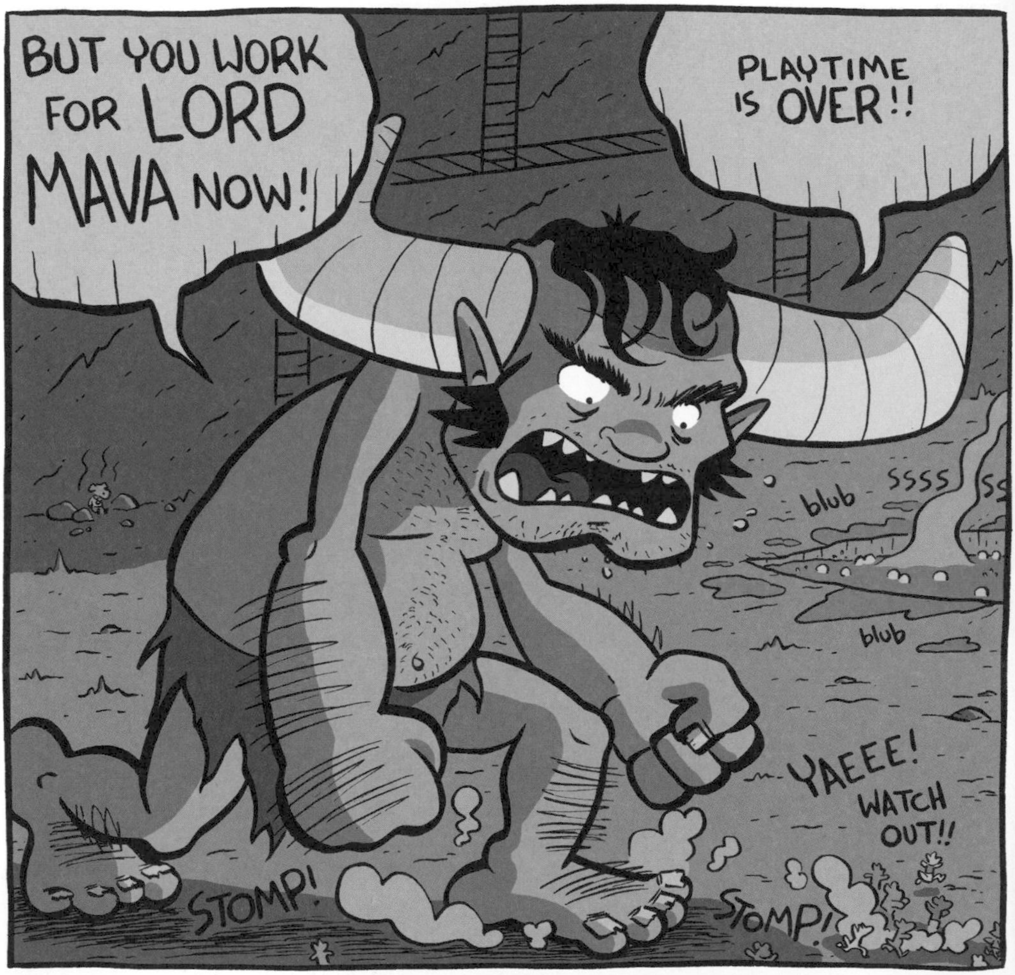
BUT YOU WORK FOR LORD MAVA NOW!
PLAYTIME IS OVER!!
blub
SSSS
blub
YAEEE!
WATCH OUT!!
STOMP!
STOMP!

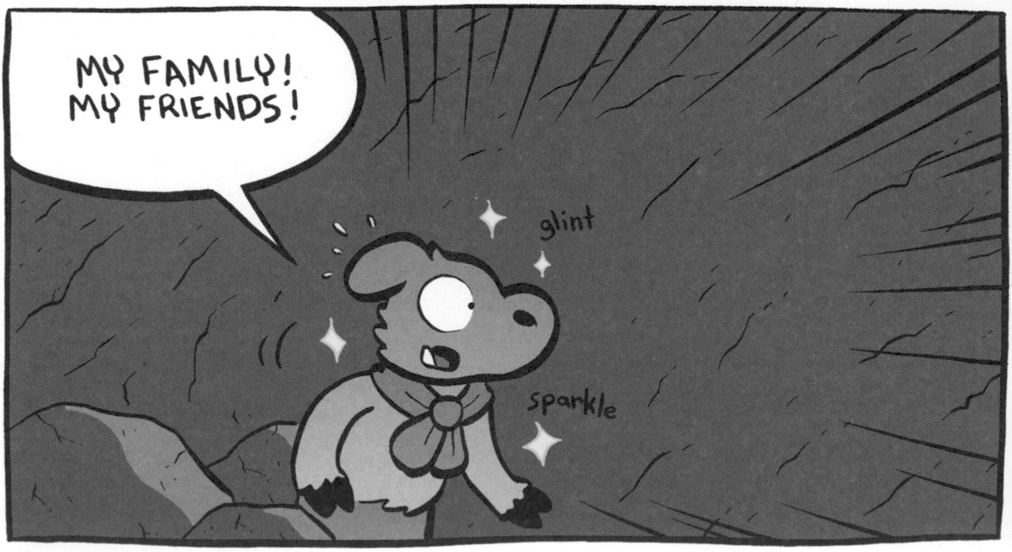
MY FAMILY! MY FRIENDS!
glint
sparkle

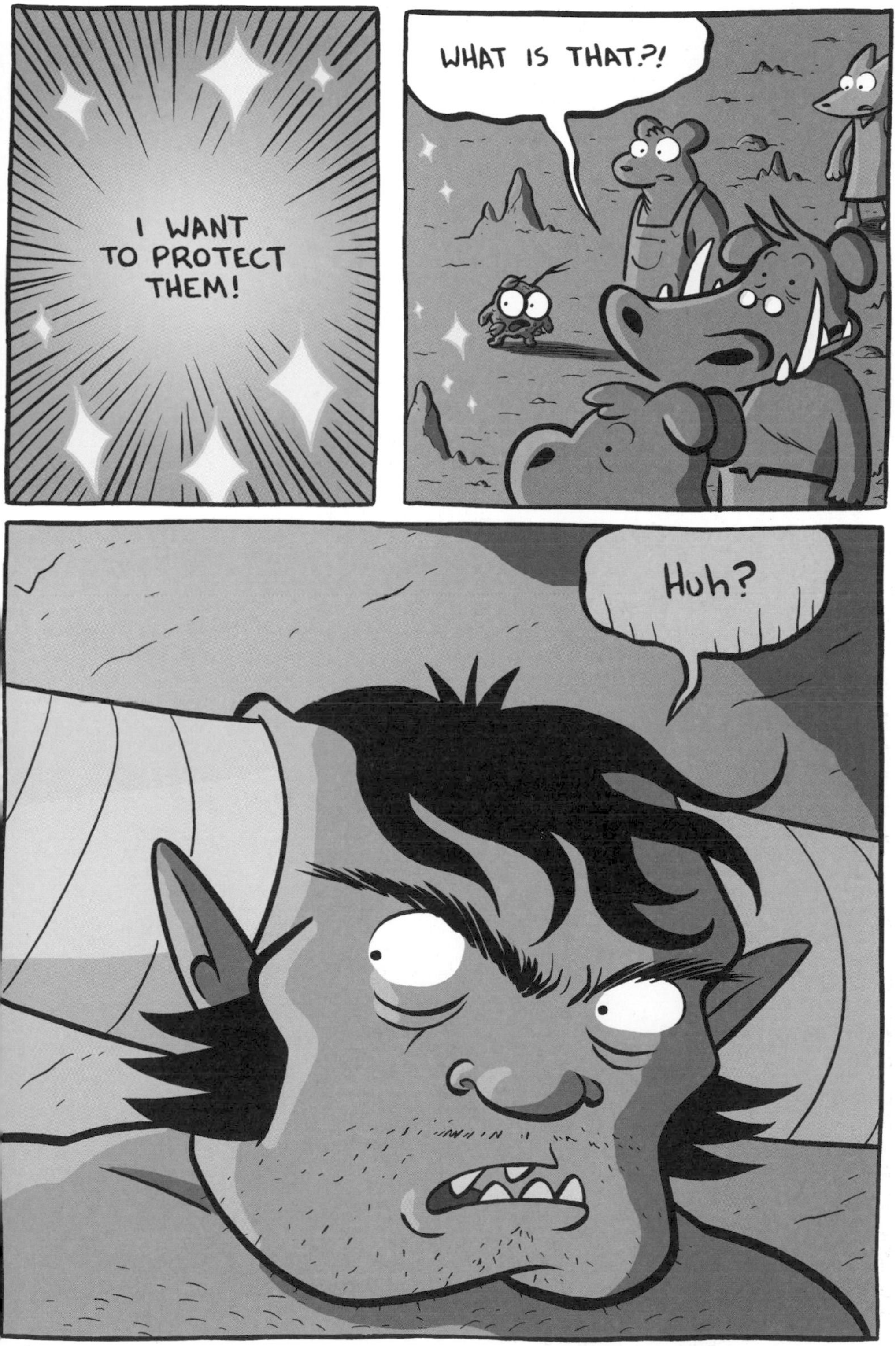
I WANT TO PROTECT THEM!
WHAT IS THAT?!
Huh?

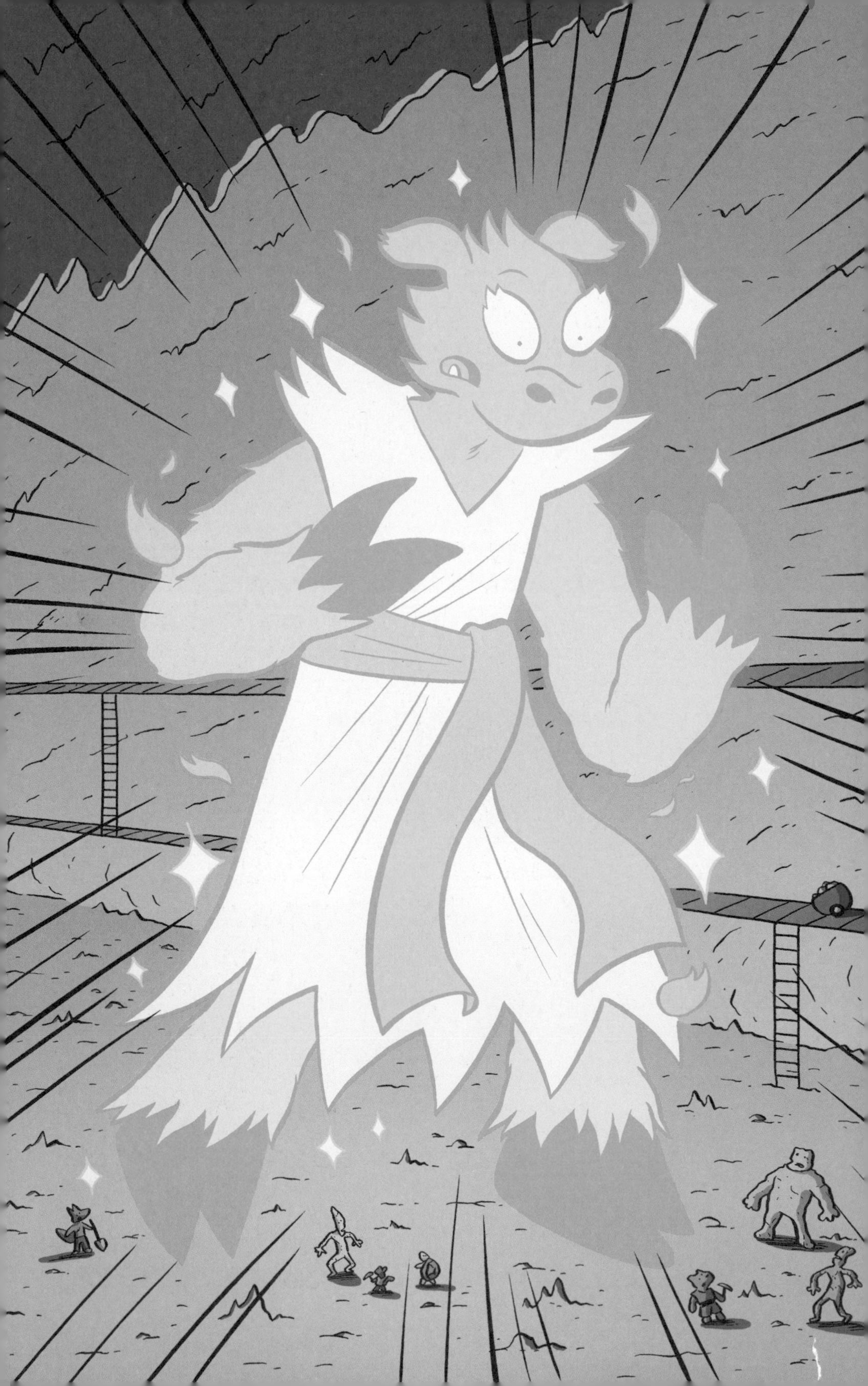

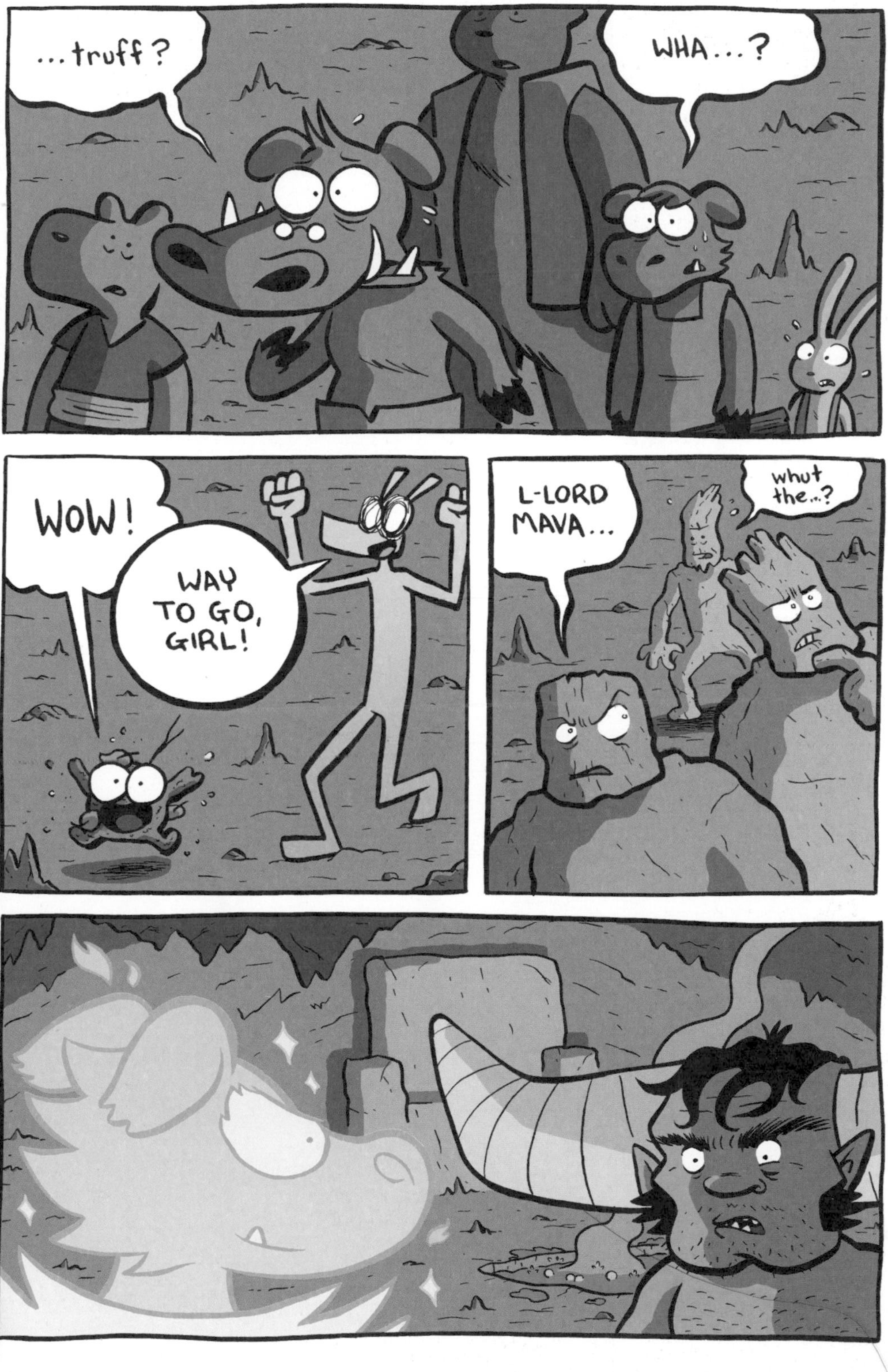
...truff?
WHA...?
WOW!
WAY TO GO, GIRL!
L-LORD MAVA...
whut the...?

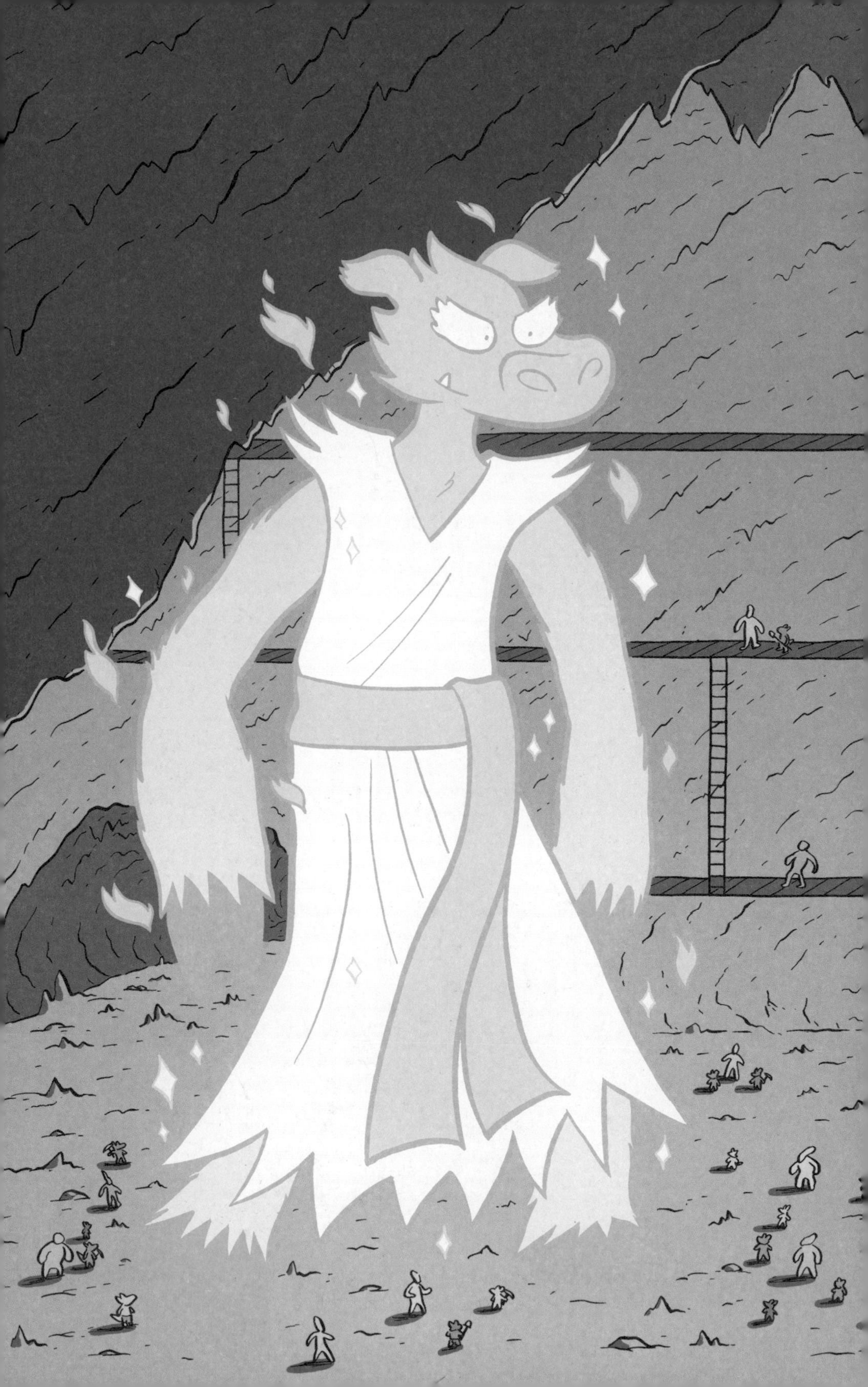

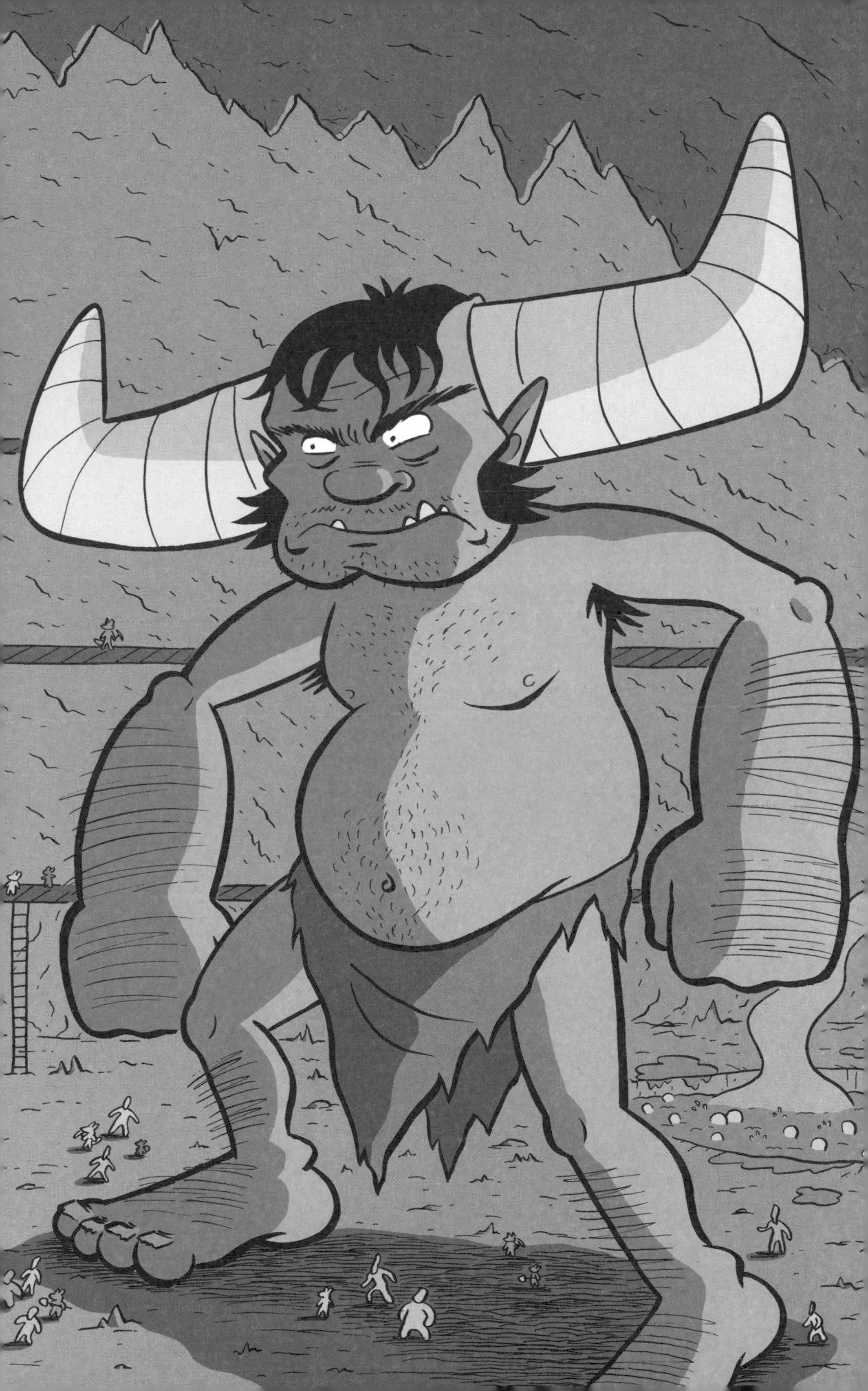

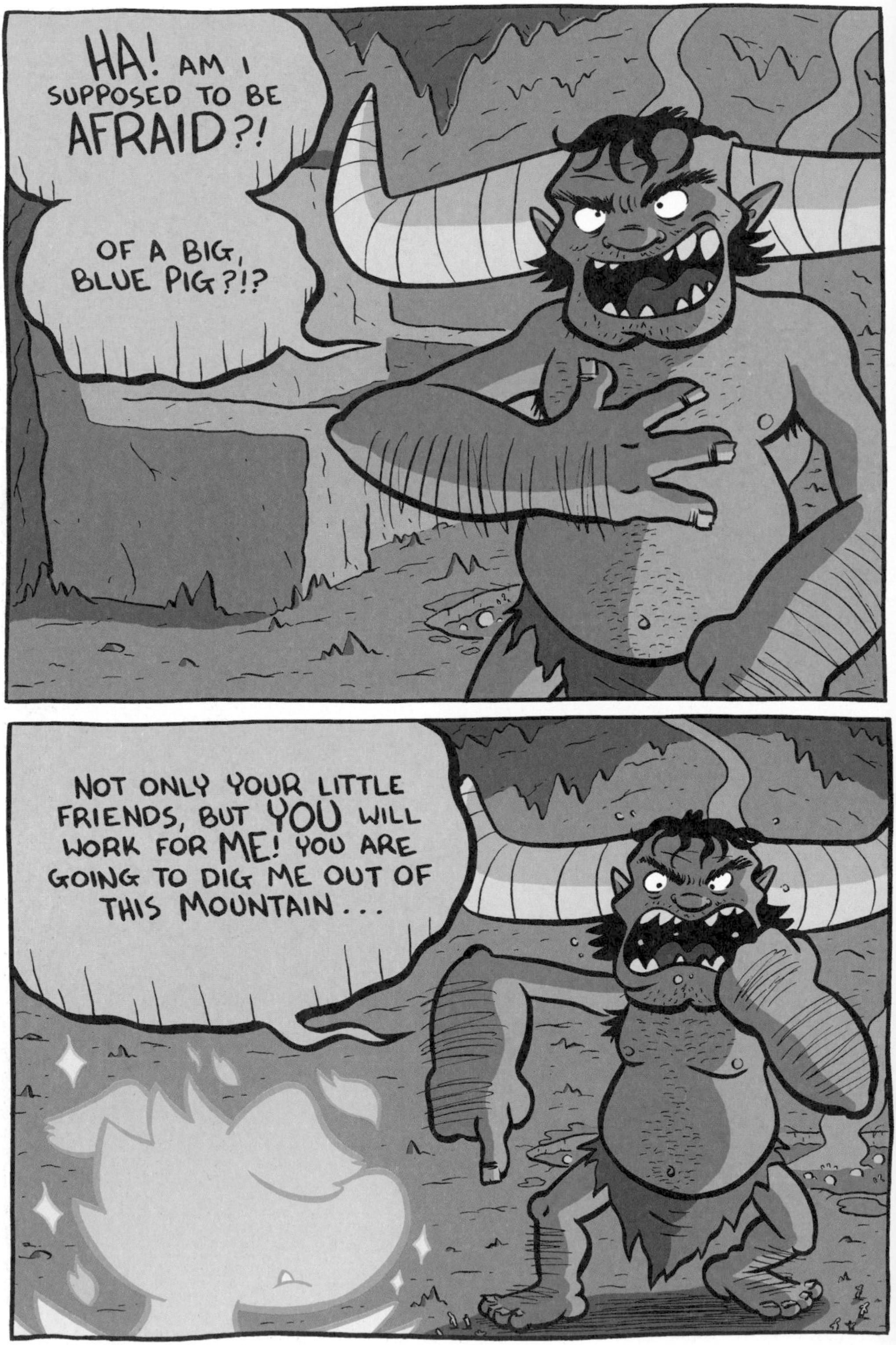
HA! AM I SUPPOSED TO BE AFRAID?!
OF A BIG, BLUE PIG?!?
NOT ONLY YOUR LITTLE FRIENDS, BUT YOU WILL WORK FOR ME! YOU ARE GOING TO DIG ME OUT OF THIS MOUNTAIN...

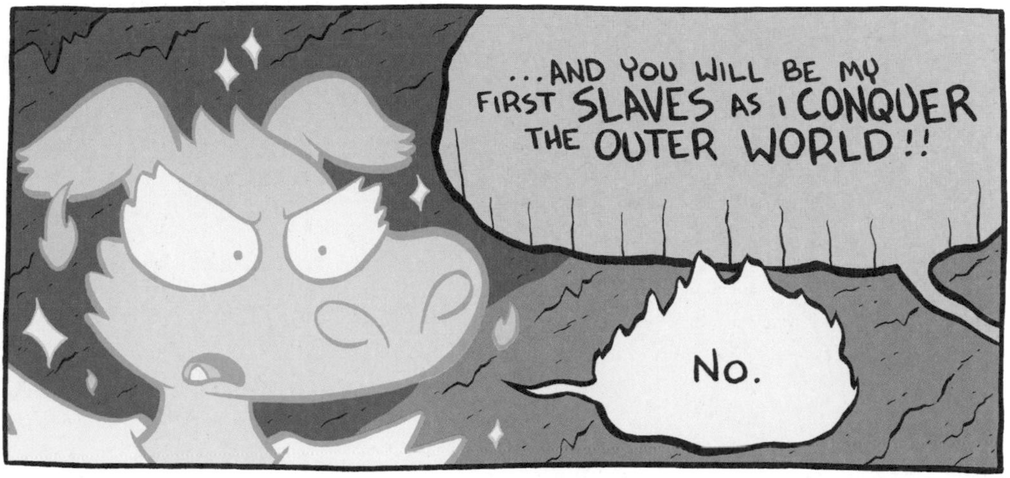
...AND YOU WILL BE MY FIRST SLAVES AS I CONQUER THE OUTER WORLD!!
No.

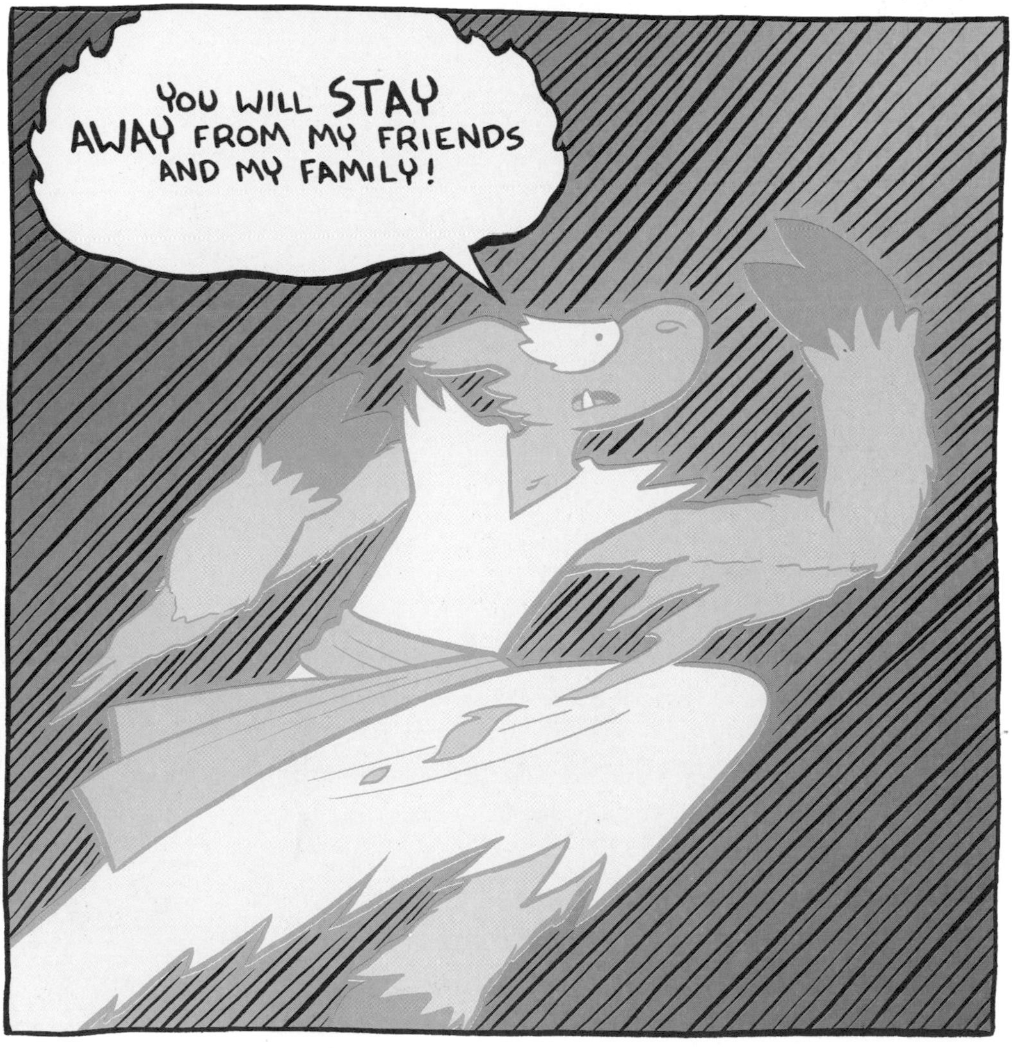
YOU WILL STAY AWAY FROM MY FRIENDS AND MY FAMILY!

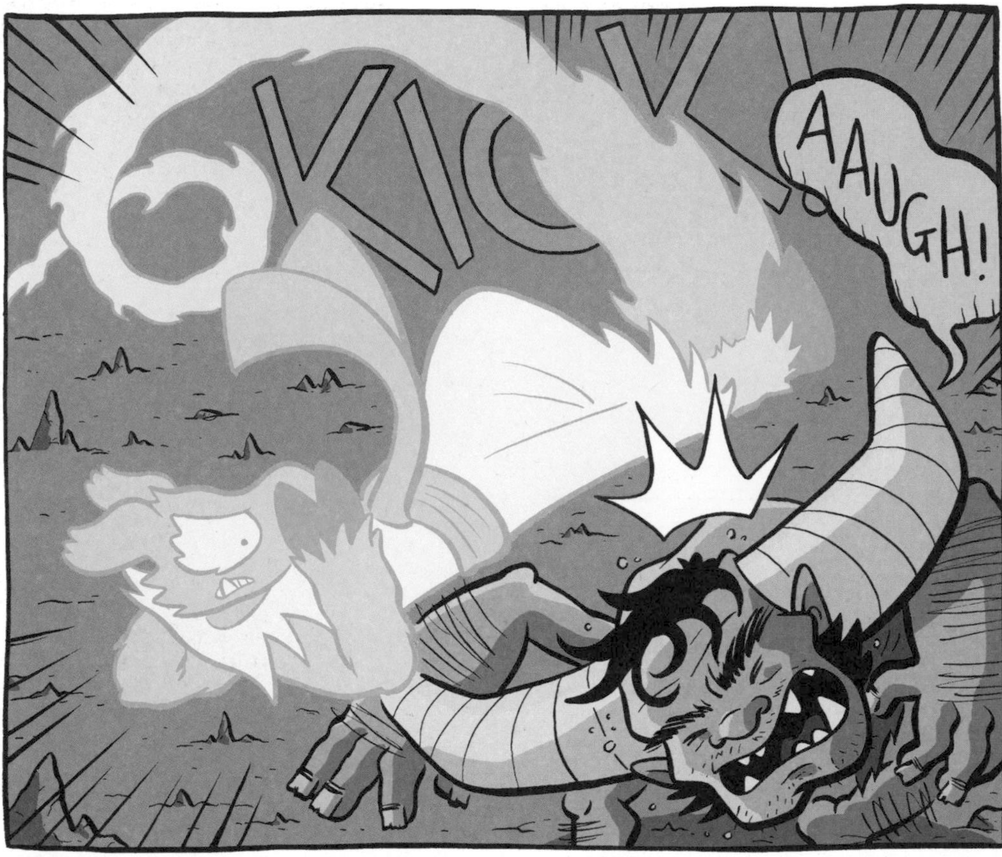
KICK
AAAUGH!

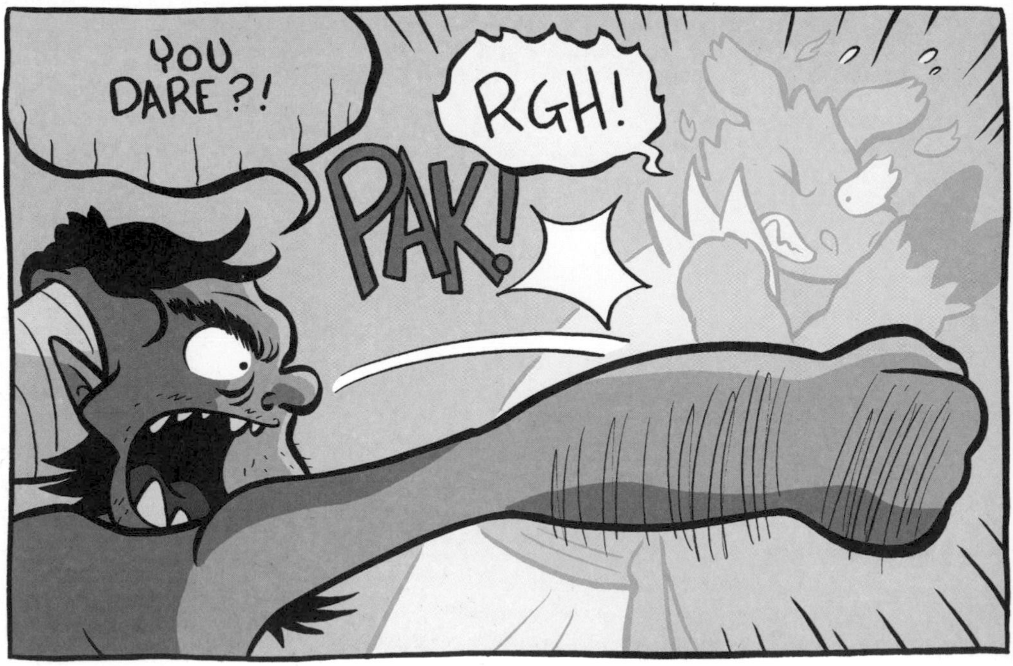
YOU DARE?!
RGH!
PAK!

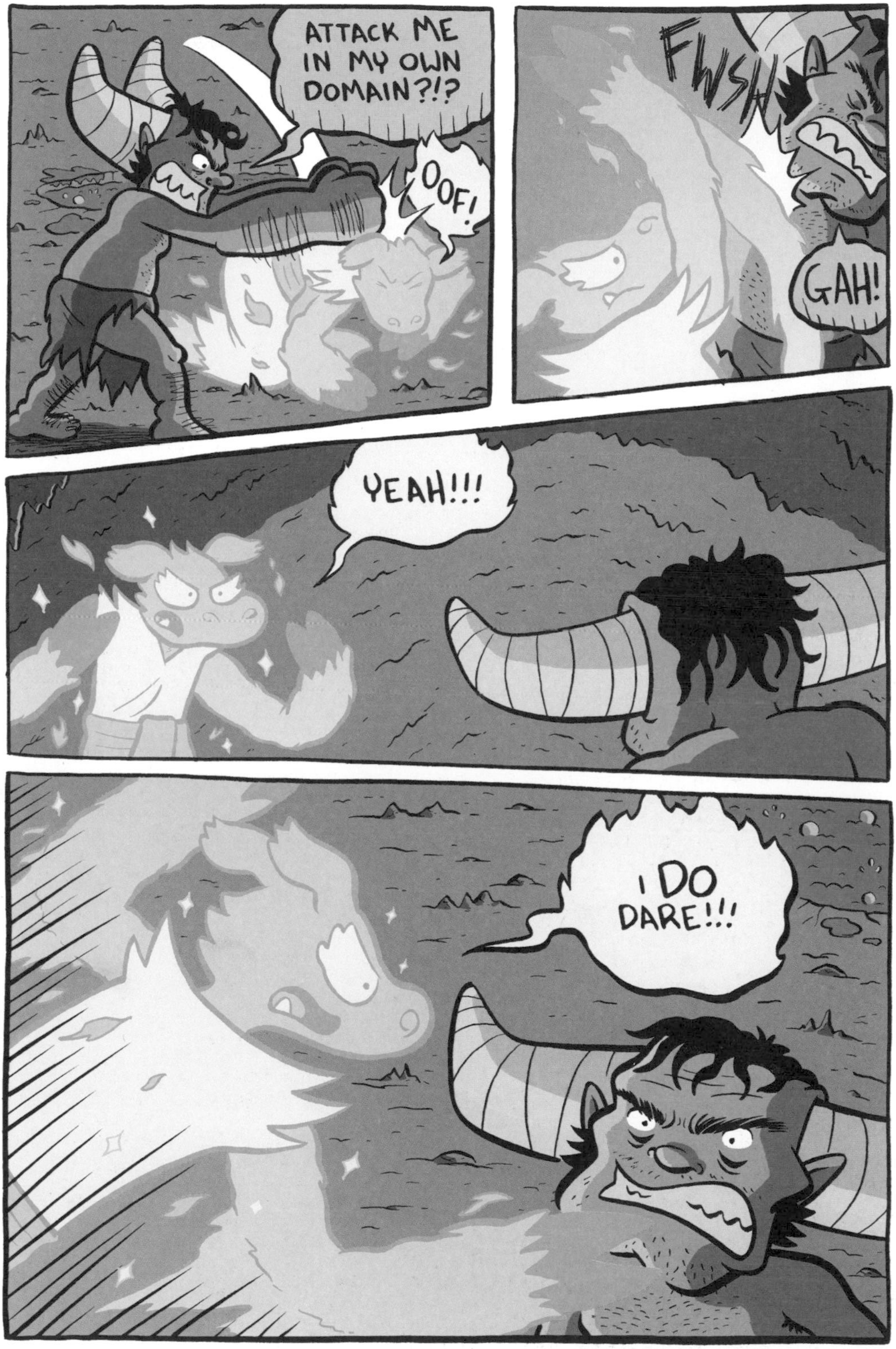
ATTACK ME IN MY OWN DOMAIN?!?
OOF!
FWSH
GAH!
YEAH!!!
I DO DARE!!!

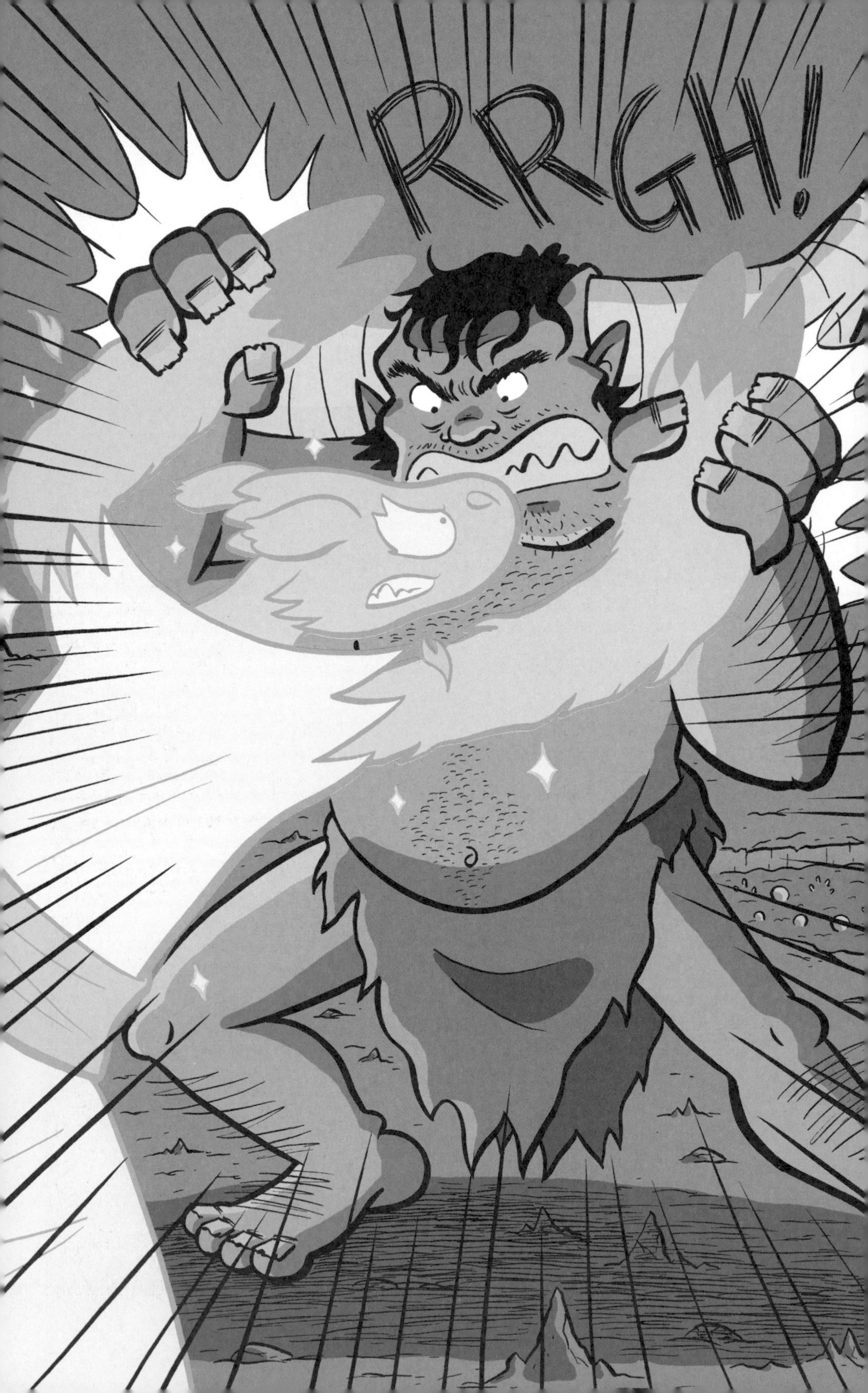
RRRGH!

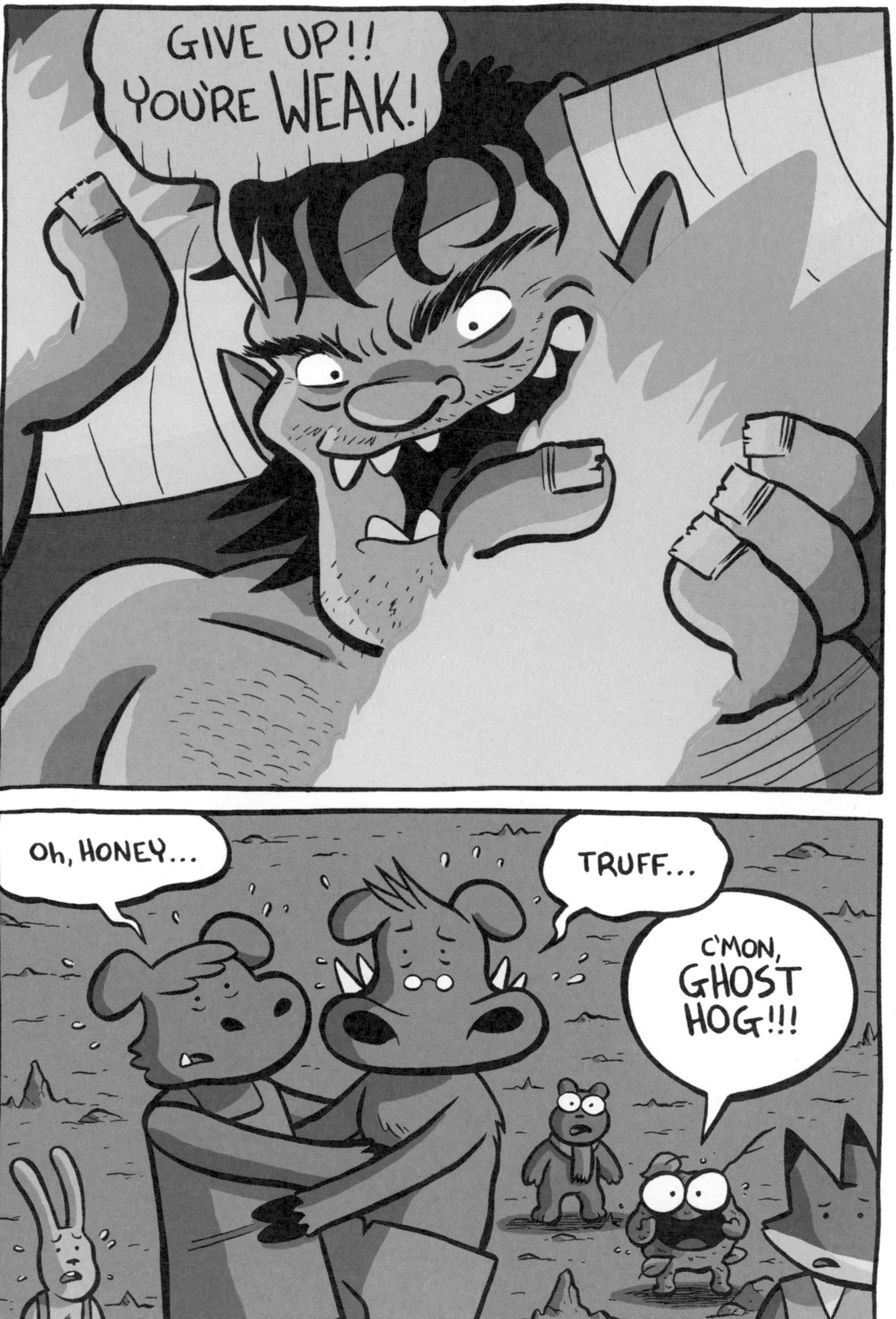
GIVE UP!! YOU'RE WEAK!
Oh, HONEY...
TRUFF...
C'MON, GHOST HOG!!!

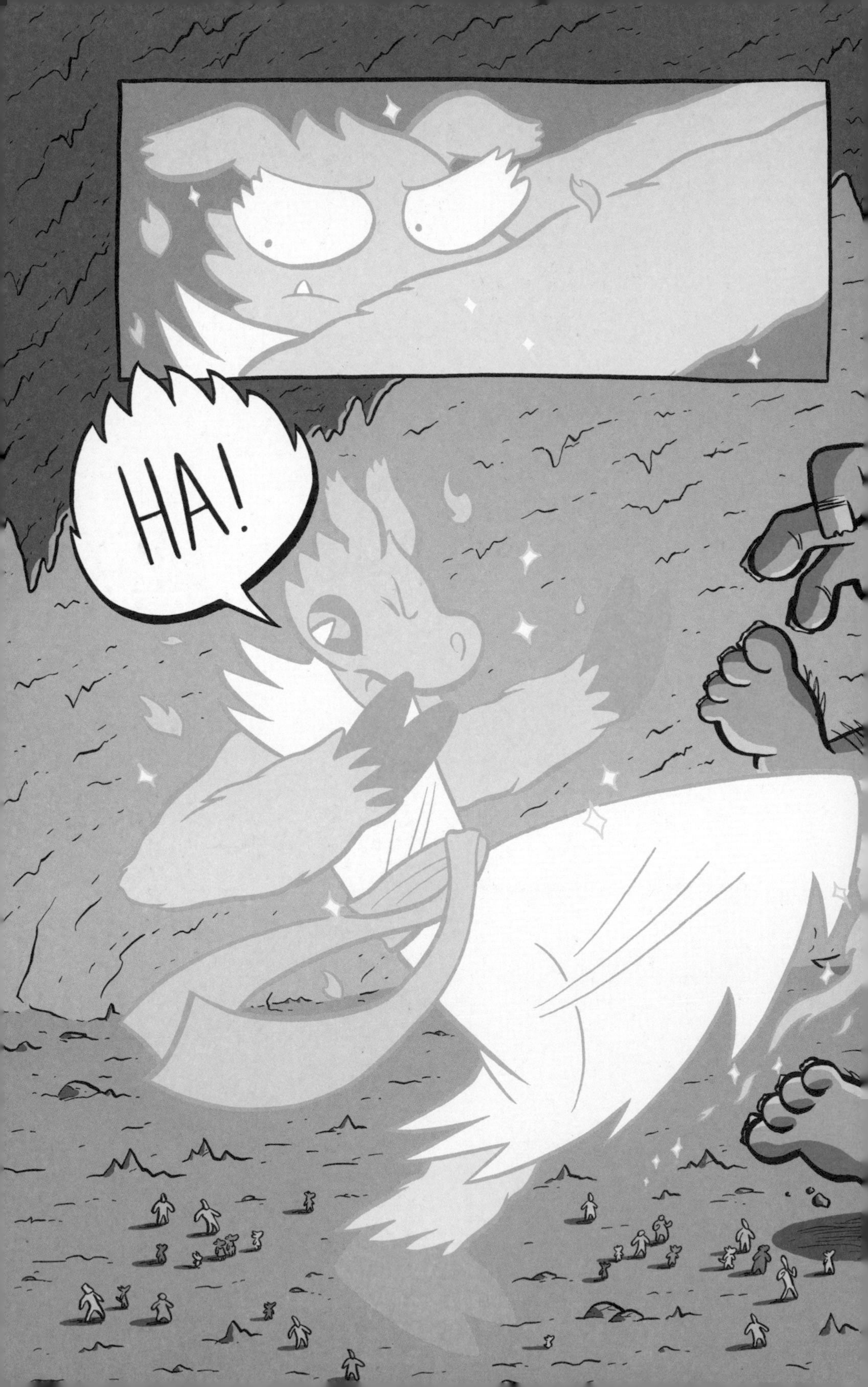
HA!

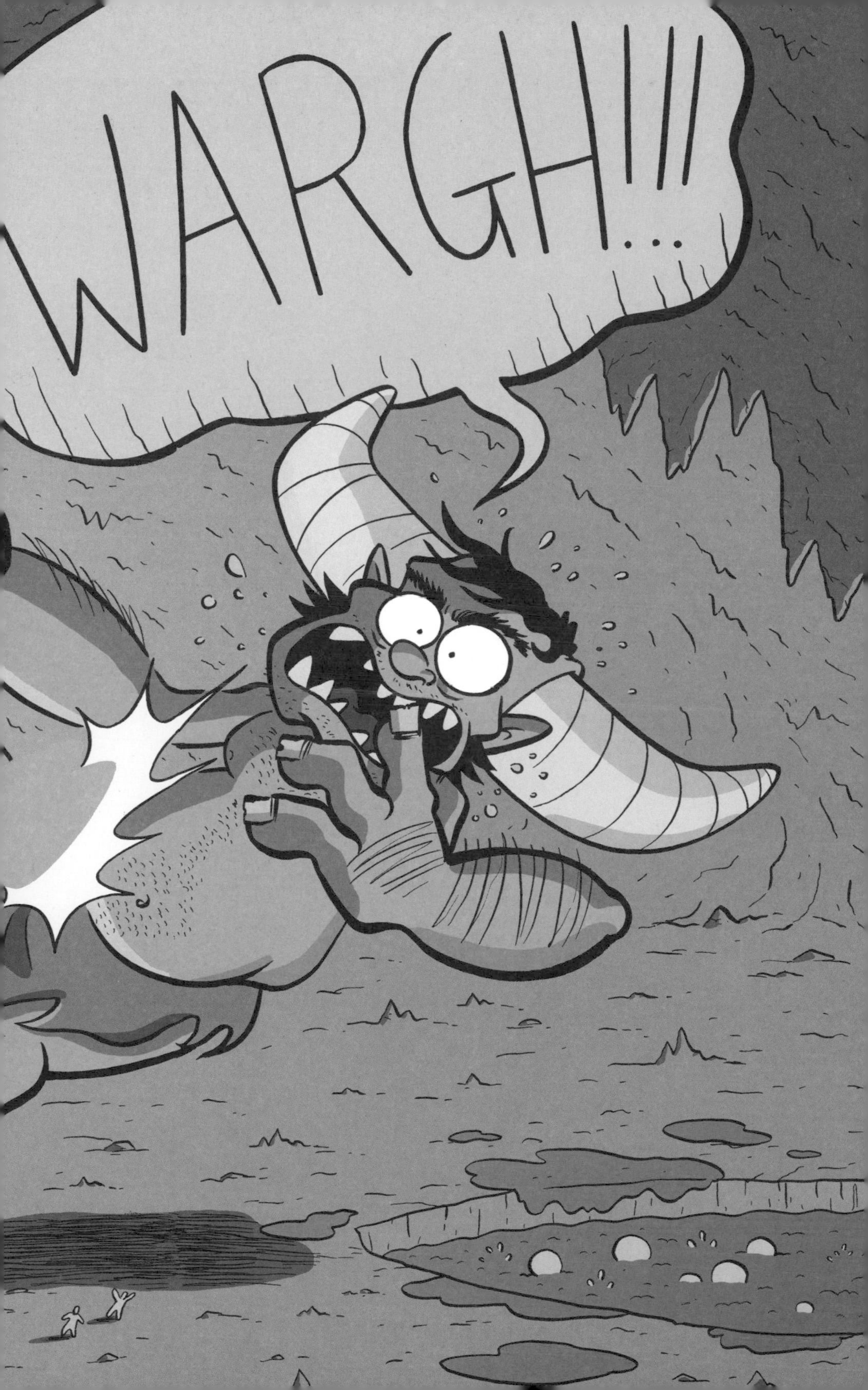
WARGH!!!...

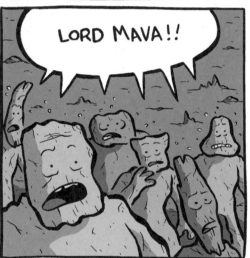

LORD MAVA!!

RIGHT IN THE MAGMA PIT!

JUST STAY IN THERE, YOU OVERGROWN TROLL!

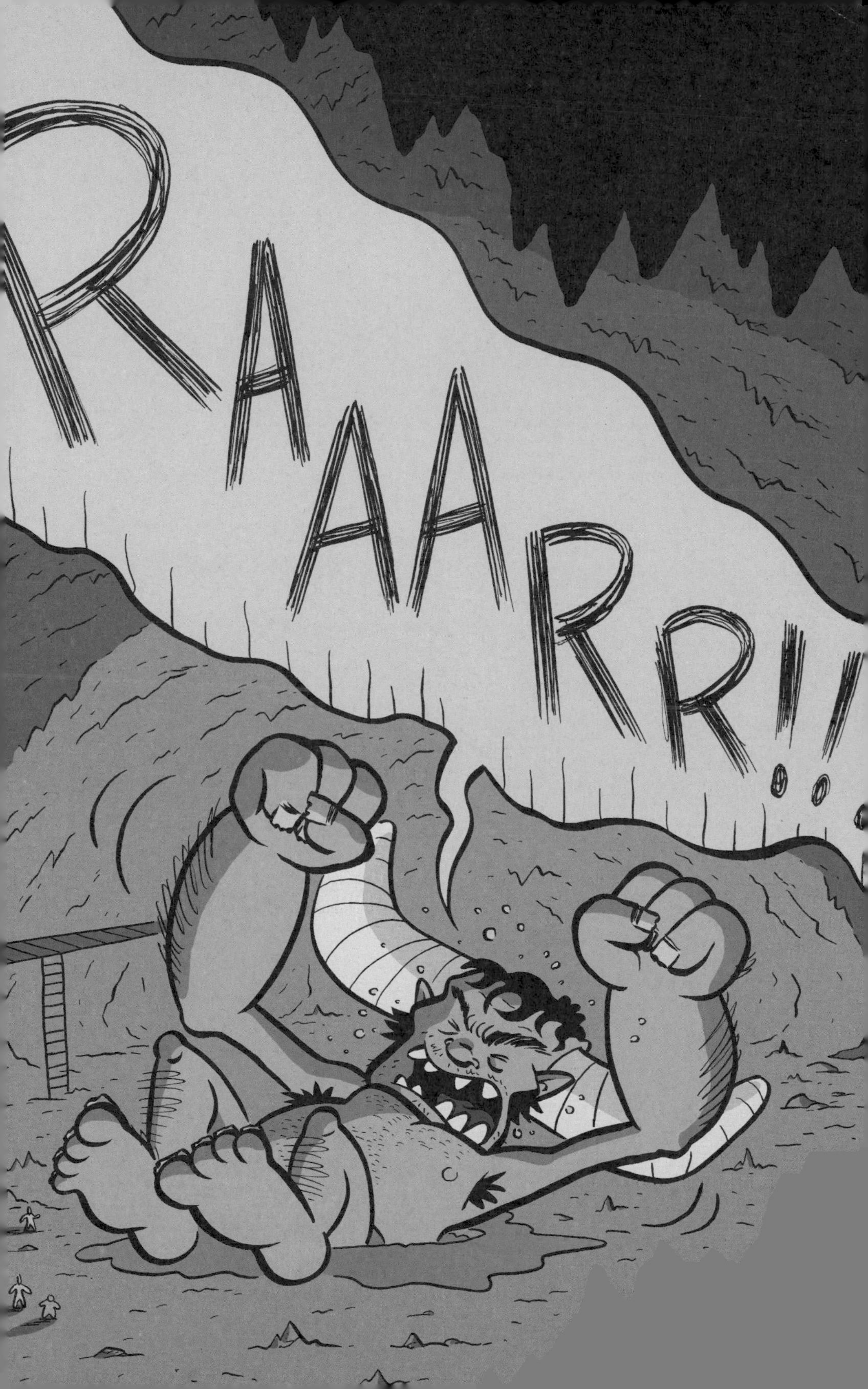
RAAARR!!!

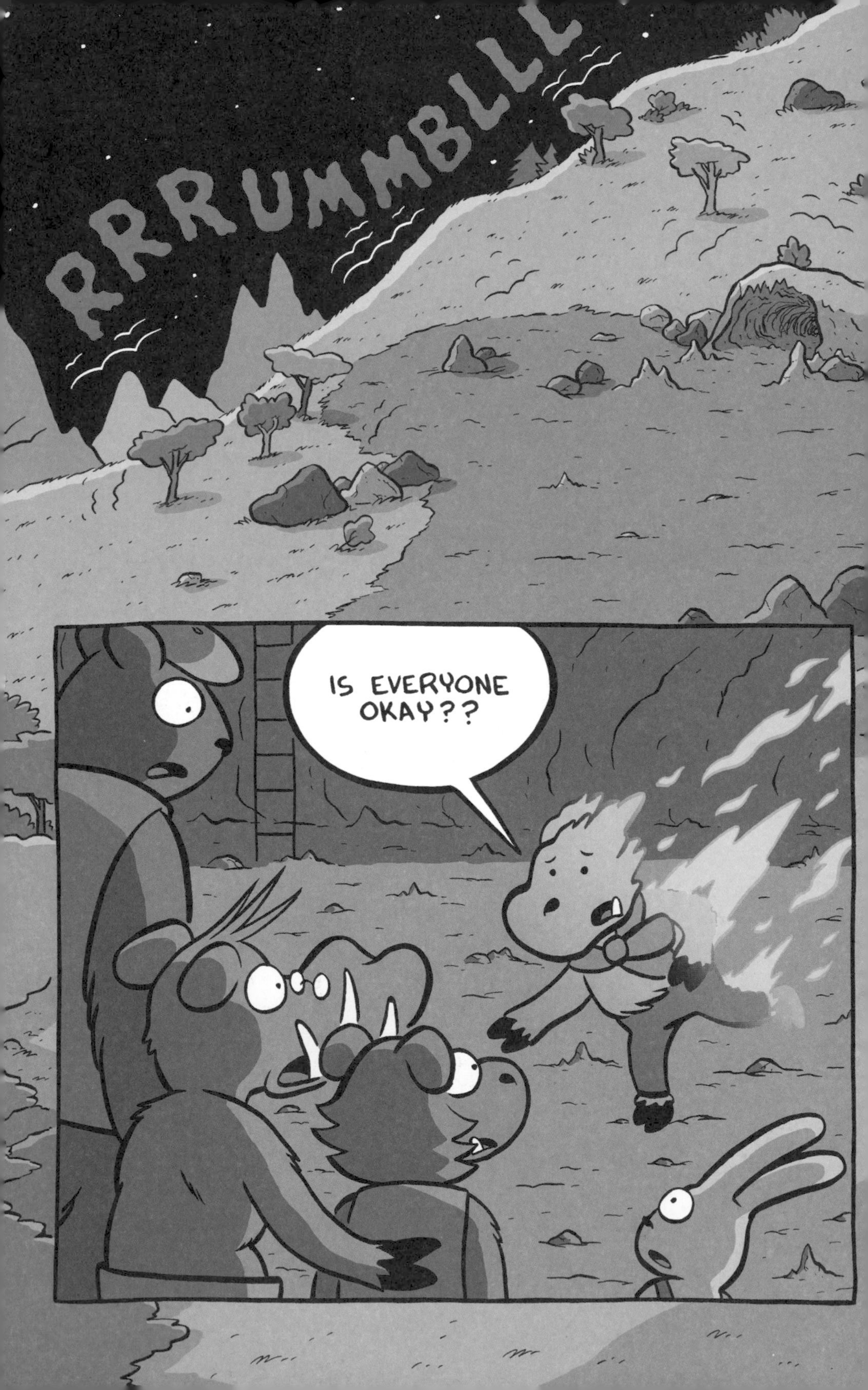
RRRUMMBLLL
IS EVERYONE OKAY??

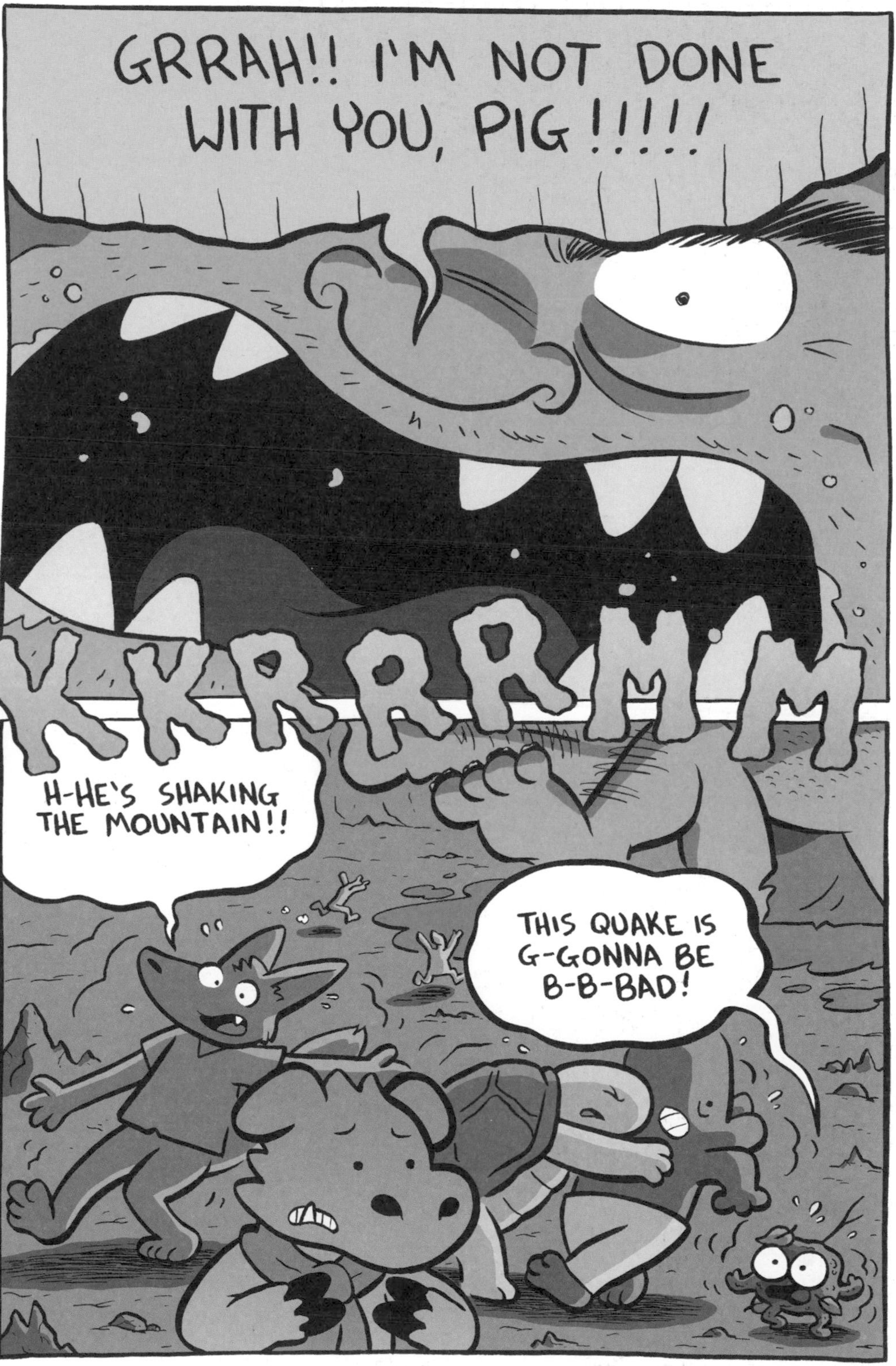
GRRAH!! I'M NOT DONE WITH YOU, PIG!!!!!
KKRRRMM
H-HE'S SHAKING THE MOUNTAIN!!
THIS QUAKE IS G-GONNA BE B-B-BAD!

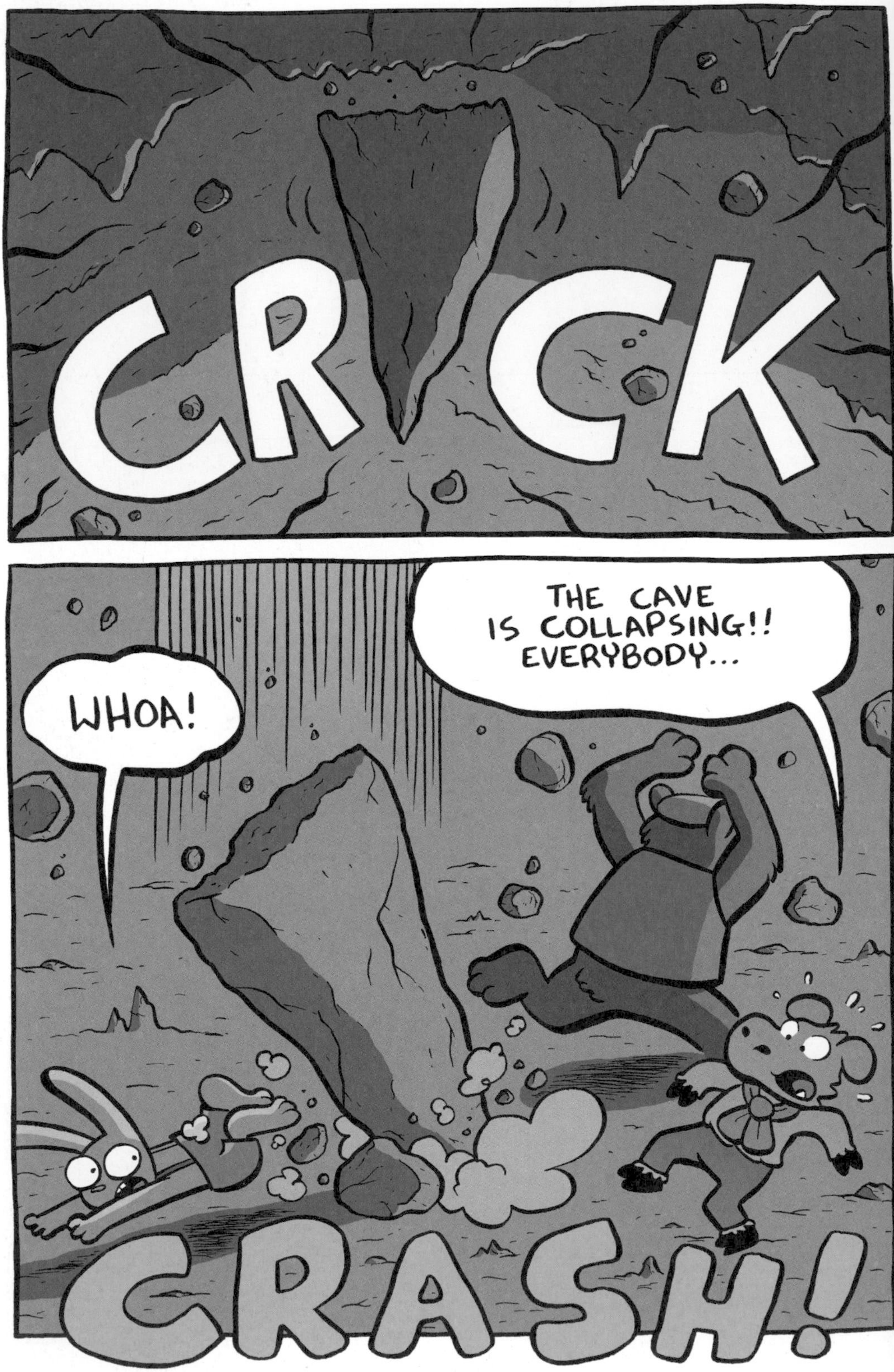
CRACK
WHOA!
THE CAVE IS COLLAPSING!! EVERYBODY...
CRASH!

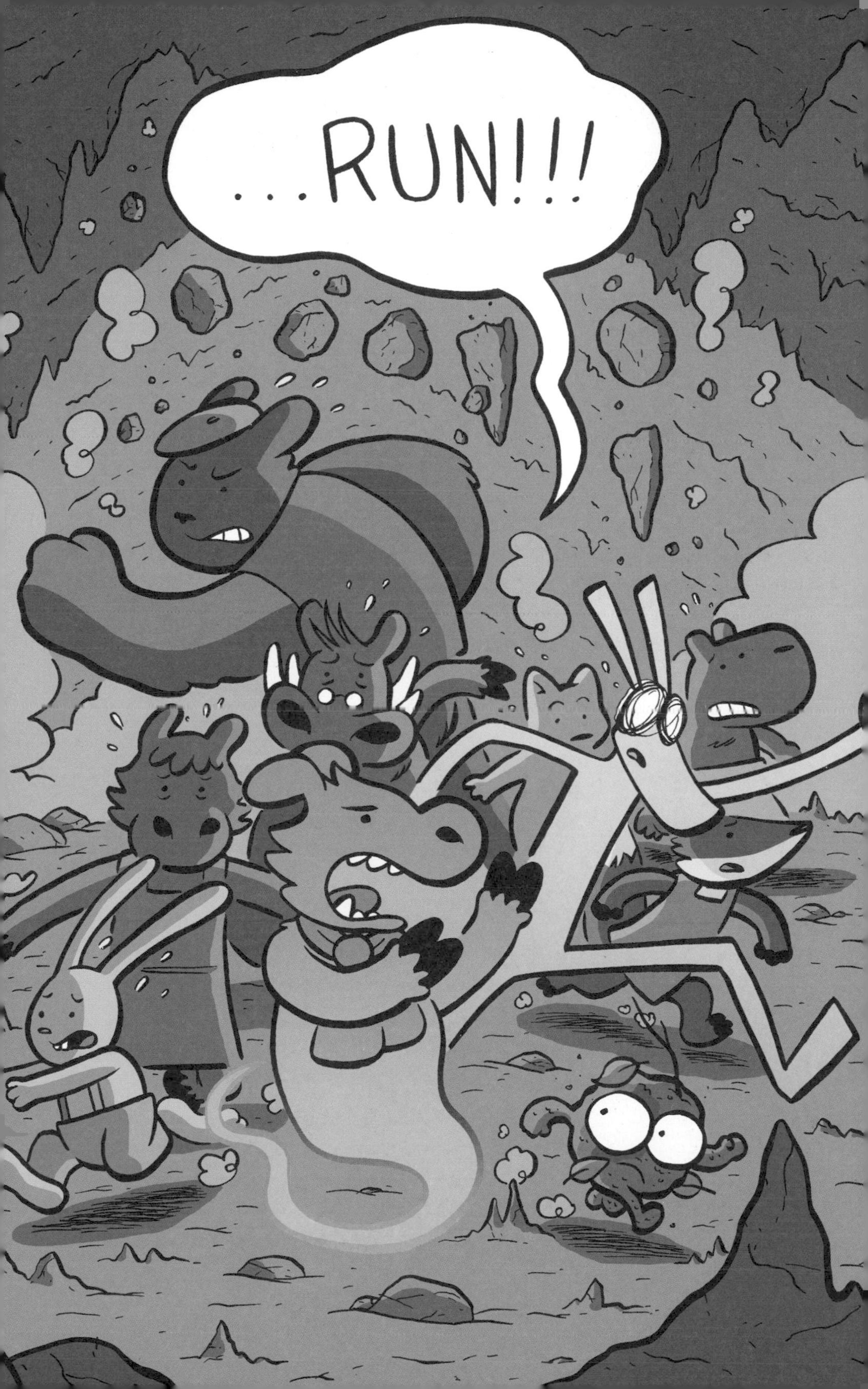
...RUN!!!

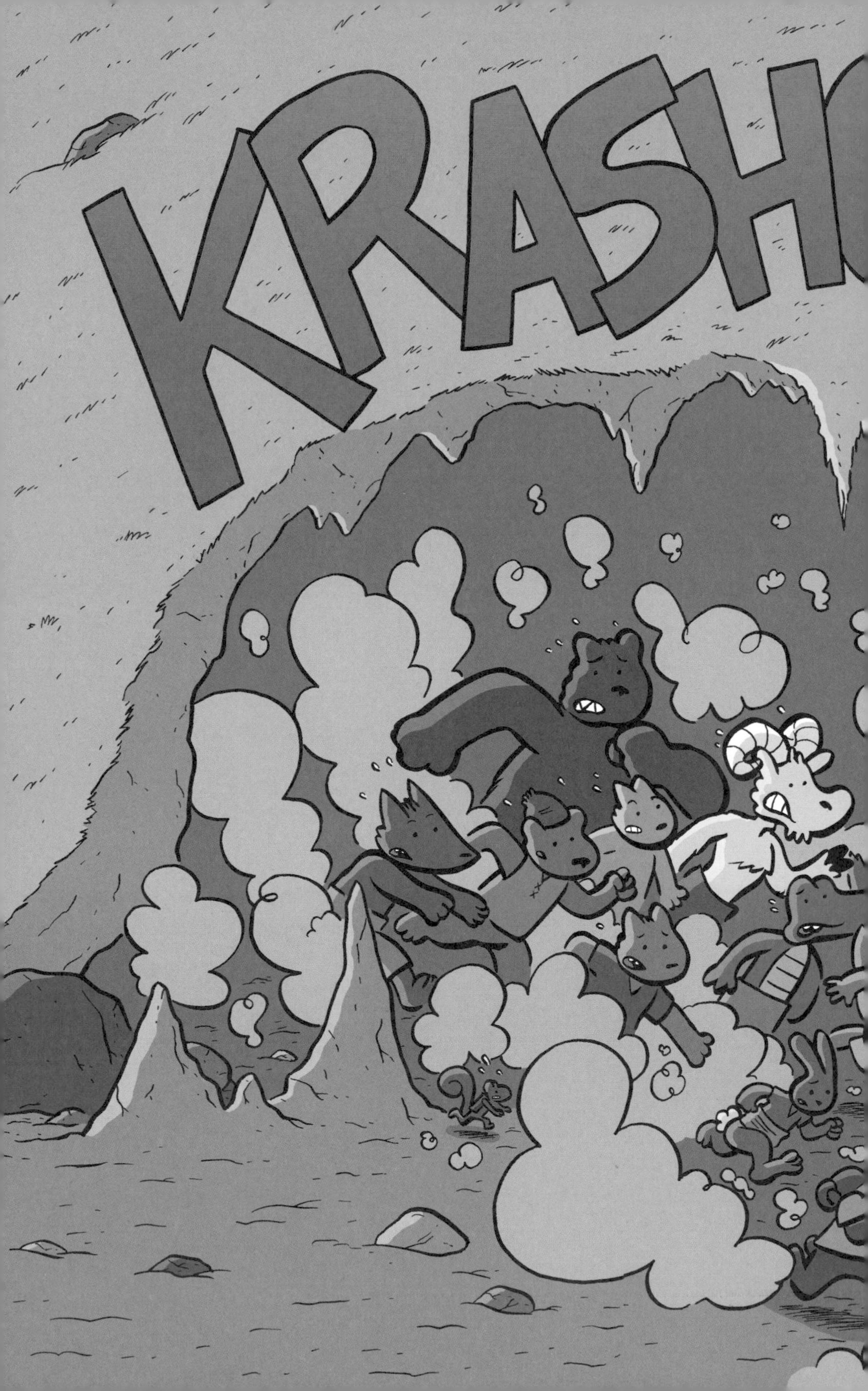
KRASH

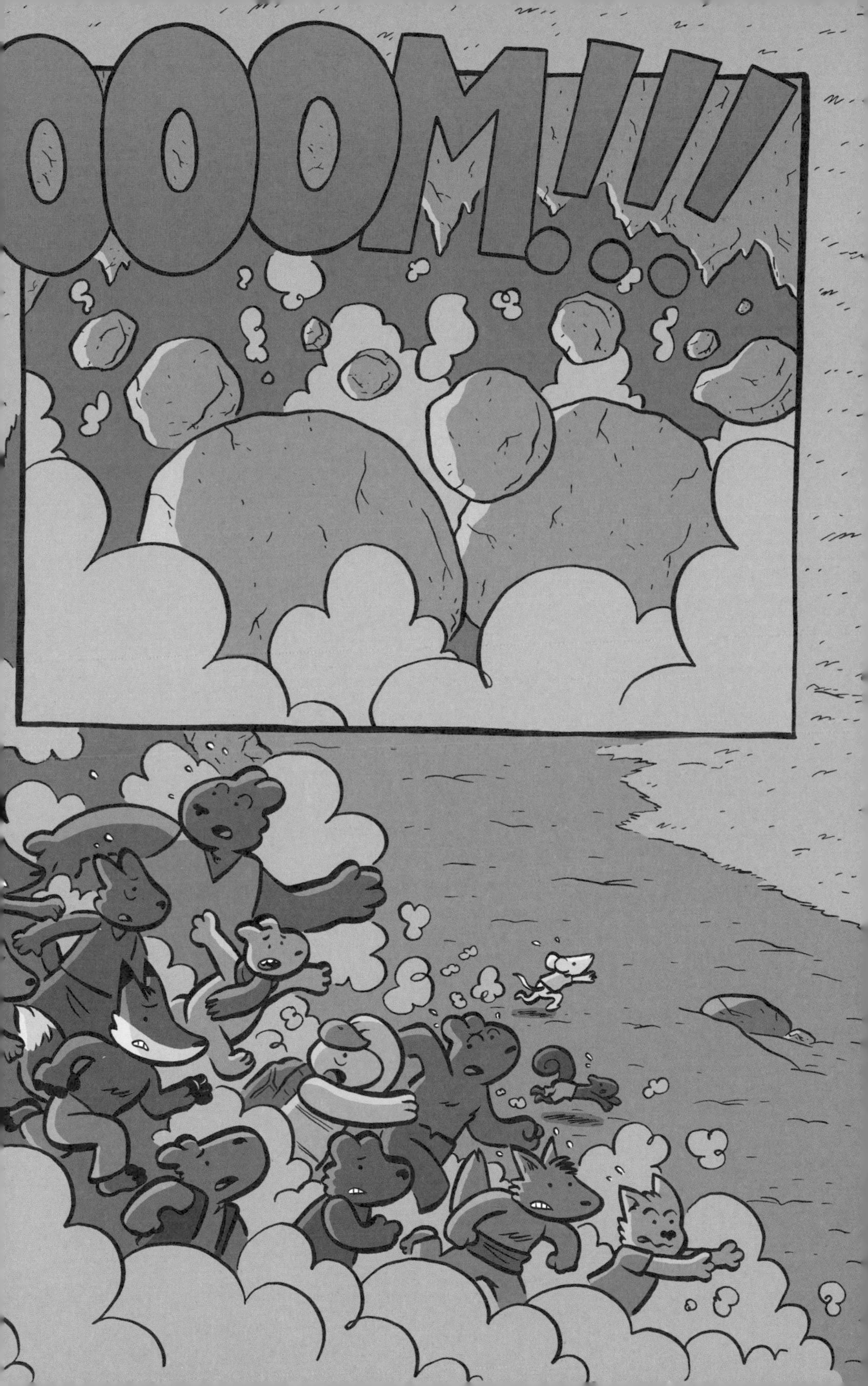
OOOM!!!!

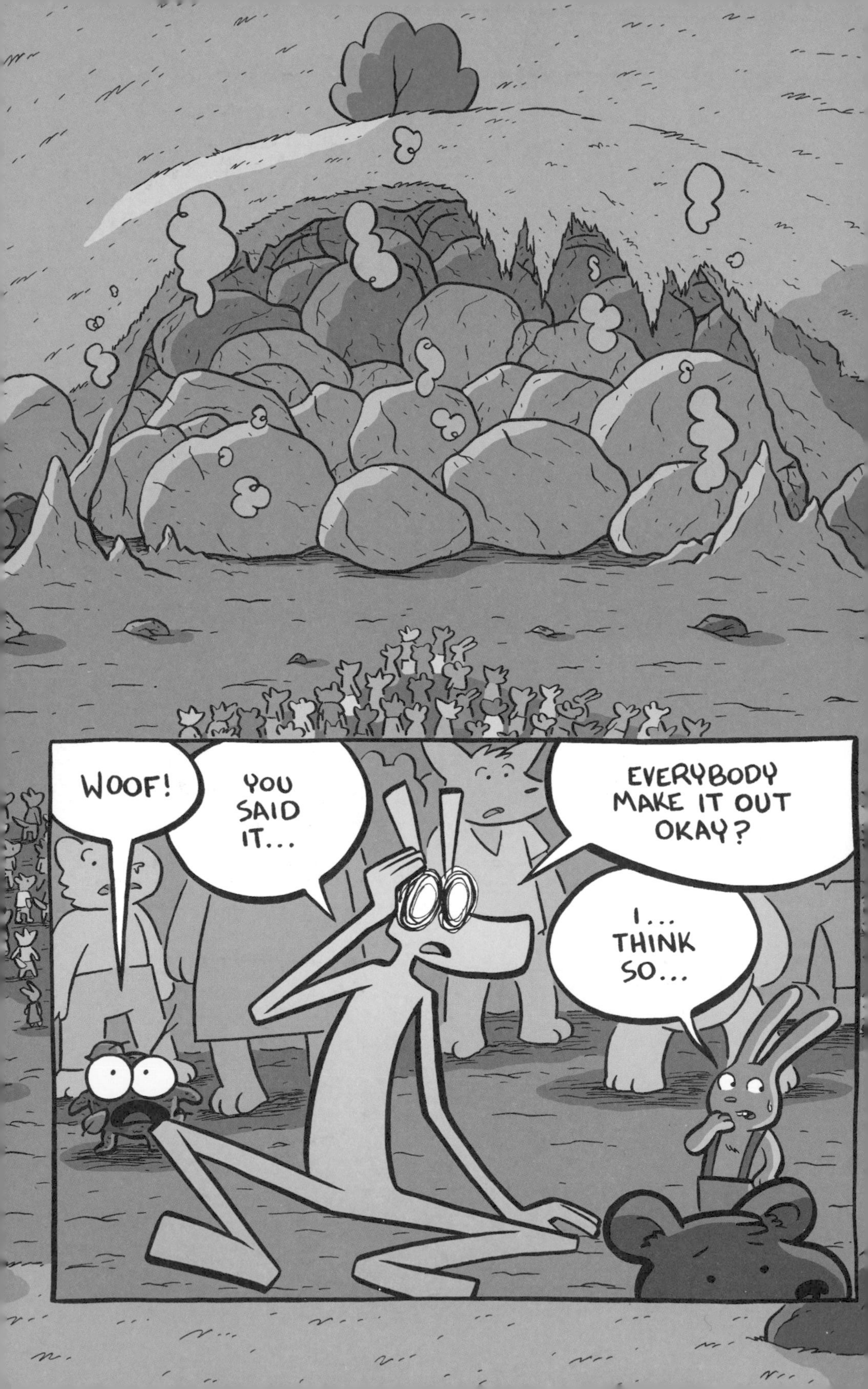
WOOF!
YOU SAID IT...
EVERYBODY MAKE IT OUT OKAY?
I... THINK SO...

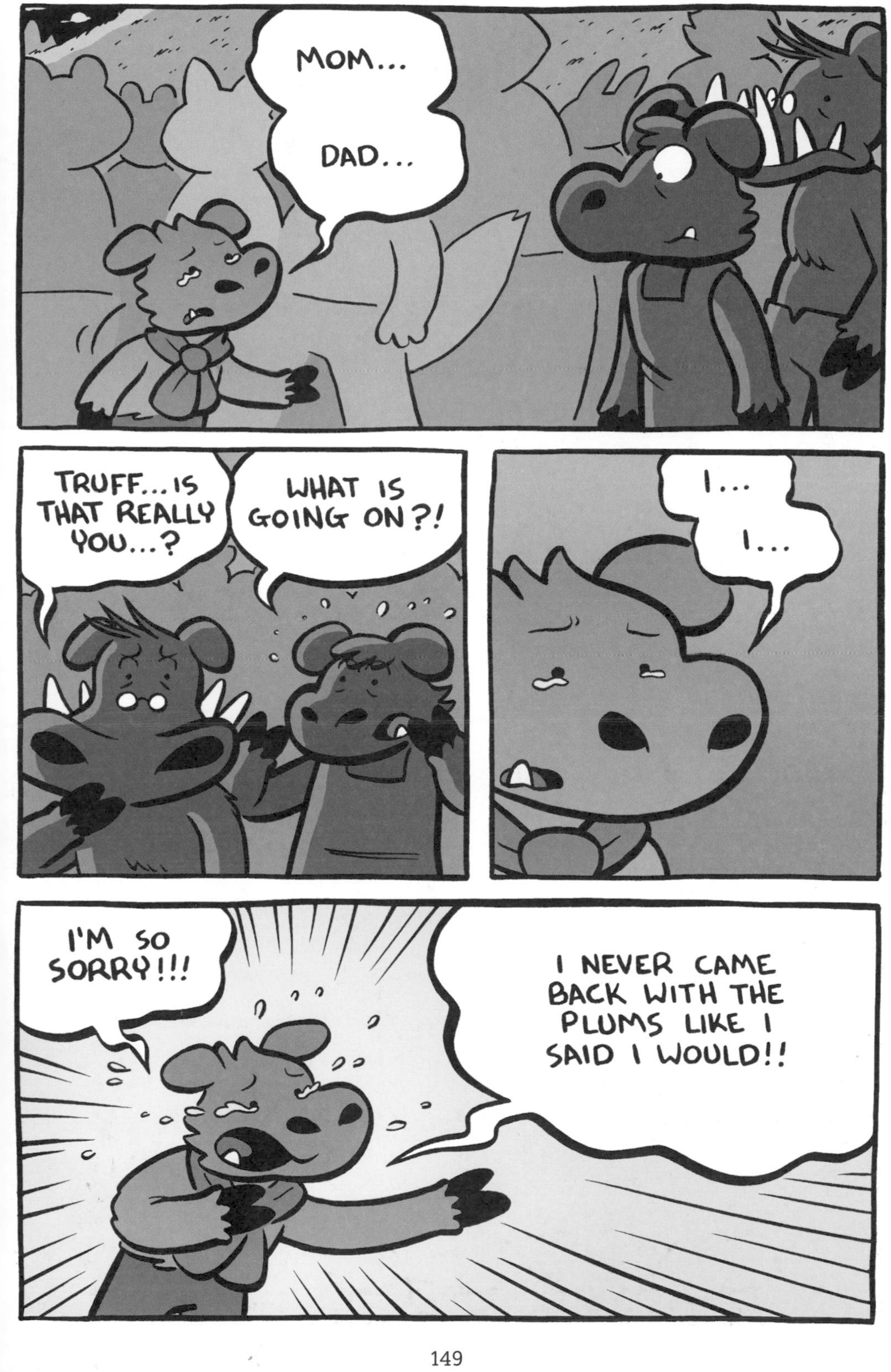
MOM...
DAD...
TRUFF... IS THAT REALLY YOU...?
WHAT IS GOING ON?!
I... I...
I'M SO SORRY!!!
I NEVER CAME BACK WITH THE PLUMS LIKE I SAID I WOULD!!

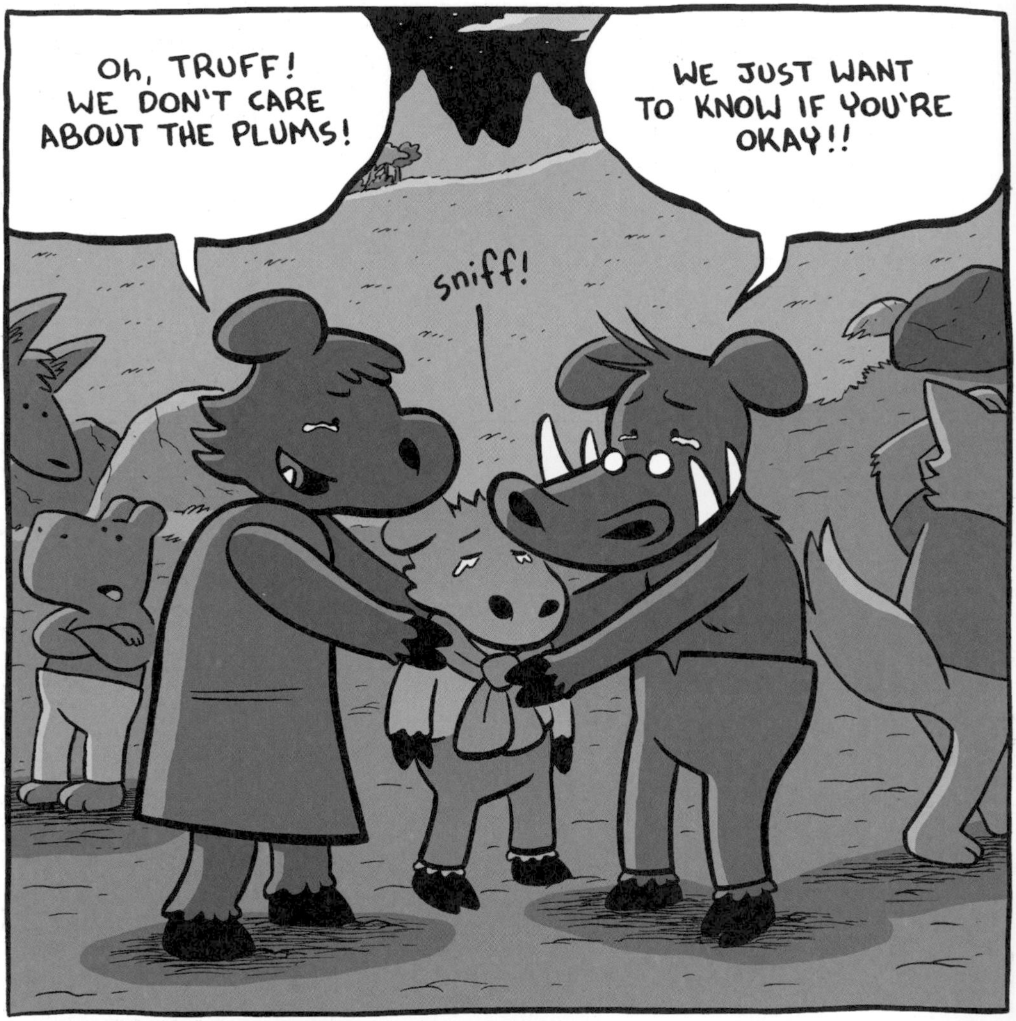
Oh, TRUFF! WE DON'T CARE ABOUT THE PLUMS!
WE JUST WANT TO KNOW IF YOU'RE OKAY!!
sniff!

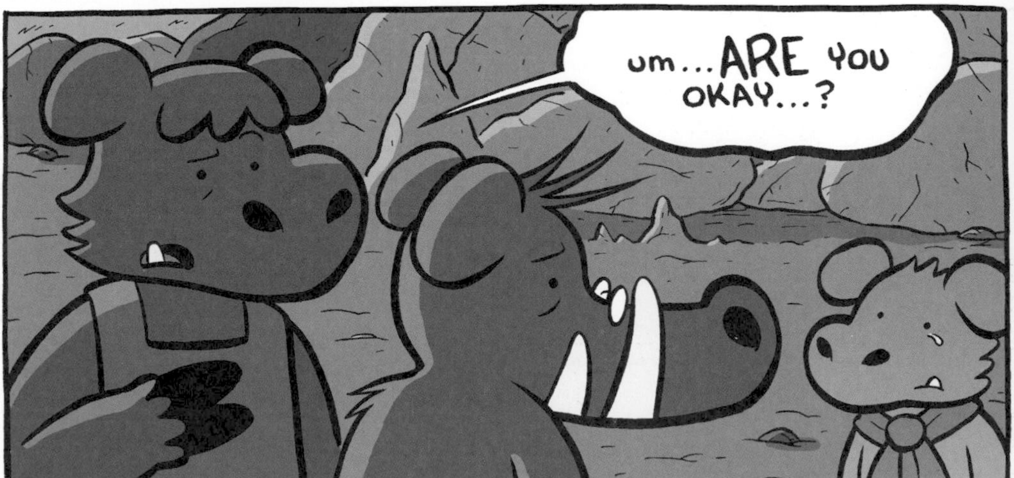
um...ARE you OKAY...?

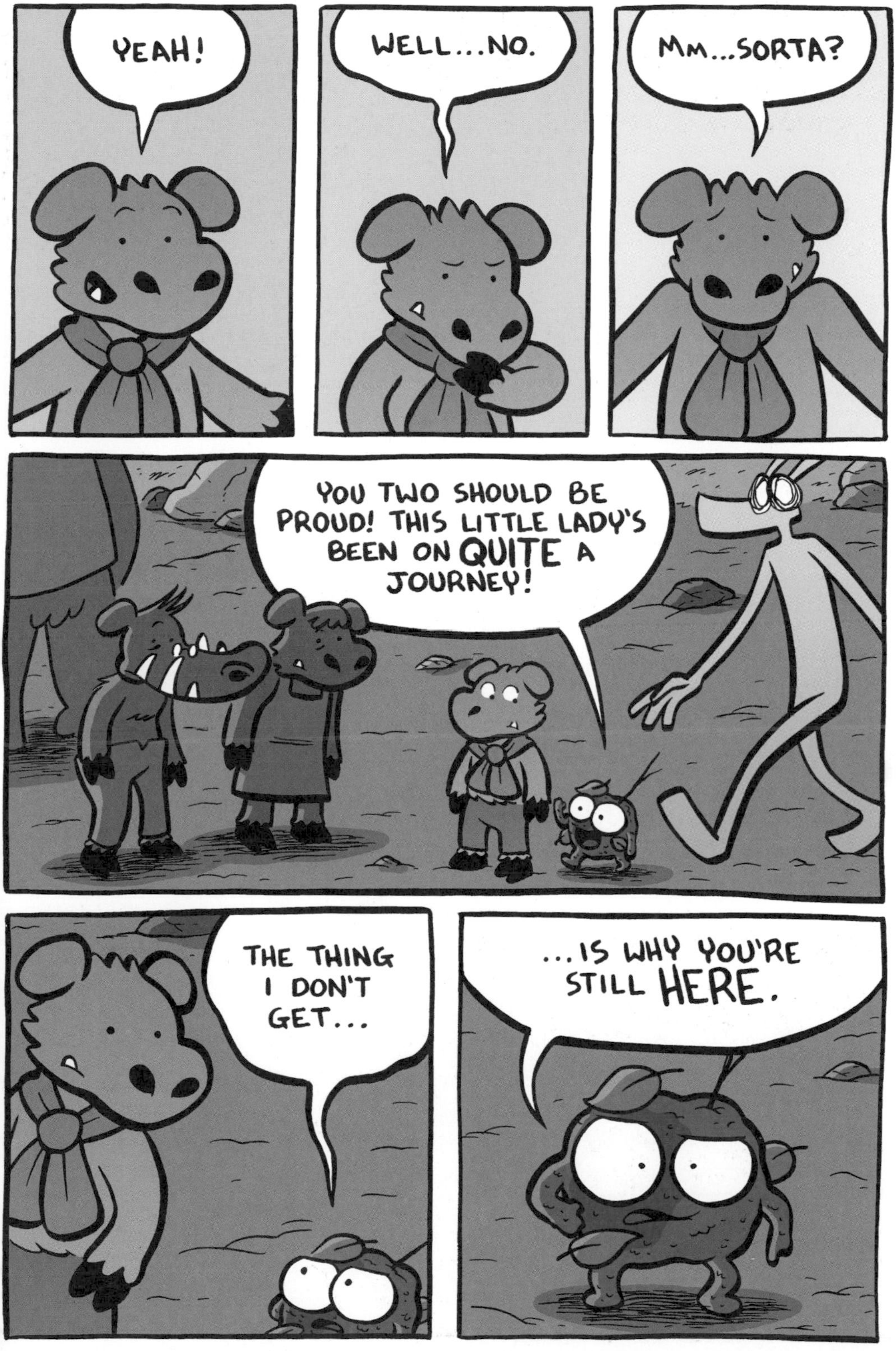
YEAH!
WELL...NO.
Mm...SORTA?
YOU TWO SHOULD BE PROUD! THIS LITTLE LADY'S BEEN ON QUITE A JOURNEY!
THE THING I DON'T GET...
...IS WHY YOU'RE STILL HERE.

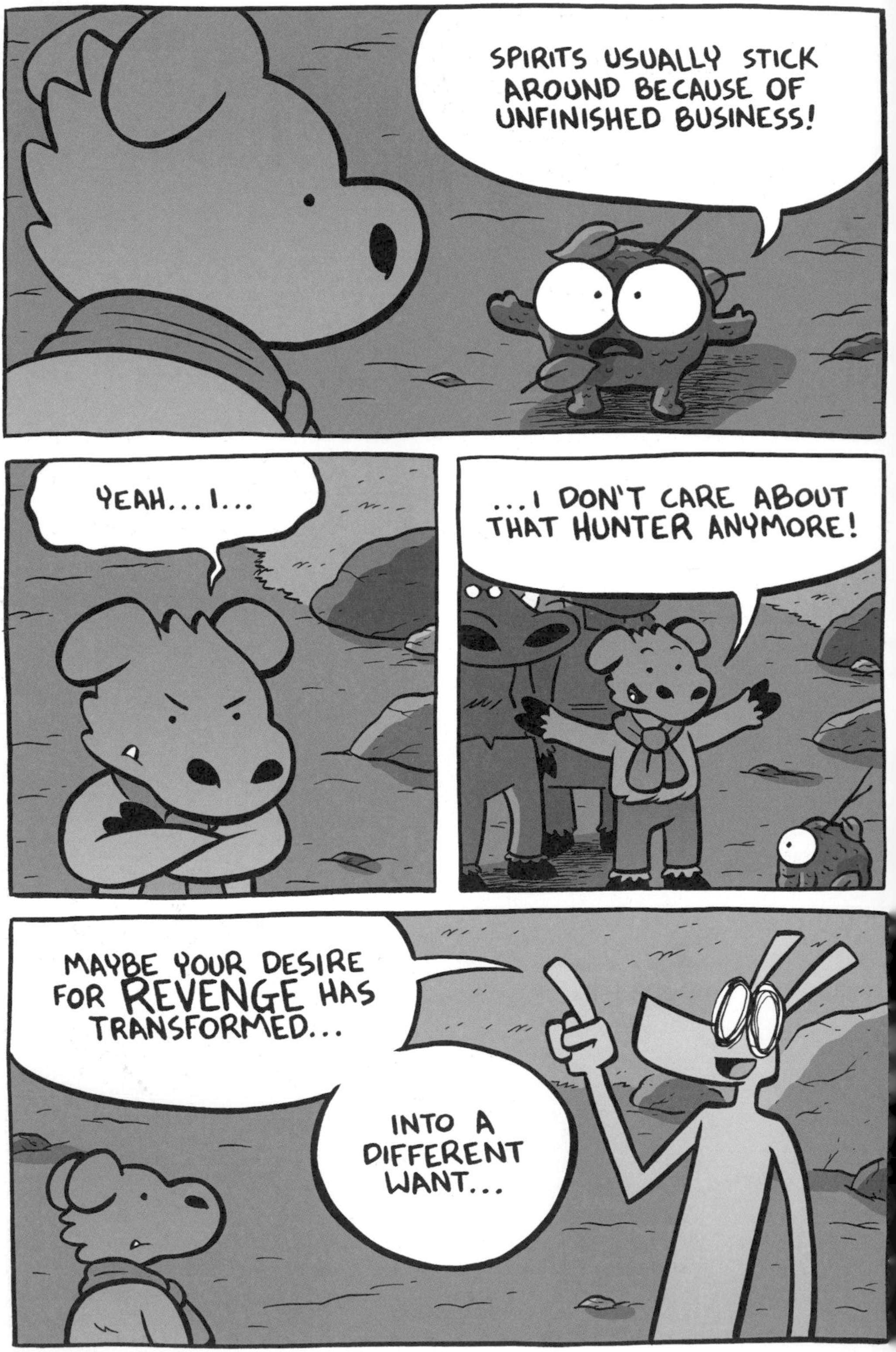
SPIRITS USUALLY STICK AROUND BECAUSE OF UNFINISHED BUSINESS!
YEAH... I...
...I DON'T CARE ABOUT THAT HUNTER ANYMORE!
MAYBE YOUR DESIRE FOR REVENGE HAS TRANSFORMED...
INTO A DIFFERENT WANT...

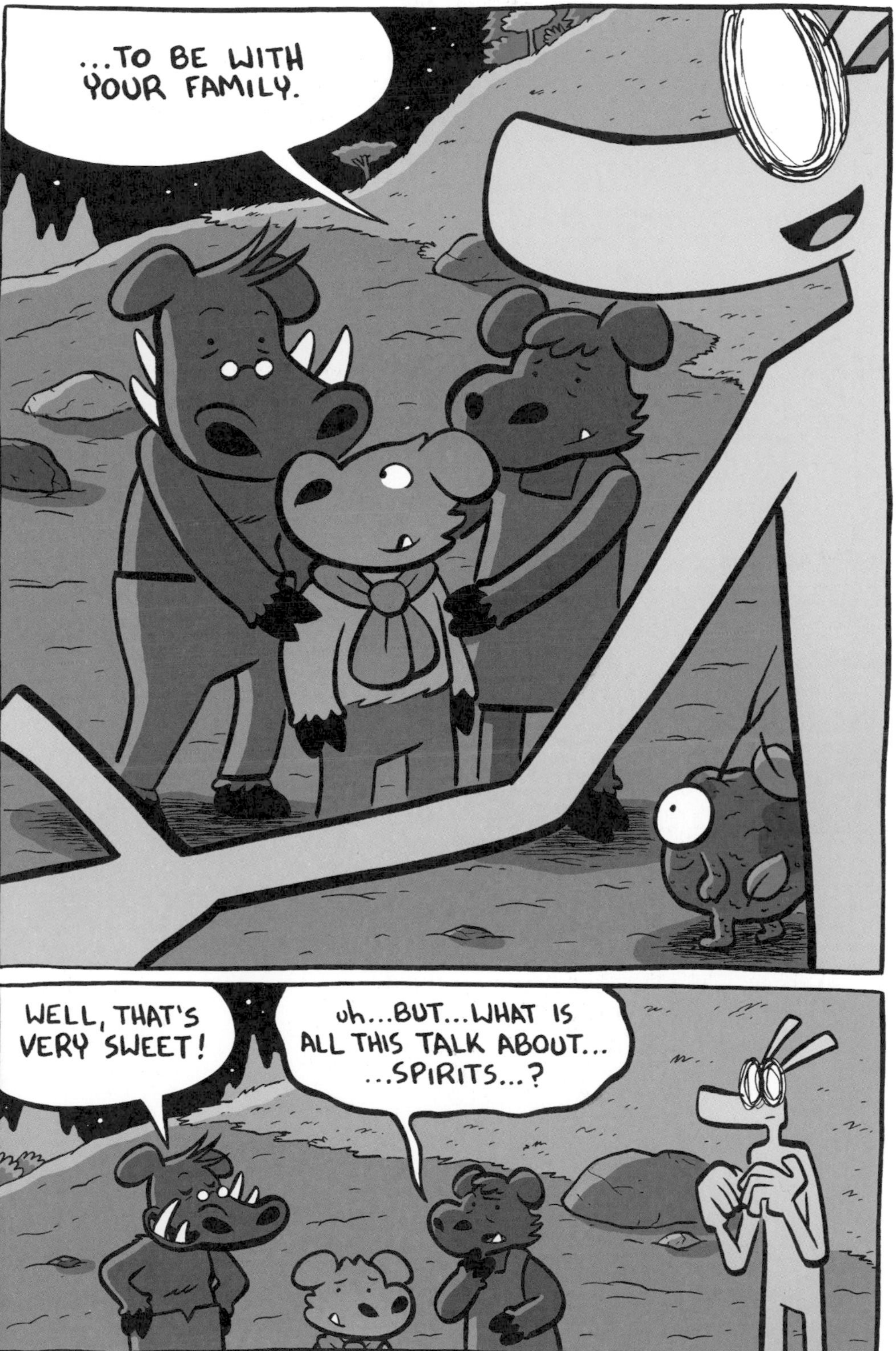
...TO BE WITH YOUR FAMILY.
WELL, THAT'S VERY SWEET!
uh...BUT...WHAT IS ALL THIS TALK ABOUT... ...SPIRITS...?

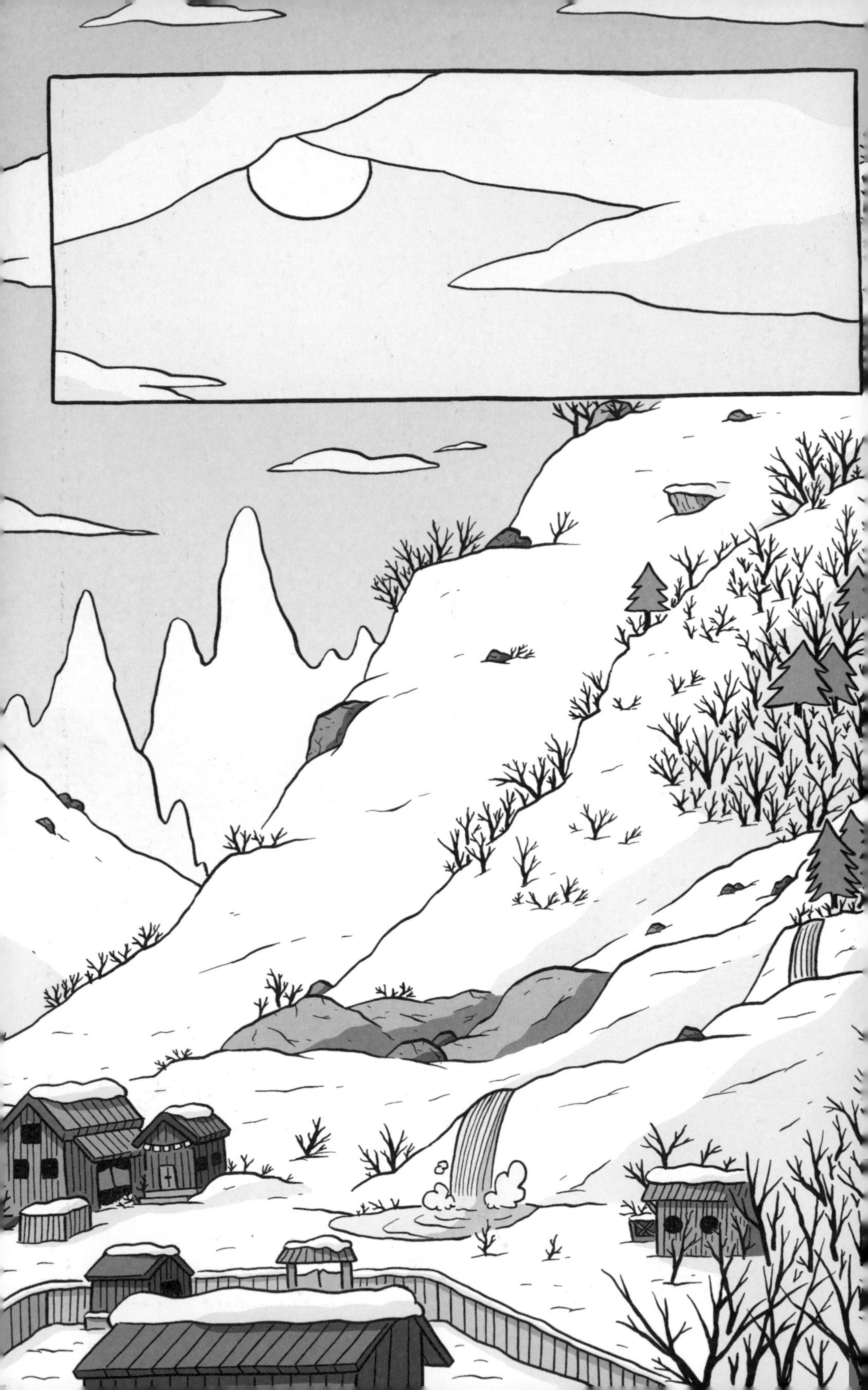

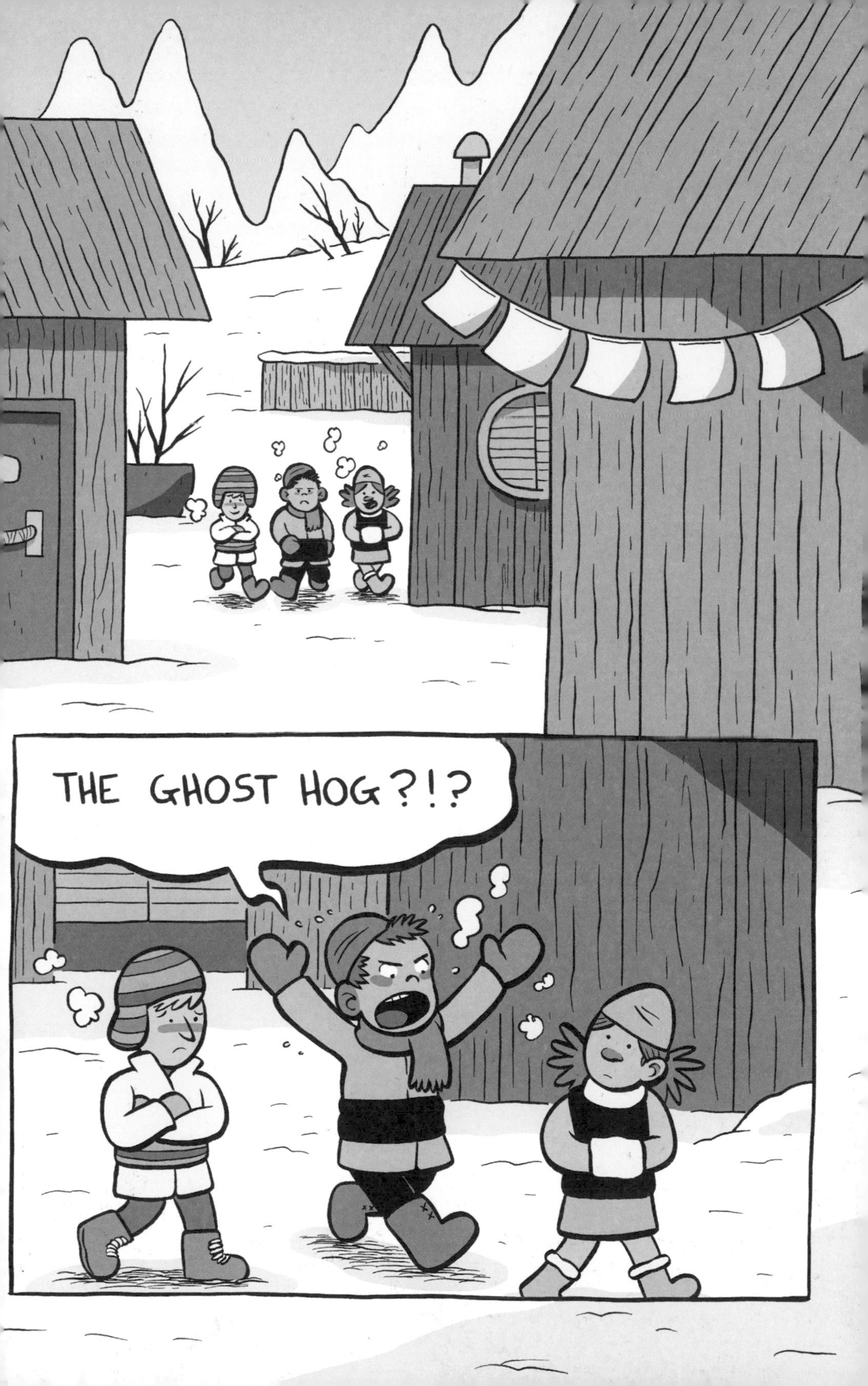
THE GHOST HOG?!?

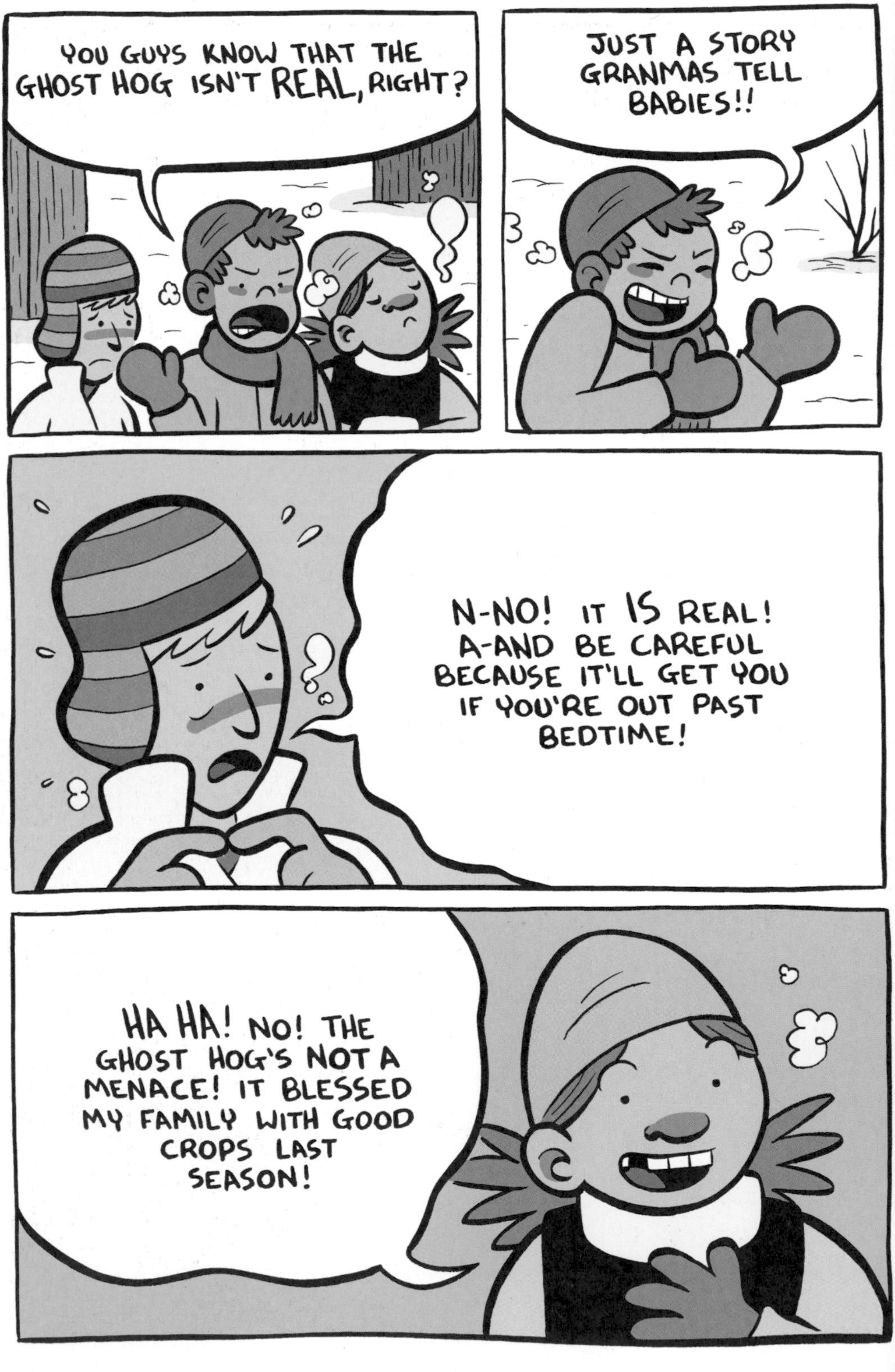
YOU GUYS KNOW THAT THE GHOST HOG ISN'T REAL, RIGHT?
JUST A STORY GRANMAS TELL BABIES!!
N-NO! IT IS REAL! A-AND BE CAREFUL BECAUSE IT'LL GET YOU IF YOU'RE OUT PAST BEDTIME!
HA HA! NO! THE GHOST HOG'S NOT A MENACE! IT BLESSED MY FAMILY WITH GOOD CROPS LAST SEASON!

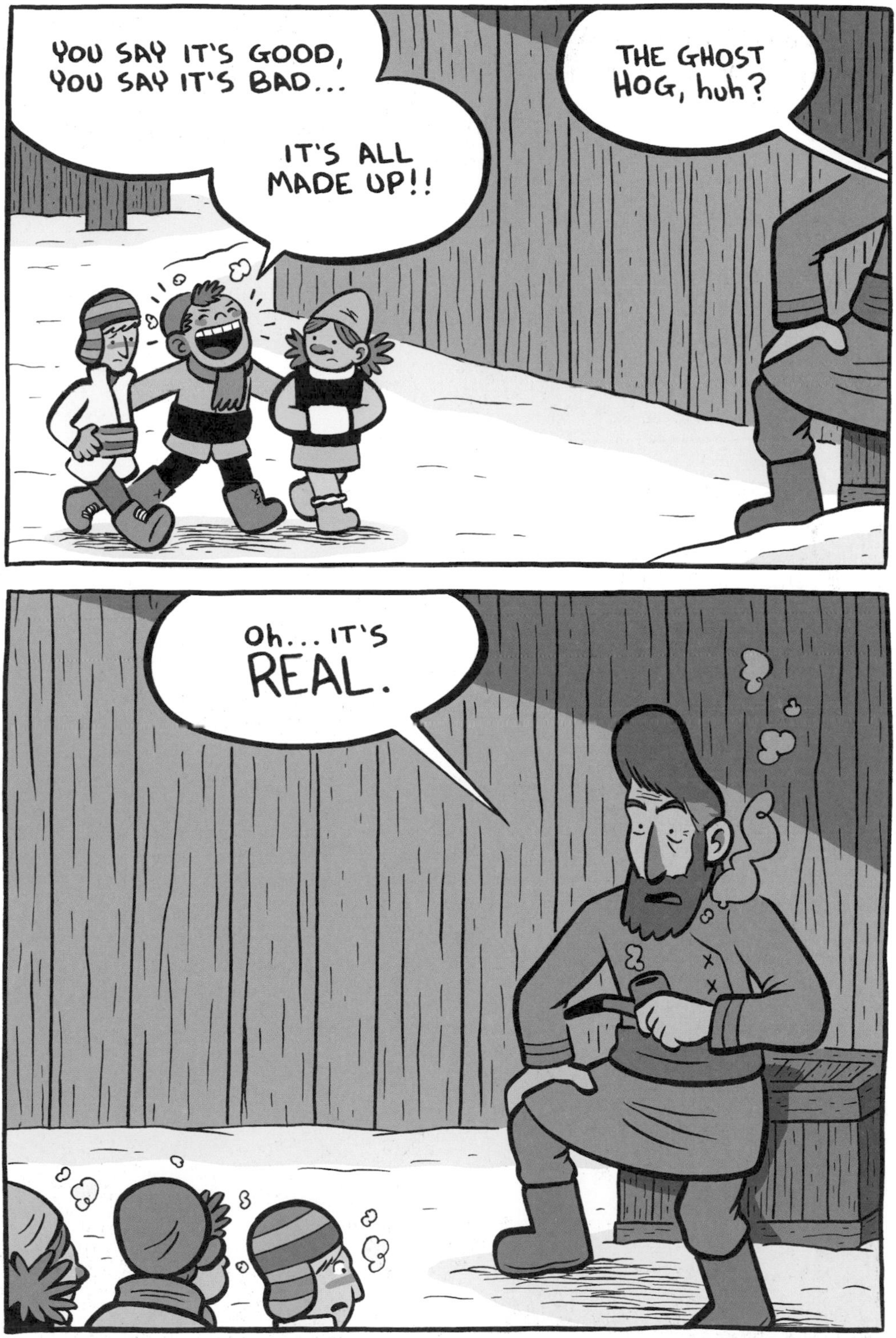
YOU SAY IT'S GOOD, YOU SAY IT'S BAD...
IT'S ALL MADE UP!!
THE GHOST HOG, huh?
Oh... IT'S REAL.

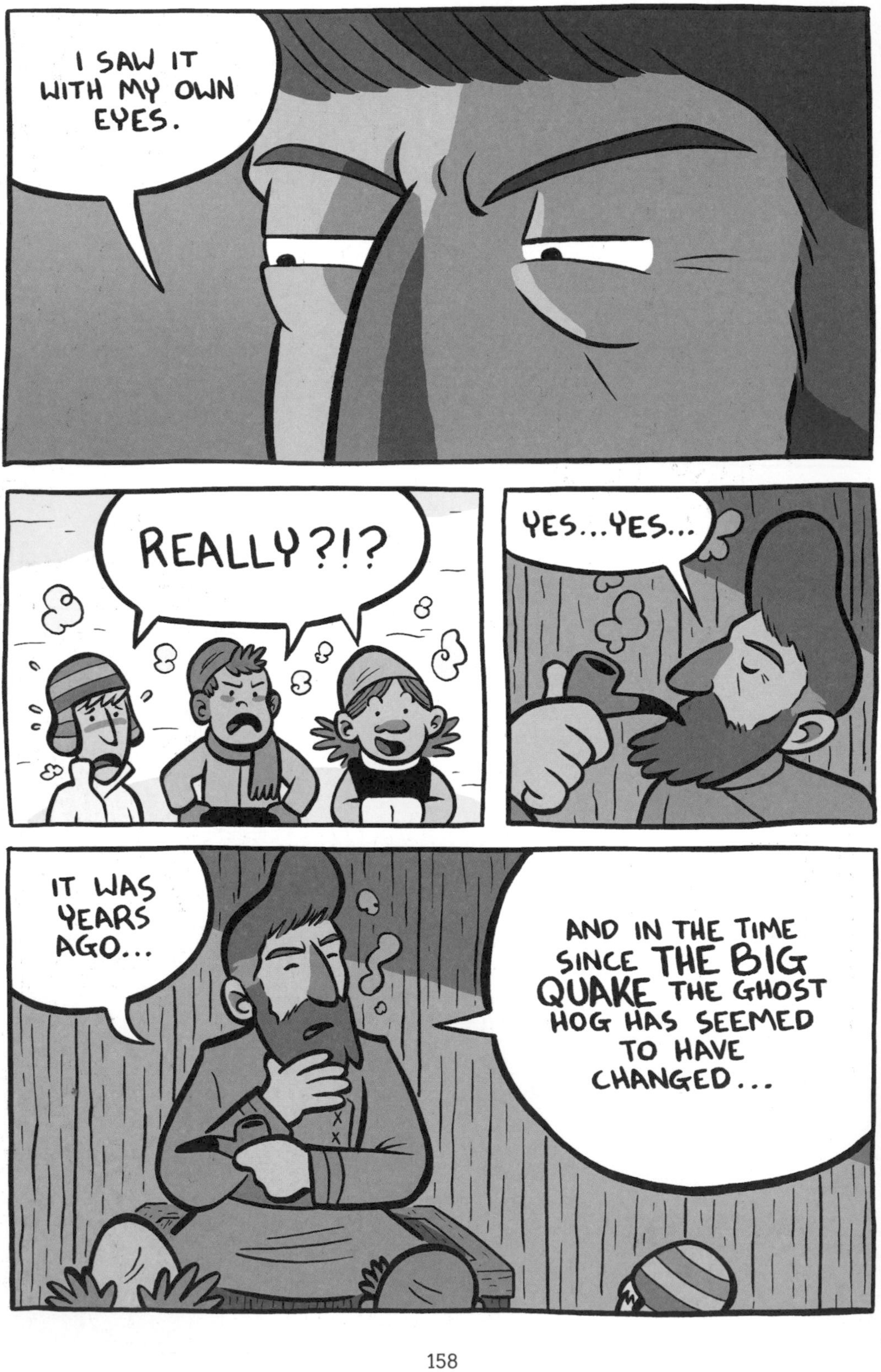
I SAW IT WITH MY OWN EYES.
REALLY?!?
YES...YES...
IT WAS YEARS AGO...
AND IN THE TIME SINCE THE BIG QUAKE THE GHOST HOG HAS SEEMED TO HAVE CHANGED...

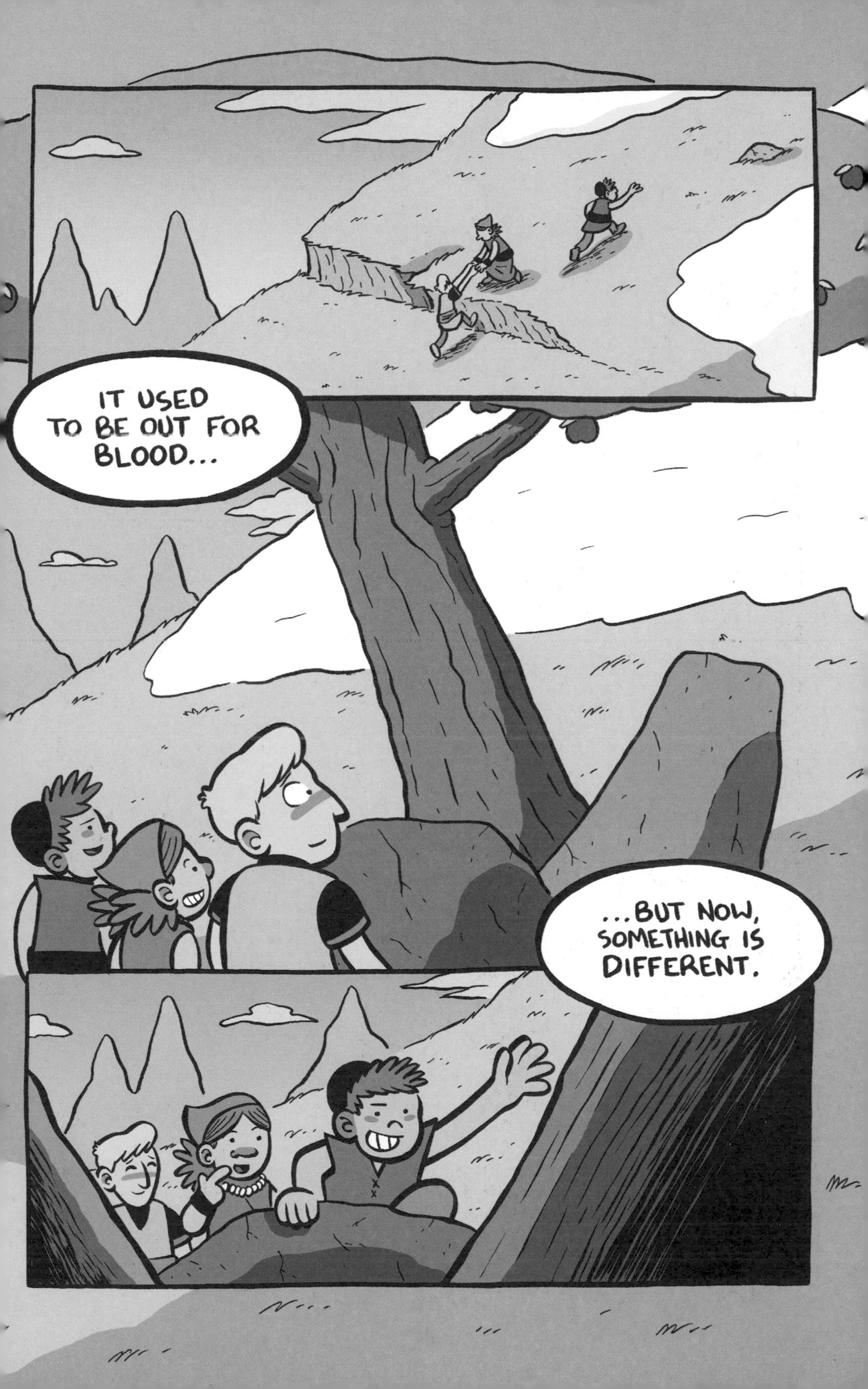
IT USED TO BE OUT FOR BLOOD...
...BUT NOW, SOMETHING IS DIFFERENT.

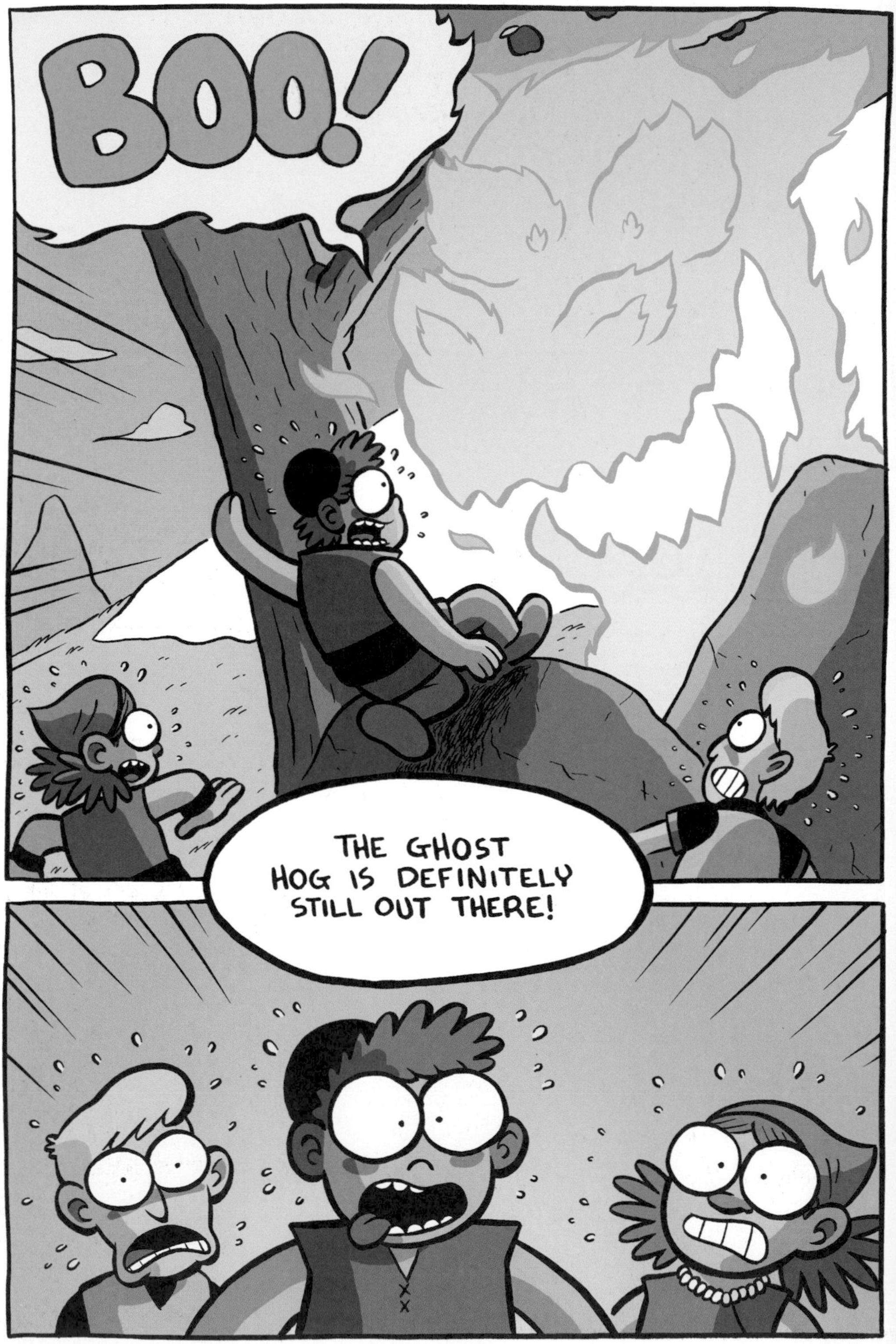
BOO!
THE GHOST HOG IS DEFINITELY STILL OUT THERE!

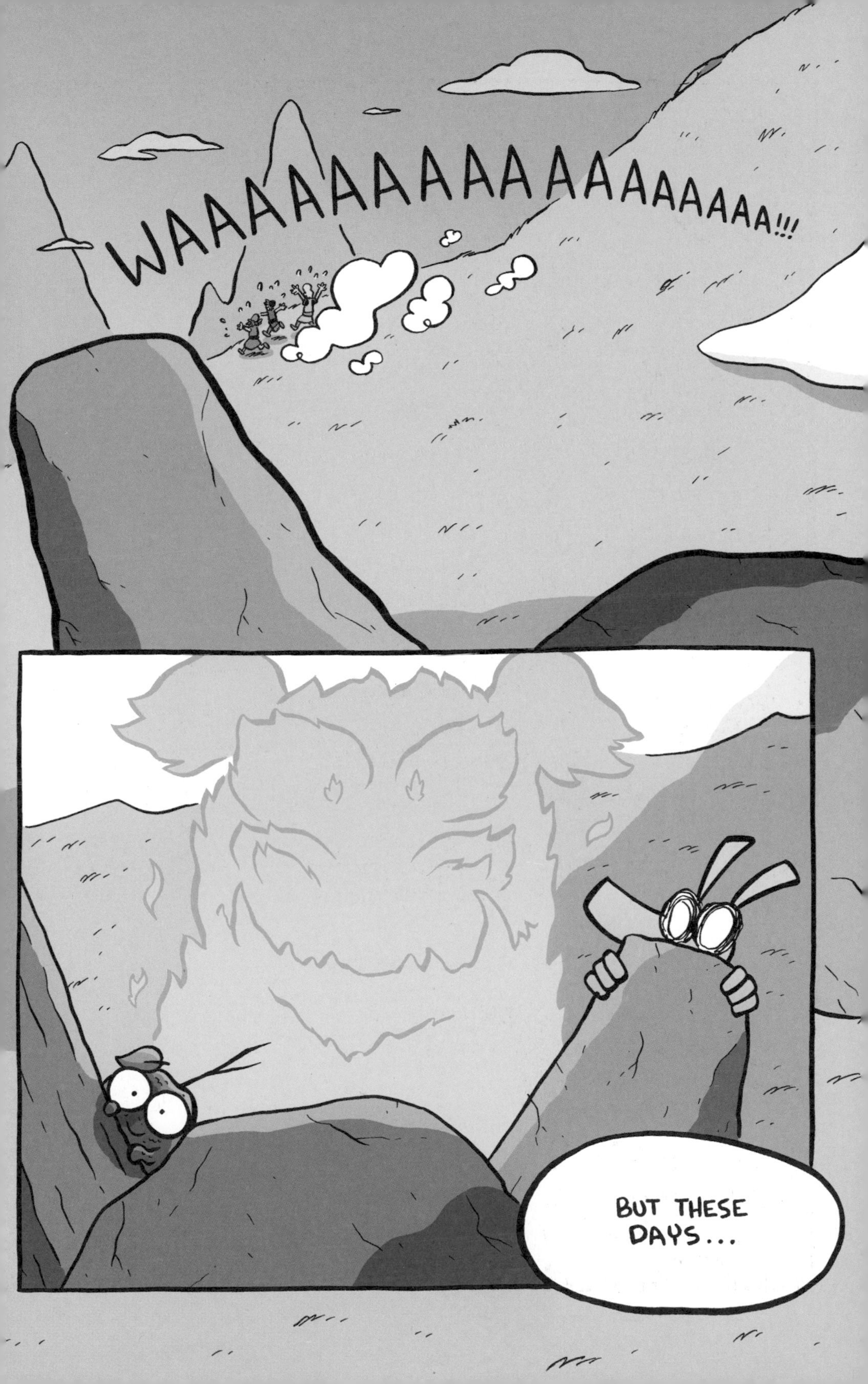
WAAAAAAAAAAAAAAAAA!!!
BUT THESE DAYS...

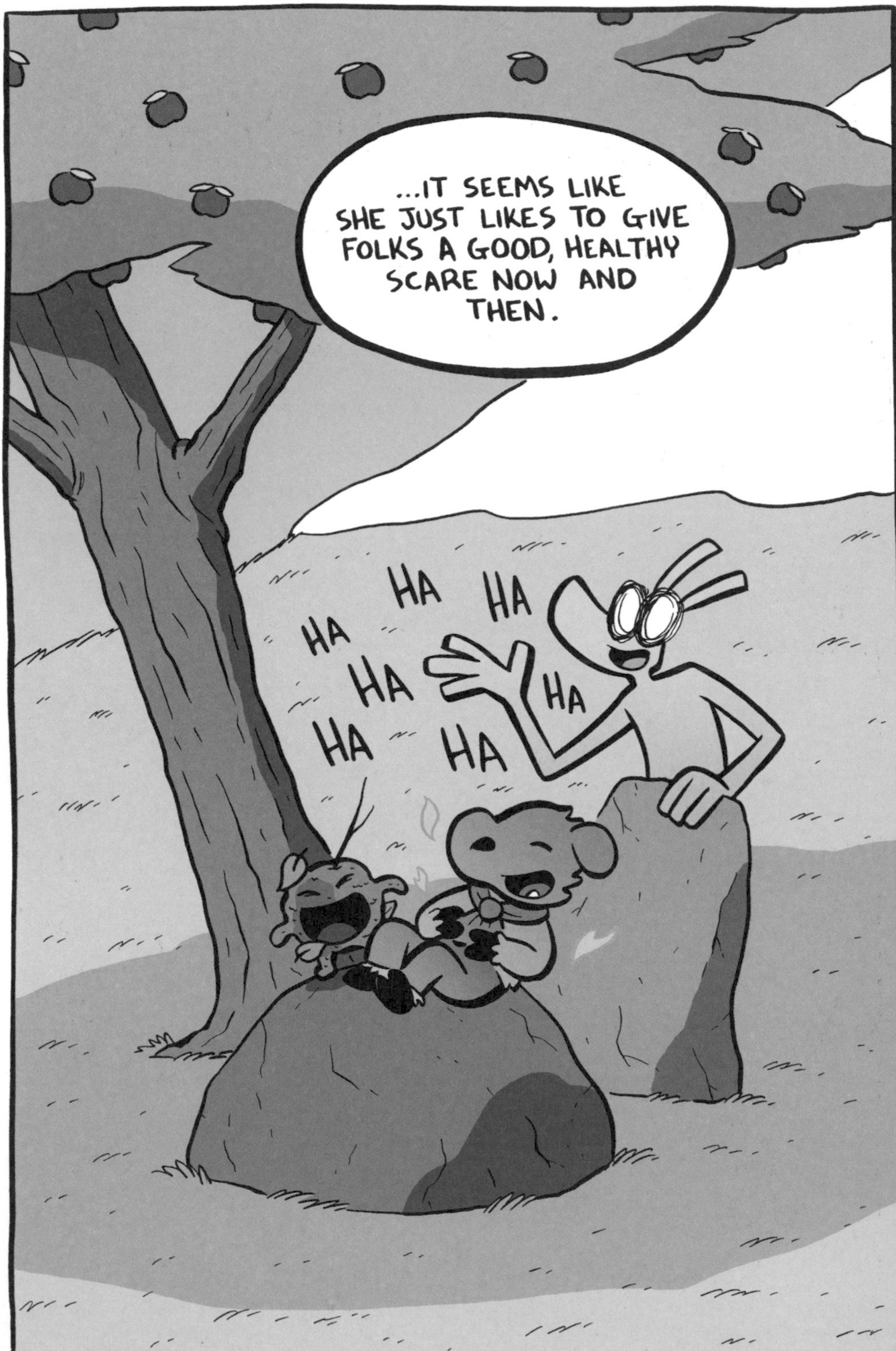
...IT SEEMS LIKE SHE JUST LIKES TO GIVE FOLKS A GOOD, HEALTHY SCARE NOW AND THEN.
HA HA HA HA HA HA HA HA

PROCESS SKETCHES!

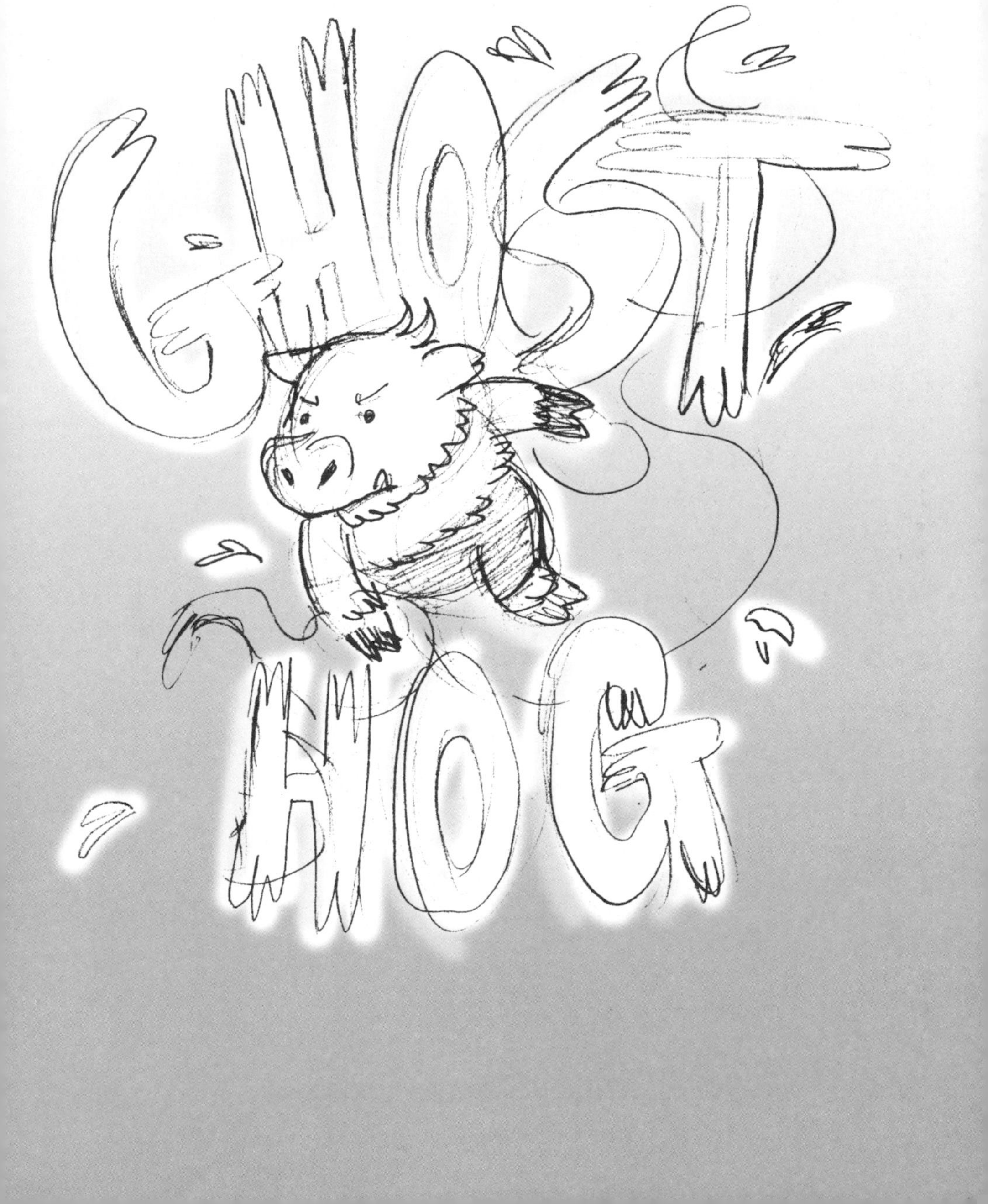
GHOST HOG

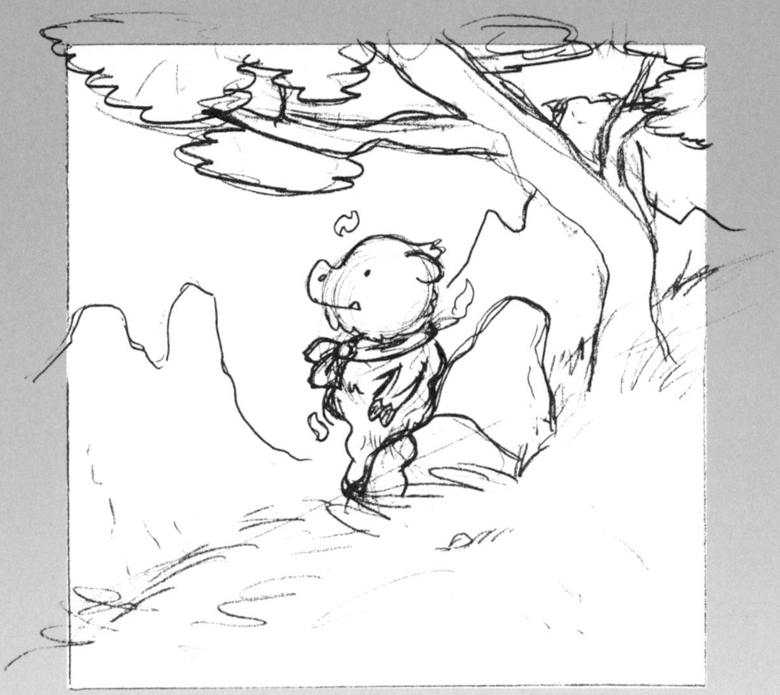

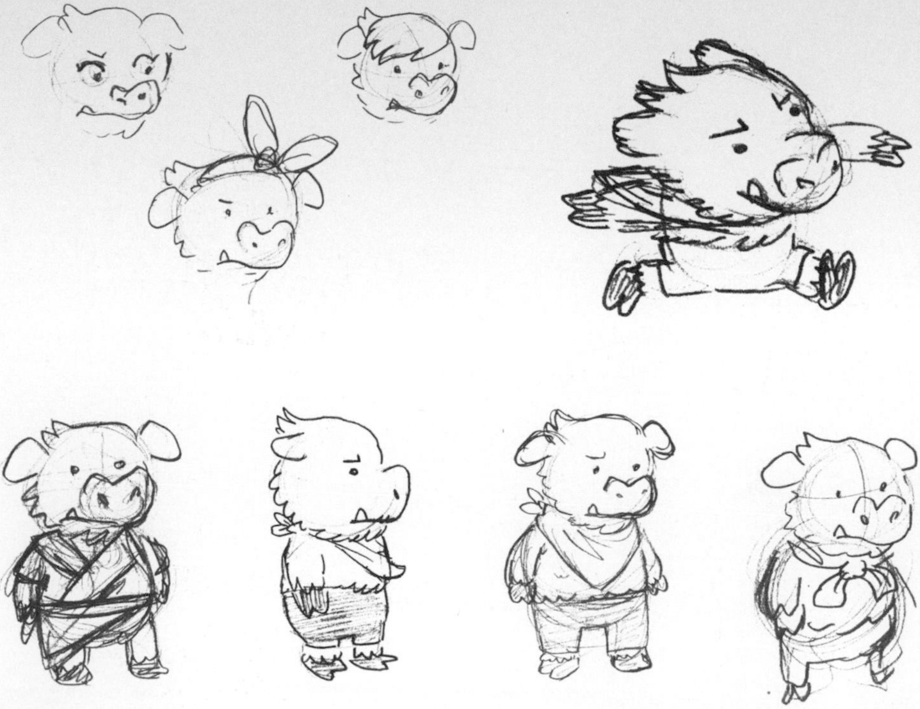

TRUFF

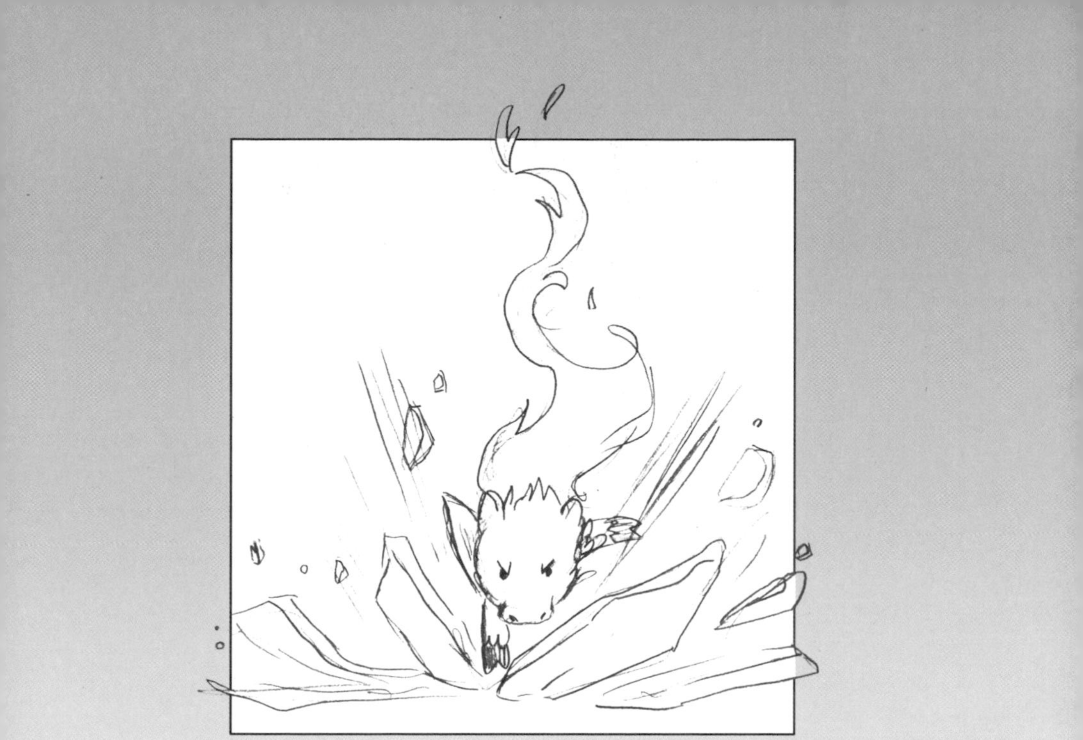

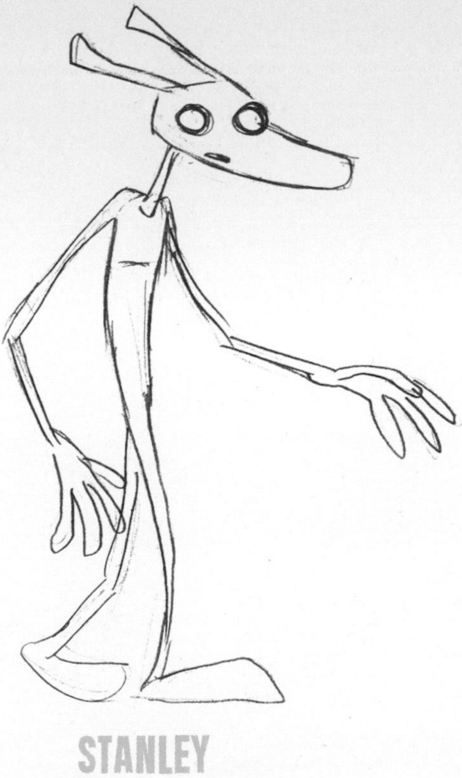

STANLEY

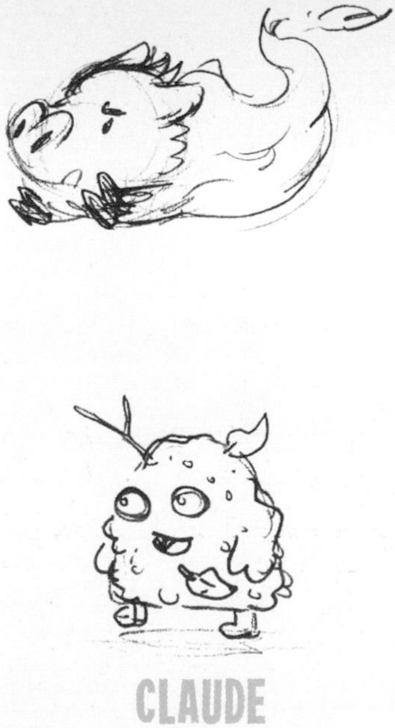

CLAUDE

HE ONLY NEEDS *ONE RACE* TO PROVE HIMSELF.

Don't miss

DRAGON RACER

an exciting new graphic novel set in the world of **GHOST HOG!**

COMING SOON!

Joey Weiser is the author of the Eisner Award–nominated *Mermin* graphic novel series from Oni Press. His comics work ranges from writing and drawing for *SpongeBob* comics to coloring the *Jedi Academy: A New Class* series. His first graphic novel, *The Ride Home*, was published in 2007 by AdHouse Books. He is a graduate of the Savannah College of Art & Design and currently lives in Athens, Georgia.

MORE books from Joey Weiser!

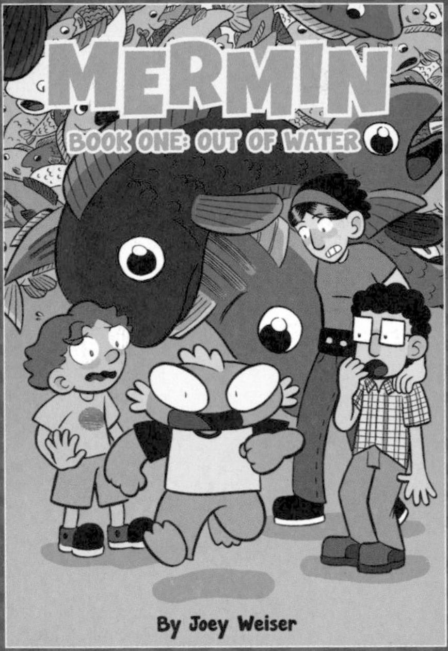
MERMIN
BOOK ONE: OUT OF WATER
By Joey Weiser

MERMIN BOOK ONE:
OUT OF WATER

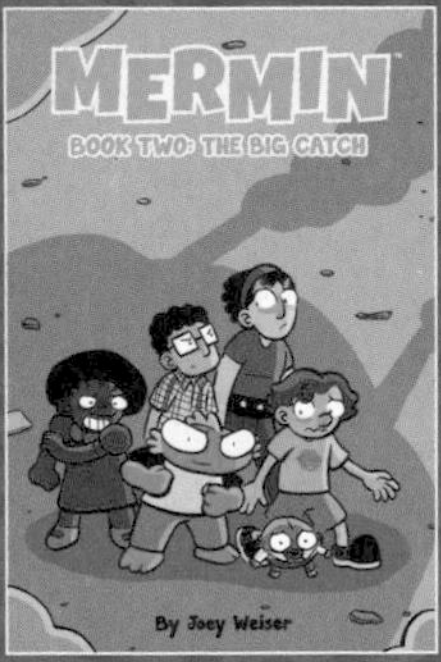
MERMIN
BOOK TWO: THE BIG CATCH
By Joey Weiser

MERMIN BOOK TWO:
THE BIG CATCH

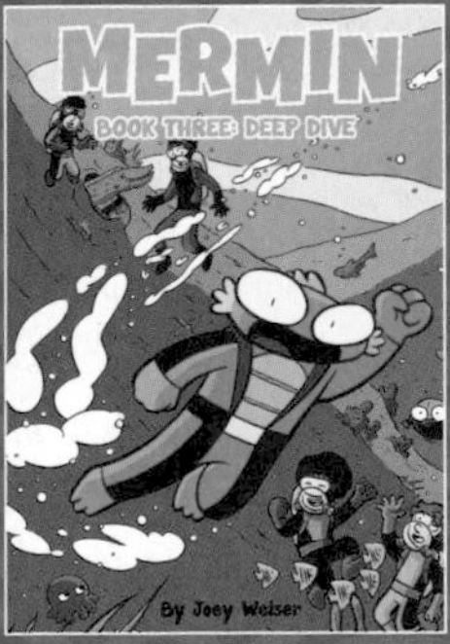
MERMIN
BOOK THREE: DEEP DIVE
By Joey Weiser

MERMIN BOOK THREE:
DEEP DIVE

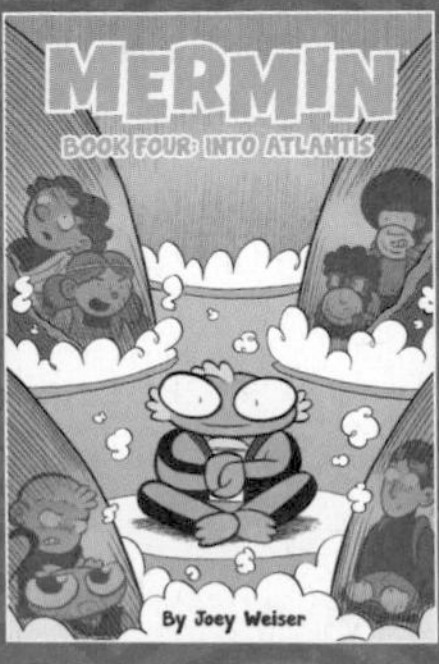
MERMIN
BOOK FOUR: INTO ATLANTIS
By Joey Weiser

MERMIN BOOK FOUR:
INTO ATLANTIS

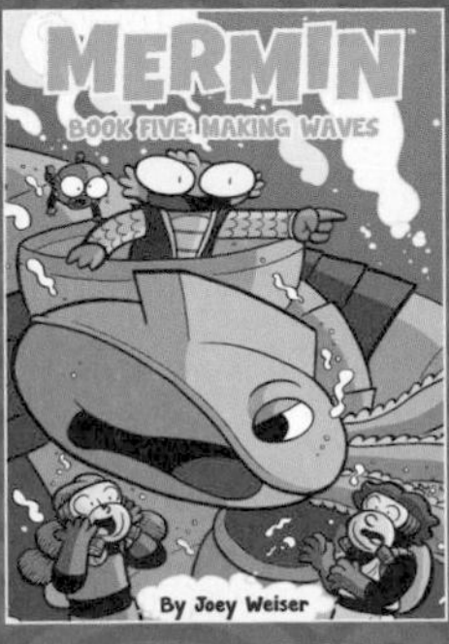
MERMIN
BOOK FIVE: MAKING WAVES
By Joey Weiser

MERMIN BOOK FIVE:
MAKING WAVES

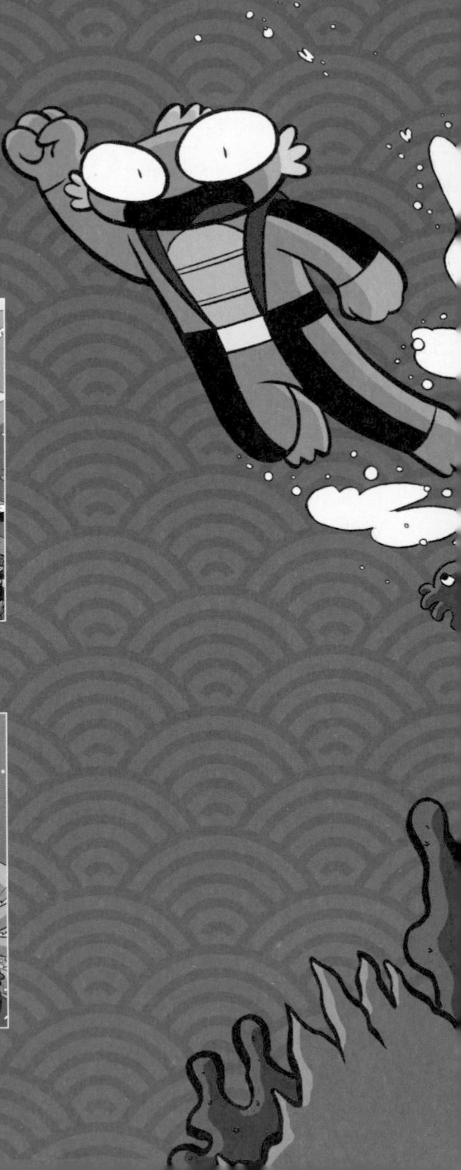